WE DARE:
SEMPER PARATUS
AN ANTHOLOGY OF THE APOCALYPSE

Edited by
Jamie Ibson and Chris Kennedy

Theogony Books
Virginia Beach, VA

Copyright © 2019 by Jamie Ibson and Chris Kennedy.

All rights reserved. No part of this publication may be reproduced, distributed or transmitted in any form or by any means, including photocopying, recording, or other electronic or mechanical methods, without the prior written permission of the publisher, except in the case of brief quotations embodied in critical reviews and certain other noncommercial uses permitted by copyright law.

Chris Kennedy/Theogony Books
2052 Bierce Dr., Virginia Beach, VA 23454
http://chriskennedypublishing.com/

Publisher's Note: This is a work of fiction. Names, characters, places, and incidents are a product of the author's imagination. Locales and public names are sometimes used for atmospheric purposes. Any resemblance to actual people, living or dead, or to businesses, companies, events, institutions, or locales is completely coincidental.

Cover by Elartwyne Estole

The stories and articles contained herein have never been previously published. They are copyrighted as follows:

THE DAUGHTER, by Chris Kennedy © 2020 by Chris Kennedy
RESPAWN, by Robert E. Hampson © 2020 by Robert E. Hampson
BOB, FROM LOS ANGELES, by Brent Roeder © 2020 by Brent Roeder
NOR WAR'S QUICK FIRE, by Rob Howell © 2020 by Rob Howell
WHY 2K, by Jon R. Osborne © 2020 by Jon R. Osborne
THE FALLOW FIELDS, PART I, by Jason Cordova © 2020 by Jason Cordova
THE FALLOW FIELDS, PART II, by Christopher L Smith © 2020 by Christopher L Smith
THE RESERVOIR, by Kevin Fritz Fotovich © 2020 by Kevin Fritz Fotovich
WARLORD, by Christopher Woods © 2020 by Christopher Woods
TEN BREATHS, by Marisa Wolf © 2020 by Marisa Wolf
MOMENTS, by Kevin Ikenberry © 2020 by Kevin Ikenberry
YOU HAVE TO GO OUT, by Philip Wohlrab © 2020 by Philip Wohlrab
EIGHT OUNCES A DAY, by Kevin Steverson © 2020 by Kevin Steverson
WRAITH, by Marie Whittaker © 2020 by Marie Whittaker
DUST TO DUST, by Jamie Ibson © 2020 by Jamie Ibson

Trouble in the Wind/Jamie Ibson and Chris Kennedy -- 1st ed.
ISBN 978-1648550607

To the men and women who form the foundation of our very civilization—everyone who keeps us fed, watered, sheltered, and healthy. We cannot do this without you.

Healthy!

Thank you for everything you (and the rest of the crew) have done for Michelle and me. It's made more of a difference than I have words to say

Jamie

Preface by Jamie Ibson

In November 2019, when I started planning the second volume of "We Dare," I didn't have the foggiest idea that the globe would be gripped with fear over the Covid-19 panic a few short months later. The first volume focused on augmentations—brain implants, nanites, cyborgs, genetic tinkering, and more. We're seeing incredible advances in cybernetic and bionic augmentation today—science fiction is becoming science fact.

When I proposed we do a second volume, I said I wanted a mix of post-apocalyptic stories that ended with some degree of hope, of positivity. I wanted stories where, whether we were fighting zombies or aliens, whether we had nuked ourselves, or suffered some other catastrophic collapse, the human spirit could not be defeated. And now, here we are, in the middle of a pandemic where it seems the panic and stress people are under is at least as dangerous as the illness itself.

Maybe some stories of hope and positivity, of what comes next, of survivors fighting and triumphing against all odds are what we need right now. After all, if our heroes can handle raiders, aliens, zombies, morlocks, shadow demons, nuclear fire, Geno Freaks, and clowns, then maybe washing our hands and keeping people out of melee range isn't so difficult.

Jamie Ibson
British Columbia, April 2020

Contents

The Daughter by Chris Kennedy 9

Respawn by Robert E. Hampson 37

Bob From Los Angeles by Brent Roeder 71

Nor War's Quick Fire by Rob Howell 113

Why 2k by Jon R. Osborne 171

The Fallow Fields, Part I by Jason Cordova 215

The Fallow Fields, Part II by Christopher L. Smith 257

The Reservoir by Kevin Fritz Fotovich 283

Warlord by Christopher Woods 317

Ten Breaths by Marisa Wolf 361

Moments by Kevin Ikenberry 399

You Have To Go Out by Philip Wohlrab 429

Eight Ounces A Day by Kevin Steverson 457

Wraith by Marie Whittaker 491

Dust To Dust by Jamie Ibson 519

* * * * *

The Daughter by Chris Kennedy

A Fallen World Universe Short Story

"Welcome back, boss," I said as Brown moved the barricade aside, allowing the convoy to cross the bridge onto Perdido Key in the territory that used to be known as Florida.

"Thanks, Williams," Luc Boudreaux said. He sighed. "It's really good to be home. It was a long and frustrating trip. We'll have a meeting tomorrow to cover all the details."

His car continued across the bridge, accompanied by a bus that sounded like it was missing a cylinder—but had acquired plenty of new bullet holes—and two other cars that had seen better days. The Agents inside them looked like they'd seen better days, too. Aside from a couple on lookout, the rest were sleeping, and many of them had obvious injuries.

Thirty Agents had accompanied Luc Boudreaux on his journey north; far fewer were returning with him. I saw the other Williams as the bus rolled by. He was alert and nodded to me as he went past. While it was nice having someone you could count on to do the right thing, it had been nice having him gone so we weren't getting in each other's hair.

He didn't look like me, of course; we just had the same imprint, which always made working with him difficult. We both had the same skill set and wanted to do the same things the same ways at the same times. It got annoying after a while. His version of Brown was with him, and he waved to my Brown, who waved back.

The meeting would be interesting.

* * *

"As most of you know," Luc Boudreaux said, kicking off the meeting in the Sandy Key Condos' conference room, "we went north to Chattanooga to find out what was still standing after the war. I took 30 Agents with me." His eyes scanned the Agents and other key supporters in attendance. "While most of the Agents who went were long-time Corporate Agents, there were also a few who were imprinted for the first time to augment our forces, since we didn't know what we'd find.

"I'm glad we took them.

"The bottom line is, it's a nightmare out there. We made it up to Chattanooga, but it got nuked. So we decided to press forward to Corporate HQ in Charlotte, but that, of course, was nuked, too. So we went up to the new regional headquarters in Philadelphia, hoping it might have been spared."

"Was it?" George Boudreaux, his nephew, asked.

"Yes, but what we saw there made me wish Teledyne had put Philly to the sword, too. The management there decided to use a forbidden imprint—the Clown—on a huge number of people, and there are Clowns guarding the headquarters who wouldn't let us pass."

"Even when you told them who you were?"

Luc sighed. "Even then. Something went wrong with the board there—I can't begin to tell you what. Maybe they were crazy to start with, maybe they snapped under pressure…I don't know. Regardless, they're now holed up in the old U.S. Mint building there, and they aren't taking guests."

He paused, and all the Agents who hadn't gone with the group glanced at each other. What could turn away a group of 30 Agents? That many had never been assembled before. A force that size could literally take on armies…and it had been turned away. "What does the Clown imprint do?" I asked.

Luc looked at the table. "It was an assassin imprint. We didn't re-alize until its first mission that the imprint was totally psychopathic in addition to being an outstanding assassin. When the Clown refused to come back in after the mission, it cost us five Agents to take him down. I won't go into the depravities he committed. When I saw the pictures, I knew that imprint had to be destroyed, and I ordered it to be done away with. Apparently, the Philadelphia board didn't delete it, and they made a bunch of them after the bombs fell.

"We had a skirmish with them where we lost a couple of the younger Agents, and we retreated when they pulled back to regroup. Even without the Clowns, though, Philadelphia is a loss—it has al-ready sunk into barbarism."

"So, what do we do?" George asked.

"We do what we can. We don't go back to Philly. We continue to rebuild here. Sometime—probably not in my lifetime, but maybe in yours—" Luc looked at George, "—maybe we can bring civilization back to places like Philadelphia. There are other places where society is looking to rebuild—like Clanton, Alabama—but those are few and far between, and all it would take is a few bad people—or a rogue Agent or Specialist—to bring them all down again."

"Speaking of bad people," George said, "as I was coming in, I heard a report come in from the western checkpoint. Apparently, someone's on the way from Gulf Shores with a request for help with some issue they have."

"Will you go find out if he's here yet?" Luc asked. "Better to deal with it now while everyone is present."

George nodded, got up, and walked out. He came back a few minutes later with a tall, broad-shouldered man. The man had an empty holster, courtesy of the check-in process anyone other than Agents went through to get to see Mr. Boudreaux.

Luc motioned the man to an open seat. "I'm Luc Boudreaux," he said. "What can I do for you?"

The man nodded. "Good to meet you, sir," the man said. "I'm Dan Codger from the Gulf Breeze mayor's staff."

"How is John?" Luc asked.

"Well, he's in a bit of a pickle," Codger replied. "We've been trying to extend our zone of control across Portage Creek to the airport and have been making good progress."

"But…"

"But we keep losing people on the west end of the island. Women mostly, who vanish in the night, along with any children they have. Any menfolk are usually left behind, slain."

"And you haven't been able to catch the people responsible?"

"No, sir. They just vanish into the night. It's like they're ghosts."

Luc smiled. "Do you believe in ghosts?"

Codger shook his head. "No sir, I don't. And I know they aren't ghosts."

"I'll bite. How do you know they aren't ghosts?"

"Because ghosts wouldn't have any reason to harvest the menfolk they come across. I've seen some of the…pieces…of the people they've left behind. They look like slaughtered animals."

Brown nudged me. "Doesn't your family live in Gulf Shores?" he whispered.

As an Agent, I have two lives. The one when I'm on the clock for the company, imprinted as an Agent, and the one where I'm the person I was before I joined Obsidian. The process for imprinting removes all your former persona and gives you the one with the skills they need you to have. When you're off the clock, they imprint your civilian persona back on you.

My wife had come looking for me once while Boudreaux was gone up north, and my alter ego hadn't come home as scheduled. When Boudreaux had left, all the Agents had been brought in "for the duration" to guard Perdido Key in his absence; we wouldn't get our normal personalities back until Boudreaux got back. I had tried to send her a message, but apparently it hadn't gotten to her.

I hadn't recognized her at the time, of course, as Williams didn't know her. She'd left, angry at me, angry with my alter ego, and angry at the world in general, but it hadn't bothered me in the slightest, aside from the peripheral knowledge that my other persona was going to be sleeping on the sofa for quite some time.

The things we do for the Corporation.

I nodded to Brown. "That's what she said." When she'd left, she'd screamed at me that she was taking our daughter and going to stay with her parents in western Gulf Shores.

"What's causing it?" Boudreaux was asking as I returned to the conversation. "Animals?"

The man shook his head. "Not unless they can pick locks."

Boudreaux sighed. "Mr. Codger, I just got back from a long, harrowing trip, and I'm running out of enthusiasm for playing '20 Questions.' What is going on, and why are you here?"

"The mayor thinks there's some sort of Geno Freak involved. Maybe more than one. The tracks they leave behind...some are men in boots, but others are...something else. The mayor knows you have people—" his eyes darted around the room, "—probably these people gathered here today, who have special abilities and special skill sets. In the interest of good relations between our two communities, he's asking—hell, he's begging—you to assist us in tracking down whatever is taking our people and to help us put a stop to it."

Luc pursed his lips and sighed. "Depending on what it is, you're probably not going to beat it on your own. If there is more than one...or they're breeding them..." He shook his head. "You're going to need help, or you're going to lose a lot more people." He glanced around the table. "This, my friends, is exactly what I was talking about. All it takes is a couple of bad people—especially powerful ones—to take down civilization in its infancy."

Luc's gaze returned to Codger. "You can tell the mayor we'll help. I'll put together a team and send them tomorrow morning. You can meet them at 9:00 on the bridge by the Florabama."

"Thank you, sir. I'll let the mayor know." Codger got up and left.

"All right," Luc said. "So let's talk about the right group of folks we need to take a look at this issue."

* * *

It wasn't a question of whether Brown and I were going; it was only a matter of which set of Williams/Brown to send. We both had the same skills; there was no need for both of us. The other Williams and I did "rock, paper, scissors" to see who would go; I lost after the 18th round. The problem with having the same personality was that we both threw the same thing the first 17 times we tried. I finally tried something new—he did too, of course—and I lost.

Our team met at the Florabama, a local bar that was enough of an institution that everyone knew where it was. We were joined by Michaelson, who was a tracker, a huge man who had the unfortunate name of Small who was our heavy weapons specialist, and Edwards, a combat generalist who specialized in the area of in-close fighting. Small could blow things up from far away, and Edwards was good at killing anything that got in close.

We piled into Small's SUV—which was needed because he brought a number of toys—and I drove the mile and a half to the bridge. I always drive; I've got the training.

Both Gulf Shores and Perdido Key had checkpoints on the bridge, not so much because we didn't trust each other but because we wanted to keep tabs on who was coming and going. There were always two Agents checking people coming onto Perdido Key, both of which had training in spotting deception in the people they spoke to.

I nodded to them when they waved, then focused on the Gulf Shores people on our side of the road. Codger was with them, and he waved when he saw us, then he jogged over to a car on the side of the road. I slowed, and he pulled out in front of us.

We followed him west until we reached Gulf Shores, then north to the end of the island, then west along Portage Creek, the waterway which separated the island from the mainland. The creek wasn't much of a barrier, as it was only 200-300 feet wide, but it would keep a lot of the riffraff on the mainland. If anyone *really* wanted to cross it, though, it wasn't much of an obstacle; all you needed was a boat big enough to bring back whatever you were stealing.

We had a similar problem on Perdido Key, but on a much smaller scale. We dealt with it through a combination of roving patrols and remote sensors. After the war, we turned away—or killed—a number of people every night until the local populace learned that you didn't try to sneak across to the island under the cover of darkness. We also had watchers on the Gulf Coast side of Perdido Key; we were serious about keeping unwanteds out. Deadly serious. If you tried to sneak onto Perdido Key, we considered you an infiltrator, and infiltrators were shot on sight.

I knew a lot about infiltration as that was one of my mission areas—infiltration and assassination, with a minor in insurrection. Brown was my infiltration teammate and, when a long-range shot was required, my spotter.

I caught glimpses of the creek to the north of us and realized how much more defensible Perdido Key was than Gulf Shores, and I made a mental note to leave my civilian persona a message to move our family to Perdido Key as soon as possible. I didn't care...but he would. And maybe it would lessen the amount of time he spent on the couch.

Codger drove to the end of the road and pulled into the last driveway. The driveway split, and he followed the one to the left. A truck was parked in front of the house, with a man sitting on the hood, facing the house. He had a rifle in his lap and looked ready to use it.

We got out and walked up to the man. He glanced at us, then went back to watching the house and the waterway behind it.

"Anything?" Codger asked.

"Nope," the man said without turning away from the house. "No one in or out."

Codger turned to us. "Want to go in?"

I could already smell decay; I didn't have to go inside the house to know something was dead. "Not really," I replied. "But I think we have to."

Codger led us up the stairs and into the house. Located only a couple of feet above sea level, the single-level house was built on stilts. Nothing looked amiss on the way up the stairs, but the smell grew. He opened the front door, and the smell hit us like a battering ram to the face.

"Oh, God," Small moaned.

"Big guy like you isn't afraid of a little smell, are you?" I asked.

"That ain't no little smell," he muttered.

He was right, of course, and I was only teasing him so I wouldn't have to think about breathing it. We all pulled our shirts over our mouths and noses and tried to breathe shallowly. It didn't help much.

The front room of the house was an abattoir. Based on the remains, it looked like two men, or maybe a man and a big woman, had been butchered. We walked through the house then back down to where the truck sat outside the worst of the stench. The house wasn't in too bad a shape—aside from the front room and blood spatters in one of the bedrooms. I spent most of the time trying not to throw up. Michaelson walked around to the back of the house alongside the creek.

"How many people lived here?" I asked when I thought I could talk without retching.

"Five," Codger said. "Husband, wife, and three kids."

"Didn't look like a man and a woman in the front room," Brown noted.

"Two men," the man on the pickup truck said. "But there ain't enough left to tell who he was." He nodded to where the next house sat, although his eyes didn't leave the creek. "The neighbors heard a shot in the middle of the night, but that was it. When the neighbors didn't come out the next day, they went and looked through the front windows. That's a helluva sight to see." He shrugged. "Same thing happened a couple of nights ago a couple of houses down. There was an older couple—"

"Hey, y'all!" Michaelson called. "Come around out back!"

We all walked to the other side of the house, except for the man on the pickup. "I ain't goin' any closer to the creek than I have to," he said.

Michaelson was standing next to the water. He pointed to the ground. "Boat came ashore here," he said. "Maybe four of five guys got out."

"No crocodile people?" I asked with a touch of nervous humor, hoping he'd agree with me.

"Nope," he said. "No crocodile people."

I smiled and opened my mouth to say something, but he beat me to it.

"The two Geno Freaks came ashore over here." He pointed to a couple of claw prints in the soft dirt about five feet away. "I'm guessing an adult and a younger one. Maybe a female, I can't really tell. Then again, I don't have a lot of experience tracking Genos."

"*You've tracked Genos before?*" Codger asked.

"Yeah. Once. Down in south Florida, near the Everglades. Had one that kept snatching people. He started with the homeless folks and would probably have been okay, except he hit a rich Obsidian shareholder and his wife who were out for a...romantic picnic. The Geno interrupted them while they were naked, killed the husband, then had sex with the woman. The man's family made the Corporation send people out to find the Geno, and I was unlucky enough to get tapped for the job.

"They updated the imprint after the mission, so now I have to live with that knowledge and some of the things I saw while hunting him. I'd have been a lot happier without it."

He shrugged. "Helps me now, though."

"So, what happened?" I asked when it looked like he was lost in his memories.

Michaelson shook his head a couple of times to clear it. "They came ashore here and went to the front. I suspect one of the humans picked the lock, and they snuck inside. They weren't quiet enough, though, and the man who lived here shot one of the intruders, then they killed him in turn. The intruders took the woman and children, like he said." He nodded at Codger. "Then they butchered the man that lived here and the man the homeowner killed."

"They butchered their own guy?" Small asked. "That's harsh."

"Yep," Michaelson said. "Food's precious in the swamp, especially now." He pointed to an open window on the back of the house. "They dropped the pieces they took with them down from the window, loaded up the boat, and left."

"Are you sure it wasn't one of the Genos that got shot?" Codger asked hopefully.

"Positive," he replied. "I've got tracks of both of them going back into the water."

"So, where are they now?" Codger asked.

Michaelson shrugged. "Wherever their base is. Probably somewhere not too far away, as they either had to paddle the boat here or have the Genos tow it. If they'd used a motor, someone would have heard it."

"How do we find them?" Codger asked. "I thought you were an expert tracker."

Michaelson smiled. "Show me where the tracks come out of the water, and I'll happily track them for you. I can only track what I can see, and they didn't leave much of a path on the water."

"How about a map?" I asked when it looked like Codger was going to say something rude and useless. "Got a map?"

It may have seemed like a dumb question, but maps were in short supply. Nearly everything went digital before the war, and now it's awfully hard to pull any of that information back out. Perdido Key only has three operational computers I am aware of, and one of those is used to run the island's security.

"Yeah, I have a map," Codger said. "It's in my vehicle."

We walked back to the cars, and he pulled out the map and spread it on the hood of his car.

"We're here," Codger said, pointing.

Michaelson studied the map. "There's an awful lot of swampland here," he noted. "That gives the Genos a lot of room to hide. They aren't going to need a lot of civilization. Some, probably, depending on how far gone they are, but not a lot."

He pursed his lips. "There's a lot of men with the Genos, though, and they aren't going to want to live in a swamp. Not for long, anyway. They're going to need access to stuff." He pointed to the area west of where we stood. "Too much swamp here. It's possible, but there isn't enough development for the humans." He swept his hand across the swampland to the north of us on the other side of Portage Creek. "This area's possible, as there are some houses. They might be holed up in a big one, or maybe in two or three that are close to each other and away from everyone else."

"Why's that?" Codger asked.

"The Genos aren't going to want to be seen," Michaelson said. "Based on the tracks they left, they have claws and tails. The tail is going to make it pretty obvious they aren't human."

"Makes sense," I said. "So maybe to the north of us…"

Michaelson tapped the map to the northwest of us, and I looked to see an island called Oyster Bay. "My money's on this island," he said. "It's the only land around here that isn't swamp, so the humans are going to like it. There are a lot of neighborhoods with only one entrance. Even the island only has one way onto it, so they can watch people coming and going. The Genos could put an observer at the bridge and then at the entrance to the neighborhood they're using. Anybody gets too nosy, *pop!* They kill them, bring them in, and dispose of the bodies. Most of the houses are a ways apart, even if there were people still living in them."

He nodded. "It's about the right distance to be using Gulf Shores as their hunting ground, too. Not too close, where they'd be immediate suspects; not so far that it would be a chore to carry people back in the middle of the night." He tapped the island again. "If I were going to bet, I'd put my money on this island."

I looked at Brown. "Let's go for a drive."

* * *

We drove back into town and left Michaelson, Small, Edwards, and Codger at an outdoor café to wait for us, then we drove off the island to the north. We received a lot of stares from people in the tent community on the mainland side of the bridge, but no one tried to stop us, which was lucky for them.

I turned left onto Waterway Boulevard, which paralleled the creek on its north side.

"What am I looking for, again?" Brown asked. "Besides lunch that *they're* getting and we're not?"

"Don't be such a baby," I replied. I handed him one of the sandwiches I'd stowed in the door pocket. "As for what we're looking for, it's anything that looks out of place."

"How about a seven-foot-tall lizard man?"

"That would be out of place," I said with a nod.

Brown shrugged. "As much swampland as they have here," he muttered around a bite of sandwich, "it wouldn't be *all* that out of place."

"Are you going to help me, or should I take you back to the restaurant?"

"I'd say, 'Yeah, take me back,' but I know you wouldn't, so why bother?"

"Why bother, indeed?"

I looked hard at him.

"Eyes on the road!" he exclaimed after a couple seconds, and I swerved to get back into my lane.

"Are you done screwing around?"

"Fine," he said. "I'll find you a lizard man."

"Good," I replied. "In that case, I'll tell you they're going to have a pizza waiting for you when we get back."

"A real pizza? With cheese?"

"And some sort of meat. They didn't say what kind, and I didn't want to ask."

Brown perked up and began looking out the window in earnest. "Okay, for a pizza, I'll find your damned lizard man."

"He's not my lizard man."

"Fine. I'll find someone else's lizard man for a pizza. I haven't had one in forever."

We drove the two miles to Oyster Bay without seeing anything that didn't look like it belonged. There were a number of old, run-down houses, but nothing that screamed "Lair!" at either of us.

That changed as we crossed the small, two-lane bridge onto the island. Two people were standing on the left shoulder of the road. Both stared at us, then one made a "slow down" motion at us. Brown pulled out his pistol, and I grabbed one with my left hand but kept it out of sight. It didn't make any sense to race past him; then we'd be trapped on the island, and they could barricade the bridge behind us.

I rolled down the window, still keeping the pistol out of sight.

"Whatcha doin' here?" asked a short, greasy-looking guy of about 30. "Don't recognize you."

"I'm looking for a boat launch to put in my boat so I can do some fishing."

The man nodded to the back of the SUV. "You ain't got no boat."

"Didn't know what I'd find," I said with a smile. "If I had to do some defensive driving, I didn't want to do it with a boat attached. I thought I'd look around first."

"There aren't any boat ramps on the island."

"There aren't?" I asked. "Seems odd an island wouldn't have any boat ramps. You sure?"

"He's positive," the second person, a large, black man, said.

"Okay, well, it won't hurt to look around and see if I can't find some place to launch it, anyway, right?"

The first man lifted his shirt and took hold of the pistol in his waistband. "It might hurt, at that," he said. "Now why don't you turn around and go find another place to launch your boat?"

"Okay," I said. I nodded up the road. "The shoulders of the road look a little soft. I'll just drive up to that cross street and turn around."

He started to say something, but I was already rolling up my window and driving off. I could see a cluster of buildings up to the left and wanted a closer look.

"Uh, oh," Brown said as we approached them. People were spilling out of the one closest to the road. Armed people.

I threw the SUV into a skid U-turn and roared off back toward the bridge.

"I found something out of place!" Brown exclaimed pointing in front of us. The two men were now in the street, and both were pointing pistols at us.

The front windscreen starred.

"You won't get any pizza if they kill us," I noted. "Perhaps you might want to shoot *them*, instead?"

"Good point," Brown said. He and I both rolled down our windows. He leaned out his window and shot at the men, and I fired my pistol one-handed out mine. The odds of my hitting anything were miniscule; I just wanted to make them stop shooting at us.

I pushed the accelerator to the floor, and the engine revved. They stood their ground longer than I would have thought, but they finally dove to the side, and we hurtled past.

They both jumped up and started shooting again, but by then we were going over 80 miles an hour, and I didn't hear any more impacts.

"Pizza time?" Brown asked as I rolled up my window.

I nodded and frowned at the bullet hole in the seat next to me. Mr. Small wasn't going to like how I'd redecorated his SUV.

* * *

"Vhat the hell?" Small yelled when we got back to the café. "You got my ride shot up!"

Codger was more sanguine. "I take it you found them."

"We found someone," I said with a shrug. "There are folks just across the bridge who aren't allowing anyone to cross it. When we did so, they took exception to it."

"I know the place," Codger said. "Used to be a retirement community before the war. Lots of old folks living in individual condos." He nodded. "It would have been pretty easy to take over. Then, once you're established, to convert any number of the condos into…whatever you wanted."

He didn't have to mention the depravities that were probably being conducted there. We were all aware of what went on in a fallen world, and, with the types of people being taken there, the things that were probably going on.

"What do we do about it?" Codger asked.

"First we have pizza," Brown said. "I was promised pizza if I found bad guys. If you look at the vehicle, we definitely did." He smiled beatifically. "Where's my pizza?"

* * *

We ordered pizza and discussed the best way to take out the complex. There was no "good" way; it was too big. An air or missile strike would have been optimal—unfortunately, those hadn't existed since the war. Also, Codger reminded us that there were hostages in there that he'd like to recover, which would have ruled out an airstrike, anyway. If we could have called one in, which we couldn't.

Codger broke out his map again which showed the area. Unfortunately, the scale it was drawn to didn't show the area in great detail, but we could at least get a general idea of the complex. The facility was on a peninsula that projected to the south of the island. It consisted of a row of small, single-family condos on both sides of the street that ran down the peninsula. To the east of the neighborhood sat Oyster Bay—the body of water, not the island—and to the west was a canal that was used to moor small pleasure craft. If we were able to capture the north end of the peninsula, we would have everyone trapped.

Except for any who escaped via the small pleasure craft or any amphibian Geno Freaks who decided to leave by swimming away.

We needed a way to trap the people, the boats, and the Genos. As the infiltration team, Brown and I had two objectives—we needed to get in ahead of the assault and pin people down on both the north and south ends of the island; no one in, and no one out. We needed a second team to secure both ends of the island, but we didn't have time to send back to Perdido Key for the other set of Williams/Brown if we wanted to hit them tonight, and Codger was pretty adamant that we needed to get the abductees back ASAP, before something happened to the latest ones.

They'd already been held two days; I was pretty sure that—if they were still alive—things had already happened to them. And, if they weren't alive, things had already happened to them. But Mr. Boudreaux had said to do things his way, so we accepted "tonight" as an operational necessity.

We made plans based on the resources we had, not the ones we wished we did. Once they were agreed on—and all the pizza was eaten—the meeting broke up. We went to prep for the mission while Codger went to gather all the troops he could find.

* * *

"**T**ime," Brown said, looking at his watch.

We had waited until an hour after midnight. Long enough for a midnight guard change—assuming there was one—and then long enough for the guards to get bored and complacent. I hated starting the assault without heavy surveillance of the target area, but taking the time to do so meant another family would probably disappear into the night.

We geared up and slid into the warm waters of Oyster Bay for the short swim across the 400-foot-wide inlet. Swimming sucks for Agents as we are incredibly dense due to our genetic modifications. We used some floats to help us along, and clouds covered the moon so there was nothing to give us away. We came ashore silently behind a screen of scrub trees and moved forward to where the men had been guarding the end of the bridge.

Unfortunately, either they increased the checkpoint manning at night—a failure which could be attributed to not enough prior surveillance—or our earlier run-in with them had raised their alert level. Either way, there were now three people watching the end of the bridge.

"What do you want to do?" Brown asked quietly.

I gave him the "hold" sign while I tried to figure it out. Before I had a plan, though, the situation resolved itself for us.

"Gotta pee," one of the men said.

"You didn't think to do that before you came out, dumbass?" a second asked.

"I was otherwise occupied," the first man said with a chuckle as he started undoing his trousers.

"Wait! Don't do it there, or we'll have to smell it all night," the third man said. "Go over into the trees, at least, would ya?"

The man walked right past Brown. He looked at me, and I nodded. Brown pounced on the man from behind, wrapped a hand over his mouth, and slit his throat. One down.

We crept up to the edge of the tree line and looked at the remaining guards. They were close enough and looking the other way. Brown and I sprang on them. The guards heard a noise and started to turn, but we crossed the distance with a speed non-Agents couldn't hope to achieve. A couple of knife strokes later, and they were both down. We dragged their bodies into the trees, then flashed a directional light twice toward the other side of the bridge.

Small, Michaelson, and Edwards raced across the bridge to join us, and Codger and his force of 20 normal men came along after them. Small was already wearing his minigun, and Michaelson and Edwards were carrying other parts of Small's weapons inventory, in addition to weapons and equipment for Brown and me that we hadn't wanted to be encumbered with on our first trip.

I pointed out which of the buildings the armed responders had come from, then Brown and I put our gear back on—including what the other members of the team had brought—and went swimming again. It was harder this time, both because we had farther to go—a half-mile, this time—and we were carrying a lot more gear, but we'd both done swims that were a lot worse, and we emerged again on the southern end of the peninsula only slightly winded. I came ashore and started to prep my gear while Brown emplaced the small, remote-controlled mine we'd brought in the center of the canal.

He finally came ashore, and we both finished gearing up. Brown looked at his watch as a detonation lit up the northern sky. "Right on time," he noted. The glow from the first RPG round hadn't faded yet when the second explosion lit the night, followed by a number of automatic rifles firing.

We gave the enemy forces another minute to start flowing toward the assault, then we moved out. Lights were coming on throughout the complex, and people were coming out of buildings and running to the north. Generally, we let them; we were looking for bigger fish—or gators—to fry.

When no one came out of the southernmost house, we broke in and found it to be a storeroom of sorts. It looked like all the loot of past raids had been stored here, both gear and valuables. We quickly left and moved up the street, keeping to the shadows.

30 | IBSON & KENNEDY

"There!" Brown whispered urgently, pointing up the street. From one of the left-side houses a little farther up, a…thing…had emerged. I knew instantly this was one of our Genos, probably the smaller of the two. Detonations continued to light up the night, and we could see the creature was green, with a tail and a small crocodile snout. It was also naked and very definitely a female.

She was also faster than shit, and she went speeding up the street before I could find her in the sights of my rifle.

"Wait for it," Brown coached as he looked through his spotter scope. "She's got to stop in a second to orient herself. Winds are calm, so no adjustment necessary. Wait for it…" The woman stopped. "Take her!"

I squeezed the trigger, and the Barrett sniper rifle barked. The supersonic .50 caliber round hit her in the left shoulder blade and ripped out her chest. She went flying forward and laid still in the sandy soil.

"That's a ki—" Brown started to say, but he was interrupted by a roar from the front of the house the Geno had come from. I spun, and there was the male Geno, easily seven feet tall, with full crocodile snout, tail, and huge arms and legs. And very definitely male.

I spun and fired, but the creature was already in motion, and the round went through the space he'd been a split-second before. I fired another time as he bull rushed me, but he dodged as he came at us. Brown whipped out his pistol and fired several times. He hit him once, but it was a glancing hit that ricocheted off.

There's no way anything should have been that tough, and even if there were, it should *not* have been that fast. I could see I didn't have time for another shot as it came straight for me, and I threw the rifle at it as I dodged to the side.

The creature batted the rifle away as he swiped at me, and my left side lit up with the fires of hell as his nails ripped through my skin. Great, he was augmented, as well as a Geno—*nothing* should have been that fast. Even I wasn't.

I rolled to my feet, drawing my pistol and knife, only to find he'd gone after Brown. Brown shot the creature once in the side as he raced forward, but the monster shrugged it off. Brown dove to the side, but the creature was ready and slashed him across the back. The Geno spun to dive on Brown, but I shot him twice before he could, and he spun back toward me.

Obviously, I needed bigger bullets, I realized as he charged back toward me. Like something built for penetrating rhino hide. My bullets kept bouncing off him.

I hit him again as he bore down on me, this time in the right hand, and he screamed as he lunged toward me. I feinted like I was going to dive out of the way to the left, then did a backhand knife slash instead. He'd bought into the feint, and my knife slid across his left bicep. His scales—I could see now he was covered in scales—turned my blade, though, and he spun back around to laugh at me.

I fired at his head. Even though the rounds weren't penetrating, they had to hurt, and maybe the blunt force trauma would damage something. I could hope, anyway. It didn't matter, though; he dodged, and I missed.

"Looks like I'm missing all the fun," Edwards said as he ran up. He drew two long, thin knives. "C'mon, big boy, let's dance."

The Geno roared and strode toward him, and Edwards dropped into a ready pose. The Geno was either starting to slow, or Edwards was *really* fast, for he made up in speed the advantage the Geno had in reach, and the two exchanged blows faster almost than my eyes could follow.

The Geno finally slapped away one of Edwards' knives, and it spun off to the side. The creature chuckled. "Now what are you going to do, puny human?"

Edwards passed the knife back and forth between his hands. "Kill you, I suppose."

"Never!" the Geno roared. He sprang forward and knocked Edwards to the ground with a massive swipe. Edwards rolled with it, then sprang to his feet, although his face was now laid open from ear to mouth where one of the Geno's talons had caught him.

Edwards settled into a martial arts stance, bare-handed, and I realized his knife was missing. After a second, I found it—he had allowed himself to be hit so he could stab the Geno in its armpit, and he had embedded the knife there to the hilt.

The Geno stared at him for a second, then his eyes glassed over, and he collapsed.

Edwards walked over, pulled out his knife, and slit the Geno's throat, before standing. "Anyone got a bandage?" he asked. He was sort of hard to understand as the words came out of his cheek, and his lips were split.

I got to work putting his face together but then Brown exclaimed, "Heads-up!"

The battle to the north had obviously been won by our side, as people were streaming toward us. A brief firefight ensued, but most of the men—and a few women—were more interested in fleeing than in watching where they were going, and we put them down. One group tried to flee by boat, but Brown detonated the mine in the canal, and the people went flying from it. We shot them as they tried to swim to the opposite shore.

Finally, there was no one left to shoot, and we began clearing the buildings. It was as bad as we had feared. The women and children had been used for a variety of evil purposes, including experimentation with different Geno technologies. We put down everything we found who wasn't human and saved the few women and children who were still alive.

As I went to enter the third building—the one the Genos had come out of—Brown came out and put a hand on my chest, stopping me. "Don't go in there," he said.

"Why not?"

He sighed. "Better you find out now, I guess." He swallowed. "Your wife and daughter are in there, and they're both dead. Trust me, you don't want to see them."

"I'm not married," I said without thinking.

"Not you, your alter ego. Your civilian family. They're dead."

"I need to see," I said, and I pushed past him.

He was right. There was enough left that I could identify them. The Genos and their human cohorts—it looked like both—had done unspeakable, unforgivable things to them. Then they'd cooked parts of them to eat. Even though I could view it clinically—I didn't feel an emotional attachment to them as Williams—it was still horrific, and I was happy my alter ego would be spared the sight of seeing what was left of them. It was easily enough to break a man.

As my eyes scanned the room, the things that had been done to them were a literal gut-punch, even without the attachment. The fact that people could do those things—especially the things done to my daughter—drove me to my knees, and I vomited on the floor of the house. I wished I could bring the Genos back from the dead so I could kill them again. A thousand deaths wouldn't make up for what I saw in front of me, though. And I couldn't even bring them back once. I wept for about ten minutes before leaving.

* * *

"I'm sorry about your family," Luc Boudreaux said after we had given him the after-action report.

I shrugged.

"I know you—as Williams—don't care as much, but I am truly sorry."

I stared at him, doing my best to forget what I'd seen in the Genos' house. Finally, I nodded. "Thanks."

"Now that the situation is less fluid, Agents are being allowed time off to be their civilian alter egos—"

"Don't want it," I said, interrupting him. It was probably the first time I'd ever done so. I shrugged again. "There's nothing for me to go back to. At some point, my alter ego might see pictures of the Geno compound or hear stories. I don't know—based on what I know of him—if he could survive it. I don't know if anyone could survive it."

"We could give you a different imprint—make you into whichever Agent you'd like to be—or we could re-imprint you with the baseline Williams imprint, overwriting everything that's happened since the war. You wouldn't have any of your memories…"

I shook my head. "No thanks. If you did that, the memories of my other family would be lost, for no purpose. You can delete my civilian persona; I'm never going back to him.

"I want to stay who I am right now. There might be other imprints with better combat skills, but I have what I need—the ability to get into places and kill the people who would hold others against their wills. I will still work for you, but I am going to dedicate the rest of my life to eradicating slavers and hostage takers. I can't do anything for my alter ego or his family to make it better or bring them back from the dead, but I can do this so other fathers don't have to see what I saw there."

Boudreaux nodded. "You've earned the right to do so. I hope you'll stay here and help me build a new society, but I understand what you want to do."

"Thanks," I said with a nod.

I had no idea what the future held, but I committed myself to bringing civilization back to this Fallen World.

* * * * *

Chris Kennedy Bio

A Webster Award winner and three-time Dragon Award finalist, Chris Kennedy is a Science Fiction/Fantasy/Young Adult author, speaker, and small-press publisher who has written over 25 books and published more than 100 others. Chris' stories include the "Occupied Seattle" military fiction duology, "The Theogony" and "Codex Regius" science fiction trilogies, stories in the "Four Horsemen," "Fallen World," and "In Revolution Born" universes and the "War for Dominance" fantasy trilogy. Get his free book, "Shattered Crucible," at his website, https://chriskennedypublishing.com.

Called "fantastic" and "a great speaker," he has coached hundreds of beginning authors and budding novelists on how to self-publish their stories at a variety of conferences, conventions, and writing guild presentations. He is the author of the award-winning #1 bestseller, "Self-Publishing for Profit: How to Get Your Book Out of Your Head and Into the Stores," as well as the leadership training book, "Leadership from the Darkside."

Chris lives in Virginia Beach, Virginia, with his wife, and is the holder of a doctorate in educational leadership and master's degrees in both business and public administration. Follow Chris on Facebook at https://www.facebook.com/ckpublishing/.

# # # # #

Respawn by Robert E. Hampson

"**H**ere you go, sweetie. Enjoy your breakfast." Jack didn't remember ordering anything, but the waitress was laying out a full spread in front of him. It was early evening, not breakfast, but he had a stack of pancakes, three fried eggs, a pile of crispy bacon, and half a plate of golden hash browns in front of him. Oh, and a tall mug of coffee.

He looked up at the waitress. She wouldn't be considered beautiful, and not necessarily pretty, but she was pleasant to look at, and she'd called him "sweetie." She'd also winked at him when he glanced her way. He looked around at the other patrons—each had a plate with some variant of hash browns and waffles in front of them.

Ah. *The Waffle Shack.*

In fact, given the unusual order of pancakes in front of him, it was *his* Waffle Shack.

He looked out the windows. Sure enough, it was daylight. The sky was the usual gray—it was always gray since the Event—but by the angle of the light, it was *morning*, not evening as he'd thought. The breakfast his waitress placed before him was exactly what he would have ordered if he'd just walked in.

Except he hadn't.

Just walked in, that is.

He remembered darkness with flashes of light.

And pain. Lots of pain.

Ah.

And now he was in his Waffle Shack.

"Honey?" he called. The waitress turned from the sink and looked in his direction. "Could I get some sugar and cream for my coffee?"

"Sure thing, sweetie. There's a sugar dispenser in front of you. Do you want half-and-half or creamer?"

"Actually, I'd like the little brown packets—about eight of them, and the creamer in the little blue cups. Four of them should do."

The waitress looked at him with a big smile. "Eight of the brown, four of the blue. Sounds like my ex. He put maple syrup in his coffee."

That was the countersign.

But first, breakfast. He'd clearly need the calories. He always did in this situation.

The eggs were just slightly crispy at the very edges and the yolks runny. The hash browns were hot and sopped up the egg yolk. The bacon crunched and broke into delightful crispy bits in his mouth. Most importantly, he had pancakes...in a place that normally only served waffles. He caught the eye of the short-order cook behind the counter and raised his coffee in a toast of appreciation. The man always did know how to do breakfast right.

The waitress brought the additives for his coffee, and he mixed them into the dark, strong brew. The resulting drink was thick and sweet, kind of like the smile the waitress kept giving him. Okay, so maybe she *was* pretty, if you didn't know her secret. Of course, to Jack, that secret just made her more interesting.

He finished his breakfast, paid the bill, and headed for the door. At the last minute, he decided to go to the restroom before exiting. The facilities were clean, just like *almost* every Waffle Shack he'd been in. Well, except for that one in the Carolinas. Still, they all had the same shape, the same menu, and the same waitresses who called you "sweetie" and "honey" and "sugar." If you knew what you were looking for, the signs were all there. If you didn't? Well, it was Southern Hospitality at its finest.

The side wall of the restroom had a supply closet locked with a combination. The waitress had used the countersign "Maple," so he keyed in 6-2-7-5-3, the telephone keypad equivalent of M-A-P-L-E. He followed it with his personal 3-digit code, turned the knob, and walked through the door.

* * *

"**N**ice to see you again, Mister C," said the man at the reception desk. He wore a simple, dark suit, but with the ubiquitous Waffle Shack nametag that read *Chris, Manager*. "Will you be needing the usual?"

"I guess so, Chris," said Jack. "Let's start with why I'm here."

"Certainly, Mister C." The manager turned his computer screen so Jack could see it. The scene showed clear outlines of white on a dark gray background. An Odin's Eye. Jack didn't entirely trust the mystical surveillance devices, but it was how the Network kept track of their operatives. There was just the slightest amount of blurring, indicating the Eye was outside the building's walls, looking inward.

There was just enough detail in the white, black, and gray for Jack to recognize himself sitting at a table with Aaron. This was the restaurant where he'd met Aaron the night before, then. A third figure

40 | IBSON & KENNEDY

walked up to the table—the time stamp said 2150, suggesting the third figure was the waiter, telling them the kitchen was closing.

The view pulled back, and a much crisper image of two figures seated just slightly below the level of the two in the restaurant resolved. There was also a *very* bright blur in front of them—a car engine. They must have been idling at the curb. One of the figures turned its head, and Jack caught a glimpse of multiple writhing lines surrounding it. The entire image turned to static. *Aw, shit, a Medusa. He stoned the Odin's Eye when he turned that way.*

The image returned from a different angle. A new Eye had joined the surveillance. Now, the second man in the vehicle out front held a long tube. There was an intense flare of light and an explosion.

Damn. Rocket-propelled grenade. Those guys weren't screwing around, they actually used explosives instead of magic.

"That was the event that triggered the respawn." It wasn't strictly necessary for the manager to say that, but it did indicate it had been quick, if not exactly painless.

Jack remembered shards of glass and the look on Aaron's face. This was Aaron's fault: if he hadn't insulted the Penguin, the alchemist wouldn't have felt the need to take him out.

* * *

"Will you be needing anything else?" Chris asked as Jack buckled on his usual gear. Three pistols, twenty magazines, and an untold number of knives disappeared onto the big man's body—plus two flashlights, a bandolier of prepackaged fireballs, and a single wand. One pistol and several "seeker" knives were attached to the armored vest, but Jack always referred to those as the "throwaway" pieces. It was the stuff the other guy *didn't* see that would kill him.

Even more magazines, knives, and pistols went into a backpack and then into an already-full duffel bag made of black ballistic nylon. "Naw, I'm good," replied Jack as he zipped up the bag.

"Sir will be needing these, then." The Network manager handed over a key ring with vehicle and residential keys. They were Jack's and had been in his pocket while he was at the restaurant. How he had managed to retrieve them and hand them over after a respawn was one of those questions you learned never to ask.

It was right up there with why you ended up at the Shack in the first place.

It had been twenty years since the Event had released magic into the world. People reacted as might be expected—they reveled in the ability to cast spells, to fly, to influence weaker minds—and they misused those abilities. That, too, was as expected; imagine road rage when you could literally cast a spell and incinerate the offending driver. Most people realized too late they didn't control their abilities, the abilities controlled them, and Magic was an angry god. The death toll was in the millions. Some societies, such as the North American Hegemony, could afford the damage and the losses. Africa, parts of Eastern Europe, and certain Caribbean islands, with their old magic and mystical traditions, were barren landscapes, radiating so much thaumic energy they might as well have been radioactive glass.

The survivors learned. If you were an Adept, you kept to yourself. If you had a small amount of skill, you apprenticed to an Adept. If you were a Normal, you stayed out of the way.

On the other hand, if you were a Normal with a *particular skillset*, you worked for the Network. Mind you, you didn't seek employment with the Network; the Network found *you* and made you an offer that it would be foolish to refuse…

…with benefits such as the Shack.

* * *

J ack took the keys, nodded to the attendant, and stepped through the exit into the Georgia heat.

It was nighttime—again—but the air was still hot, muggy, and filled with strange energy. It had reached almost a hundred degrees during the day, and the inevitable late day thaumicstorm did nothing to abate the heat. Orange and purple lightning and blue-green raindrops might look pretty, but the truth was storms simply raised the humidity and made it even more uncomfortable. That was one reason Jack had left Atlanta. The summers in Detroit were better, although the winters sucked. The fact that the city was a wasteland—Jack could go all day without seeing another Normal, let alone an Adept—was simply a bonus. However, Aaron had asked him to come. *"It'll be fine,"* he'd said. *"The Convention will cover our tracks,"* he'd said. Jack snorted; obviously, that hadn't worked, given that the Penguin had taken them both out with an RPG.

He frowned. He'd been complacent—the Penguin's operating network was in California and wasn't supposed to be this far east. He wasn't about to make that mistake again.

Naturally, he was in the parking lot of a Waffle Shack, but it was a two-story building that used to have a club above the restaurant. Though his pancakes had told him where he'd started, his trip through the back room took him out a *different* Shack, albeit one that seemed passingly familiar. He looked back in the windows and didn't see the pretty waitress or his regular cook.

Shit. He never got her phone number.

Then again, she might not have been one of the "ordinary" workers.

Somehow that thought didn't help. The idea that she might be one of the Extraordinaries—the Ex-Tee-Ohs, in the trade—made her that much more interesting.

He unlocked his car and threw the duffel in the back seat. Yes, it was his car, it even had the right dents, scratches, and yesterday's half-empty coffee cup. Again, one of those things you didn't ask about. As he climbed in, he wondered about Aaron. Did he respawn as well? He knew Aaron was something of an operator, a minor Adept working on his journeyman card. What he didn't know was whether he was connected in *that* way. In the Network, you respawned at a Waffle Shack near where you died, although in Jack's experience, it initially seemed to be the one he usually frequented—he just came out somewhere near where he had been before. If Aaron did something similar, he might just come walking out that door…?

On the other hand, there also seemed to be a delay of up to twenty-four hours between death and respawn. That was a good thing, and, in the past, it had helped him stay away from cops. On the other hand, you often saw cops in a Waffle Shack or walking out, but you never saw them walk in.

Don't ask, Jack. Don't ask. You *really* don't want to know in case you have to off one as part of a job.

If Aaron was going to respawn, it may have already happened, or it could be who knows how long until it happened. There was no point waiting around here. He needed information, and the best place to find that would be the Speakeasy.

* * *

J ack's appearance didn't garner any reaction when he walked into the hotel lobby. He'd put some red plastic plugs into the barrels of the throwaways and blended right in with the superheroes, TV and movie soldiers, and even some of the more— *ahem*—furry creatures in the soaring atrium. It was another one of those things you didn't question. Ever since the Event, time, itself, had gotten twisted; if you were headed to Eddie's Speakeasy, there would be a science fiction convention going on.

Atlanta seemed to have survived the Event and its aftermath pretty well. Jack suspected that it was due to the Convention. Before the Event, it had been one very long weekend a year. Now, it seemed that the Convention was happening any time he was in town. If the various Magicals and Normals wanted to throw a 365-day convention to cover their activities, the people of Atlanta would certainly welcome the business.

The glass-sided elevators were crowded, as was the lobby where guests waited for them. Jack looked up and down. There were five elevators in use and on various floors, each one filled to capacity, and nearly fifty people waiting to board them. After all, this was *the* Convention. The crowd was okay, though. The Convention had concerts, shows, some of his favorite authors…and girls. Girls in costume. Girls practically *out* of costume. Girls in costumes made of duct tape and dental floss.

It also had the Speakeasy.

Jack bypassed the main elevator lobby and went to the one in the adjacent tower. Again, you didn't ask how or why this worked. You just followed instructions and you got to the Speakeasy. If you tried to find it on your own, it wouldn't be there.

There were a few other people in the elevator car, so he punched the button for the sixteenth floor. This was a much quieter tower and didn't connect to the main atrium, so the elevators were never as crowded. People got on and off at the lower floors, but the numbers trailed off the higher the elevator ascended. A couple got off at the twelfth floor, then three more at fourteen.

Jack was the only one getting off at sixteen. That's how it always worked. There never seemed to be anyone else at sixteen, either on the elevator or at the floor. His instructions were very specific about what to do if someone else was present, but he'd never had to use them.

There was a house phone on a table opposite the elevator bank. He picked up the receiver, punched in 1-6-3-5, and waited for an answer.

Someone answered on the other end but didn't speak. It was ringing, then it clicked, and the line opened. That was fine, Jack had his instructions.

"This is Jack. Brown-eight. Blue-five." He also entered his personal code on the keypad.

He heard three beeps. The code was accepted.

The call disconnected, and the elevator behind him chimed. It was the same one he'd exited a few moments before, but instead of glass walls, it had plain metal, plastic sides, and it was empty.

The new elevator car shimmered slightly. If you had The Sight and knew what to look for, you'd see that the walls were covered with runes to ward against unauthorized use. He was just about to step into the elevator when two men in long coats came out of the corridor that presumably led to the guest rooms on this floor. Given that Jack had never explored this floor and never seen anyone else, he'd always assumed the rest of the floor was empty.

They were non-descript, costumed as members of the libertarian-cowboy-space-opera fandom, complete with the long brown coats favored by those costumed players, or "cosplayers." Jack had been known to wear that costume at a con. The long coats could—and usually did—conceal a lot.

He paused. His skin itched. The runes were activating, and there were explicit rules regarding what to do if there was someone else present when the elevator arrived to take you to the Speakeasy.

Explicit rules. No exceptions, no negotiations.

Jack grabbed a gun off his chest rig with his off-hand, and a pair of seeker-charmed throwing knives with his strong hand just as the libertarian space-cowboys swept the long coats aside to reveal large black wands.

Crap.

This wasn't supposed to happen. Did this mean the Speakeasy was involved? Or compromised? Or was it the Penguin?

Since the knives were in Jack's strong hand—his left—he planned to throw first, then shift the gun over from his weak hand. He could shoot ambidextrously, but he'd be more accurate with the gun in his left hand. On the other hand—he grinned at the unintentional pun—unless the pair knew a lot about him, they'd consider a gun in his right hand to be the main threat.

As expected, the pair saw his grin and misinterpreted his reaction, levelling their wands and backing up slightly at the sight of the big man grinning for no good reason.

He released the first knife as one of the pair got off his first shot. The other man never got an aimed shot off, given the knife that had flown unerringly and embedded itself in his throat. Aimed was the operative word, a spray of fireballs ripped past Jack and tore into the wall and ceiling. A heavy slam behind him signaled a security door closing off the elevator.

Shit. With the elevator in lockdown, he'd have to use the secondary route to get to the Speakeasy. If he got there at all.

He felt heat and a pair of impacts on his vest. *Quit daydreaming, Jack. You still have a threat in front of you.* He threw the remaining knife but rushed it. It flew true, magically seeking its target, but the man raised his left arm and the knife bounced off the coat. The first man was down and thrashing. No threat for now, but he needed to even the odds against the wand.

Jack tossed his gun from right hand to left and retrieved a second pistol from his vest. The other man might have the advantage in rate of fire, but full-auto wand bursts were notoriously inaccurate. Jack was a crack pistol shot and, at less than twenty feet apart, the distance favored him—unless the other guy was armored.

Apparently, the long coats were magically reinforced. His bullets tore the surface, but never penetrated. Moreover, the loose coat dissipated most of the impact. The two traded shots, Jack taking a few more impacts on his own enchanted armor, while all his shots were either absorbed or deflected. He tried for a headshot, but his opponent merely raised an arm and wielded the brown coat like a cape. Jack was running low on bullets and would soon need to reload; his opponent's wand did not need reloading.

This exchange wasn't working, so Jack ducked his head and plowed into his assailant, taking him by surprise and knocking him down. The two were tangled up in each other and the long coat.

Jack had a hand inside and a knife up his sleeve. A twist and the other man stopped struggling. In death, his body shifted into the shape of an aquatic mammal—slick black skin, short flippers, round head with no external ears.

Damn it. Selkies.

Slowly, Jack stood up and surveyed the scene. Two unknown assailants, dead on the floor. Numerous bullet holes, charred spots, and a knife sticking out of the table with the telephone, still quivering.

The phone rang.

"Do you need cleanup?" The voice on the other end spoke without introduction. Of course, Jack didn't announce himself when he picked up the receiver, either.

"Yes. Two down."

"Very well, get into the next elevator car. Go to the top, get out, and follow the lights."

Almost as soon as he hung up, the elevator chime sounded, and the doors opened once more. Jack stepped in, and the doors closed. There were no buttons or indicator lights, just an immediate sensation of movement in multiple directions at once. The sensation lasted for one minute, then it slowed, and the door opened.

The floor was unfinished, with only bare steel beams, concrete floor and ceiling, and strings of bare incandescent lights. The lights began to blink in sequence, leading away from the elevator bank. The lights would illuminate an area ahead of him and extinguish behind him. He walked for several minutes in a small pool of light, shadows of construction debris just out of view. There was also a hint of movement in the dark, as though he was being shadowed.

The lights stopped at another elevator bank. As he approached, one of the doors opened. Again, it was a featureless steel and plastic box. He entered, the door closed, and the box began to move. After several more minutes of vertical—and horizontal—movement, the door opened again.

He was on a high floor of the main hotel atrium. He could hear the noise from below and see costumed congoers on the floors above and below. Doors lined the corridors to the left and right of him. He was in one corner of a large, open square, with hotel rooms all the way around. He could see people going in and out of the doors on other floors, but never on this one.

He turned to his right and went around a short wall separating the elevator from a corridor that led to a door recessed from the main hallway. The number on the door read 1-6-3-5, and it was covered with convention-appropriate signs and flyers.

He knocked on the door and was ushered into another short hallway. There was a strange effect such that he couldn't actually see into the suite. Everything more than three feet from his eyes was blurry. A medium height, fat man was standing in front of him with his hand out.

"Credentials."

Jack reached into his pocket and felt four large, heavy disks. He pulled them out and looked at the faces of the coins. Each would serve to identify him, but they each also had a secondary meaning in identifying his purpose here tonight.

The one with the dragon meant he was off-duty and just here to relax. The one with the mushroom cloud meant he was claiming sanctuary under the Network's compact with the Speakeasy and was not to be disturbed. The one with the cat's paw meant he was working and on contract. Speakeasy rules said he couldn't actively pursue a target here, but unlike some places, they'd understand if the target found him, and he had to act.

The one with the rocket ship meant he needed information and was there for the contacts. That was the one that Jack showed the man. "I'm looking for Doc."

"Very good, Jack." The man looked up at him and smiled. In all, he was probably as large as Jack, just not as tall. That didn't mean Jack would want to try to match wits or skill with the man. It was rumored that he might have had something to do with the Event. That was before he'd retired, though. Now Eddie ran the Speakeasy and brokered information.

"C'mon in and relax. Get Ginger to mix you something at the bar. Doc's on the smoking deck; he told us you'd had a respawn and said he was expecting you. Oh." Eddie laid a hand on Jack's arm. Normally, he wouldn't tolerate that from a guy, but this was Eddie, after all. "I have to warn you; I'm expecting the Penguin later tonight. I don't want trouble from you two. He's a friend, too. I don't want to have to throw one or both of you out of the suite via the balcony."

Jack swallowed his first response. It wasn't an idle threat. He'd been in the suite the year the scrawny elf had claimed to be "the most casually dangerous" person in the room. Eddie had walked right up behind the elf, lifted him up over his head as if benchpressing a barbell, and thrown him off the smoking deck. It was fourteen floors down to the top of the hotel entrance, and the fae crashed right through into the lobby. An ogre came up about an hour later, a hotel cop, that is. He spoke briefly to Eddie and then left. No one ever spoke of the event, but everyone knew that it had happened.

You didn't mess with the Speakeasy or its proprietor.

Jack decided on the simplest response. "Yes, sir."

Eddie moved out of the way, and the effect lifted, allowing Jack to see into the suite. It was much larger than it should be for a room at the corner of this hotel. There was a rather large seating area and a full bar to one side. Through a doorway, he could see another seating area with a large screen TV and several game controllers. From previous experience, Jack knew there were two more social areas and at least two bedrooms beyond that. He opted for an energy drink mixed with vodka from the bar and headed to the glass doors that opened onto the smoking deck.

On the way, he spotted some familiar faces. *Oh, shit.* They were powerful Adepts. One was the head of House Sabaton, and the other, House Heinlein. They seemed to be chatting amiably in the living room, but he'd have to pass between them to get to the sliding doors. He shuddered. He'd used the rocket ship coin of Heinlein as his credential. With *her* here, that meant he'd declared an allegiance. He'd never been on the bad side of the other wizard, but they were people you did *not* want to cross, and he wasn't entirely certain he'd avoided their shit list.

He needed to be *very* careful. The Lady turned to look at him. She knew. She knew he'd used the coin; of course, it was probably enchanted such that she would be aware of its presence. She was well-known for returning "unacceptable" items—documents, magical items, tribute—covered in red…and it wasn't ink.

As carefully as he could, Jack edged past the Adepts. There might have been a time when he would have stopped to give the obligatory pleasantries—after all, the Network was officially neutral—but again, he wasn't certain he hadn't pissed off one of them. They wouldn't do anything here, of course, although one always had to be cautious of that whole "if looks could kill" thing.

He managed to get past with just a nod of acknowledgement from the Lady. She was wearing a neutral expression, so it probably meant there would be no immediate repercussions.

"Hello, Jack."

Oh shit. "Tay." She was probably the one person he *shouldn't* have run into in the Speakeasy. His Sight was definitely not up to spec. This Penguin business still had him rattled.

<SMACK>

He was expecting the slap—it was penance.

"You broke my heart, Jack."

"You broke mine first, Tay."

"I heard you got blown. Up." She didn't need the pause to turn the phrase into double entendre. She did *that* as naturally as breathing.

On the other hand, Jack could watch her breathing all day long.

"Yeah, I've still got some memory loss." He gave her his best boyish grin. "I can't remember…were we supposed to have a date?"

She reached up to slap him again, but instead, grabbed his ears and pulled him in close for a long, deep kiss. So deep, she could probably taste the pancakes, and so long, he might need them again, soon.

Before they both ran out of air, she broke the kiss, then leaned in close and whispered in his ear. "This isn't over, Jack." Then she bit his earlobe. Hard.

When she pulled back, there was blood on her lips. She licked it off slowly, giving him another one of her looks, then spun and took off through the suddenly crowded room.

Jack needed a moment to regain his balance. Tay *always* had that effect on him, and frankly, he never truly knew where he stood with her.

When he could stand at all. Oh well, she would have to wait until after this business was finished.

He stepped out onto the balcony and saw three men. Doc…and two other men sitting with Doc, smoking cigars. Doc gave him a nod, and Jack approached.

Sitting in the corner was Johnny Reeve. Rumor said that he'd once been in the same business as Jack but had retired. It hadn't been an easy retirement, or at least that was part of the rumor. The dog lying at his feet was supposed to be part of it, but people usually didn't talk about the dog. He wrote science fiction now. The rest of the rumor had it that he had something to do with the Network. Every time Jack had been in the Speakeasy, Reeve had been there, smoking a cigar, drinking an iced coffee drink, and telling stories.

Reeve nodded to Jack and motioned to a chair.

The other person on the deck was Aaron, and he was spewing a nonstop stream of complaints. "…she placed a regular waffle in front of me. Regular! I told her the contract says *pecan* waffle, not regular. So, she took it away. All of it. By the time she came back with my pecan waffle, the guy comes out of the back and tells me I must go, that I'm expected here. I mean, she had *just* served me my pecan waffle, and I didn't even get a bite! That's got to be against the rules!"

54 | IBSON & KENNEDY

Doc shook his head, while Reeve pointedly ignored Aaron. "Jack? I heard you had a bit of trouble on the way up?"

He might have known that Reeve would already know, and the way Doc was nodding in agreement told Jack he knew as well.

"Yeah, couple of SEALs over in the other tower."

"They're not supposed to be there," Aaron said. "Tower two is Army country, not Navy."

"Well, supposed to or not, they didn't want to go sailing. It's as if they knew I was coming…and seeing as you're already *here*, Aaron, I have to wonder just how much trouble you've gotten me into."

The other man held up his hands. "Hey, not me. I did *not* start this, the Penguin did."

"Oh, bullshit, Aaron," Doc said. "I heard you question his loyalties on the Army-Navy game. International regimes have fallen on less provocation."

"Look, how was I supposed to know he's Navy? He's an *alchemist*, that's Air Force territory for Ghu's sake! He should be a natural Army ally!"

"He's a shifter, you idiot, and he works with the brain. That makes him Navy. Besides, you insulted his alchemy." Reeve tsked. "That makes two branches mad at you. Not good, man, not good."

Once the initial chaos of the Event had settled down, the surviving military commanders fought to harness the magic for military uses. Physical magic such as spells, wards, and artifacts became the province of the Army. Mental magic, mind control, and shapeshifting were Navy. Alchemy, as well as the fae and aetheric realms, were Air Force.

"Yeah, especially considering what he's been working on lately." Doc grimaced as he thought about what he'd seen the last time he'd visited the Penguin's lair. He'd called it a lab-OR-a-tory, just like in the movies, but it was clearly an evil alchemist's lair.

"Actually, it's not really the Penguin I'm worried about," said Jack. "It's that assistant of his, Caitlin, that scares me."

"She's harmless," said Doc.

"Yeah, Cate assures us of that…constantly," added Reeve.

"I can handle the Penguin—" Aaron started.

"No, you can't," Jack, Reeve and Doc interrupted, simultaneously.

"—yeah. Okay." Aaron agreed sullenly.

There was a disturbance inside the main part of the suite. Jack glanced in through the glass doors and saw a short, round man in a tuxedo, all black and white. If you knew anything about the man, you knew he was the head of an international crime syndicate. His illicit network of laboratories manufactured the most horrifying alchemical weapons, and for all of his dapper appearance, he gave the impression of some sort of evil penguin.

"Aaron, you're on your own. I don't really want anything to do with the E.P.," Jack said. "Doc, can you support me in this? Reeve?"

"Hey, I'm staying out of this," Reeve replied.

"It *would* be better if you weren't here," Doc said. "I called in a Dragon, but CK was already here."

"…and I'm solidly off-duty," their Dragonrider, CK, said from behind them. She pulled up a chair and toasted Jack with her own vodka and energy drink. Sugar-free, of course. "It's *gauche* to hand Eddie one coin and then change your mind mid-stay. Sorry, Jack."

Jack looked back through the glass doors but didn't see the Penguin. He tried to see through to the more remote rooms of the Speakeasy, but the blurred morphic field appeared to be back.

"Eddie put the fog field back up, Jack. I think that means you and Aaron need to head back inside if you don't want the Penguin surprising you out here." Reeve blew a smoke ring and cocked his head toward the glass door. "Go on, I don't like the sight of blood."

"Wait, that's not what I heard—" began Aaron before Doc smacked him on the back of the head.

"I'd rather not be looking at anyone's blood tonight. I'm off duty, so get in there and apologize to the Penguin, or *I'm* punching your ticket tonight," said Doc.

"You know it hurts like hell every time I die, right?" whined Aaron.

"Yeah, why do you think I said I'd do it? I'm hoping you learn a lesson."

"What's Rule Number One, Aaron?" Jack asked.

"Don't piss off Jack?"

"Actually, that's number four. Number one is 'don't piss off a wizard.'"

"Oh."

"And number two is 'I don't have time to take you to the hospital tonight,'" added Doc.

"Wait, so what's rule three?"

"Something about not buying delivery pizza on the night after garbage pickup."

"Oh, yeah, I suppose that makes sense."

"Momma's rules, Aaron, and right now, Momma says you've broken one and four by dragging her blue-eyed baby boy into this mess." Jack grabbed Aaron by the collar. "Come on; let's get in there."

Once they were back inside, Jack was somewhat surprised to find that the room looked much like an unmodified hotel room. There was no sense of being bigger on the inside, no prickling of the skin suggesting magic, and most surprising of all, no sign of the Penguin or his minions.

The only one present in the room was Lady Virginia of House Heinlein. She was positioned to block further movement into the suite. Jack and Aaron had no choice but to come face-to-face with the powerful Adept.

"You have invoked my protection, intentional or not, Jack."

Jack nodded but did not reply. Aaron opened his mouth, but Jack held up a hand to silence him.

"I have no desire to be involved in this conflict, but neither will I deny one of my Champions," she continued. "Neither will Edward tolerate a blood-feud in his demesnes. Therefore, I have disconnected us from the pocket dimension in which the Speakeasy resides." She waved toward the door. "Outside that door is the Real World, such as it is. You will exit and take your conflict with you, Aaron. Jack, you may stay or go. If you stay, you have my protection for this night only. If you go, you are on your own."

Jack nodded again and looked around. Normally, there were at least three doors in this part of the Speakeasy, plus the sliding glass door to the balcony. Now there was but a single door, and a blank wall behind him. There were only two choices.

Stay. Or go.

"I decided to see this through. I'll go with Aaron."

"Very well. I can grant you two hours. Get where you need to be, then settle this." With this final pronouncement, the Lady faded from view, leaving them in a blank, empty room with just the single door.

The room wasn't entirely empty. There were two black duffle bags on the floor at their feet. Jack's was identical to the one he'd loaded up in the Shack—he thought he'd left it in his car, but once he opened the door to hallway, he realized why the Lady had granted them this favor.

Outside the door was the post-apocalyptic landscape of the *Real World*.

* * *

J ack looked around at the tall, dark buildings with their crumbling concrete and broken glass. The sky was red, and the air smelled vaguely of fire and soot. This was still Atlanta—but Atlanta the way it *really* looked, without the eldritch glamour that turned the shattered landscape into the glitz and glory of the Convention.

Aaron just stared, mouth open. It was clear he was unfamiliar with this scene, considering he kept turning to look behind—and up—at the blasted wreckage of a hotel that ended at the fifteenth floor.

"Yeah. This is how it really looks," Jack said. "I take it you don't spend much time on the Zero Level?"

Aaron's mouth moved as he tried to count the floors to identify the location of the Speakeasy.

"Don't bother. It's not there. It hasn't *really* been there since the big blow-up in 'Nineteen."

"But…but, where *were* we? There's no sixteenth floor?"

"Didn't you pay attention to the Lady? It's a pocket dimension. A Level Nine, full-featured phantasm." Jack paused and looked at Aaron quizzically. "You really *don't* spend any time on Level Zero. Have you ever?"

"I vaguely remember growing up on a farm. It was dry and parched, so it was probably real. My father was a Journeyman Adept, but my mother was a Normal. I take after her. He gave us drops for our eyes to allow us to see at least Level Two, and Level Three on holidays. When I turned seventeen with hardly any magical ability, I joined the Army—thaumic tanks—and they trained me and showed me how to use enchantments and potions to make up for the lack of ability. The Network recruited me straight out of the Army."

"Huh, well, I was born around here, the bastard son of an apprentice sorcerer and the heiress of House Huntsman. I was five when the Lord of Huntsman banished me and removed my nascent power. He had been planning on a dynastic pairing between his daughter and the Knights of Raven. Her having a bastard kid hanging around didn't factor into his plans, especially when it became apparent I'd inherited hers—and his—level of power. He stripped me of my power—or so he thought—and made my mother send me away. My father's sister and her husband took me in and raised me in Detroit." Jack stretched out his arm and indicated the ruins around him. "It takes a Level Four glamour to make my old neighborhood look this good."

Aaron shuddered. "So, how did you end up in the Network?"

"As a kid, I ran errands for the local warlords. I was a little guy, then, and I had just enough magic to make me a really good street urchin." He slapped his barrel chest and laughed a deep laugh. Aaron's eyes widened at the thought of Jack the Mountain as a scrawny kid. "But one day I came across a library and found books about the Old Gods—Heinlein, Clarke, Asimov, Campbell. I dedicated myself to the masters, while becoming the best thief, bouncer, fixer, and procurer in Detroit." Jack started walking, picking his way over and past the shattered concrete and twisted ruins. They reached an intersection. The traffic lights were long gone, but the street signs remained. Both signs read *Peachtree*. They turned right. "Then one day I stumbled across one of the Great Coins. I'd been hired to 'relieve' a potions merchant of some of his stock. Hidden at the bottom of a case was a Challenge Coin from House Heinlein. I stole it, and as far as I know, the owner never found out, because some of the folks he did business with whacked him that same night. The Lady Adept knew, however. She visited me the next night and questioned me at length. I don't remember everything she asked, but I must have convinced her that I was not involved in the death of her operative. She let me keep the coin but insisted I change careers…or at least employers."

"The Network?" Aaron hung back as they approached another intersection. Again, both street signs said *Peachtree*. Jack looked up and down both directions of the cross street, then continued straight across the intersection.

"Partly. Mostly I just freelance. Fixer, problem solver, literal troubleshooter. I make connections and help people find things they've lost. Then they owe me. I take payment in coin, weapons, amulets, charms, bottled spells…and pancakes."

At the next intersection, Jack saw a broken signpost with a familiar sign resting on the pavement. "Up here. This should be the respawn point."

The Waffle Shack looked like every other building around them, broken and abandoned. "Why do we need a respawn? Are you planning on killing me to solve your problem?"

"No, although that would be one solution."

"Why then?" Aaron asked as Jack opened the boarded-up outer door, then crossed the darkened diner to the kitchen door.

"Because we need to get back into at least Level Two before the Penguin finds us." Jack punched the combination into the door lock. "Anyone with even the slightest ability to weave glamour is effectively invisible to us as long as we are in Level Zero."

"Oh," said Aaron as the door opened onto a brightly lit room with a man in a dark suit standing behind a reception desk.

* * *

"Nice to see you again, Mister C," said the manager. "Will you be needing the usual?"

"Nope, not this time, Chris. We just need a reset, not a full respawn." Jack made sure Aaron was completely inside, then pulled the door firmly shut until the latch clicked.

"Very well, sir. Will you be needing anything else?" Chris acted as if Jack hadn't been there just a few hours before.

Jack turned and squinted at the manager. He had a funny feeling. Nothing seemed out of place, it wasn't that kind of feeling, but he had a very strong urge to repeat all of the conversation and actions from his earlier encounter. He'd never felt such a strong sense of *déjà vu* with any of his previous respawns as he did this time. It must have been a side effect of being dumped out into the Real.

"Naw, I'm good," replied Jack as he turned back to the door.

"Sir will be needing these, then." Chris held up a key ring with vehicle and residential keys.

Jack slapped his pocket and realized his keys were not where he'd put them after parking his car at the hotel.

"Sure. Thanks." He took the keys, opened the door, and stepped out into bright sunshine.

* * *

"Okay, now this is different." Aaron squinted up at the sun, shading his eyes with his hand.

Jack opened a pocket in his vest and pulled out a pair of sunglasses. They weren't usually necessary outdoors but were sometimes useful in a club or on a job. Bright sunshine and a clear, blue sky were quite unfamiliar. "This is it, then."

"Where are we?" Aaron asked.

Jack sniffed the odor of dust and held out a hand, palm up, feeling the intense heat of the air. "Texas, I think."

"Oh crap, not Killeen."

"Nah, I think we're further south. There's too much green. San Antonio or down in the Valley."

"Why here? We were originally killed in Atlanta."

"I'm not sure. We're in unfamiliar territory. I haven't been through the Network without a respawn, before. Let me look." Jack held up his left arm and turned a dial on his watch. "Huh. Level Five glamour. Also, we're in Air Force country."

"Shit. We're on the Penguin's home turf."

"Yeah, pretty much." Jack looked around. Instead of standing in a parking lot outside one of the ubiquitous Waffle Shacks, the two men were standing beside a dirt road. Jack's car sat nearby with both doors open. There was only one building visible, a structure with an old windmill that appeared to be several miles away, down the road. Around them were fields of grass and small shrubs. A faint tang of cow manure filled the air. "Okay, ranching country, but still too green. Probably down in the Rio Grande Valley."

"Head to that building?" Aaron pointed down the road.

"I guess." Jack held up his keyring and showed it to Aaron. "There's an extra key on here, so if this key fits a lock in that place, it's likely our next step."

The building turned out to be a small ranch house. It was old and weathered, and parts seemed to be falling apart, but there was a storm cellar entrance with solid wood, new hinges, and a new hasp and padlock. Needless to say, in this magical world, there were no coincidences.

The key fit the lock.

Aaron turned to Jack. "In all of this, you never asked me why."

"Why the Penguin? Or why you involved me?" Jack turned the key and removed the padlock from the hasp.

"Both, really."

"Well, I figured it wasn't really about the Army-Navy game."

The two men moved to either side of the double door, and each grabbed a handle and pulled, opening the doors wide without standing directly in front of the opening.

"Funny you should mention that—" Aaron stopped as a half-dozen black and white rats erupted from the door. They continued past the two men, and he watched for a moment as they passed, then turned back to address Jack. "Rats. I hate rats."

"No, wait," Jack cautioned. "Those are lab rats…"

The distinctive black and white markings on the rodents blurred as each shifted into a full-sized human. Jack had a brief flash of thought, wondering about conservation of mass, but quickly dismissed the distraction. This was magic, after all.

"Shit," both men said simultaneously.

Jack pulled two pistols off his chest rig. He didn't fire both at the same time; he shot the one in his left hand, dropped it when empty, then transferred the one in his off-hand to his dominant hand to continue shooting.

Aaron reached across with his right hand to cross-draw what was either an awfully long knife or a really short sword from his belt. His left hand also went to his belt and opened a pouch, removing several marble-sized objects. Given that neither scabbard nor pouch had been evident a moment ago, the Normal operative was using enchanted gear. Jack wasn't sure he approved but then he *did* use seeker knives on occasion. It's just that they still had conventional points and edges, effective even if the magic failed or was suppressed during a fight.

Ah well, not his place to criticize.

The rat-men formed a semicircle behind Jack and Aaron. They'd have to turn their backs to the doorway to engage, and that made Jack nervous. Jack edged sideways, instead, and looked carefully at the shifters. The men were unarmed except for very long claws on their hands and feet and large buckteeth. If these were anything like normal rats, the claws were the main danger, not so much being cut, as being infected. Since they were up against the Penguin, it was likely to include a fast-acting neurotoxin.

So, stay away from the claws, then.

Jack opened fire, and Aaron threw one of the small spheres. There was a pop as the object hit the first rat-man, and that creature abruptly disappeared.

"Black Holes! Damn it, Aaron, what are you doing carrying around miniature Black Holes?"

"It seemed prudent at the time, Jack."

"Look, it's a magically charged environment. Those things could fizzle, or they could lose containment and wipe out half of Texas." Jack emptied his first pistol. Two more rat-men were down. "I can take these guys. Put those dangerous toys away and conjure that pouch-of-holding back to where you were keeping it. I don't want them anywhere near me."

Two more rat-men were down, but Jack's second pistol was empty. He thumbed the release with his shooting hand, grabbed a magazine from his belt with his right, and reloaded. The last rat-man was down and dissolving into goo while Jack pivoted to check his surroundings and orient back on the open doorway.

"I guess this means that Adeptus Moseley isn't interested in negotiating. Again, why's he so pissed at you, and why are you even bothering him in the first place?" Jack bent to pick up his discarded pistol, reloaded both with fresh magazines, then placed one back on his chest rig, and pulled out a flashlight for his off-hand. "Oh, and if you're going against shifters, you need something bigger than that overgrown toothpick."

"But it's Hanso steel," Aaron pouted.

"You still need something longer to keep the vermin at a distance. I don't care if it's Hattori Hanso's thousand-layer katana. You're a Normal. You can't trust magic to get you out of a fight."

Jack sighed. "Now. Tell me now, before we go inside. What's going on between you and the Penguin?"

"He wants my Stone, Jack," a new voice said. "The great Houses hired him to steal it."

Jack turned and saw a small penguin with bright orange eyebrows emerge from the entrance to the below-ground space. Before his eyes, the flightless bird shifted into the tuxedo-clad man he'd last seen inside Eddie's Speakeasy.

"Moseley." Jack nodded. He normally had nothing against alchemists, even one as notorious as the Penguin.

"Clemson." The Adept nodded back. "You don't have to be involved."

"Sorry, but Aaron invoked my Network Obligation."

"Too bad. You, of all people, would benefit from the Stone. I could give you your magic back." The man waggled his orange eyebrows.

"Um, no thanks." Jack edged over toward Aaron. The younger man was bound to try something foolish.

"Too bad, really. Your cousin is in charge of Huntsman these days. A weak, venal fool. You would make a much better High Adept, and you have a better claim to his seat."

"You can't tempt me, Moseley. I'm happy where I am."

"Ah yes, the favored of Lady Virginia. Fortunately, she's practically the only one of the High Adepts who does *not* want my Alchemists' Stone."

Jack had heard of the near-mystical object. It stored and transferred magic—not spells, but actual magic. If the alchemist had created a Stone, he was a threat to *all* the Adepts.

As they had been talking, Jack had continued to shift his position to be closer to Aaron. In the meantime, Aaron had been shifting slightly to be partially obscured from their adversary's view. There was movement in Jack's peripheral vision, and he dove for the ground.

"Eat hot lead, you Evil Penguin!" Aaron shouted as he pulled the trigger on a rather large, black rifle.

Jack would have shaken his head if he hadn't been covering it. Aaron should know better than to spray full-auto; it was notoriously inaccurate.

On the other hand, there were tiny 'BAMF' noises each time a bullet hit the ground or the building.

Crap. Not again. That boy doesn't learn.

The banishment rounds had no effect on the Adept, but they certainly did on the building, windmill, and environment. The bright sun faded, and the blue sky turned to gray. The buildings and fields disappeared, leaving the three men on a featureless gray plain.

"Shit. Not even Level Zero," Jack observed as the battle rifle's magazine went dry.

As Aaron fumbled to change magazines, the Penguin raised one hand, and lightning shot out, transfixing his opponent. A small stone glowed red, then orange, then white-hot in the Adept's other hand.

Aaron collapsed on the ground, sparks leaping from his fingertips, his eyebrows, his teeth. He was surrounded by an intense white glow that was somehow black around the edges.

"You will not have the luxury of a respawn, Aaron, nor will any of the lords and ladies who hired you," the Penguin gloated as more lightning shot out. "Whereas I…I will live forever."

Jack raised his off-hand. A wave of force lashed out, knocking Moseley off his feet, interrupting the attack on his friend.

"You!" gasped the Penguin. "How are you doing this?"

A shimmer of force appeared around the evil alchemist and started to shrink. The Adept struggled and tried to break through the barrier. Energy discharges sparked throughout the rapidly contracting sphere.

"I said I didn't trust magic. I didn't say I don't know how to use it."

The force sphere contracted all the way down, destroying both the mage and his too-powerful Stone.

Mom was right. Wizards are not to be trusted. Something Granddad should have remembered when he tried to strip my power. She and Aunt Emily and Uncle Jeremy had the right idea getting me out of House politics.

Jack stepped over to Aaron. He was severely burned and twitching all over. The discharges had probably overloaded his muscles and nerves. He looked at Jack and croaked out one word, "please."

Jack pulled a knife from the sheath on his belt, then reconsidered and picked up the tanto that Aaron had dropped earlier. He inspected the blade and felt for the soul inside the steel.

Yes. This will do.

He held the blade to Aaron's throat, and the man closed his eyes. A quick motion and the body went limp.

He began to gather up the detritus of the battle. It was never a good idea to leave human artifacts on one of the nether planes of existence. He was gathering up the last of the rifle casings when Doc and Chris arrived. A duffel bag had appeared at his feet, and Jack put the last of Aaron's belongings in the bag and zipped it closed.

The two men zipped Aaron's body into a black bag. Doc passed a hand over the prone bundle, and it levitated to about three feet and started to move off in the direction from which the two had appeared. Jack handed the duffel to Chris, then nodded to Doc. "Give my regards to the Coast Guard, gentlemen."

Jack turned to head in the opposite direction as the skyscrapers of Atlanta began to fade in around him. It was time to find Tay and...apologize.

He turned back, remembering something from an earlier conversation. "Oh, and Chris? Make sure he gets his pecan waffle this time."

* * * * *

Robert E. Hampson Bio

Dr. Robert E. Hampson wants your brain! Don't worry, he's not a zombie. He's a neuroscientist who is working on the first "neural prosthetic" to restore human memory using the brain's own neural codes. As a nonfiction writer and consultant, he uses his PhD to blog about brain science and to advise over a dozen science fiction writers. As an SF writer himself, he puts the science in hard-science & military SF, and looks for the SF influences in science. While not a zombie, he does know a few things about them and will keep them away from your brain...at least until he can use it for his own nefarious purposes! He is a popular convention panelist who makes science—and science fiction—interesting and accessible to the public. Find out more at his website: http://REHampson.com.

# # # # #

Bob from Los Angeles
by Brent Roeder

"Is Mike here?" a monotone voice asked.

"Whahowshidahuh," the sentry sputtered, jumping up and spinning around. Up to that moment, it had been a quiet watch for Jack. Then the guy had appeared out of nowhere and spoken to him. The man just stood there, looking at the sentry. Between his large frame and his clothes, which were made for someone a hundred pounds heavier and hung off his frame, he resembled a scarecrow.

Or someone who'd been on the edge of starvation, like so many who had been lucky to survive since society collapsed.

The clothes were obviously well cared for and showed signs of having been mended, but they were stained, ragged, and threadbare. He was wearing a chest rig covered in pouches, a gun belt with multiple magazine pouches, and a pistol on each hip. On his back was a surplus field pack, or a hiking pack of some type, but between the wear and tear and the stains, Jack couldn't be sure without examining it closer. In his hands was a rifle, the muzzle pointed safely down and to the side, with a loose sling looping around his neck.

"Who are you?" Jack demanded after taking a moment to collect himself.

"Bob," the man replied in the same uninflected tone as before.

"Where did you come from?" Jack asked.

"Los Angeles," Bob replied.

"Los Angeles?" Jack exclaimed. "That's over two thousand miles away! How'd you get here?"

"Walked," the man replied. After a pause he asked again, "Mike here?"

Jack was beginning to get over his shock and realized he was going to be in trouble for failing to spot the man before he got so close, so he decided to gather some more information before calling Mike back at the farm to let them know about this enigmatic and reticent visitor.

"Why do you want to talk to Mike?"

"Need a part," the man said and raised his AR15 for inspection. He pointed at the rear retaining pin, which had been replaced by...a bent cleaning rod? The cleaning rod was bent down so it couldn't be removed, and it almost looked like the ends had been hammered into place. Between the worn finish, mismatched furniture, and noticeable bite marks on the stock, it was obvious the rifle had seen heavy and unusual use, so the repair wasn't readily apparent until it was pointed out.

"What happened?" Jack asked with raised eyebrows, knowing there had to be an interesting story behind this bizarre field repair.

"Dropped it."

"What?! Where? No, wait. *How*? That pin isn't supposed to come out."

The man paused and thought before finally answering, "Houston. Busy."

"Alright, I'll call up to the house," Jack said, pulling out his radio and shaking his head in disbelief, "but they're going to want to know who you are."

The man cocked his head at the sentry as if slightly confused, then responded in his monotone, just slower and more deliberately, "Bob. From Los Angeles."

Jack keyed his radio and spoke, "Hey guys, this is post four, and I got a guy here asking for Mike."

"Yeah, Jack. This is Mike." The radio crackled. "Who's there?"

"Guy says his name is Bob," Jack answered. "Bob from Los Angeles."

"Only Bob from LA I know is a fat guy. No way he could make it all the way here," Mike radioed back.

"They're vanity pounds," Bob muttered, mostly to himself.

"Uh, Mike. He says they're *vanity pounds*."

"Holy shit! That *is* him," Mike crowed in surprise. "Tell him to head on up to the house. He's been here before. He'll know the way."

"Will do, Mike," Jack said before putting his radio away. He turned to the ragged man and said, "Over the crest of the hill…"

"Second left. First right. Third house on right," Bob said as he turned and started trudging up the street.

"Nice to meet you," Jack's voice trailed off as he realized he was waving goodbye. The past few minutes had been surreal and left him so off balance, he had forgotten he was in the middle of an apocalypse.

* * *

74 | IBSON & KENNEDY

"**B**ob!" Mike cried as he spotted the gaunt figure walking toward his driveway. "Good Lord! Is that really you?"

Bob ignored the shortcut worn across the front lawn that most people took and meticulously turned at the edge of the concrete driveway. The extra distance gave Bob time to wonder if Mike had intended to ask a question with such an obvious answer, or if he had meant to ask something else. When Mike didn't follow up, he answered, "Yes."

"What are you doing here? Hell, how'd you get here?" Mike asked.

"Need a part. Walked," Bob responded, raising his AR15 to show the cleaning rod retaining pin substitute to Mike and the group of people with him.

Mike cocked an eyebrow in surprise at Bob's flat tone. The Bob he'd known from conventions had been outgoing and verbose. "When was the last time you ate?" he asked, looking at Bob's much thinner figure.

Bob paused and thought before responding, "Springfield."

"Springfield…" Mike repeated dumbly, recoiling in shock.

Again, Bob paused, seeming to consider his answer, then responded, this time adding a slight nod for emphasis. "Springfield."

"That's over two hundred miles from here," Mike said. "How'd you end up going through Springfield if you are coming from Los Angeles?"

"Detour," Bob answered.

"Around what?" Mike asked curiously.

"St. Louis."

"That makes sense," Mike mused. "Probably easier to avoid the city. Where did you pass through before that?"

"Memphis," Bob answered.

"You came through Tennessee and detoured through Illinois to get to Indiana?" Mike asked confirming what he thought Bob was telling him.

"Tennessee, Kentucky, Missouri, then Illinois," Bob corrected.

"That is a hell of a route to take from LA, just to get here," Mike said.

Bob gave a ghost of a headshake. "Going to Savannah," Bob said as he lifted his rifle again. "Need part."

Mike began to feel a little like his sentry had felt. He asked, "So, you are walking from Los Angeles to Savannah, Georgia, and you came up here, to Indiana, to get a part?"

Bob thought about his answer and finally replied, "Yes."

Mike looked at the cleaning rod that was now a semi-permanent part of Bob's rifle, and he just had to know. "So, what happened to the takedown pin?"

"Dropped it."

"How!?"

"Busy."

"Uh-huh. And where were you so busy, you dropped it?"

"Houston."

"Houston," Mike echoed in disbelief.

After he stopped to think over his answer, Bob decided he needed to give more information, as it seemed Mike was having trouble understanding him. "Downtown Houston. By river."

76 | IBSON & KENNEDY

"The river doesn't really go near downtown," Frank, one of the group that had been silent up until now, said with a note of suspicion clear in his voice.

Bob thought this over and finally responded, "Downtown. By port."

"That's not considered downtown," Frank responded, openly suspicious of this odd arrival and his claims. "Anyone familiar with Houston knows that."

Bob looked at Frank long enough to set him even more on edge, then answered, speaking extra slowly. "From Los Angeles. Not Houston."

"Ok," Mike said, taking control of the conversation and buying time to think as well as to acknowledge Bob's answer. "Frank, I've known Bob for years. Bob, why don't you come inside and get something to eat? Then you can grab a shower, and sometime after that, we will look at the rifle."

Bob slung his rifle and considered the proposal. In a rare display of emotion, he shrugged slightly and, almost muscle-by-muscle, as if he had to remember how, cracked a small grin. "Sure."

* * *

"I don't know how he snuck up on me," Jack admitted in confusion. "It's like he appeared out of nowhere. Suddenly, he was just *there*, asking about you."

"I knew Bob before The Fall. He didn't have the skills to sneak up on people like that," Mike said, his voice full of frustration. "Obviously, this is a problem with your situational awareness."

"I swear I was paying attention," Jack insisted. "I don't know how he did it."

"You were on damned sentry watch," Mike snapped. "The hilltop is the only major thing within a mile that blocks the view from the house! That means you need to fucking *watch* it. That's why we put a damn sentry on the other side of it!"

"I was! I was watching, and I was concealed, and he shouldn't have been able to see me!"

"Obviously, you fucked up," Mike yelled, turning and slamming his fist onto the desk behind him. "He must have seen you, since he found you!"

"Radio," Bob said from over by the side of Mike's desk.

"Shit," Mike yelled in surprise, recoiling back from Bob and half falling backward onto his desk. "How the hell did you get in here?"

Bob looked at Mike and then at the only door into the office, then turned back to Mike. "The door."

"How long have you been here?" Mike demanded.

Bob thought and responded, "About five minutes."

"How?" Mike asked, half to himself.

Bob turned to the door again and then looked at Mike for several seconds. He pointed to the door and said, "Door."

"What did you mean 'radio'?" Mike asked.

"During check. Heard radio," Bob said.

"Uh, ok. Um, hey Bob, could you give us some privacy?" Mike asked.

Bob thought about this for a moment, nodded, then walked out, closing the door behind him.

"See? *See?* I told you!" Jack said, pointing to where Bob had just walked out.

"Was he really in here for five minutes?" Mike asked, bewildered.

"I have no idea. I didn't notice him until he said something," Jack answered. "It was just like what he did to me when he showed up!"

"How the hell is he doing that?" Mike asked rhetorically.

* * *

Bob focused on slowly and carefully shaving with the brand-new razor Mike had given him. He was content to let his thoughts wander. He realized he hadn't had hot water to shave with since sometime in Texas. Then, the water was only hot because the steel canteen cup it was in had drawn the heat from the sun baked rock it was sitting on. That day had been a real scorcher, at least a hundred degrees, Bob figured, although he wasn't sure as he didn't have a thermometer, and there weren't any convenient weather reports anymore. He had been able to keep his beard and hair manageable with a pair of scissors, but he felt there was no substitute for a nice, hot shave to help him feel clean and refreshed. This shave was especially enjoyable, he thought, as it was coming right after his first shower in months. Mike had been able to retain the trappings of civilization better than almost anyone else Bob had seen on his journey. Most of them were doing well to survive. None of those doing really well, like Mike, had let Bob stay with them. Mike was a bit of a survivalist, and his place was in the middle of nowhere, meaning he'd come through The Fall nearly unscathed. There was plenty of food to eat and clean water to drink. Showers were rationed to once a week, and you were supposed to conserve hot water, but they were still heavenly to have available.

A young woman in a bathrobe opened the door and walked into the bathroom. Bob stopped shaving, and his thoughts wandered. Bob was surprised but didn't show any outward reaction. He'd seen the young lady earlier, during the hasty introductions in the dining room, and he had heard someone call her Christine. He was glad he had his towel wrapped around his waist.

He paused his shaving as he watched for a reaction from Christine, but she ignored him, put the bathmat down, and placed her shower stuff in the shower. As she shrugged out of her robe and stepped inside, Bob returned his attention to shaving. He heard the shower curtain close behind him and the water start, and he gave the most minuscule of shrugs and continued. He realized there must be a high demand on facilities with the extra people Mike had here. He guessed, because they only had one working shower, they'd simply gotten used to having to share facilities, and they ignored each other to give the illusion of privacy. That was fine with him as it was still far better than no weekly showers and hot shaves.

After a minute or so in the shower, Christine in an exasperated tone said, "Shit. I forgot a towel."

Bob thought about it and decided to try to be friendly. "Can get you one after shaving," Bob offered.

Christine let out a shriek, then stuck her head out from behind the shower curtain. "What the hell are you doing in here!? Damn pervert! Get out of here," she screamed.

In confusion, Bob turned to face her to try to clarify what she meant. He thought shaving was pretty self-explanatory.

As Bob opened his mouth to try and explain that he was shaving, Christine started to scream at him again. "Fucking pervert! Get the hell out of here!"

The bathroom door suddenly flew open, and Mike, followed by Phil and Frank, filled the doorway. "*What the hell is going on in here?*" Mike demanded in a roar.

"He snuck in here! He's spying on me," Christine yelled, pointing at Bob. "Maybe he was going to try more than spying. He's half naked!" she pointed out, noticing he was wearing only a towel.

"Bob, what the hell is wrong with you?" Mike demanded. "I don't care how long you've been out on your own, you can't just walk in on people without asking."

At this pronouncement, Bob cocked his head in confusion and looked at Mike in obvious non-comprehension.

Mike noticed his confusion and repeated slower, in a calmer tone, "You can't walk in on people in the bathroom without asking first, Bob. Do you understand?"

"Yes," Bob answered slowly, still confused about why Mike was telling him this and not Christine.

"So, why did you walk in on her?" Mike asked, trying to figure out why Bob was still looking confused.

"Didn't," Bob answered.

Mike tried to hold his temper and responded, "Yes, Bob, you did. That is why Christine is mad at you."

Bob, even more confused by Mike's apparent anger, thought carefully about what to say and finally responded, "Didn't. Here first." As he finished his answer, Bob raised his hand with the razor in it and pointed to his half-shaved face that still had shaving cream on the other half.

"Lying pervert," Christine yelled before stopping at an abrupt gesture and look from Mike.

Mike looked back at Bob and then did a double take. He took in the partial shave, the fresh washed look, the damp hair, the damp towel around Bob's waist, and the shaving kit laid out by the sink. The collection of scars from bite wounds, slashes, and other less identifiable injuries that covered Bob's haggard frame and must have been new since The Fall, caused Mike to pause. He tried not to wince at the site of them and realized his friend had gone through hell on his journey. He had thought losing so much weight had been hard on Bob, but it was obviously not the worst he had faced.

"Christine, how long have you been in here?" Mike asked.

"About two minutes, but—" she responded before Mike cut her off with a raised hand.

"Bob, how long have *you* been in here?" Mike asked.

Bob looked at the clock on the wall, calculated how long, then responded, "Seventeen minutes, forty-three seconds."

"Bullshi—" Christine was again cut off by a gesture from Mike, but this time, it was an angry one.

"Christine, he's fresh out of the shower and half shaved, and all his toiletries are laid out next to the sink. There's no way he could have snuck in, wet down himself and his towel, spread out his stuff, and shaved in that time. You must have walked in on him," Mike told her.

"No way," she snarled. "I didn't see him there. And if I did walk in on him, why didn't he say something instead of spying like a pervert?"

"Bob?" Mike asked as it was a reasonable question.

"Shaving, not spying," Bob said, once again lifting his razor. He thought for a second, then continued, "She was quiet. Only working bathroom. Guessed had to share. So…was quiet."

Mike sighed and turned to the small crowd behind him and waved at them to go away. "Everyone, go back to what you were doing. Show's over here." He turned back to Christine and Bob and continued, "Christine, you can either get out and wait for Bob to finish, or you can keep showering while he finishes shaving. It's up to you. Unless, Bob, you want the bathroom to yourself?"

"Don't care," Bob answered with a slight shrug. "Just shaving."

"Fine," Mike said turning and walking out. "Christine, figure it out," Mike called over his shoulder as he closed the bathroom door.

Bob turned back to Christine and figured he should say something to try to patch up the misunderstanding. "Still want a towel?"

Christine let out a shriek of frustration, snatched up her shampoo bottle, and flung it at Bob, hitting him in the chest.

"Guess not," Bob said and turned back to the mirror to finish shaving. He rinsed his razor and discovered his hot water was now only warm. He was disappointed the interruption had allowed the water to cool, but he cheered up as he reminded himself it was better than not being able to shower or shave at all. He ignored the muttered curses coming from Christine who was still hiding behind the shower curtain, and, as he finished his shaving, he felt an urge to whistle.

He hadn't whistled since before Houston.

* * *

"Mike! Mike?" Sarah called, tearing down the hall to his office and bursting through the door. "I can't, I can't, I can't—" she stammered before pausing to catch her breath between hysterical sobs.

"What is it? "Zombie?" Mike demanded, standing up from behind his desk so fast, his office chair flipped backward. "Did one get through the perimeter watch?" he questioned while dragging his plate carrier off its stand.

"No!" Sarah choked out, shaking her head frantically. "She's gone!"

Mike stopped putting on his plate carrier, and the color drained from his face. "Who's gone?" he whispered.

"Alyssa," Sarah answered.

Mike grabbed Sarah by the shoulders, stared directly into her eyes, and as calmly as possible, forced out the question, "What happened?"

"She finished her lunch, so I put her down for her nap," Sarah got out as tears streamed down her face. "About twenty minutes later, I was in the bathroom, and I heard her wake up. She was crying the way she does when she has one of the nightmares that started when Julie died. I was finishing up in the bathroom so I could go and get her, and she stopped crying. You know how she won't stop crying after a nightmare until she tires herself out? She stopped, suddenly."

"But you said she was missing. What do you mean she's missing?" Mike finally snapped in frustration that Sarah wasn't getting to the point.

"When she just stopped, I knew something had to be wrong. I ran to her room, but the crib was empty."

"You know she can climb out."

"I checked the whole house. I can't find her anywhere!" Sarah said, finally getting to the important part of the story. "There's no way she would have stopped crying yet, but I can't hear her anywhere in the house."

"She shouldn't be able to get out of the house. There is no way she can reach the new locks we put on after The Fall," Mike countered. "She *has* to be in the house."

"She's not! That's what I'm telling you! She's gone!" Sarah said and collapsed into a sobbing heap.

"Frank! Jason!" Mike bellowed at the top of his lungs as he grabbed his rifle and charged into the living room. "Phil! Christine! Get your asses in here!"

"What the hell's going on?" Frank asked, running into the room.

"Alyssa's gone. She has to have out somehow," Mike explained, finally closing his plate carrier. "Frank, go to the front yard. Jason, go down to the stream. Phil, search the left side of the house. And Christine, you've got the right. I'll check out back, the garden, and the shed. Go! Go!"

As everyone charged off in their assigned directions, Mike snatched up his radio. "Stephen, Jack, you guys stay where you are but keep an eye out for Alyssa. She's missing."

"Shit, copy that," Jack radioed back from his post.

"Same here. Good luck, Mike," Stephen radioed from his.

Mike barreled through the back door, nearly tearing it from the frame in his haste. As soon as he was outside, he ran across the back patio and straight to the shed next to her sand pile where they kept her outside toys.

"Alyssa? Come to Daddy, Alyssa," Mike called quietly, trying to keep the fear out of his voice so as not to scare her. "Come here, baby girl," he continued as he searched the garden. He didn't find any sign of her in the garden, so he scanned the backyard and the field that ran up to it, but he still didn't see his daughter.

He ran back to the house and cried out desperately, "Alyssa, where are you?"

"Quiet. Don't wake," Bob said.

Mike crashed to a halt in response to Bob's words. He charged back out found Bob sitting in a chair by the back door he had just run past twice without noticing his friend. "You found her!" he gasped in relief. "Guys, she's on the back patio," Mike yelled into his radio.

"Quiet. Don't wake," Bob repeated.

"Where was she?" Mike asked. He started shaking as he started to come down from his terror fueled adrenaline high.

"Crib," Bob said.

"You took her from her crib?" Mike asked, starting to get angry.

"Was crying. No one around," Bob answered.

"Why didn't you let Sarah take her?" Mike demanded.

Bob looked at him, thinking over his last answer, and repeated, "Was crying. No one around."

"Oh, thank God," Sarah sobbed, as she and everyone else piled through the back door and saw that Alyssa was safe.

"Quiet. Don't wake," Bob said.

"What did you do to make her stop crying?" Mike asked through gritted teeth as he fought back his temper.

"You better not have hurt my niece," Sarah threatened, moving forward and taking the sleeping Alyssa from Bob who carefully handed her up from where he sat.

"I asked you what you did to stop her crying," Mike said with menace clearly audible in his voice. As he said this, Alyssa started to squirm in Sarah's arms and began to wake up.

"Held her," Bob said. "Seemed tired," he elaborated after a pause.

"Impossible," Sarah snorted. "No one can stop her crying after a nightmare."

Bob thought about this, then gave a slight shrug. As he did, Alyssa woke up fully and began to shriek, tears running freely, twisting in Sarah's grip. Mike moved close to his sister, and the two of them tried to calm Alyssa down by whispering to her. Alyssa struggled and twisted in Sarah's grasp into a position that let her see Bob. As soon as she saw him, she reached toward him and struggled even harder. Her shrieks redoubled.

"Shit," Phil said. "She's too loud. We need to get her inside in case any zombies are close enough to hear."

"Yeah, good point," Mike said, starting to shoo Sarah into the house. As Sarah passed Bob, Alyssa reached out as far as she could and was just able to lock a fist onto the sleeve of Bob's shirt.

"Let her go," ordered Sarah.

"Let her go, Bob," Mike echoed.

Bob looked from Mike to Sarah, then down to his hands resting on his knees, then back up to Mike. He slightly tilted his head in confusion, "How?"

Jason looked at the scene and interjected with some hesitation, "He's just *sitting there*, boss. Alyssa is holding on to *him*, not the other way around."

Mike listened to Jason and forced himself to take a pair of calm, deep breaths and look at the scene again. He then focused on Bob, who was sitting still and calm as if nothing were happening. As calmly as he could, he asked Bob, "How did you stop her crying?"

Bob, confused by Mike's seeming incomprehension, tilted his head slightly further to the side with just a ghost of a confused look on his face, then repeated, "Held her."

Mike stepped back and ordered, "Sarah, hand Alyssa to Bob." As she opened her mouth to object, Mike quietly snapped, "Just do it."

After a long moment, Sarah finally relented and, with a look of great reluctance, handed the screaming and struggling Alyssa to the sitting man. As soon as Alyssa was in Bob's arms, her cries began to die down, and in less than a minute, she was asleep with her head resting on his chest, over his heart.

"How'd you do that?" whispered Sarah in shock and disbelief. "She never stops like that for anyone."

The ghost of the confused expression returned as Bob looked at Sarah and tried to figure out how to answer. He shrugged one shoulder slightly, careful not to disturb the sleeping toddler and repeated once more, even slower, "Held. Her."

* * *

"Bob, come into my office and let's talk," Mike said gesturing for Bob to follow him from the living room. Mike walked around his desk and resisted the urge to simply collapse into his chair, as well as the appeal of the bottle hidden in his lower desk drawer.

As Bob followed him into the office, Mike pointed to a chair and ordered, "Sit." Bob sat, facing Mike's desk, and waited passively. After a couple of minutes spent watching him, Mike finally spoke up.

"The number of zombies seems to have dropped noticeably since winter started. It hasn't been a bad one, but apparently it's been enough for them to start dying off or, who knows, maybe eating each other," he said with a grimace. After waiting and not receiving a response from Bob, Mike continued, "We mapped some places we thought we might find supplies when The Fall hit, and we've started doing some light scouting. We think it is safe enough for us to hit some of the locations we had our eyes on."

After Mike paused again for a bit, it seemed to occur to Bob that Mike might be waiting for an acknowledgment that he understood. Without saying anything, Bob slightly nodded his head.

Mike sighed and ran a hand over his face. "The first place we want to check is the pharmacy in the town about eleven miles from here. Since you were a biochemist back in LA, I would like you to go with the team, as you'll be able to sort through what medications are still left. You can figure out what's safe to use and, therefore, worth the trouble of carrying back. Sound good?"

After a pause to think it over, Bob again nodded slightly and said, "Better than before."

Mike hesitated at the odd response but decided he could live without hearing the details of Bob's trip before he arrived. "Ok, good. Let's see if any of the plate carriers we have left will fit you," Mike said, getting up to head to the room he used as an armory and gesturing for Bob to come with him. "How are you fixed for supplies? How much ammo do you have for your rifle?"

"Three," Bob said.

"Three mags? That's not bad."

"No. Three."

Mike stopped and turned to face Bob. He asked, "You mean three rounds?"

Bob nodded slightly.

"And pistols?"

"Empty."

"How did you end up with only three rounds?" Mike asked, again wondering how Bob had survived.

"Saved them."

"Saved them for what?"

"Emergency."

Mike was starting to get a bit of a headache from his conversation with Bob. He turned and started for the armory again. "So, what did you do instead of shooting them?"

Bob thought for a moment and responded, "Hit them, mostly."

"Of course, you did…"

* * *

90 | IBSON & KENNEDY

"Everyone gather 'round," Jason quietly called out to the rest of the team.

The half dozen people huddled together just under the crest of the hill to listen to the team leader.

"As you can see from here, it isn't much of a town," Jason said, waving in the general direction of the hill's crest. "Mainly a grocery store, a pharmacy, and a few other shops and what not, so the locals didn't have to drive all the way into the city for things they needed. As we discussed before we left, we hope the town is pretty well stocked for being so small," Jason said as he reiterated the plan.

He picked up a stick and began sketching a diagram of the nearest part of the town on the ground, then continued the review. "Our target is the pharmacy. When we were scouting around after things went to hell, we discovered the grocery and hardware stores had been raided. At that time, the pharmacy hadn't been. We might come back to see if anything is left in the other stores, but the main things we want to get our hands on today are any medical supplies and drugs left in the pharmacy. We don't need much, yet, as we have a decent stockpile back at the farm, but we don't want to have to go raiding for something once the need becomes critical."

At this, everyone except Bob nodded or muttered agreement. They had faced few, and no serious, medical problems so far, and they had all been handled with the supplies Mike had stockpiled before the world went to pieces. They'd been absurdly lucky, but that luck would run out someday, like it already had for so many people. Just being alive at this point made you absurdly lucky.

"The plan," Jason continued, "is to move in quietly to the pharmacy. We don't want to wake the dead, or we will get swarmed.

We're going to hook around the alley behind the building and try to force our way in. The stairs to the second floor are near the back entrance, so Frank and I will sweep the floor level while the rest of you hold the ends of the alley, the back door, and the stairs inside. There are enough of you to cover those locations while Frank and I are clearing."

Jason finished his sketch, including the path they would take, and tossed his stick away. "Once the ground floor is clear, Frank and I will move to the top floor and clear it. If there is access to the roof, we will clear that too. After that, we'll pack up the drugs in the pharmacy and get out. Questions?"

"Why not try the front door?" Christine asked, leaning forward and pointing out a slightly different route on the sketch. "We'll risk drawing rezzies, but we are less likely to get trapped on the main street than in a back alley. Besides, it looks clearer than we expected. We haven't seen a single rezzy yet."

"This is the first time we've tried raiding a place like this, so we don't know which way is better. The decision to try the back was mine. I figure, at the very least, we will be out of sight," Jason explained.

Christine settled back on her heels and nodded.

"Alrighty everyone, let's—" Frank started before being cut off by a shriek that made everyone jump.

"Fucking hell! What was that?" Joseph demanded, looking around.

"It's a rezzy, dumbass," Christine scoffed, pointing her rifle at the empty fields. "You've heard them before; you should know that."

"Calm down everyone," Jason said, trying to settle the group. "I know being away from the house is freaky, but everything is fine. It sounded like the noise came from the town. Still, check your sectors, and let me know if you see anything."

"Uh, guys," Jack started, "where's Bob?"

"Huh?" Jason muttered as he whipped around. "How the hell does he do that silent appearing-disappearing crap?" he demanded.

"Take a look over there," Frank said. He had risen up high enough to see over the crest of the hill and was pointing at the town. "He's down at the pharmacy. I think a zombie spotted him..."

* * *

Bob tugged on the Halligan tool, trying to determine how well it was wedged into the door frame. He'd never used one before and wasn't sure if he was doing it right. *Better safe than sorry.* He gave the Halligan one more solid whack with the mini sledgehammer. When he struck it this time, the sound was louder and had a new metallic undertone to it. The noise attracted the attention of a zombie, but Bob ignored it as he inspected the face of the hammer. Jason had coated the hammer's head with spray-on rubber to keep it from making noise when driving it in, but it seemed to have partially worn off. The zombie closed to within fifty feet in its shambling gait, and Bob let go of the Halligan. The oversized crowbar/pick was stuck in the door frame, and Bob placed the hammer on the ground so his hands would be free for weapons.

The zombie lunged, and Bob dodged to the side, then turned and shoved the zombie in the back, causing it to sprawl face first on the concrete. Bob reached into his front pockets with both hands. When he withdrew his hands, they were armored with heavy brass knuckles. The outsides of the weapons were scarred and pitted from heavy use, and the insides were worn smooth. Bob pivoted toward the zombie as it tried to scramble back to its feet. He dropped his shoulders down and tackled the rising zombie, knocking it flat, and landing on top. He rose so he was kneeling on the zombie, pinning it down, and he began hitting it, over and over until it stopped moving. Bob climbed back to his feet and cleaned off the blood covered brass knuckles on his shirt, then tucked them away. Bob had fought a *lot* of zombies.

Bob turned back to the Halligan, tugged on it, and decided it was in solidly enough. He grabbed the tool tightly with both hands, planted both feet against the wall of the building, and heaved.

* * *

"Should we go down and help him?" Frank asked.

"I'm not sure," Jason replied, staring, half in consternation and half in awe.

A crack like a gunshot broke the quiet stillness. Part of the door frame cracked, and the door flew open.

The Halligan came free, and Bob went from having his feet braced against the wall to sprawling flat on his ass. He got back on his feet, put the Halligan and the hammer in his duffel bag, and entered the pharmacy.

"Shit!" Frank pointed to a group of zombies who appeared to be wandering toward the pharmacy to investigate the noise.

"That decides it," Jason said. "We can't risk getting swarmed. That dumbass is on his own. We'll hold here for now and see if we can sneak in after the zombies are done with him."

"Why did Mike think it was a good idea to send this guy along?" Christine asked.

"Apparently, he was a chemist or something," Stephen chimed in. "Personally, I think he's off his rocker."

The half dozen zombies sped up and began keening at the sight of the body, excited by the prospect of food. As they started to fall on the corpse, several of them paused and looked at the doorway.

Three of the zombies turned from the corpse and entered the pharmacy. Faint banging and shrieks could be heard from inside. The noise caught the attention of the remaining zombies, who joined the fray.

The volume of shrieking and banging grew noticeably.

As the noise continued, Jack muttered to himself, "That has to be it. They're probably finishing off each other now."

The noise had been sufficiently loud that it attracted more zombies from further out in the town.

A second wave arrived, and a reprise of what happened with the first group played out. The group started to descend on the original zombie's corpse, and as before, whatever was going on in the pharmacy attracted the attention of some, so they went inside to investigate. The banging and shrieking increased in volume, drawing the remaining zombies inside.

The noise and commotion caused by the second wave were enough to draw a *third* wave.

"That's it, I think," Jason said. "There are too many for us to sneak in."

"Let's hang around a little longer," Frank suggested. "We can, at least, get an idea of how many zombies will be left in town after this cluster fuck."

"Good point," Jason agreed grudgingly. "Let's give it about thirty minutes, then we'll start back."

"Damn waste of time," Christine complained, "all because of that ass."

"At least it's the last time we'll have to deal with him," Jack said, trying to look on the bright side.

"Alright, everyone, let's settle down," Jason said. "We'll just wait a bit to see what the zombies do and then we can get out of here."

Everyone settled down and made themselves as comfortable as they could, considering the small horde of swarming zombies less than half a mile away.

As the noise from the third wave was dying down, the fourth wave arrived, and the noise resumed. After the fourth wave, there was a slow trickle of newcomers in ones and twos.

"I think this is the best information we're going to get," Jason said after standing up to peer over the hill crest and check what was going on outside the pharmacy. "Let's get—" he said before his voice suddenly cut off.

Jack stood up. If Jason wasn't going to explain what he'd seen, he'd just have to see for himself. "Well, I'll be damned."

Bob came around the corner from the back of the pharmacy and headed toward the hill where the team was hiding. On his back was a full duffel bag with the Halligan sticking out sideways through the closed top. In each hand was a mostly full duffel bag. Bob and the bags were liberally splattered with blood.

Bob walked right by the mob of zombies who were fighting to get into the pharmacy, not even turning his head to look at them. He and the zombies ignored each other, like they didn't know the other existed.

Bob walked up to the group and stopped when Jason demanded, "What the hell did you think you were doing?"

Bob looked at Jason in slight confusion, thought about the question, and finally answered, "Went. Got stuff."

* * *

"Mike!" Christine hollered down from the top of the attic ladder. "Get up here! Someone is launching fireworks. I think they're trying to call for help." She shook her head and muttered, "So much for having a nice, calm day after that shit show at the pharmacy."

As he ran toward the ladder at the end of the hall, Mike yelled for help. "Jack, grab the spotting scope and meet us up on the roof."

Because Mike had a well, the plan had always been for people to hole up at his place in case of a disaster. With fresh water, they could hold out for quite a long time, but without it, they were as good as dead. When the president appeared on television to talk about how bad things were, they started modifying Mike's house. And once the collapse appeared inevitable, they scaled up the modifications far beyond their original plans. They fortified the house with armored doors and windows, and they built an observation platform on the roof. Mike's house stood on the only hill in the area. Between the height of the hill and the added elevation of the observation platform, they were able to see a little over eight miles in every direction.

They had laid in provisions and stockpiled—mostly legal—firepower. Since then, they had eliminated singletons and small bands of roaming zombies, and otherwise buttoned up and avoided drawing the attention of larger hordes. Most of the time. The few times they hadn't been able to wait out a passing horde, someone had snuck out and drawn them off with decoys.

Mike climbed onto the platform, and another skyrocket went off to the northeast. "Damn it," Mike snapped. "If they keep that up, who knows how many rezzies they are going to attract. It's bad enough that it's daylight. We'll be fucked if they keep it up at night."

"How do we get them to stop? Signal them somehow?" Christine asked. "That's about where we saw the vultures the last few days. There were some there this morning, but I don't see them now. Maybe the fireworks scared them off?"

"Scope's coming up," Jack called and handed them a case from halfway up the ladder.

"Give me that," Mike ordered. He opened the case and set up the scope facing in the direction of the fireworks. "Which house is it, Christine?"

"Look past the fields. See that cluster of about half a dozen houses?"

"Yeah, I see them. White with blue trim, right?" Mike answered.

"That's them. Find the road and trace it north, past the second cluster of houses. It is the second singleton. The green and white one that's on a slope. It has trees around it, so it's hard to see much except the top floor."

"At least there haven't been any more fireworks," Jack added, hopefully. "Maybe they're out."

"We can only hope," Christine said. Mike grunted in annoyance.

"Ok, got them," Mike said.

* * *

"So, here's the situation as best as we can figure it," Mike started. "Six miles from here, the ...MacPhersons or the MacPhees, I forget which, launched a bunch of fireworks. I assume they're a signal. They got our attention, but also that of the rezzies. The house is surrounded, but it is too far away and there are too many trees between us to get an accurate count."

"Have we seen many rezzies moving between us and them?" Phil asked.

"Yeah, a few more, but it's been like that for the last few days," Christine answered. "We've seen some vultures over in that direction, and you know how they seem to attract zombies."

"So, we know they've been moving around, but we don't know if the fireworks really changed anything," Mike continued. "The plan is to gear up for a rescue mission. They're closer than the pharmacy, so we'll have time to get there and back on foot. We'll take our time approaching and try to lose any trailing zombies we pick up. Ok. Let's pack, rest up, and head out at dawn."

"Why wait?" Christine asked, and several of the others mumbled in agreement.

"All, right. Quiet down," Mike said. "We need to wait and see if those fireworks attracted any large groups of rezzies. If they did, we can't do anything to help, because we'll have to hunker down ourselves. Even if they didn't attract a bunch, we don't have time to get ready and get there before dusk, and I don't want to fight zombies in the dark. So, there's no point rushing."

"This sounds like a good way to lead a mob back here," Frank interjected. "We had plenty of time and distance to make sure we weren't followed back on the pharmacy raid."

"We'll only try to rescue them if it looks like we can get in and out unnoticed. I have plenty of decoys in the garage, and we can use them to draw the rezzies away if need be," Mike replied. "The main thing is to stay safe. It does us no good to save them if we end up getting swarmed a little later."

"Who is executing this mad plan?" Phil asked.

"You, me, Frank, Christine, Bob, and Stephen," Mike answered. "Jack will stay here with Sarah and Alyssa to make sure we have a place to fall back to."

* * *

"Okay, so it looks like we can get them out." Mike quietly dropped into a squat. "There's a driveway leading from the road to the house, with trees and shrubs between the house and the road. There are a few scattered zombies in the bushes, but I think we can sneak in and take them out if we have to. The real problems are the back of the house and one side."

Why's that?" Phil asked as Mike paused to get a drink from a canteen.

"There's a shit ton of zombies down there. At least three dozen."

"Crap," Phil swore.

"This doesn't sound doable, boss," Frank chimed in.

"It's not as bad as it sounds," Mike replied. "There's a garden, which is probably where they got a lot of their food, and they were probably picking off the rabbits and squirrels that were raiding the garden to get some protein. There are also a pool and a trough that look like they were fed by that windmill. The windmill looks broken, and there's a bunch of partially eaten bodies around it and between it and the house. It looks like one or two had clothes on, so they weren't zombies."

"Sounds like they were trying to fix the windmill and attracted some unwanted attention," Stephen said.

"That's what it looks like to me," Mike agreed.

"How are we going to take out all of those and the ones out front?" Frank asked.

"We're not," Mike said. "We're going to distract the rezzies and pull them off to the west, then lead the folks inside back this way."

"You're talking about using the decoys," Christine said. "I thought those were to help us get home safely."

"They'll work for that too; we'll just set them off earlier than originally planned."

"I'm getting a bad feeling about this, boss," Phil said warily.

"It's simple. Christine, you and Bob take the decoys and set the first one up about half a mile from the house, then keep setting them up in a trail heading west. When you set them off, they will draw the main body of zombies," Mike explained. "We can sneak up on any that stick around in the trees in front and take them out. Then we'll go into the house, grab whoever's inside, and get out of there."

"And what happens to us?" Christine asked.

"Once you set off the last decoy, the big one made from the fire alarm bell, circle around southeast and meet us at the nearest cluster of houses on the way home. That bell is loud as hell, and it'll ring for at least an hour on the batteries it's got. We'll hoof it home once we meet up. The zombies will have plenty to pay attention to here and no reason to follow us."

"Fine," Christine said, shrugging.

Everyone but Bob murmured or nodded agreement, although most looked more resigned than enthusiastic. "Bob?" Mike asked.

Bob looked at Mike and shrugged.

"Ok. Stay off the radios unless it's critical. We don't want to be heard. Let's plan on moving at ten to twelve. Everyone good with that?"

Mike got up and gestured for his team to follow. "Good luck, Christine, Bob," he said quietly over his shoulder.

* * *

Christine watched their back, while Bob watched their front. She hoped none of the zombies would show up, because having to set off the first decoy before the scheduled time would be a good way to screw things up and a bad way to rescue the people inside.

"Like the name Christine. Always thought it was pretty," Bob said, using more words than Christine had ever heard him use.

Afraid Bob was trying to hit on her, Christine asked warily, "And that's why you like the name? It's pretty?"

"Yes," Bob said. After a moment he added, "Daughter's name."

Bob's initiating the conversation already had her off balance. His admission that he had a daughter who shared her name threw her even further. "Where is your daughter? Savannah? You said you were going to go check on family."

"Under carnations. Parts I could find," Bob said. "Susan too."

Christine dreaded the answer, but she had to know. "Who was Susan?"

"Wife," Bob answered.

"They died from the virus?" Christine asked, hoping that was the answer, but fearing it wasn't.

"Susan turned. Got Christine."

"And Susan?" Christine asked.

After a long pause, Bob finally responded, "Strangled Susan." Then Bob added, "Both under carnations. Both loved carnations."

Throughout the entire conversation, Bob's voice remained his normal monotone. Christine wasn't sure whether that was sad, scary, or some combination of the two. She did know she would never look at carnations the same way.

About five minutes later, Bob checked his watch and stood up. "Time," he said and flipped the cover off the power switch. He looked at Christine to be sure she was ready.

"Okay," she said, standing up and quickly settling her gear on her shoulders. "Let's go."

At her confirmation, Bob flipped the switch and slapped the cover back over it. A moment passed and then the speaker emitted a high-pitched, oscillating squeal. Their first decoy was in place, and they had to move fast. They had five more to deploy like a trail of really loud breadcrumbs.

Christine took point, leading the way toward their next planned stop. Bob shouldered the duffel full of decoys and followed her, keeping watch behind them.

* * *

"Mr. Oz," Johnny cried out. He reached back toward the stairs as his stuffed koala bounced away. "I need to get Mr. Oz!"

"Grab the kid and keep him quiet," ordered Phil. "We have to be *quiet* if we are going to get out of here."

"Mr. Oz!" Johnny screamed as he tried to duck past his mom, who grabbed him around the waist and clutched him to her.

"Shush, Johnny, shush. Mr. Oz will be ok." Jennifer, his mother, tried to soothe him as she lifted him into her arms and followed their rescuers.

"I'll get him," Rebeccah volunteered, starting down the stairs to the basement. "It'll quiet him!"

"Shit! Get back here!" Frank yelled and charged after her as the rest of the group moved toward the entrance to the house. Near the top of the basement stairs, a zombie entered the hallway from the kitchen. It knocked the basement door closed and slammed into Frank. The two fell to the floor, but Frank landed with his shotgun barrel pointed toward the shambler. The zombie snapped at him and struggled to shake off Frank's weight. Frank pulled the trigger. The twelve-gauge shot boomed in the short hallway, leaving him half deaf.

"What the *hell* is going on?" Phil demanded. He ran back into the hall and spotted a group of zombies climbing through two partially broken windows in the kitchen. He shouldered his rifle and started firing—Frank's shotgun blast meant the time for stealth was gone.

Phil piled up dead zombies in the hallway. Frank scrambled to his feet and added to the fire long enough to put down the first rush.

"Guys!" Mike called from the entryway. "We're starting to pull zombies back from the decoys! Get the girl, and let's get out!"

"We're trying!" Phil called back. "We got leakers getting into the house!"

"Shit," Mike swore. He put one hand on Stephen's shoulder and pointed through the door to the tree line. "Get them going, the rest of us will catch up."

"Boss," Stephen started to protest, but Mike cut him off with a gesture.

"No arguing, just go."

"Yes, boss," Stephen said, turning and grabbing Jennifer, who was holding onto Johnny. "Time to go," he said, hustling them out the front door.

"But…Rebeccah!" Jennifer cried looking back toward the basement door and the piled bodies keeping it shut.

"They'll try to get her out, but right now, we have to take care of you two." Stephen tried to soothe the mother while urging her toward the tree line.

As Stephen got the two refugees moving, Mike linked up with Phil and Frank. Phil kept shooting the zombies entering the hallway, and Frank dragged the bodies out of the way. Frank, who was trying to keep from getting shot by Phil, couldn't remove the bodies fast enough to clear the basement door.

"What the hell is going on?" demanded Mike. "Why are you fucking around with dead zombies, and where is the girl?"

"She's trapped in the basement!" Phil answered. He swapped the empty magazine in his rifle for a full one and fired one handed while shoving the empty magazine into a dump pouch.

"We've got to get her and go," Mike snapped, trying to push past his frustration and think of some way to help.

"That's what we're trying to do," Frank said before grunting and yanking a zombie out of the hallway. "The door to the basement is blocked by dead zombies."

Mike heard a snarl behind him. He spun around and shot a charging zombie before it could reach him. He finished off the still-thrashing zombie with a pair of headshots, then turned back to the two men, realizing what needed to be done. "We have to go. They're coming in behind us. If we stay any longer, we're going to get swamped."

"But the girl!" Frank objected. He pulled another corpse from the pile blocking the door.

Mike carefully edged past Phil, got as close to the basement door as he could, and yelled loudly and slowly, "Too many zombies! Wait there, and we'll come back!"

Mike moved behind Phil and pulled out something that looked like a giant smoke grenade from a fireworks stand. "Frank, make sure the front door is clear. Phil, get ready to pull back when I toss this. I don't know how long it will be before it goes off once I throw it."

"What is it?" Phil asked.

"Homemade flashbang. I made it while tinkering with the decoys, but I'm not sure I got the mixture right," Mike said as he put his finger in the pull ring.

"Front is clear for now," Frank yelled.

"Everyone, get ready! It's going to be loud and bright," Mike yelled. "Phil, I'll throw it on the count of three. Back around the corner right away. Hopefully, this will distract them."

"Ok," Phil said, sounding a little uncertain. He continued shooting the zombies who were coming down the hall toward them.

"One. Two. Three," Mike counted. When he reached three, he yanked the pull ring that ignited a friction primer, then he threw the flashbang past Phil into the kitchen, praying it would actually work.

Phil backed up and had just cleared the corner of the hallway when a small bang and flash could be heard and seen.

"Well, cra—" Mike started before being cut off by a flash of light that seemed as bright as a dozen lightning strikes and an ear shattering boom that was felt as much as heard. Mike blinked his watering eyes and shook his head to regain his senses, then grabbed Phil, who seemed more stunned than he was, and dragged him toward the front door. "Let's go!" Mike called to Frank.

"What?" Frank shouted as he followed the other two. The ringing in his ears muffled and distorted his hearing, like he was underwater; he only barely made out that Mike had said something, but he hadn't understood a word. "I can't hear you!"

"I think using it inside made it louder!" Mike yelled, as he pulled Phil through the door with him.

"What?" Frank yelled back.

* * *

"Don't worry." Mike tried to comfort Jennifer but failed. He was too loud; his ears were still ringing. "We're going to go back for her. We just have to wait a few days for the zombies to calm down."

"You have to get her! You can't leave her," Jennifer quietly wailed, turning her tear-streaked face toward Mike. She feared for her daughter's safety, but within her, that fear warred with the need to stay quiet in case one of the rezzies heard her and found the group.

"You said there is plenty of food and water in the basement," Mike continued. "She just has to sit tight, and everything will be fine."

"What's going on?" Christine asked Frank as she and Bob finally met up with the rescue team.

"The stupid girl went back for her brother's stuffed animal," Frank answered. He'd meant to keep his voice down to avoid upsetting Jennifer, but his hearing was still screwed up from the homebrewed flashbang. Jennifer unleashed another wave of tears, while

Frank explained what had happened inside. "She went down into the basement, and we were swarmed by rezzies. We killed a bunch in the hallway, but the bodies blocked the door so we couldn't get her out."

"They were getting into the house so fast! They were swarming us!" Phil added. "We had to kill zombies or move bodies out of the way, but we couldn't do both quickly enough."

"So, you guys *left her behind?*" Christine snapped.

Both men winced, but Phil continued. "We tried to get to her, but we were losing ground. Mike told us to pull back. He realized we had to choose between staying and getting swarmed or making sure the mother and son got out. I feel awful we couldn't get the daughter out, but we did the best we could."

"We were able to save the boy and his mother," Frank added. He sounded like he was trying to convince himself more than anyone else. "It's better than nothing."

Christine opened her mouth to snap an angry retort, but a hand on her shoulder interrupted her. Bob stood behind her, holding out his rifle.

"Take," Bob said.

"Why?" Christine asked.

"Going back. Don't need it," Bob answered.

"Hell, no. You're not going alone. I'll go with—" Christine started before Bob cut her off with a single shake of his head. "What? Why the fuck not?"

Bob paused a moment, looking at Christine, then finally tapped his chest. "Outsider. Expendable."

Bob held his rifle back out to her. Christine's face fell. Her heart broke as she finally understood how he thought of himself, and she took the rifle without comment. Bob shrugged out of his pack, reached in and pulled out, of all things, a mace. It was almost two and a half feet long with four steel flanges that ran the entire length of the weapon from the tip down to the leather wrapped hand guard to the ball pommel. Christine took the backpack from Bob, speechless, and Bob turned back toward the house.

Christine turned around to speak to the others. "We need to go. *Now*." She shoved past Frank and Phil and looked into Jennifer's eyes. "Bob has gone back to get your daughter, and we need to get you and your son to safety."

"Shit! Where is he?" Mike demanded, looking around for Bob.

"He's already gone, and we need to *go*," Christine said.

"Fine, let's get out of here," Mike snapped. He rubbed his temples—between the concussion of the flashbang and Bob being Bob, he had one helluva headache.

"She'll be fine, I promise," Christine said to Jennifer, trying to calm her. "I trust Bob." To her surprise, she actually meant it.

* * *

Rebeccah sat huddled in the corner of the basement farthest from the stairs. Tears streamed down her face, but crying silently was one of the survival skills she'd learned since The Fall. Even though it was pointless to stay quiet, now that the zombies had broken into the house, she still kept silent out of habit. The erratic pounding and keening at the basement door that had continued since the rescue attempt told her it was simply a matter of time until she died. The men who rescued Mom and Johnny had said they were coming back to get her, but they wouldn't be in time. The basement door would collapse before the zombies lost their interest in the possible meal downstairs. Her only comfort was knowing everyone else had made it out.

Clutching Johnny's stuffed koala and her .38 revolver to her chest, she debated whether to use the gun now or wait. The pistol would be so much quicker and less painful than the alternative. If she waited too long, the zombies would take that choice away from her. She had four rounds left, so she might even take some of the zombies with her. Depending on how fast they were, though, she might not get a chance to kill herself before they got to her.

It wasn't fair. She knew she was going to die, but she wanted to *live!*

Rebeccah flinched as the zombies' shrieks redoubled upstairs. There was more slamming and thumping, but not at the door anymore. The volume died, slowly, until the house grew silent.

A loud *thunk* broke the silence, then metal hammering on metal—once, twice, three times. She heard the creaking of the splintering wood and then a *crack* that sounded like a gunshot. She had no idea what was going on upstairs, so she raised the revolver to her temple in case zombies crashed down the stairs. She wouldn't let them take her alive.

Rebeccah huddled in the corner, holding the pistol to her head. She heard slow repeated thumps—someone was walking down the basement stairs. From where she huddled in the corner, she could only see the lowest third of the stairs. First, she saw a pair of heavily worn, blood splattered boots, with pants tucked into the tops. *Clothes!*

It's a live person! Not a zombie! She dropped the pistol and clutched the stuffed koala even tighter as a sob of relief broke through.

The man who came down the stairs was bleeding from bites and other wounds on his arms, chest, and head. His clothes were torn and soaked in blood. Far more blood than could be explained by his injuries. He'd tried to clean some of the blood off his face and hands and the weapon he held in one hand.

The man stopped at the foot of the stairs and scanned the basement. His gaze rested on Rebeccah. He stretched out his free hand toward her as he spoke. In a flat tone, he said, "Come. Live."

* * * * *

Brent Roeder Bio

Brent Roeder is a neuroscience PhD candidate, researching how to restore damaged memory functions. A life-long geek, he enjoys writing sci-fi and fantasy to relax from work. Very occasionally, he even remembers to finish a story.

# # # # #

Nor War's Quick Fire
by Rob Howell

"Fiat lux," whispered Marcus Allardeck.

"But this light brings the end of all things, not the beginning," snapped Eva Fielding.

The passengers on the SPSS *Tempest* sat on their acceleration couches. The couches limited their vision, but the planners had thoughtfully provided vidscreens above each.

That meant they could all watch the horror unfolding below them. Points of nuclear light turned into massive mushroom clouds along the west coast. Another cloud rose above the USS *Missouri* in Pearl Harbor. The light bathed the core of the American maritime infrastructure in the Pacific in fire and shadow.

The news networks were already showing Chinese officials proclaiming the light an "appropriate response to American aggression."

"Probably not the end of it," said Marcus. "The Chinese are counting on the American president and people not having the will to respond with overwhelming force. Even if the US responds in kind and takes out Qingdao, Zhejiang, and Shanghai, the People's Liberation Army Navy isn't working that well. That's why they were desperate enough to do this."

"How can you be so sanguine? Are you so—"

Dick Fielding interjected, "Eva, let's at least introduce ourselves before arguing. Especially now. Since we all rushed to the *Tempest* to get away from the nukes, I'm not sure who is in this chamber with us. My name is Dick Fielding and I'm—"

"Deputy Dick!"

"Yep. And who are you?"

"I'm Jason Allardeck."

"Let me see. As I recall, you were a freshman at Texas A&M, studying geophysics, and a cadet in their ROTC program before joining us."

"Yes, sir."

"Oh, great, another—"

Dick cut Eva off smoothly. "And that means the voice with the English accent, discussing the reasoning behind the Chinese strike, is Marcus Allardeck. William told me your research might have people putting you in the category of Linus Pauling someday."

"William exaggerates."

"Perhaps, but what you've done after such a decorated career in the Royal Marines is impressive."

"That was a long time ago. A time I'd like to forget."

"Good," snapped Eva.

"I assume Frances is here too, right?"

"Right here," she replied.

"I'm told your research into lasers is revolutionary."

"Thank you."

"My daughter, Sarah, is next to Jason, I think. That leaves three more couches. Who else do we have?"

"I'm Sung Li," said a clipped, angry voice.

"We're going to need as many hydroponics experts as we can get." Dick paused. "Wait, you were at UCLA. I'm sorry about your friends."

"Not the first the Chinese have killed."

"Oh?"

"My family escaped when I was ten."

"I see. Who else do we have?"

"I don't see anyone on either of the couches next to me," said Sung.

"Shit. That means at least two people got left behind, and I haven't heard anything from the other decks."

"It's not your fault. Emergency exfil never goes smoothly," said Marcus.

"Those are people's lives," snapped Eva.

"Yes…" he trailed off.

"Yes what?"

"Never mind. Some things are better left forgotten." Marcus sighed.

"You—"

Frances interrupted, "Please don't get him started, Eva. It's tedious, and I've heard it too many times."

Positional thrusters on the *Tempest* engaged, stopping conversation for a couple of minutes.

"Mr. Allardeck, the Chinese did this because their navy lost to ours?" asked Sarah.

"Probably."

"So, they killed millions instead of stopping the war?"

"Human lives don't mean much to the Chinese government, even their own," answered Sung. "Never have."

"She's right. What matters to them is that it'll probably be decades before the US can support a Pacific fleet again, by which time they'll have gotten Taiwan and everything else they want in the western Pacific."

After the thrusters stopped, Dick added, "Hopefully, we've left all that behind. In a month, we'll be on another planet, making a new life."

"That would be nice."

"God bless eccentric billionaires," said Sung.

The thrusters blasted once more and were followed by an announcement from a monotone, artificial voice. "Initial thrust phase complete. Trajectory within acceptable parameters. Primary thrust vector calculated and approved. Passenger couches operational. Passenger vital signs within acceptable parameters. All personnel, prepare for hibernation."

Then the drugs flowed into their bloodstreams and stilled their senses in Lethe sleep.

* * *

"Attention, all personnel." The computer repeated the message every five seconds until the passengers escaped their land of dreams.

When their vital signs reached appropriate levels, the computer's message changed. "Primary braking phase complete. Passenger vital signs within acceptable parameters. Trajectory within acceptable parameters. Approaching Mars orbit. Prepare for orbital insertion."

The *Tempest* headed directly toward Tharsis Montes with the Vallis Marineris canyon system stretching off in the distance.

Frances whispered, "Amazing."

"We made it, my love," agreed Marcus.

A series of lateral rocket thrusts and fission microbursts pushed the passengers around. Finally, the computer voice continued, "Orbit achieved. Passenger couch restraints released. Please commence disembarkation procedures. Shuttles inbound."

As the sudden weightlessness lifted them off their couches, a human voice came over the *Tempest*'s speakers. "Welcome to Mars! How you feeling, Deputy Dick?"

"Is that you, Felix?"

"Sure is. I'm on the shuttle approaching you," replied Felix Baker.

"We're doing great, as far as I can tell. We're here, after all."

"This is definitely the place to be."

"What's happening on Earth?" asked Eva.

"We live in interesting times." Felix's voice went cold.

"Ironic time to use a Chinese curse," said Dick with a sigh.

"Yeah, but that's where we're at."

"We left just after the bombs fell on the west coast," said Marcus. "Any more nukes after that?"

"Yeah, the Americans took out some of the Chinese ports, but so far, that's it. In fact, right now, the two sides are playing laser tag in space, and that's about the extent of the conflict."

Eva asked, "Did the *Falstaff* make it?"

"She arrived ten days ago, right on schedule."

"Any cargo damage from the higher gee accel?"

"Not much. It looks like one of the secondary nuke plants took a little damage in transit, but we should have a year before we try to bring it online. All the heavy equipment is dirtside and working. Eva, your crates of prototypes arrived sealed and unmarred, but we haven't opened them to confirm there's no damage inside."

"If my equipment is still in their packaging, they should be fine."

"When are you sending the *Falstaff* back?" asked Dick.

"William said to hold off until we figure out what's going on Earthside. Doesn't matter how fast the ship can accelerate, if there's no Shakespeare Project to fill her back up."

"What's the status with the base?"

"We haven't started extending Scotland Wing, but both first-stage nuke plants are up and doing well. And all the first-stage hydroponic farms are constructed and operational. Had our first harvest before the *Tempest* left orbit, in fact."

"Excellent!"

"Is that you, Sung?"

"Yes."

"They'll be glad to see you. They've been busting their asses."

"I'm ready to get to it. What about water?"

"The first two water plants are online, with the third and fourth in progress. Better yet, the aquifer under Endeavour Crater is bigger than initial estim—"

Suddenly, they heard nothing.

"Felix, say again, your transmission stopped," said Dick.

"Sorry, I got distracted."

"What's wrong?"

"We just spotted a pulsed nuclear flare. Damn."

"Another ship?"

"Two flares boosted from Earth after you left. We hoped they were going somewhere else, but it looks like they're headed our way."

Marcus sighed. "We're in the middle of a shooting war, and at least one of the combatants assigned someone to follow us?"

"Looks that way." Felix sighed. "William thinks the worst case is they are warships about the size of the *Falstaff*. They don't have as much lift capacity, of course, because they're armed, armored, and carry more fuel, but they can still carry a company of space marines."

"How far behind us?"

"If they stick to their current course and decel, they'll be here in about 35 hours. However, they could be here in little more than a day."

"There's good news, though," said Frances with a harsh laugh.

"Oh?" muttered Eva.

"They don't want us dead. We're on a known, static trajectory. They've had the past few minutes to fire a laser at us."

Marcus snorted. "We'll live to get to the ground, but that's only because Stratford Base has become a much bigger pawn in the strategic game."

"Yeah," said Felix. "We have to get you off the *Tempest* as quickly as we can."

"When did the *Horatio* launch?" asked Dick.

"They're initiating launch tomorrow. At least, that's the current schedule. It'll probably change when William hears about these ships. William stayed behind to keep an eye on things."

"Damn."

The passengers took another deep breath. William had recruited every single adult on the ship. He wasn't a brilliant scientist or talented artist, but his ability to organize and lead, combined with his engaging personality, had made him billions of dollars and thousands of true friends.

Including every member of the Shakespeare Project.

"In any case, it's time to get you all dirtside."

* * *

Felix waited for them at the ramp of the shuttle bay after they landed. He pulled Dick and Marcus off to the side and handed each of them a data pad. "It's confirmed, the flare was a braking ship. Our last hint of its course would put it in orbit in about twenty hours. Also, we saw another ship behind it."

"I wish we had something to defend the base with," said Marcus.

"We do." Felix smiled. "William had trouble with pirates over the years, and he always knew a Mars colony would be a target, so he got someone to produce modified X153 battle rifles, optimized for the Martian environment. We've got several hundred, a bunch of ammo, and all we need to make more."

"That's good to hear. Bullpup design?"

"Yes. He thought that form would be best in these warrens."

"Probably right. What kind of ammo?"

"We've got solid, pellet, or tungsten-carbide sabot separating rounds."

"Excellent. We'll face marines in battlesuits, and that means we'll need armor piercing."

"Those rounds will punch right through the walls," protested Dick.

"Yes, but we *have* to penetrate their armor," replied Marcus.

Felix raised a hand. "Hold on. Yes, the sabot rounds will go through the walls, but they're designed to leave small holes. The walls have self-sealing insulation. There's no way that'll be sufficient, of course, so we'll have everyone in vac suits, which have their own self-sealing feature, and we've got plenty of insta-patch foam canisters and vacuum tape." He smiled at Dick. "William and I talked about that when we chose the ammo."

Dick blew out his breath. "How that man juggles all those details, I'll never know."

"True." Marcus smiled. "How many people are up here now?"

"Counting you all, 823." Felix grimaced. "Now, if you're asking about military trained, that's a different question."

"There were nine on board the *Tempest*," said Dick. "Assuming all the veterans made it."

"That gives us over a hundred with military training, though many are older than military service age."

Dick turned to Marcus. "You're the highest ranking officer, by the way."

"I am?"

"Yes. It was William's plan, all along, for you to take charge should the need arise."

"What? He didn't tell me that," snapped Marcus.

Felix snorted. "You're a great scientist, but everyone on this trip has at least two important skill sets. Even the teenagers. Your son, for example, will probably be a great chemist, and I don't need to tell you how good his ROTC instructors think he is."

"That's exactly the sort of thinking I'd expect from William. I just wish he'd talked to me about making me senior."

Dick smiled wryly. "Would you have come if he had? You know he looked at your Royal Marine records, including the redacted stuff."

"Yes!" Marcus sighed. "Maybe." After a moment. "No, I probably would have stayed home."

"But you'll step up to the plate and do whatever's needed, won't you?"

"Stupid Yank."

"I guess you'll have to lift that stiff British upper lip." His smile faded. "Do you think we have enough to hold off a company of marines?"

"It'll be a close-run thing, but I think so. Now we have to ask ourselves, do we fight?"

"Good question. I think it's time for me to send a message to William. Just in case, you two start preparing."

"Will do," said Felix.

"While you're in the comm room, try to make contact with both ships," added Marcus. "See if you can buy us more time, but at the very least, get an idea of what they want."

"Right." Dick left.

Marcus turned to Felix. "Any weapons other than the X153s?"

"No. We never anticipated an attack so soon. We do have some mining explosives, but not many."

"Why not?"

"We use heavy mining lasers with power packs that are charged from the nuke plants, so as long as we have power, we're set."

"Mining lasers, eh? How powerful are they?"

"Now that's an interesting question." Felix punched up the specs. "Hmmm. The specs don't tell me anything. Fortunately..." He called Frances over and handed her the pad. "I've got a project for you."

"You want me to see if I can make these mining lasers usable as weapons." She grimaced.

"Yes, my love. I know you wanted to leave war behind, but..."

"Not your fault, my dear." She turned to Felix. "Is someone in charge of the miners?"

"Linda Puig. She's running that forklift right now." Felix called her over and explained what they wanted to do.

The short, heavy-set woman shrugged. "Better 'n sittin' around with my thumb up my ass."

Marcus nodded. "Alright, you two figure things out. Felix, help them with anything they need. If you do come up with something, talk to me about placement. Otherwise, since we don't have much time, do whatever might work. Any questions?"

They shook their heads.

Marcus reached out and grasped Frances's hand, then the women left. He turned to Felix. "Now, let's see what we can do to fortify this place."

"The nuke and desalinization plants are buried deep; if they're destroyed, we're all dead anyway."

"That's good to hear." Marcus glanced out one of the transminium windows. "I assume there's no real difficulty landing shuttles on the Meridiani Planum, right?"

"Not really. It's flat about everywhere." Felix sighed. "It's dusty, and we saw some issues with our shuttle engines after landing, but…"

"So, yes, they could land anywhere." Marcus grimaced. "How many ways into the base?"

Felix pulled up the map and pointed. "The two main wings, Denmark and Italy, each have three airlocks. Scotland Wing has two at the far end in case people need to evacuate. Stratford Core doesn't have any outside airlocks, except for the shuttle bay."

"Eight?"

"We didn't plan on building a fortress." Felix shrugged. "Of course, they're airlocks, so they're armored against depressurization."

"Good point." Marcus studied the schematic. "Now that I think about it, I bet the Chinese force breaches at points where there aren't airlocks. Can the walls hold against C4 or laser torches?"

"Not a chance."

"So, they can come in where they want."

"We do have secondary airlock-rated doors all over the place so we can isolate an area."

"Those will help." Marcus studied the pad. "Felix, we've got a bunch of heavy vacuum-rated cargo containers, right?"

"Yes. We get as many as we can with each shipment because we use them as building material."

"Good. We can use them as firing points and bastions. You know this place better than anyone, so I'll leave that to you. I'm going to concentrate our forces here, in Stratford Core, meaning we should set up our defenses pointing outward."

"OK." Felix tapped his pad. "I've got some ideas."

"The next thing we need to do is hide the *Tempest*."

"The *Falstaff* is still up there, too."

"That will help. Get some people to figure out new orbits for them. Goal one is to keep them from being easy targets."

"Makes sense."

"Precisely. Goal two is to position them to watch as much of the surface as they can. Ideally, they will have line of sight on both the American and Chinese bases as well as around as much of Stratford Base as possible. I have no idea if it can be done, but that's my hope."

"Got it." Felix narrowed his eyes. "Won't both sides be able to see the ship's radars?"

"If they're in geosynchronous orbit, they can shut everything off except passive sensors and a point-to-point laser comm with us. Optics can tell us a ton, but they'll be a tiny hole in space and can relay information to us without broadcasting their position."

"OK."

"The Americans and the Chinese will be able to find them if they want, but hopefully not without using active sensors and giving away their own positions."

Felix tapped on his pad. "I sent a message to the crews of both ships to make ready."

"Excellent."

Dick's voice came through the overhead. "Felix, bring Marcus to the comm room."

Once they arrived, Dick said, "I've sent the message to William. The timer on that screen shows the earliest we can get a message back from him. In the meantime, you need to hear this." He punched a button on the computer.

"Attention, Stratford Base. This is Captain Geoffrey Abrams of the USS *Puller*. Please respond immediately."

Marcus started. "We might have gotten lucky."

"Oh?"

"I know Geoffrey well. We served together on a couple of ops."

"Good. We've got to wait for William's response anyway. Answer him."

Marcus punched the button. "Attention, USS *Puller*. This is Marcus Allardeck from Stratford Base."

"Marcus, is that really you?" came the response after about six seconds.

"Sure is. It's been too long."

"Damn right it has. What the hell are you doing down there?"

"Well, I thought I was going to focus on my research, but it looks like I'm wearing a second hat. That's assuming you're not here just to say hello."

"I've got orders to occupy Stratford Base or, failing that, do anything I can to prevent the Chinese from taking the base. Space Command said they saw their Type S174 *Tian Shan* boosting out toward Mars, which is why we followed."

"That would be the ship about a day ahead of you."

"Yes."

"This is Dick Fielding, deputy governor of Stratford Base. You're ordered to do *anything* to keep the base out of Chinese hands?"

"I wish I could allay your fears, Mr. Fielding, but I can't. The order specifically includes destroying the base."

"But we're mostly scientists and families," he protested.

"I know. Believe me, I don't want *any* civilian casualties, but I've got orders, and the brass is clamping down on anything remotely resembling insubordination after the nukes landed." He sighed. "Everything's a little crazy back on Earth, so I don't have any choice."

"Why don't you just destroy the Chinese ship and leave us alone?"

"If I get a shot, I'll take it, but it won't be easy. They went silent as soon as they completed their main decel, same as we did. Even so, that doesn't solve anything. Space Command wants me to take Stratford Base or destroy it. No other options."

"The Chinese captain probably has similar orders," mused Marcus.

"Probably. The *Tian Shan* is much like the *Puller*."

"Not the ship to send if they just want to destroy the base."

"Not this time, no." Abrams paused. "Marcus. I heard what you said about another hat. Be smart. I've got over a hundred leathernecks up here, and I can drop them in one wave. Everything we know about the *Tian Shan* suggests they can do the same."

"I know, Geoffrey, I know." Marcus sighed. "But we're not going to stand by and lose everything we're trying to do."

"We've got some time before anything happens," said Dick. "We're expecting word from Earth in a few minutes, and maybe that'll tell us something new."

"We can hope. Abrams out."

Marcus sighed. "So, it's the worst case."

"And now we wait for William."

They stared at the incoming message board until the message received signal popped up. With a deep breath, Dick punched play.

William's face appeared. He had allowed his brown hair to recede instead of getting treatments, and he wore a Shakespearian-style beard. He sat at his desk in Stratford-upon-Avon with a grim look in his eyes.

"Well, ladies and gentlemen, what I feared has come to pass. I knew it might happen sooner or later, but this war made everything happen sooner. The *Horatio* will be boosting within the hour, and she's crammed with everything I could think of. Keep our ships in Martian space until this clears up. Worst case, Felix has plans to convert them into asteroid mining ships, and ships are just too valuable to risk."

William took a drink of water. "I planned to someday get international recognition for Stratford Base as a new nation-state. I have receptive ears in the American government and in the governments of all the other spacefaring nations, except the Chinese. I'm staying here to see if I can make my plans work, though it's happening much sooner than I intended. It's a good thing I'm rich because this plan costs a bunch in bribes."

He smiled. "Anyway, if you can hold those ships and marines off, you'll prove Stratford Base can protect itself, which is the most basic job of a nation-state. Then, since Mars is far enough away that neither side can afford to repeatedly send ships back and forth, both sides will probably think it's too much of a hassle. It's worth a shot at least."

William shuffled some papers and looked uncharacteristically out of sorts. "Marcus will know what to do, and you have the skills and weapons to hold off their troops. I know it's not going to be easy, but I'm asking you all to pitch in and do your best."

He paused. "Nothing can destroy us, not even war's quick fire. William out."

The men in the comm room looked at each other.

"So, that's that," said Marcus.

Dick nodded slowly. "Felix, gather everyone who's not doing something crucial in the gymnasium and set up camera feeds."

"We need to set up the stage. Take about ten minutes."

"OK, make it happen."

Marcus sat down at his desk and poked at his pad. "That's ten minutes for me to come up with some sort of unit structure."

"Do it right the first time," said Dick with a wry smile.

"If I don't, at least I won't have to live with my failure very long."

$$* * *$$

Dick looked out on nearly every member of the Shakespeare Project. "As you all know, two warships followed us here. We sent a message back to William to get his guidance. This is the message he sent back to us."

After it played, Eva snapped, "By hold them off, you mean fight them, right?"

"Yes, dear, I'm afraid that's exactly what I mean."

She turned her glare to Marcus. "I had hoped, when we left Earth, we'd leave jingoistic myrmidons like him behind us."

Marcus took a deep breath. "Mrs. Fielding, I never wanted this to happen. In fact, had I known it might, I wouldn't have come."

"Bullshit."

"Eva, he *didn't* know until he got here. William thought he wouldn't come if he knew, which meant Frances and Jason wouldn't have either. He respected what the Allardecks could contribute too much to risk their staying Earthside based on something which, at the time, seemed unlikely."

She opened her mouth to continue.

Sung Li interrupted her. "None of this matters. We might be able to negotiate with the Americans, but the Chinese can't be reasoned with. We have to fight them or let them take over the base. And if we do that, there'll be no place like America for us to flee to, meaning we'll become slaves of the Chinese government forever. We *have* to fight."

"We can shut the doors and not let them in," said a tall, lanky man in the back.

Marcus shook his head. "They'll just cut through the walls."

"What? That's likely to kill some of us!" He looked outraged.

Sung snorted. "They nuked the American west coast. You think they're worried about walls?"

"Madness! We're just scientists."

"We're a *project*," said Dick. "William built Stratford Base because he didn't want all of humanity's eggs in one basket, which, given that nukes were just used, is a real smart thing. Both the Chinese and the Americans want to control that basket."

"Both want a bolt hole," agreed Marcus.

"What about their installations on Mars?" asked another man.

"Neither is self-sufficient. For both nations, a presence on Mars was secondary to a space navy capable of dealing with the other side. But things have changed."

Eva snapped, "That's ridiculous."

"I'm sorry, Mrs. Fielding, but they don't think like reasonable people." Sung glared at the other woman. "That's because they're *not* reasonable people, by our terms."

Dick raised his hand. "This is not terribly helpful, nor is it pertinent." He glanced at his wife. "I'm sorry, my love, but our choices are to defend ourselves or to allow ourselves to become controlled by one side or the other."

The tall man yelled, "But there's no way we can fight—"

Marcus cut him off. "Not true. Those ships carry at most 150 troops each. Probably more like 120 or even less."

"But they're soldiers!"

"There are over a hundred of us who were in the military, all of whom had exemplary records, or William wouldn't have chosen us." He sighed. "And there are a bunch of you who are able bodied and can fight at their sides, even if you haven't served."

"Like me!" said Sarah.

"Like us," said Jason, stepping up to stand at her side. The two looked shyly at each other.

Marcus smiled sadly at them. "Thank you."

"And we have weapons," added Felix. "William made sure of that."

"My wife, Frances, is working on finding a way to use the mining lasers to defend us. She's one of the best laser physicists I know, and she's done this sort of thing before." He noticed her waving from the back. "In fact, here she is now. Any news?"

"Yes. The lasers can be scaled up to be useful. We're working on running lines to the plants."

"That's great news," said Marcus. "What about aiming?"

"That'll be more of a challenge, but we're on it."

"We'll leave you to it," said Dick. He looked out over the crowd. "There it is, folks. We know our choices. We know we *can* fight. Now, we need to know, should we fight?"

Nearly every arm rose.

"Those against?"

Eva's arm shot up, as did the tall man's in the back and a few others.

"Clearly, then, we fight," said Dick.

Sarah looked up at Marcus. "You'll be asking for people to help fight, right?"

"Yes. Anyone who is willing and able," he replied.

"What? I won't have it!" snarled Eva.

"Can't you hear what Dad's saying?" Sarah turned to her mother. "We either fight or let them take us over. That's it."

"Be quiet!"

"No!" Sarah balled her fists. "The Chinese bastards killed my friends, and now they're trying to take this place away from us. I didn't want to come here, but now that I am, I'm going to make the best of it. Living under Chinese rule or in an American military base is not the best of *anything*."

"But—"

"She's made a choice," Marcus said. "And I thank her."

Eva stood there fuming. "I'll not forget this."

"Neither will I." He looked at the audience. "Sarah brings up an important point. We won't force a weapon on anyone who isn't willing, but we *will* take everyone who is."

Felix forestalled Eva's next outburst. "We'll need help for other things, though. We're going to have wounded to tend to and damage to the base to fix. You don't have to fire a gun to do your part."

"Yes." Dick stepped up to the front of the stage. "Let's get this clear. This is going to take all of us, not necessarily holding a gun but making sure as many of us survive as possible so we can make Stratford Base what we all hoped."

The crowd muttered and snarled and issued more than one curse. Eva ranted at Sarah, who shook her head.

Marcus raised his hands. "People. People!" After getting their attention, he said, "We have much to do. Those of you who want to fight, stay here."

"Those with medical training, report to the infirmary, and the docs will get you organized," said Felix. "The rest of you, join me in Warehouse Denmark Alpha. We have a ton of work to do, and we don't have much time."

As people made their choices, Frances walked up to Marcus.

He hugged her. "Great work."

"We'll see."

"What do you think of Linda?"

"Sharp cookie. Those miners respect the hell out of her."

"Good. Tell her she's in charge of Heavy Weapons Group One, Weaps-One on the comms."

"I thought you'd do something like that." She kissed him. "I love you. I may not get a chance to say it again."

"I love you too." He sighed. "I'm sorry."

"We'd already be dead if we hadn't made the choices we did. It's clear as day. At least, this way, we have a chance. Eva Fielding is an idiot."

"I don't blame her. I went straight to rage when I saw the first bomb hit Puget Sound."

"You're much nicer than I am," Frances said with a harsh smile. "I think I'm going to have a *conversation* with her when this is all done. There aren't enough people up here for there to be any...misunderstandings."

He grinned. "I love you."

She kissed him. Hard. "I love you, too."

Marcus watched her walk away, then jumped back on the stage. "Now, for the rest of you." Marcus took out a pad, tapped on it, and displayed a list on the wall screen. "I'm breaking us down into four companies, one for each wing plus a reserve company. Then we'll assign twelve platoons to those companies. Here are the commanders. The rest of you..."

The next twenty minutes were a full Charlie Foxtrot getting everything organized, but in the end, the platoons all had about the same number of people and knew who commanded what.

"Alright, everyone," said Marcus after everything settled. "The commanders will break you into sections, give you weapons, and bring you up to speed on using them. Any questions?"

None came.

"Look, I'm not going to bullshit you. You're not going to be as good as the Chinese or the American marines. Not even close. However, we've got several advantages. There are more of us than them.

We know this place, and they don't. And…" He paused. "They can retreat. We've got nowhere else to go. We fight, or we die."

While they filed out, Dick asked, "And what are you going to do?"

"Right now? I'm going to get an X153 and learn how to fire it. Then I'm going to think about our options. It would sure be nice if we didn't have to face them straight up, where their training and equipment will matter most."

"Good luck."

"I'll need it."

"*We'll* need it."

* * *

Eva stomped around her new lab, emptying packing crates and putting experimental parts in various cabinets. Her preparations for the upcoming battle had taken almost no time, and now she had too much time on her hands.

Time for her temper to take over, which, like always, kicked her genius into overdrive.

She stopped suddenly. "That's it!"

She searched through the stack of crates, leaving haphazard piles of items around the lab, until she found what she wanted. She connected it to a diagnostic pad.

Throughout the process, she never stopped cursing Marcus.

Once she got the diagnostic results, she snapped, "I'm such an idiot! I'll have to get the chem cocktail right to avoid brain damage, but *this* is how we get the hardware and software to sync with the nervous system in an emergency. So damned simple."

She pulled out the pad that held her huge pharmaceutical database. She went to one drug, but shook her head almost immediately

"No, not that. That needs the patient's genome to work, and that would slow everything down."

She continued her hunt, taking notes here and there. "Now this series *could* work." She paused, drumming her fingers on her desk. "But how do we test it to get the right balance?" Suddenly, another idea came to her, and she typed into her pad.

"Would you like some help?"

Eva turned toward the door and saw her daughter, and her rage flared again. She pointed at the gun slung around Sarah's neck. "Aren't you supposed to be learning how to use that *thing*?"

"It's surprisingly easy."

"So, you're the perfect warrior now," spat Eva.

"Mom…" A tear ran down Sarah's face. "Mom, it's not like that."

"What's it like?"

"I can't not…" Tears started flowing. "I love you, Mom, but this time you're wrong."

Eva leaned back, stunned. Then the rage returned. "Then go. Go fight your little war."

"It's not *my* little war. It's *our* war. It's the only way you get what you wanted."

"Bullshit."

"You told me you wanted to come here so you could *really* do your research! Dad wanted to come because he wanted to please you, plus it was such an opportunity for him. But me? I came because of you guys. I wanted to go to prom! I wanted to go to Stanford! I wanted to go to Daytona Beach for spring break! I wanted to be a *girl*, not Eva Fielding's daughter."

"You don't have to be my daughter anymore."

Sarah started toward the door.

"Wait—" yelled Eva. "I'm sorry. I didn't mean that. I'm just…"

"Yeah." Sarah turned back and looked around the lab. She noticed the components and pads strewn about. "So, what did you discover?"

"What?"

"Every time you get really pissed, you figure out something brilliant. I've never seen you this pissed before, so I bet it's something amazing."

"I'm not like that!"

"Oh, yes, you are. Dad and I have known for years." Sarah chuckled. "So, what did you figure out?"

"Uh, now that you mention it, I finally found a way to insert prosthetics for wounded people extremely quickly."

"See?"

"Whatever." Eva glared at her daughter. "It's just that Allardeck is such an asshole."

"Maybe, but he's right."

"But it doesn't make any sense!"

"Did you hear the Chinese woman at the meeting? They *think* differently."

"Stupid." Eva paused. "But even stupider would be to let my temper drive you away."

Her daughter embraced her.

They sniffled when they stepped back.

"Uh, you know Sarah, if you've, uh, got time to help, some of the larger prototype limbs are heavy and awkward for one person to carry, even in Martian gravity." Eva stared at the ground.

"I'd love to."

They pulled them out, and Sarah held them while Eva plugged them into their charging and diagnostic cradles.

"Now they'll be ready when I need them."

"Good." Sarah grimaced. "I love you. I gotta go. They told us to get some food and sleep, so we'd be alert when it's time."

"I hate all this." Eva's eyes flared. "But I do love you, Sarah."

They embraced, weeping.

Sarah stepped back. "See you later, Mom."

Eva nodded, but she didn't trust herself to say anything.

Sarah picked up her X153 and left.

In the next few hours, Eva unloaded more crates, though her anger diverted her time and again. She theorized over a bunch of nagging issues for fast insertion that resulted in an innovation that would make later generations remember her alongside Mendel, Darwin, and Hampson.

But it was all so stupid!

* * *

Marcus walked into the comm room.

"You look like hell," said Dick. "Did you get any sleep?"

"Some. Even ate some food."

"How long until the Chinese reach orbit? About an hour?"

"Haven't seen anything from the *Tempest* or the *Falstaff*, but yes, about that. They're probably braking pretty solidly right now."

Dick fiddled with a keyboard. "What do you really think?"

"Honestly?"

"Yeah."

"I don't know." Marcus shrugged. "Felix has done a fantastic job setting up strongpoints, and we'll outnumber the Chinese at least two to one, but we're just militia. Worse, every person who dies is someone William thought Stratford Base would need, and we're going to lose more than I'm comfortable with."

"What about the lasers?"

"Linda and Frances have done wonders, but they need more time." Marcus shrugged. "They've got two batteries hooked up with decent aiming optics, but no more. They're the ones guarding Stratford Core because they had the easiest power runs to connect."

"Those will help, right?"

"Some. We want to prevent shuttles from coming directly at Stratford Core, but elsewhere? They *might* be able to aim on shuttles that are landing, but only if they come in high or on certain arcs. Otherwise, they simply won't have line of sight." He sighed. "Give us another eight hours, and we'd have a battery attached to each wing, but the Chinese aren't going to wait that long."

"Probably not." Dick pointed at some screens running continuous feeds. "There's more bad news. The most recent news reports from Earth are not good."

"Damn."

Felix piped up. "It's not all bad news. The kids and the elderly are suited up in the plants down below," said Felix. "The infirmary is ready. The mobile medical teams are ready, and we have more supplies than I realized. I've got wall patching teams ready to go. We're as prepared as we can be."

"Speaking of doing wonders," said Dick.

"Indeed," agreed Marcus.

They stared at the screens flickering with fresh images of nothing new.

"You said the laser batteries need more time," said Felix. "What can we do to delay the Chinese attack?"

Marcus blinked. "I've been so focused on getting the units ready, I hadn't thought about that. *We* can't do anything, but maybe we can find someone who can."

"Oh?"

138 | IBSON & KENNEDY

Marcus punched the comm. "Stratford Base to USS *Puller*, come in please."

"Abrams here. What do you have for me, Marcus?"

"How secure is this comm?"

"Hold one." The communication link light blinked out and then blinked back on again. Abrams said, "Now, it's a point-to-point laser with standard encryption. The Chicoms could break that encryption easily, of course, but they'd have to be between us to intercept it, and that's unlikely."

"We'll have to chance it. We need your help."

Abrams' reply took much longer than the lightspeed lag required. "How many people you got down there?"

"Over eight hundred."

"How many kids?"

"Almost fifty under the age of ten."

"And I'm sure you've got Jason there too. Along with Frances."

"He's not a kid anymore. He's nineteen and already good enough that I made him my reserve company commander."

"What? When the hell did that happen? Last time I saw him he was, what, eight?"

"About that."

"Helluva kid."

"There are lots of great kids up here. And people."

There was another long pause. "What do you need?"

"The Chinese are going to attack soon, right?"

"Probably. I don't know exactly where they are, but they're less than an hour from orbit. Once in orbit, it's merely a question of launching at the best time."

"Can you do anything to prevent that attack? Or, failing that, hinder it in any way? It would fall under the section of your orders about preventing the Chinese from taking us over."

"Did I mention I'm just a sub driver?"

Marcus chuckled. "A good one, as I well remember."

"OK. I'm not saying we'll do anything, but I'll talk with my XO. We'll see what happens. I'll keep this link open just in case."

"Thank you."

"Don't thank me until this is all over." Abrams sighed. "I might still have to drop my marines on your head."

"I know, Geoffrey, I know."

"Abrams out."

The next hour lasted forever. The occasional status report arrived. They dealt with it. One of the agronomists brought sandwiches and some of his gigantic radishes, along with fresh-pressed lemonade. Mostly, the three just stared at the optical feeds coming in, flicking between the *Tempest* and *Falstaff* feeds and the news from Earth.

"It's amazing. I would have never expected telescopes focused on nothing in particular to be more engrossing than 24-hour news," Marcus murmured.

Felix snorted. "I did."

At the end of the hour, nothing happened. More minutes ticked by.

Then the incoming message light came on.

"This is Stratford Base," answered Dick.

"The People's Liberation Army of Space assumes control of Stratford Base. Any resistance will be dealt with according to our procedure." The message repeated.

"Shut it off," growled Marcus.

"Not yet." Felix manipulated the comm computers.

"Why?"

"I might be able to get enough of a fix on the *Tian Shan* to point the optics at the right spot in space. Finally, Felix leaned back with a smile. "Got it." He pointed at the screens showing the feeds from the *Tempest,* and there she was, a thick tube with a set of huge, air-tight doors running down one side.

"We still have that link to the *Puller,* right?"

"Yes."

"Send this feed, along with the location data on that link. We'll see if that helps them."

"You betcha," said Felix with a grin. "Done!"

"Can Abrams destroy it now?" asked Dick.

"Unlikely," replied Marcus. "We've got them pointed at a spot in the sky, but it's too far away for a good laser lock with whatever passive sensors are on the *Puller.* They won't light their active sensors, I don't think. That means they'd have to fire missiles, which are even less stealthy than assault shuttles."

"Will they fire on the *Tempest?*"

"Both of our ships are prizes, so I doubt they will, even if they suspect we're using the ship's optics to help keep an eye on things."

They waited for something to happen.

Dick sighed. "It's times like this, I wish everyone thought about war like Eva does."

"Me too," said Marcus. "More than she'll ever understand."

Dick nodded.

They watched the feed from the *Tempest*'s monitor. As the seconds passed, a hope came to each that maybe, just maybe, nothing would happen.

And then the huge shuttle bay doors started to open.

"Well, that's that," said Marcus.

"What the hell?" snapped Felix. He pointed at a screen aimed at Earth. Two large flares showed on the screen.

Marcus smacked his hands together. "You sneaky sub driver. Those look like shuttles that punched their drives as soon as the *Tian Shan* cracked her doors."

"I thought you said launching shuttles was obvious."

"It is, but he didn't *launch* them. I bet he pushed them outside the *Puller* and then continued his braking maneuvers to get into orbit, letting them coast along ahead of him. It's tricky and dangerous, but he did something like that with our landing team once. It was a slow, bumpy ride, but no one knew we were there until we announced ourselves."

"Just like here."

The flares suddenly got brighter.

"And now they've launched missiles." Marcus smiled.

As they spoke, the *Tian Shan* rotated on her axis and closed her bay doors. It took minutes for the missiles to arrive, but both exploded before getting within ten thousand klicks.

"Laser point defense," murmured Marcus.

"So now we're back where we started?"

"Not exactly. The captain of the *Tian Shan* knew the *Puller* was out there, but he hoped to drop his troops in one load. Now, with the American shuttles configured for space-to-space fighting, he's got to adjust. His deck crews are changing the loadouts on some of their shuttles to match."

"He gave us some time."

"Yes. Better yet, it means their assault on us won't be *all* of their marines."

After about fifteen minutes, the *Tian Shan*'s doors opened. A shuttle launched from the bay, her launch flare obvious on the screen. Then another.

"The Chinese captain was ready for something like this, or his munitions people are incredibly fast. My bet is he's damn good *and* so are his deck crews," said Marcus.

The *Tian Shan* rose to a higher orbit and moved off to the side.

"Now, he's trying to go back into hiding. It'd probably work, too, except for the *Tempest*. Ships are hard to see."

A half-hour later, six more shuttles launched, accelerating down and around the planet.

"At least it's two shuttles fewer than they might have sent," said Felix.

"Maybe more. I'll bet two are configured for escort duty."

The shuttles passed the *Tempest*'s line of sight.

"And now we wait until the *Falstaff* can pick them up, assuming they don't do something sneaky while we can't see them."

Dick punched the comms. "I'm live-streaming everything back to the Project on Earth. They're ten minutes behind us, but it might help William."

Marcus thought about contacting each unit commander, but he'd met with all of them while they organized. They'd already worked out the best possible deployment plan they could think of.

Can't micromanage.

He thought about other options.

Can't dither.

He thought about saying something inspirational.

Never was something I could do all that well. Always just came off as nervous. Can't do that either.

Felix monitored the readouts. "The *Falstaff* has them. Coming right in where we expected." He announced on the overhead comms, "Everyone double-check everyone else's vacsuits."

Marcus added, "The Chinese are incoming. Repeat, the Chinese are on the way. Commence your final preparations."

"Tell me when they're over our normal, visible horizon, Felix," said Dick.

"Will do." He stared at the screen. "Clearing the horizon…now!"

Dick leaned into the microphone. "Attention incoming shuttles. You're approaching Stratford Base airspace. Please state intent."

No answer.

Marcus hit the comm. "Weaps-One, do you have line of sight on any of the shuttles?"

Linda replied, "No. They're coming in too low."

"OK, unless something changes, I don't want you to fire. Repeat, do not fire."

"Uh, did you say you don't want us to fire if we get a shot?"

"Yes."

"Why the hell not?"

"Because if you do, it'll be a hard shot and probably won't do any good. Odds are we're going to have to fight off at least one more shuttle attack. It's possible, by then, *all* of the batteries will be available. That means they might have a chance to do serious damage, but only if no one knows they're there."

"I guess I understand that."

"Good. Don't worry. You're my hole card, and if I can play you, I will."

"Got it."

Dick spoke again. "According to international law agreed to by the People's Republic of China in the 2042 Geneva Space Colonization Accords, we are allowed to claim a territorial presence up to 25 kilometers out from our installation's walls."

Still no answer.

"If you do not answer, under international anti-piracy laws, Stratford Base may legally fire upon you when you are within our territorial perimeter."

"Nothing," said Felix.

"How far?" asked Marcus.

"Two hundred klicks. One hundred. Fifty." Felix took a breath. "Within the 25-klick limit."

"Now what?" asked Dick.

"We let them land. Nothing else we can do right now."

Suddenly, four of the shuttles slammed on their thrusters and curved to land next to Scotland Wing.

"Damn!"

"What?"

"The Chinese commander knows his business."

"What the hell does that mean?"

Marcus ignored him. "Denmark and Italy Companies, set one of your platoons to watch the wing, then send the rest back to Stratford Core as fast as you can." After they confirmed the order, he continued, "Scotland Company, Scotland Company."

"Scotland here," answered the lilting voice of a former US Army captain.

"You've got four shuttles of Chinese marines heading for your wing."

"I love target-rich environments."

Marcus chuckled. "Don't try to stand up to them. I'm bringing as many troops as I can to the first warehouse on that wing."

"Where Felix set up strongpoints."

"Exactly. Slow them down if you can, but—"

"But we aren't a match for them. Got it."

And then the shuttles were on the Martian surface. Heavily armed and armored elite marines of the People's Liberation Army of Space charged out. As Marcus had expected, the PLAS eschewed the airlocks and breached the walls.

"Felix, close every airlock-rated door outside our perimeter in Denmark and Italy."

"Got it."

Jason leaned his head in. "Dad, all the other platoons are here."

"Right." Marcus turned to Felix. "You take over here. I'm taking the reserve to the Scotland Wing. When I get to the warehouse, I'm going to need to know all I can about what's happening further up-wing. Got it?"

"But—"

"I've been a trigger-puller before. Just keep an eye out."

Felix nodded and turned back to his screens.

Marcus grabbed a rifle and left the comm room. "Platoons, advance to the first warehouse in the Scotland Wing. On the bounce!"

When they got there without contact, Marcus went to a wall comm. "Felix, what's our status?"

"Our people are essentially running at this point. They'll be on you soon. The Chinese are advancing methodically, so they'll be there in a few minutes."

"Good. How many cargo container fighting points did you set up in this first warehouse?"

"Three, one up to the left that has a line of fire on both the incoming entrances and two others near the inward doors."

"Right." He turned to the platoons. "I'll take a platoon up to the flanking position—"

Jason cut him off. "No, Dad."

"What?"

"You have to be able to retreat, so you gotta stay back. If you get cut off and killed, we're all dead."

"But—"

"You taught me, so I know what to do. I'll take the platoon."

"But—"

"Dad, you can't say no because it's me."

"And me." Sarah stepped up next to him.

"I..." He stopped, looking at the other defenders around him. *Most of them aren't soldiers. Jason's right.*

He took a deep breath.

"I hate it when kids are right. OK, take that position. Remember, our guys are coming back fast. Don't fire at the first thing you see. Got it?"

Jason smirked. "As if." They moved off.

"Arrogant punk."

"I get it from my dad!"

Marcus laughed and pointed at a platoon. "You take that position." He pointed at another. "You take that one. Set your X153s to three-round bursts. And remember what I said about the good guys coming back. Aim at battlesuits, not our vacsuits. You hit one of ours, and I'll let my son tell you how to do your jobs too. He's *really* annoying at that."

A series of laughs answered him as they moved.

Marcus looked at the remaining platoons. "Arrange yourselves inside those doors. My guess is Scotland Company is going to come back running. Let them through, then attack."

"Uh, why not keep us all out here?"

"There's not enough cover, and you'll come out from two firing positions. It won't surprise them much, but I'll take every advantage I can get."

They settled into their positions just before the remnants of Scotland Company slammed open the far doors and ran through the warehouse.

"Check fire! Let them through!" yelled Marcus. "Jason, the Chinese'll throw flashbangs when they come through the door."

"I already have firing lines marked and extra mags ready. We'll close our eyes and spray and pray. I told them to be Tri-V heroes."

"Good call. We'll back you up."

"You better, or Mom's gonna be pissed."

Marcus laughed. "The rest of you, keep your eyes closed and stay in your cover until I tell you otherwise."

Two eternal, breathless minutes later, there was no more time to think. The anticipated flashbangs popped into the warehouse.

Marcus heard Jason's people fire. When they paused, he commanded everyone else to open up. His people looked over and around the crates, sending a hail of tungsten-carbide sabot rounds toward the door.

He felt the warehouse losing pressure. Fortunately, the armor-piercing rounds shredded the Chinese battlesuits. A half-dozen PLAS marines fell in the initial barrage.

Unfortunately, that didn't stop them. The remainder threw a spread of grenades and pushed into the warehouse.

Shrapnel ripped through a number of defenders.

Marcus sent a three-round burst into a marine. The attacker after him fired to his left, cutting through an entire section of defenders. Marcus shot him before he could turn his weapon against more of the defenders, but more Chinese followed.

And then the defending platoons burst from behind them, spitting tungsten at the PLAS. A bunch of attackers fell.

Heavily outnumbered, the Chinese commander called his troops back, and they retreated out of the warehouse.

"Cease fire!" shouted Marcus. "Cease fire!"

For a long moment, the hiss of air escaping the warehouse was the only sound.

Marcus jumped on the warehouse comm system. "Felix, what are the Chinese doing?"

"Looks like they're carrying their wounded back to the shuttles."

"Good. Get med teams here now. Hole patching teams, too."

"Already on the way."

Medical personnel ran into the warehouse.

"Mr. Allardeck! Marcus!"

He turned and saw Sarah frantically waving at him, and he rushed over to her. A medtech was working on Jason's leg.

Marcus fell to Jason's side. "Son..."

"Hi, Dad. Guess I didn't pass the final, did I?"

"It's not over yet. Keep working, dammit."

"Get out of our way, Mr. Allardeck. He'll be fine if we can get him to the med section," snarled the medtech. They lifted Jason onto a gurney and wheeled him out before Marcus could really understand what was going on.

Sarah grabbed him, and they rocked back and forth, crying.

Felix's voice came through on the overhead speakers. "Marcus to a comm station. Marcus to a comm station."

"OK, I've got to go," said Marcus. "Go help the others."

She nodded and squared her shoulders.

Marcus went back to the warehouse comm station. "What's going on, Felix?"

"It's confirmed; their shuttles are already lifting off."

He looked around. The Chinese marines, especially their grenades, had hammered the defenders. He stared at his son's blood on his suit's gauntlets. He whispered, "Otherwise we should grow too fond of it."

"What was that?"

"Nothing. I'll be back at the comm center as soon as I get us organized."

* * *

WE DARE: SEMPER PARATUS | 149

Blood stained Eva's lab coat. She yanked off her gloves and yelled, "Bring me the next one!"

A medtech pushed a gurney in front of her. Shrapnel had shredded the patient's leg. An IV ran into his arm, where the vacsuit had been cut away.

"Help me get his helmet off." Her eyes widened when she realized it was Jason Allardeck. "What do we have?"

"His leg's hammered, but he's stable, and the vacsuit seals kept him from losing as much blood as he could've. He was awake until I gave him a sedative for the pain."

"Good." She looked at the ravaged leg. "Damn, it's ripped to shreds."

"Yeah. Even Johns Hopkins couldn't save that."

Suddenly, Marcus's voice came through the overhead speakers. "OK, everyone. Here's where we are. We drove off the Chinese assault. That's the good news. Unfortunately, we took a bunch of casualties, and the Americans are still coming. And I don't think the Chinese are done."

Eva's rage returned as she heard his voice. "Sacrificed his own damn son for his pride."

"What?" asked the medtech.

"Never mind," she snapped.

Marcus continued, "I told you earlier we wouldn't ask anyone to fight who isn't willing. I hold to that. We've got lots of other things to do. However, if you've reconsidered, we can use every trigger-puller we can get. It's going to be a close-run thing."

"He needs everyone, eh?" asked Eva.

The medtech grimaced. "We took a lot of casualties. We've kept most alive, but still…"

"Right." She bared her teeth in a feral grin. "Get him to my lab with as much blood as you can scrounge up. I'll be there in a few. I need to grab some things from here."

He hesitated.

"Do it. I'm going to take care of his leg. And wait for me there."

The medtech shrugged and pushed Jason out of the infirmary.

Eva grabbed what she needed, growling at anyone who stood in her way.

This is stupid, a little voice kept nagging her. *It all looks good in theory, but you've not tested anything. Nothing!* Rage overrode the little voice, and she rushed to her lab.

She pointed at the medtech. "We're going to put him on that table." After that, she asked, "What sedative did you give him?" At his answer, she turned to the pharmaceutical reference pad and nodded. "Good. That'll be fine. In fact, that's probably the one we'll use as a standard."

"A standard for what?"

"Fast insertion."

"What?"

She moved to one of the storage cabinets. "Never mind. Come help me with this." They set a prototype leg next to Jason.

"You're going to replace the leg?"

"Yes, and I'm going to do it quickly."

"Can you do that?"

"It's something I've been working on."

"OK." He glanced around. "Do you still need me?"

"Probably not. Thanks."

"Sure, doc, that's what I'm here for."

After completing the preparations, she hesitated. "This is stupid, Eva. You've not done any testing. It ought to work, but how many people have died because it 'ought to work?'"

She took a deep breath and started to turn away. Then Marcus's voice came over the speakers again, this time with initial casualty reports.

"None of that would have happened if those fools hadn't fought in the first place," she snarled, and her rage drove her to action. Soon, Jason's shattered and ripped leg filled a hazmat recycle bin. She applied her first great invention, a special nanotech, bioelectric, connective fluid. Then she fit the prototype leg to the stump.

She leaned back and checked the readings on her monitors. Everything looked good...for a normal insertion.

Still a chance to stop, said the nagging voice. *At this point, he's stable, and you can do the same insertion you've done a hundred times before.*

"He said we need more trigger-pullers *now*," she snarled to the emptiness.

She inserted the drugs. While they took effect, she readied the pad with her new installation sequence. When all was ready, she took a deep breath and turned the artificial leg on. Jason's body stiffened as the feedback from the leg ran up his spine. The pad flickered as it synced with the leg, the nanotech fluid, and the diodes attached to his head. She punched the icon for her freshly written, crash install sequence.

Jason's body flopped as the data hammered into his brain. She threw herself down on him, struggling to hold him still.

The installation took about fifteen minutes.

Fifteen long minutes.

By the end, Eva was bruised and battered. And terrified by what she'd done.

Screwing up her courage, she looked at the readouts. They all looked right, but only one thought ran through her mind.

What have I done?

* * *

Eva was sitting next to Jason, staring at her pad, when Marcus came in.

"What have you done!" he demanded when he saw his son on the table.

Her rage flared. "I replaced his leg so you can have another trigger-puller."

"What? That's impossible. I'm just a chemical engineer, but I know bioreplacements take months and the right genetic combinations!"

She stood and jabbed a finger into his chest. "They used to. Now they don't."

"When the hell did that happen?"

"I just figured out the process."

"When?"

"Today!"

"What? When did you test it?"

She looked down. "I didn't have time."

Marcus bunched his fists. "You did this to my son without *any* testing? I thought you were a scientist!"

Eva stared up at him with angry, dark eyes. "You took my daughter!"

"She made her own decision!"

"You said you needed all the trigger-pullers you could get!"

"Not if it means using some untried experiment—"

"What's all the shouting?" Jason asked in a blurred, thick voice.

"Jason!" Marcus leaned over his son.

"Dad?"

"How do you feel?"

"I hurt." He suddenly yelled. "My leg!"

"It's right there," said Eva. "Better than ever."

Marcus glared at her.

"Is it?" Jason looked puzzled.

"Yes. Let me help you up, and you can see." Marcus's eyes burned as he lifted his son to a sitting position.

Jason saw the prototype leg. It looked extremely human, but not quite. "Huh."

Marcus gritted his teeth but didn't say anything.

"My head hurts," said Jason.

"That's to be expected," said Eva. "Can you move the leg?"

He lifted it and yelped in pain.

"Son?" Marcus reached out.

"It's OK, Dad." He blinked. "It's really OK. I mean, it hurts, but like it's sore. And I have one hell of a headache."

Marcus glared at Eva.

Eva handed Jason a handful of pills. "It's simple ibuprofen. In other patients, the main cause of pain is inflammation."

Jason swallowed them. He lifted his leg again. He grimaced but didn't yelp. "Huh."

"What?" asked Marcus.

"It feels weird."

"I'm not surprised," said Eva. "Here, let us help you up. The best thing is to use it. Your brain and leg are synced as best as the software can, but nothing beats using it."

He stood up. Then he took a step and blinked. He glanced at his dad with a hint of a smile. "It works." He took another step, but when he pushed off the artificial leg, he suddenly bounced up and went sprawling.

"Jason!" Marcus rushed over.

Jason was laughing as he pushed himself up. "That was weird!"

"What happened?" He turned to Eva. "What did you do to my son?"

Eva ignored him. "Jason, the leg I gave you is not simply a replacement. That leg is augmented."

"What do you mean?"

She glanced up at the ceiling. "Let's go to the gymnasium." Once there, she pulled over a large cushion and instructed him to jump off his human leg. "OK, now try the new one."

He touched the ceiling.

He landed with a roll and rose with a huge smile. "That was amazing!"

Eva smiled. "Run around in here and try things out. You'll need to adjust to get your balance because you'll have to push less with the new leg, but eventually, it'll be second nature."

"Thanks, Mrs. Fielding!" Jason returned to the mat, experimenting.

Marcus took a deep breath. "Thanks, Eva."

"Don't thank me," she hissed. "In a few hours, he'll be a useful trigger-puller again."

They heard Dick's voice over the speakers. "Marcus, I need you in the comm room *now!*"

Marcus stared into Eva's eyes. "You can't possibly fathom how much I hate what I have to do now," he said. "But I'm going to do it anyway because I have a son, and you have a daughter, and we have a chance up here."

He ignored her response and went to hug Jason. Then he left.

He never noticed the puzzled look in her eyes, nor did he see Jason bring her to tears later when he thanked her for helping him get back to his unit.

* * *

WE DARE: SEMPER PARATUS | 155

In the comm room, Dick took one look at Marcus and asked, "What happened?"

Marcus shook his head. "What do you need?"

Felix pointed at the screen streaming news from Earth. It showed three mushroom clouds. "Washington's gone. Beijing and Moscow too."

"What?"

"That's all I know."

Dick snorted. "That's all anyone knows. It happened about a half hour ago in all three cities."

"Terrorists?"

"Probably. Who knows?" Dick sighed. "Everything's going crazy. Congress was in session. We don't know the status of the American government, and we know even less about the Chinese and Russians."

Marcus stared at the screen. The reporters were talking without saying anything useful. The scrolling feeds at the bottom added data but provided no answers.

"What does this mean for us?" asked Felix.

Marcus shook his head. "I don't know. But we're a bigger game piece than ever before."

"Yeah."

The message received light popped on. With a deep breath, Dick punched the button.

William's face appeared. This time, he wore a vacsuit, but he was clearly standing in an underground area, not a spaceship. "If you haven't seen the news, what the hell am I paying you for?" His face twisted into a smile. "I don't have much to tell you that you don't already know. Things are going crazy down here. You need to hold onto Stratford Base no matter what. It may be all humanity has left."

He shook his head. "Look, I don't know when, or if, it will be safe to send a ship back to Earth. Dick, you're the man now. Make whatever calls you think are right. I doubt I'll be in any shape to criticize."

A boom sounded behind him.

He turned back to the camera. "Just...take care of my baby."

All of them wept as the message ended.

Then Abrams' voice came over the open channel. "Marcus, I need you to talk to me as soon as you can."

"I'm here."

"Since you're answering in English and not Mandarin, I assume you held off the Chinese?"

"Your trick made a huge difference. I don't know if we could've held off their entire complement."

"Good." Abrams paused. "I assume you've heard the news from Earth."

"Yes."

"It's worse than you know. I've received reports from Space Command. Some of the captains in cislunar space went crazy. Civilian, military, ours, theirs. They just freaked out. Nobody really knows what's going on."

"Damn."

"Yeah. A helluva situation."

"So, what now?" asked Dick.

"Space Command hasn't given me new orders, and I've got a crew to think about. I'm going to *have* to take Stratford Base."

"The Chinese commander is probably thinking the same thing. Are you still going to nuke us if they manage it first?"

There was a long pause.

"Geoffrey?" prodded Marcus.

"I don't know, Marcus."

Dick leaned in. "What if we can help each other?"

"I'll take any suggestions."

"The uh…" He hesitated and then smiled. "The Martian Republic is open to anyone who wants to request asylum and citizenship."

"The Martian Republic?" Abrams chuckled. "Has a good ring to it."

"Doesn't it? It has an ancient and honorable tradition of treating immigrants well."

It seemed, at that moment, the most humorous thing ever to all of them.

Abrams caught his breath. "I'm their captain, but I can't make this decision for them. For that matter, I'm not yet sure what my own decision is."

"We'll make the offer to the Chinese, too."

"That makes sense. They won't take it, though."

"Probably not," agreed Marcus. "My guess is they're going to attack us again, this time with everything they got."

"Yes."

"They're not as strong as they were," said Felix. "We counted almost thirty dead or wounded from the first assault."

"Don't be too sure about that," said Abrams. "They're desperate. They'll send every rating who can point a gun along with the marines."

"Wonderful."

"It'll take them some time to get everyone organized, though. Let me talk with my crew." He hesitated. "Whatever happens, Godspeed to all of you. Abrams out."

The three men looked at each other.

"The Martian Republic, eh?" asked Marcus. "Damn Yank couldn't even choose a proper monarchy."

Dick laughed. "I was pressed for time."

"Might as well send the message to the Chinese captain. Won't do any good, but there's a chance."

"We can hope, right?"

"We can always hope."

* * *

"Abrams to Martian Republic, come in please." Dick punched the comm hastily. "Martian Republic here."

"You have a collection of tourists and immigrants up here."

"As everyone knows, we have a thriving tourist industry. Lots to do. You can even visit Opportunity."

"Opportunity is always a good thing." Abrams chuckled. "Let's be clear, though. I need assurances that any sailor or marine who wishes to return to Earth is welcome to do so."

"As soon as travel is safe."

"Agreed. Also, when that happens, you'll grant passage and immigrant status to any family members of my people who choose to stay up here."

"We wouldn't have it any other way," said Dick. "If this is going to succeed, it's going to be because people stick together."

"Yes." Abrams paused, and they heard him say something to someone else on the *Puller.* Then he spoke into the comms again. "Well, we're committed."

Felix pointed at the screen, where a huge flare showed on the path from Earth.

"Thanks, Captain Abrams," said Dick.

"You're welcome. Now I gotta go. I got other things to do."

"Oh, like what?"

"Save my ship. A launch like that makes us a big ass target. I'd like to be around to see if we can help a little more. I might have another surprise or two coming."

"Stay safe, you old sub driver."

"Abrams out."

The men on Mars turned their eyes to the screen showing the *Tian Shan* from cameras on the *Falstaff*. She rotated on her axis and skewed her trajectory slightly. Then nothing much happened.

About ten minutes later, the doors opened, and all eight of the Chinese shuttles launched in quick succession.

"Damn, that sub driver's smart!" said Marcus. "They launched shuttles sooner than they wanted, I bet. Can't take a chance a missile gets lucky. Too much at stake."

Felix tapped his pad. "And their trajectory is awful. They'll take at least an extra fifteen minutes to get dirtside."

"Good."

"I've got a track on those missiles," continued Felix. He pointed at a screen from the *Tempest*. "They're burning fast." An even larger flare appeared behind it. "There's the *Puller*."

"What's he doing?" asked Dick.

"He's charging," said Marcus grimly. "That's his main drive. He's following the missiles, and there's no way the Chinese can miss him."

"Can they destroy him?"

"Depends on how well he can dodge." Marcus grimaced. "Larger spaceships like the *Puller* are not known for their maneuverability."

"Maybe they'll distract the Chinese long enough."

Marcus looked at the screen. His eyes narrowed. "Maybe."

"What?"

"Nothing we can do anything about. We've got to get ourselves ready for the Chinese."

"Hey, Marcus, this is Linda...uh, I mean, Weaps-One. You out there anywhere?"

"I am. What do you have?"

"What I have are lasers on all three wings, with power and optics to aim them."

Marcus took a deep breath. "That's great to hear. You've done great work. Pass that on to your people."

"Will do. Oh, hold on."

Another voice came on the comm. "Take care of yourself, love."

"You too, Frances."

"And watch over Jason..."

"As much as I can. I love you both."

Linda's voice returned. "Damn, you too are sickeningly sweet. Got all my lads and lasses about ready to puke."

"Tell them they're assholes, and if they don't treat Frances right, I'm beating the hell out them after this."

Linda laughed. "I'll tell them."

"Shit." Felix pointed at a screen. "Two shuttles just took off from the Chinese Mars Base."

Marcus looked. "Do they have any troops on Mars?"

"Apparently."

"Let me guess, the Chinese shuttles will get here about the same time as the *Tian Shan's*."

"Why do you always have to be right?"

Abrams popped up. "Marcus, did you see—"

"The Chinese shuttles from their base? Yes."

"Nothing I can do to stop them, and we don't have anything at our base up there to help you."

"We'll do our best. You stay alive."

"We're trying. They clipped us with a laser before we went back to silent running, and we're not sure of the EM trail we're leaving. Abrams out."

"Can you see them, Felix?"

"No, but I'm only using the visible wavelengths. If they're running especially hot, the Chinese might see them on IR or something like that."

"Right. Well, back to the waiting part of tonight's entertainment."

"So much fun."

"Yes."

"The *Falstaff* caught the shuttles on screen again. Still on the same landing profile, so the timing is about right," said Felix.

"Can you show their projected trajectories in relation to the base on the screen? All ten of them?"

"Sure." He punched some buttons.

Marcus stared at the screen, then he pointed at various spots. "Highlight and mark these points."

"OK."

"Now put countdowns on each one."

Felix complied.

"Weaps-One, this is Marcus. Felix is going to send your batteries an image of the Chinese shuttles' projected landing trajectories. We've highlighted targeting opportunities for them and added countdowns."

"Oh, that's smart. Yer not as dumb as most bosses."

"Good hunting."

"Back atcha."

Waiting for the Chinese shuttles to curve around Mars this time was worse than the first time, even though they had a good lock on the trajectories and timing.

The shuttles popped over the horizon right on time.

"They're coming in, Weaps-One. Open fire when they get to those points."

"Got it, boss. Now shut up and let us work."

"Right."

Dick glanced at him. "You're letting them get awful close."

"I'm letting them get to where all five batteries have a target before opening fire. They don't have a clue we have these lasers, or they'd dodge them."

"Makes sense."

The timer reached zero, then the lasers fired.

Linda and Frances had managed to get five batteries of two lasers organized.

Two batteries were confused by Marcus's targeting parameters, and all four of their lasers targeted one shuttle. Three of their lasers hit, and the shuttle exploded immediately.

The other batteries targeted properly. One shot a shuttle's tail, and it smashed down into the Martian dust. Another separated a wing, sending that shuttle careening off into the distance. The other missed completely.

"Best we could hope for, I think," said Marcus. "Worth the trouble at least."

"Oh, shit!" muttered Felix.

"What now?"

Felix pointed at a screen. The *Tempest*'s optics showed a bright flare out of Martian orbit. Then the message received light appeared.

"Marcus, take care—"

Another flare appeared, and the message ended.

"Look!" said Dick. He pointed at the screen following the *Tian Shan*. A line of fire intersected her. The bow and aft portions spun away from each other, with smaller pieces flowing outward.

"Does that mean what I think it means?" asked Dick.

"If you think it means both warships are gone, then yes," snarled Marcus. The shuttles reached the Martian surface and the Chicoms charged out. "Damn. Four shuttles are attacking Denmark Wing."

"Can we hold against that?" asked Felix.

"Going to have to. I don't dare pull any platoons from Italy or Scotland until the Chinese attacks on those wings are stopped," said Marcus.

"What are you going to do?" asked Dick.

"Same thing I did last time."

"You remember where the strongpoints in Denmark are?" asked Felix.

"If I don't, it's because I'm an idiot." He grabbed his X153. "Keep me apprised of what's going on in the other wings, Felix. Use the overhead speakers. It's not like the Chinese won't know what's happening."

"Got it."

Jason stood at the head of the reserve platoons.

"How are you?"

"The leg still feels weird, and this new vacsuit pinches." He grinned. "But I can do some cool stuff."

Marcus put his hand on his son's shoulder for a moment, then they moved out.

Denmark Wing was the longest, widest, and most built up of Stratford Base's wings. It included a number of labs, hydroponic farms, and two of their big 3D printing manufactories. Only Stratford Core's access to the hydroponic and nuclear plants meant more to Stratford Base's long-term survival.

It also had as many bastions as Felix could cram into it.

"Listen up, everyone. We're going to advance as far as we can, probably the other side of Hydroponics Two. When the Chinese press, we'll fall back to the new line of defenses. This won't be easy, but it's our best shot." He assigned platoons and sections to each strongpoint as they passed them.

Good thing Felix has a solid eye for terrain.

He found a wall comm. "Felix, we've taken position at the far side of Hydroponics Two. What's the status up ahead?"

"They're pressing Denmark Company like mad."

"Command Denmark Company to fall back to here on your mark. Repeat the order a couple of times. Then wait for a few seconds and call it. Do it on the overhead."

"Won't that let the Chinese know what we're up to?"

"Yes. I'm hoping we can get them to overextend themselves."

"If you're sure…"

"Do it!"

While Felix made the announcement, Marcus reminded everyone to set their X153s to three-round bursts and to watch their targets.

A section of Denmark Company appeared ahead of him. They took cover behind a wall I-beam. The rest of the company came running with the Chinese at their heels. The area ahead of Marcus became a swirling mass, better suited to the superior training and heavier armor of the Chinese.

"Open fire on my mark," he growled.

"But we'll hit our own!" yelled one man.

"Try not to, but we've got no choice! Fire!" Marcus squeezed off a burst. One of his bullets ripped through a defender, but the other two sent a marine spinning. He fired again.

A cluster of people dropped to the ground. He didn't know if they were hit or just trying to get out of the line of fire.

He had a clear shot at two more Chinese and nailed both.

Out of the corner of his eye, he saw Jason kill one. So did Sarah. But the Chinese were desperate. They jumped forward as fast as the low Martian gravity would allow.

Too fast!

"Fall back by sections!" he yelled. "Jason, go now! Back to the corridors."

Jason's section fell back smoothly. Then Marcus and his section followed, moving out of the large hydroponics area back to a series of corridors. They passed a line of strongpoints held by another platoon, who slowed the Chinese with heavy fire at the chokepoint.

Felix's voice came on the overhead. "Marcus, we've got a situation in Italy Wing. The Chinese only sent one group there, but they must be the best they've got. They're only a couple hundred meters from Stratford Core, and it looks bad."

Marcus yelled to Jason, "Cover me!" Then he dove toward a wall comm. "Tell Scotland Wing to retreat back to Stratford Core, then close the airlock doors behind them."

"Give up Scotland Wing?"

"They're pressing us hard here, and we *have* to hold Stratford Core."

"Got it."

Marcus rolled back to cover just as the Chinese marines burst out from Hydroponics Two. Again, the defenders took a toll, but the Chinese sent grenades over the defending positions. The shrieks of the wounded filled the air.

Marcus killed two charging attackers. So did Sarah.

The Chinese kept coming.

"Fall back to the manufactory by sections!"

They fell back. Some of the wounded defenders stayed. They died, but not before giving Marcus and his people time to take cover in the manufactory. The defenders who remained in Denmark Wing had time for two deep breaths before the Chinese reached them.

Many defenders flipped their selectors to full automatic. Doing so helped blunt the initial charge, but most couldn't keep their rifles from rising. Their rounds ripped holes in the upper walls and ceiling instead of the attackers.

Again, the Chinese threw grenades, but the larger area reduced their effectiveness. However, they did make many of the defenders duck for just a moment.

And that was all the PLAS marines needed. They jumped in with knives that easily ripped through the vacsuits. With their superior hand-to-hand training and heavier suits, they ravaged the defenders. Marcus killed two as they charged him, but a third flipped him against the wall before stabbing his knife into the defender next to him.

Marcus launched himself at the attacker and landed on top of him. The knife skittered away. He pressed his X153 to the marine's helmet and sent three rounds through it, through the floor, and six feet into the Martian red dirt.

Another collision sent him sprawling. Marcus saw Jason pick up a Chinese marine who was standing over him, and with a weird one-legged hop, he punched the attacker through the ceiling where he dangled with his legs flailing.

Jason rolled and launched himself at another marine. This time, he jumped at a low angle and used the marine's helmet as a battering ram. He smashed the helmet into another attacker, who spun away with his head at an awkward angle. Jason jumped again, this time crushing the marine's head into an I-beam.

A huge explosion rocked everything.

Marcus jumped to a wall comm. "What the hell was that?"

"Five more shuttles just landed. Well, six, but the last one didn't have the best landing ever. Looks like the Chinese had more reinforcements."

"The hell it does! That Yank sub driver hid his shuttles right behind his missiles."

"Yes! You're right!"

"Call Sung Li on the overhead, tell her if she knows Chinese, now's the time for her to tell them about the Americans. Tell the Chinese we have a place for them if they surrender."

Marcus didn't wait for an answer. Marcus heard a loud shriek of pain and saw Sarah gripping the stump of her arm. In the light gravity, her forearm hadn't yet settled to the floor.

Her attacker raised his knife to finish her off.

Marcus killed him with a three-round burst.

Jason tackled two other marines who were rushing her. He grabbed a knife and stabbed both of the Chinese before they could catch their breath.

Sung Li's voice came through the overhead speakers.

Then, a complete section of Chinese marines charged Jason.

Marcus flipped his X153 to full auto and emptied his mag at them. He had just punched another mag in when something slammed into his back.

He fell against the wall, twisting his rifle around. He pressed the trigger, and his attacker fell away.

He staggered to his feet and saw an attacker standing over Sarah. He jumped with all he had left in him. The attacker saw him coming and stuck his knife out. The knife entered Marcus's ribs as he landed on him. They fell to the ground.

Marcus opened his eyes and realized his X153 was pointed at the attacker. He pulled the trigger.

Sarah collapsed next to him and cradled his head in her lap. They watched as Jason and the remaining defenders fought for their lives.

Then, suddenly, everything stopped.

The Chinese backed off and laid down their weapons.

Marcus smiled. He reached up to touch the side of Sarah's helmet.

168 | IBSON & KENNEDY

Time floated as he watched Jason disarm the Chinese.

Then the medtechs ran in, one of whom ran to him and Sarah.

He looked up and saw Eva Fielding's eyes through her helmet visor. She knelt beside them.

"Marcus saved me, Mom."

"I know. Dick told me he watched this part of the fight on the monitors." Eva placed a patch to bolster the seal from the vacsuit on her arm.

"Jason saved me too."

"He said that too."

Marcus touched Eva's arm. "Jason…"

"Hush, you're hurt." Eva slapped a bandage on his chest.

"Jason…" he repeated. "A good man. Thank you, Eva, for saving him." He touched her helmet and then his arm fell in the light Martian gravity.

The scientist wept as the myrmidon died in her arms.

* * *

Dick held Eva's hand as they stood on the stage. Over a hundred caskets, a replica of the *Puller*, and a bust of William Shakespeare sat in the center of the gymnasium. All had been hastily designed and printed in one of the big manufactories.

Everyone who wasn't in the infirmary encircled the items.

The surviving veterans, including those William recruited, the American marines and sailors, and a dozen Chinese, stood at attention. They had insisted on a color guard, which meant the survivors had to hastily agree upon a flag.

The color guard stood on the stage bearing that flag. Red with golden, crossed spears wreathed in laurel leaves.

They watched as vacsuited bearers carried the caskets outside and placed them in graves hastily dug in the blood-red dirt.

There was no trumpet on Stratford Base, but one of the people William picked had been the world's best flautist before making the journey. Once all had been interred, she played Taps.

Dick stepped forward. "Ladies and gentlemen. Today we remember the people who defended William's dream. He will never join us, but we will never forget him. He is a founding father of the Martian Republic. Thank goodness for eccentric billionaires."

A chuckle ran through the crowd.

Eva stepped forward. "But there is another. Marcus Allardeck stood for everything I hated, all I wanted to leave behind on Earth. I considered every warrior stupid, for I *knew* violence never solved anything. That their egos drove them to this idiocy. That they created this code of honor to hide their arrogance and pride."

She paused. "It's not easy for a scientist, one who's been told she's a genius, to admit she's wrong."

The audience laughed.

"But I was. Marcus Allardeck proved to me I was wrong. I know, now, we wouldn't have survived without him.

She looked down at her daughter, who stood close to Jason.

"That my *daughter* wouldn't have survived without him."

She pointed at the color guard.

"So, let everyone see our new flag. Let them see the leaves of peace entwined on the spears. Let them know peace is all we want."

She turned to Jason Allardeck, who wore a hastily designed military uniform.

"But let them also see the keen points on those spears, the spears of Mars. Let them never forget we'll unleash the war god's wrath on those who attack us!"

* * * * *

Rob Howell Bio

Rob Howell is the creator of the Shijuren fantasy setting (www.shijuren.org), an author in the Four Horsemen Universe (www.mercenaryguild.org), and editor of "When Valor Must Hold," an anthology of heroic fantasy. He writes primarily epic fantasy, space opera, military science fiction, and alternate history.

He is a reformed medieval academic, a former IT professional, and a retired soda jerk.

His parents discovered quickly books were the only way to keep Rob quiet. He latched onto the Hardy Boys series first and then anything he could reach. Without books, it's unlikely all three would have survived.

His latest release in Shijuren is "Where Now the Rider," the third in the Edward series of swords and sorcery mysteries. The next release in that world is "None Call Me Mother," the conclusion to the epic fantasy trilogy The Kreisens.

You can find him online at: www.robhowell.org, on Amazon at https://www.amazon.com/-/e/B00X95LBB0, and his blog at www.robhowell.org/blog.

\# \# \# \# \#

Why 2K by Jon R. Osborne

April 17, 2019

A classic country tune caught Holden's ear. He took it as a good omen as he ascended the beaten, wooden steps. The solar-powered lights aimed at the wooden sign over the door hadn't kicked on yet despite the fading sun. Like so many things in the world, maybe they had finally broken down.

Several patrons looked up as Holden pushed the door open but quickly lost interest. He crossed the dimly illuminated floor to the bar. In the corner, an old-fashioned jukebox switched to another song with the *ka-klunk* and hiss of a needle dropping onto vinyl. The lights and jukebox meant electricity, and electricity meant cold beer.

The bartender spotted Holden. "What can I get you?"

"Two cold beers, preferably bottles." Holden surveyed the tables. Farm hands and factory workers filled a quarter of them. Good. More signs of civilization.

"Forty bucks." The bartender held the bottles out of reach while Holden dug out a small fold of bills and peeled off three. He set the money in front of the bartender, who relinquished the beers.

"I'm passing through, heading west. Can you recommend somewhere to hole up for the night?" Holden twisted open one of the bottles and gulped a third of it. It was bland but cold.

"Are you heading out US-30 or 224?" the bartender asked.

"I'm planning on 224, unless there's a problem," Holden replied and took another swig. States charged exorbitant tolls to use the interstates unless you drove a fuel rig, and bandits knew better than to screw with the well-guarded semi-trucks. Solo vehicles, however, were a different matter.

The bartender frowned. "That takes you by the old Highway Patrol and Transportation yard. The bad news is they'll hit you up for a toll, but on the upside, if you pay them, they won't rob you."

"Are these actual cops?" Holden asked. He didn't want to tangle with law enforcement.

"No, they co-opted the facilities when the state police abandoned the site. They charge the farmers coming into town and trucks passing through," the bartender replied. "You might be able to bypass them on side roads if you're not driving a big truck."

"What about fuel? I don't think I'll find any across the road," Holden said. The gas station across the street had been razed at some point, along with the big box store behind it. Taking back roads to cross three states took more time and fuel than before Y2K.

"There's a truck stop and a motel a couple blocks south of the interchange with US-30. Truck teams use it, so expect prices to match. If you go into town, the gas will be cheaper, assuming they have any." The bartender lifted his head to peer past Holden.

A few appreciative remarks mingled with the music as boots tapped across the wooden floor. "Start without me, Old Man?"

Holden slid the beer to the woman half his age as she took the stool next to him. "At least I saved you one. How long does it take to check the trailer?"

"Thanks, Dad." Amanda twisted open the bottle. "Nice, quiet place. I was worried we might have trouble."

Holden scanned the locals. While a few watched Amanda, none seemed inclined to approach. He suspected the sword across her back dissuaded any interested parties more than his presence. "Seem like civilized folk. Why would we have a problem?"

A burly man in a leather jacket shoved open the door. "There's the bitch!" Two more men followed him in.

Holden sighed. "What did you do now?"

"I think I hurt his feelings. I thought using big words would soften the blow until he had time to look them up in a dictionary." Amanda took a drink and turned to face the arrivals. "In case you couldn't figure it out, I'm not interested, you inbred troglodyte."

"Stop right there, Austin," the bartender warned as he reached below the bar. Metal scraped across wood.

The big guy jabbed a thick finger at the bartender. "Stay out of this, Borland, or we might forget you paid your insurance this month."

Amanda laughed. "A thug shaking down local businesses for protection money, and you people tolerate it? How cliché can you get?" She took another gulp of beer and hopped off the stool.

Holden shook his head, reached into his denim jacket, and unsnapped his holster. The bartender met his eyes and gave a small nod. You could only push people so far. Holden grinned. "I bet you a beer she kicks his ass."

"It will be worth a beer to see it," the bartender replied under his breath.

Amanda stopped a couple paces away from Austin and crossed her arms. "So, what's it going to be? You need to prove your dominance by beating up a woman?"

"Austin, this smells like a set up." One of his companions eyed Amanda nervously.

At five eight, she only stood a hand shorter than Austin. Granted, he had a hundred pounds on her, but did he know how to use it? "What's wrong, big guy, getting cold feet? Like your boyfriend?"

"You bitch!" To Austin's credit, he threw a solid jab, not some cartoonish haymaker. As Amanda snapped her head out of the way, the thug followed with a body blow from his other fist.

Amanda blocked the punch, but it carried enough force to shove her back a pace. Master Park would have chastised her for getting cocky.

Holden watched Austin's buddies and eased his .357 free of its holster. For the moment, they appeared content to remain on the sidelines. "Don't do the spin kick," Holden whispered under his breath.

Amanda's boot heel whipped in an arc as she twisted her body. Austin blocked the back of her leg with a beefy arm and lunged forward, sending Amanda sprawling. Her sword hilt smacked loudly against the wooden floor. She managed to roll over her shoulder before Austin could pounce and pin her. Amanda sprang to her feet and met Austin's charge with a snap punch to his face and an elbow to his throat.

The big man bellowed through the pain and let his momentum carry him into her as he threw his arms around her. Holden winced;

if the fight devolved to a grappling match, Austin would have an advantage. Amanda twisted before Austin could secure his hold and seized his right hand. His thumb popped, and Austin reflexively jerked back his hand.

Austin's other hand found the sword handle, and he yanked Amanda to him. "When I'm done with you…"

Amanda slammed her head into Austin's face. His nose crunched into a bloody mess, and he staggered back. Her roundhouse kick snapped in from his right, and the toe of her boot cracked into his temple. The big man crumpled.

"So, these guys shake you down every month and harass any women who strike their fancy?" Holden asked without taking his eyes off Austin's buddies. They watched Amanda standing over the fallen man but did not make a move.

"That's the size of it," the bartender replied. He placed another cold beer on the bar.

Holden drained his first beer. "How many other people do these assholes extort? How many sisters, daughters, and girlfriends have they hassled?"

"They squeeze my dad's store."

"I can't bring my girlfriend in here."

"They cost me most of my profits."

"My sister is afraid to go outside."

One by one, patrons rose from the tables and stools. The flunky who had remained quiet reached into his coat but froze at the *clicks* as hammers cocked, and both Holden and the bartender aimed at him. "You boys pull a gun or a blade, you'll be dead."

"What are you going to do, take us to the sheriff?" the nervous fellow asked.

"He won't do nothing," the bartender said. Louder, he added, "It's up to us to throw out this trash." The crowd swarmed Austin and his pals and dragged them outside.

Amanda plopped back onto the stool, breathing heavily, and grabbed her beer.

"What did I tell you about those spin kicks?" Holden asked as he opened his fresh bottle.

"I know, Dad."

* * *

December 31, 1999

"Has Amanda given you any trouble?"

"No more than I'd expect out of a five-year-old," Holden replied, cradling the telephone's handset on his shoulder. The television displayed the New Year's Eve countdown from Times Square, but Holden had lowered the volume so he could talk to his girlfriend. "She misses her mother, and so do I."

"I miss you both. I'm in Bogota for three more days," Olivia said.

"So, sixty more episodes of Scooby Doo and Sponge Bob?"

"I'm surprised she didn't stay awake for midnight," Olivia remarked.

"She tried, and if she had known you were going to call, she might have made it, but she conked out an hour ago," Holden said. "The countdown is running—twenty seconds."

Holden raised his beer and called off the seconds. "Happy New—" The lights blinked, the television went to static, and the phone went dead. "Liv? Are you there?"

The television switched to the test pattern. Over the tone, Holden could make out the chug of the backup generator. The power cutting out must have interrupted the phone connection long enough for the international call to drop. Holden hung up and tried again, but it remained silent.

"Perfect, a tree must have taken out the lines," Holden muttered. After turning off everything but a single light to conserve juice, he stepped outside. Stars gleamed in the cold, clear winter sky. All but one of the neighbor's houses were dark. No glow from Yorktown illuminated the horizon to the east. He walked the 200 yards to the lake. Only a handful of lights dotted the shore on the other side. Whatever the problem was, it extended beyond his dead-end road.

When Holden returned home, he double checked the locks on his workshop, garage, and house. Olivia indulged his survivalist streak, so provisions didn't worry Holden. Out of an abundance of caution, he checked his pistol before turning off the last light.

* * *

January 1, 2000

Holden stared dumbfounded at the old radio from his workshop. An AM station, full of static and hiss, recited the latest news reports. Something had gone terribly wrong with the vast majority of computers on the planet, and they had shut down. Olivia had poo-pooed the hyped Y2K bug, stating the error had long been patched and, at worse, a few computers would need to be restarted. Since she worked in software, Holden considered her advice solid. According to the radio, the Y2K bug had brought the planet to a screeching halt.

"Why 2K?" Amanda asked from the doorway to the kitchen. She rubbed her bleary eyes. "Is it why it's cold?"

"I turned the heat down. Bundle up if you feel chilly, and I'll stoke the fire in the fireplace." Holden collected a bowl and cereal. "Do you want some breakfast?"

Amanda nodded and climbed onto her favorite chair at the table. "When will Mommy come home?"

"She has three more days of work in Colombia," Holden replied. "Hopefully this Y2K nonsense doesn't delay her long."

"I wish Mommy was here."

"Me too, kiddo."

* * *

January 13, 2000

"Holden, when will Mommy come home?"

"Not soon enough, kiddo," Holden replied. One of the Youngstown television stations had returned to the air. Despite Amanda's protests, Holden only switched on television an hour a day. He unplugged everything else in the house except the refrigerator and switched the overhead lights to the lowest wattage bulbs he could find.

According to the news, most of the power plants and the electrical grid had crashed. Everything dependent on a computer had shutdown. Millions of vehicles cluttered the road, refusing to start. Only the most primitive planes and helicopters could fly, and none out of major airports. Hundreds of billions worth of stock holdings evaporated.

"Do you think Mommy is okay?"

"Of course, kiddo." At least Olivia had not been flying when the clock hit midnight. According to the news, jetliners had fallen from the sky or soared off over the ocean until they ran out of fuel. "I'm sure she's working her butt off to get back to us, but since planes can't fly, she'll have to find a boat."

"Why 2K?"

"Yeah, because of Why 2K," Holden replied.

* * *

February 3, 2000

Holden joined several neighbors on the beach. Cries and gunshots carried across the water.

"They hit the other side of the lake," Todd Martin said. He lived at the corner of the dead-end road and Grandview, which ran along the west side of the lake. Like Holden, Todd carried a rifle.

"What about the police?" someone asked, chattering against the cold.

"The township police department has, what, six cops?" Todd shook his head. "I bet these guys hit the police station right after the grocery store. Sounds like a big group, probably out of Youngstown."

"Looters have hit that store a couple of times, so there couldn't have been much for the raiders," Cheryl Meadows remarked. She puffed on a cigarette—they'd gone fast over the last five weeks.

"Those thugs set to looting the nice houses on the east shore. You can see flames near the interstate." Staccato gunfire popped in the distance.

"This is why we need to fortify the north and south ends of Grandview Road," Holden stated. "I already helped Mike Andover secure his store, but it won't thwart a larger group, and they could pillage our homes."

"They could try." Todd spat on the ground.

Cheryl snuffed the cigarette. "I heard Mike say the only reason he got the last shipment for the store was because the truck driver refused to go into the city."

"According to the radio, Pittsburgh and Cleveland have collapsed. The government isn't even trying. They flagged the big cities as no-go zones."

"Wait until the survivors start spreading out in search of food." Holden turned as a large car slowed to a halt.

Chief Ross leaned out the window of the rumbling Oldsmobile. "A few of you guys with guns want to come down to the bridge? Jacobs and Cougan are already headed there. A show of force should dissuade these assholes if they decide to try their luck on our side of the lake."

"Cheryl, can you send your daughter to sit with Amanda?" Holden asked. "She's asleep, but I want someone there in case this takes a bit, and she wakes up."

"Sure thing, Holden."

"Chief, by 'show of force,' do you mean 'preemptive return fire?'" Holden climbed into the front seat as three more men filled the back.

A scream from across the water rose above the chugging engine. "Yeah. If they show up, don't wait for them to shoot. No time to get squeamish."

* * *

June 12, 2006

"**H**appy birthday!" Holden set the wooden board on the table.

"What is it?" Amanda asked, wrinkling her nose.

"I baked you a pizza," Holden replied. "I mean, it's not Luigi's."

"Round and flat doesn't mean it's pizza. Where's the pepperoni?" Amanda protested.

Holden's spirits sank. "The venison sausage crumbles too much to slice it like pepperoni. I couldn't get mozzarella, so I used a mix of Swiss, Colby, and goat cheese." Holden slid a slice onto Amanda's plate. "Come on; it's better than that month we spent eating oatmeal and jerky."

Holden served himself a slice and took a bite. The crust resembled toasted flat bread, the sauce, made from canned tomatoes, had lumps, and the cheese and sausage added ample grease. Not as good as old-school pizza, but it was better than oatmeal.

Amanda reluctantly chewed a mouthful and swallowed. "It's okay. Thanks, I know you worked hard on it."

"Maybe your present will cheer you up."

Amanda perked up when Holden set a shoebox on the table with a bow on it. "Shoes?"

"Better. Open it."

Amanda flipped open the lid, and her eyes went wide. She carefully hefted the pistol, mindful of where she pointed it. Amanda checked the chambers of the .357 Python. "This is Mom's gun."

"She's not back yet, and you should have a sidearm," Holden said. He had taught Amanda gun safety when she turned nine, and she had already practiced with her mother's Colt. "From now on, it's your job to keep it clean."

"What about when Mom comes home?"

"You can give her that gun back, and we'll buy you a new one, or we'll buy your mom another one," Holden replied.

Amanda rounded the table and hugged him. "Thanks, *Dad.*"

Holden blinked away a tear.

* * *

August 7, 2010

"What did I tell you about spin kicks?" Holden reached out.

Amanda grabbed his hand and hauled herself to her feet. "Showing off will get me knocked on my butt."

Holden peeled off his sparring gloves, then his sweat-soaked head gear. Holden was pushing forty and finding it harder to keep up with the teenage girl. "Work on your sword drills for half an hour."

Amanda snorted as she removed her sparring gear and checked it for tears. Duct tape covered half the pads. "You and Master Park are running me ragged."

Master Park and his family had retreated to their lake house shortly after the crash. Master Park's wife, Min-Ji, brought valuable medical experience to the community, but Holden and others recognized the worth of Master Park's skills. Before the crash, the martial arts instructor had also trained law enforcement officers in close combat techniques.

"We're getting you ready for the world," Holden countered. Master Park deserved as much credit as Holden. Holden had taught Amanda how to handle guns, but Master Park had taught them both how to fight. "You can't count on anyone to protect you. You have to be able to protect yourself."

"Fine."

Holden looked over his shoulder when he reached the corner of the house. Amanda was working through her first sword kata. Holden shook his head; if not for Y2K, she'd be worrying about high school drama, not fighting bandits and worse.

* * *

March 12, 2019

"Dad, what is it?" Amanda asked.

Holden held the letter in trembling hands, sitting at their kitchen table. Tears blurred the cursive script. "It's from my mother. My father died a few weeks ago."

Two decades ago, the letter would have taken a couple days to arrive. Now, mail crawled through a network of regional post offices, which in turn collected and delivered mail to county post offices. Holden made the trip once a month.

Amanda hugged him from behind. "I'm sorry."

Holden patted her arm. "It's a miracle they made it this long, especially since my father smoked until the crash. Y2K forced him to quit."

"What do you want to do?" Amanda pulled a chair around to sit next to him.

Holden shook his head and collected himself. "What can I do?"

"We could go there," Amanda suggested. "I know your mother is tough as iron, but she's also in her 70s."

"We can't leave," Holden said hoarsely.

"Dad, she's not coming back. We've waited almost twenty years."

"You don't know that," Holden protested.

"When I was fourteen, I made up a story I would tell myself when I missed her. Why 2K trapped my mother in South America—you know she wasn't on a boat or train when the computers shut down," Amanda said.

Holden nodded. "Right, I was on the phone with her."

"So, she survived the initial midnight crash," Amanda continued. "She was stuck with no way home, but she's strong and smart, so she would have made it through the first winter since it was summer there. For a few years, she tried to find a way home, but no one could get through Central America.

"Eventually, she admitted Colombia was her home, and she made a new life there. She found a kind man with useful skills, fell in love, and had a family." Amanda sniffled. "Even though she found happiness, she never forgot us, but she knew she could never come back. She moved on."

Tears welled in Holden's eyes again. "Why didn't you tell me this story before?"

"Because you weren't ready to move on, and in a way, neither was I." Amanda leaned her head on his shoulder. "When Trisha Burns tried to seduce you, and you turned her down? You should have let go then."

"How do you know about that?"

Amanda laughed. "Everyone this side of the lake knew about it. Trisha would mess up her car so you would have to go and fix it."

Holden broke the silence that settled over them. "I need to go to Abingdon. I might not come back."

"We're going," Amanda corrected. "I'm not letting you cross three states solo."

"What about letting go? Maybe it's time you got on with your life," Holden countered.

"Let's get your mother squared away. Maybe I'll take a liking to one of those Illinois farm boys," Amanda said.

* * *

April 16, 2019

"You're sure about this?" Todd Martin asked.

"I expect to be gone a long time, if not for good," Holden replied. "Junior apprenticed with me, so I know the shop will be in good hands. Lord knows, you could use the space."

Todd nodded. Three generations crowded into his house. "I love the grandkids, but they're underfoot and stacked like cordwood."

"We're hitting the road in the morning. Fair warning—I'm taking the best tools and supplies. Junior will have to sift through what's left," Holden said.

"Even if you stripped them to the walls, you're still giving Junior a bargain on the house and shop," Todd remarked. "The town will miss you."

"Junior can use the work." As it stood, Junior fixed cars, trucks, and tractors for those who couldn't wait for Holden.

"It's a shame Amanda never found someone to settle down with," Todd said. They had joked about setting Amanda up with one of the Martin boys, but nothing came of it.

"This will give us both a clean break. As long as we stayed in this house, we harbored some hope Liv would come back," Holden said. "It's time we both move on."

* * *

April 19, 2019

"We'd be there by now if you hadn't stopped for the tractor job," Amanda groused.

Holden shrugged. "And we'd have had a smoother trip if you hadn't picked fights at every bar we stopped at. Not to mention, I didn't hear you complaining about spending the night in a soft bed as part of our payment for the job. *I* slept on the couch."

Amanda ignored the jibe about Austin and his cronies and consulted the map. "What about Gilman? Should we scoot around it on the country roads and catch Highway 24 before it meets I-57?"

"Think we can go through a town without you getting in a fist fight?" Holden asked.

"You started the last one. I thought the guy would wet himself when you pulled out your mutant spear-sword." Amanda laughed. "How could he miss the haft jutting over your shoulder?"

"He did piss himself. Let's give the town a try. The intersection with the Interstate means a good chance for gas." The sign ahead read 'Gilman—Population 1727 900ish.' Small rural towns weathered the Y2K collapse better than the cities. In urban areas, famine, disease, and violence wiped out 80% of the population.

"We have plenty of fuel," Amanda protested. Every stop presented a risk.

"You know my mantra," Holden retorted. The government had taken over oil companies after the fall, but supplies remained unreliable.

"You can never have too much fuel, food, or ammo," Amanda parroted. "If we get into a dust up because some hilljack decides he wants me to replace his sister niece, I'm blaming you."

"Duly noted. Uh-oh, they have a welcoming committee." A semi-trailer formed an ad hoc gate flanked by derelict trucks. A pair of armed guards waited at the gate. If they hadn't had the trailer behind the pickup, Holden could have turned around.

One of the men approached while the other unlimbered a semi-automatic rifle but kept it lowered. The man stopped ten paces away. "Howdy. You have some horses to trade?"

"Not exactly," Holden called back. "I'm a mechanic and an ironmonger, so my tools take up a lot of space. I'm passing through with my daughter."

The man's eyes shifted to Amanda, and he smiled. He couldn't see the Rossi M92 carbine in her lap. "Passing through? That's a shame. There's always work for a mechanic."

"We're going to see my grandmother," Amanda added, smiling sweetly.

The man nodded and made a circling gesture with his hand. A winch and pulley system dragged the semi-trailer far enough to open a lane. "My folks own the grocery store, so if you stop by, tell them David sent you."

Holden nodded, and Amanda waved. Holden kept an eye on the rearview mirror in case an armed gang lurked beyond the gate. Two men operated the crank on the gate system, but no bandits lay in wait. "See, honey works better than vinegar," Holden remarked.

"Until you get stung," Amanda countered. "Are we stopping at my new in-laws' grocery store?"

"Tempting, but the Rutledge's generosity put us in good shape for provisions," Holden replied. As with most small towns, most of the homes near the main roads remained occupied, and several showed evidence of fortification. "As Mayberry as this place appears, let's try to get some gas and move on."

* * *

April 20, 2019

"Sonuvabitch." Holden thumped the steering wheel. "I should have guessed Peoria would be a shit show."

"What now?" Amanda asked. They had stopped in Eureka, a small town along Highway 24, and the locals had warned them against trying to cross the Illinois River in Peoria unless they were willing to pay the exorbitant toll on I-474 and risk bandits in the city.

"The three central bridges are gone. Either we go south or north, and either could be dicey." Holden studied the map. "The south route puts us on Highway 136. It connects to 41 which takes us into Abingdon. The north route takes us through Galesburg. Y2K hit it hard, and bandits grow like weeds in the city. I say we steer clear."

"Abingdon isn't even ten miles from Galesburg," Amanda noted. As a small city surrounded by farm communities, Galesburg should have weathered or rebounded from Y2K better than the big cities but sustaining any sort of urban population meant getting food through trade or force.

"They've held out this long. Once we get there, we can evaluate whether it's tenable or whether I need to convince my mother it's time to move," Holden said.

"How long has she lived there?" Amanda asked.

"Only 74 years."

"Good luck getting her to move."

* * *

Between controlling the bridge across the Illinois River, having a functioning power plant, and possessing grain elevators able to load river barges, Havana had turned into a fortress town. Holden stewed for half an hour before deciding to follow a semi to the gates on Highway 136.

Havana's stockade and gates were permanent constructions of concrete, steel, and timber. The guards at the entrance wore blue uniform shirts and ballcaps. One guard approached their truck while the others watched with military grade rifles held at port. Satisfied Holden and Amanda didn't present a threat, the guard waved them through.

On the other side of the fortifications, Havana could have passed for a small town before Y2K. A few older cars cruised the streets, and patrons dined outside a converted fast food restaurant. Holden gazed longingly at the auto parts store but resisted the urge to shop and pump the employees for information.

"You could lead a normal life here," Amanda remarked as they passed another restaurant. "Pizza House? I don't even remember pizza."

"I made a pizza for your twelfth birthday," Holden said.

"That was pizza?"

"*Ouch.*"

* * *

They slowed before the south entrance to Abingdon. As opposed to the solid stockade of Havana, barbed wire and cattle fence marked the perimeter. A pair of watchtowers flanked IL-41 before the American Legion. Young men wearing blue armbands milled in the Legion's parking lot.

A middle-aged man in a police uniform approached from a shack at the base of one of the towers. Holden gestured for Amanda to keep her carbine out of sight while he rolled down the window. "Good afternoon, officer."

"Good afternoon. Mind if I ask what you're hauling?" Behind the policeman, a couple of youths eyed Holden suspiciously.

"A couple of motorcycles and as many tools and parts as I could cram in the trailer," Holden replied. "I'm a mechanic and a metalworker."

The policeman nodded. "What brings you here? Looking for work?"

"I received a letter from my mother, Barbara Clark. She lives on Main." Holden checked the man's nametag. "Fisher? Larry Fisher?"

The policeman broke into a grin. "You're Mrs. Clark's son? I'm surprised you remember me. You were two years ahead of me."

"It has been a long time, but it's a small town," Holden said. "What's with your junior squad?"

Officer Fisher leaned on the door of the truck. "Citizens' Committee volunteers. The manpower comes in handy, even if they tend to hang out here instead of at the north gate."

"Galesburg giving you trouble?" Holden asked.

"They control two-thirds of the county. The state considers it a local matter they don't have the resources to deal with." Fisher shook his head. "I guess it could be worse. At least we aren't near Chicago."

"True. So, do I need to pay to get in, or what?" Holden asked.

"I'm not charging Babs Clark's son. You might as well be a citizen." Fisher stepped back to let Holden drive through the checkpoint. One of the Committee hurried over to Fisher and muttered in Fisher's ear, while glaring at them. Fisher shook his head. "We went to school together, and his mother still lives here. I'm not charging him."

Holden drove forward before any of the youths could move to block him. "Welcome to Abingdon."

Amanda watched in the side mirror. "Something about those guys gives me the creeps."

* * *

The trees had changed, but Holden recognized the houses. Life after computers left little time or inclination for remodeling, especially if you had to build security perimeters and fortifications.

"What's the crowd ahead?" Amanda reached for her carbine.

"Shit, they're in front of my folks' house." Holden resisted the urge to gun the engine. A dozen people milled in front of the gate in the barricade fronting the house. They shouted at someone past the wall. He could have run over half of them before he had to swerve to miss the idling pickup truck.

Holden stopped a dozen yards away. A couple of youths with blue Citizens' Committee armbands hung in the back of the crowd. "Cover me," Holden said as he stepped out of the truck.

He could pick out his mother's voice cursing the crowd. "Go to hell! You're not going to tell me what to do with my land!"

One of the Committee boys spotted Holden. "Sir, this doesn't concern you. Get in your vehicle and move along." He turned to show off the 'CC' band on his arm.

"She's my mother. Clear those people out, or I'll do it." Holden squared his shoulders.

"Your mother refuses to comply with the Citizens' Committee request." The young man appeared to be 20 and fit.

"I drove across three states because my father died. Get them out of my way," Holden growled. A few people in the crowd noticed his presence.

"Fine, but this matter isn't over." The man whistled and gestured to their truck. Two Committee men climbed into the cab while the rest of the group piled into the back.

"Holden?" Once the crowd cleared, his mother spotted him.

"Hey, Mom." Holden went to the gate without taking his eyes off the departing throng. Past the gate, Oscar cradled a shotgun while his son Dan held the leash of a German Shepherd. No fence separated the neighbor's house from his childhood home. "I'm sorry it took so long to get here."

His mother snapped her holster. "You arrived in the nick of time. These damned Committee punks don't like to be told 'no.' Is that Amanda in the truck?"

"Yeah. She insisted on coming with me."

His mother nodded and turned to her neighbors. "Let's get this gate open."

"So much for Illinois farm boys," Amanda muttered. She scooted over to the driver's side and pulled the truck into the compound.

"The last time I saw you, you must have been four or five," Holden's mother said as Amanda returned from parking the truck.

"I remember that Christmas. It's good to see you…Mrs. Clark," Amanda said as Holden's mother hugged her.

"Nonsense, call me Babs." She turned to Holden. "Did you bring horses? The stable is still in the pasture, but we use it for goats now."

"No, we have a couple of motorcycles, and as much gear from my shop as we could load," Holden replied.

"Well, your father left behind a garage full of tools and parts." Holden's mother took a deep breath. "Let's get you two unpacked and inside. Dan can turn Bruno and Zeus loose if the Committee goons come back."

Holden's mother led them through a side door into the kitchen. The aroma of cooking meat and spices wafted from a pot on the stove. "Dinner is almost ready, and I don't want to hear you've brought some rations or other nonsense." Holden's mother checked the pot. "I'm making a big batch of venison and goat chili."

"Some home cooking sounds great," Amanda said. "Dad's a pretty good cook, but we've been on the road."

"So, what can you tell me about those Committee yahoos?"
Holden asked.

"Get unloaded. We can talk about those assholes over dinner,"
his mother replied.

* * *

"Ten years ago, we rebounded enough to keep kids in school if they didn't apprentice out. A few even went to college in Monmouth." Holden's mother ladled out bowls of chili.

"College? No offense, Mom, but ever since Y2K, I figured learning a trade or working a farm would trump higher education, especially in these parts."

"Doctors, vets, and teachers still come in handy," Amanda said.

"Monmouth got some food processing plants running using antiquated gear and duct tape. They struck a deal with Burlington for electricity in exchange for food and feed. Monmouth reopened the college, not only for the skills Amanda pointed out, but they also touted it as the best hope to recover civilization."

"What? Rely on computers again?" Holden scoffed.

"I can't imagine we'll ever go back to the 20th century, but some folks remember when life was easier. Families sent their kids to college, and some came back with notions about how to make society 'better.' It started out innocently enough—gathering donations and volunteering for projects to help the unfortunate. They raised funds to cover Mrs. Adair's taxes, and they built the Coolidges a new barn after theirs burned down.

"Two years ago, they added a volunteer corps to supplement the police force. I'm sure you saw some of those armbands at the gate.

They began recruiting kids out of high school—filling their heads with nonsense. Reminds me of my parents talking about communism and socialism in the 50s."

"Great, not only did Y2K knock technology back to the 50s, it knocked politics back 50 years as well," Holden remarked, waiting for his mother to take a seat before digging into dinner. "I suppose these kids missed the part where communist and socialist countries oppressed and starved their citizens?"

"A victim of the crash. A curious student could go to the library and research the matter, but most students relied on what their teachers told them and took it as gospel. Remember the Sanders family?" Holden's mother asked, taking her seat.

"Yeah, Ellis Sanders was a rich jerk. I hated him in high school," Holden replied.

"I sense a story," Amanda remarked while blowing on a steaming spoonful of chili. "Did he steal your prom date?"

"A mob torched the Sanders' mansion," Holden's mother interjected. "No one could prove the Citizens' Committee led the gang, but everyone knew. Even after Y2K, the Sanders found ways to stay on top. They reopened the local bank and bought out several farms. The Committee objected to their using their wealth to make more wealth and not help the 'less fortunate.'"

"So why were they here? Do you have a bank?" Holden dug into the chili.

"No, but they think I have too much land and that they should decide what I grow," Holden's mother replied. "They can fuck right off."

Amanda giggled at the septuagenarian's profanity, before asking, "What gives them the authority?"

"Mob mentality. Someone speaks out against them, they rally people to brow beat the offender. It's what they were doing at the gate. I've been working our plot for 50 years. I know how to manage it, but these fools want to plant kale."

"I enjoy a good salad as much as the next person, but all kale?" Holden tried to imagine his chili with kale instead of beans and tomatoes—unappetizing. "So, they don't have official authority, right?"

"Not yet. Rumor has it they're going to harangue the mayor and town council into giving them some sort of oversight powers," Holden's mother replied.

"You'd think no one ever read Orwell," Amanda remarked between spoons of chili.

"They haven't. And it's no accident they waited until your father died before they started pressuring us again. The neighbors are as old as I am. They hope to tire us out, but the bastards don't realize I'm *more* inclined to shoot them than your father. Maybe I should have set an example today." Holden's mother mopped up her chili with a hunk of bread.

"That could bring in legitimate authorities," Holden remarked. "I need to talk to some folks."

"Try not to get shot, dear," Holden's mother cautioned.

* * *

April 21, 2019

Holden brought the motorcycle to a halt in a cloud of gravel dust. "I figured as much."

"Are we looking for the police?" Amanda asked,

pulling off her helmet and shaking out her hair. She dropped the kickstand and swung off her bike to follow Holden.

"This place was famous for breakfast and coffee," Holden remarked. "The old guys would argue over the newspaper while the cops caught up on the day's gossip. Bet it still holds true."

"At least I'll know where to find you," Amanda jibed as they reached the door.

"Very funny." Holden led them through the doors. Strangers drew attention, especially armed strangers. The chatter from a quartet of policemen faded as they watched Holden and Amanda go to the counter.

Gone were the days of chocolate frosting and rainbow sprinkles. The fanciest offering was maple glazed, but Holden opted for a regular glazed donut and a coffee. Amanda mimicked his order. Holden gave the cashier a 20-dollar bill and told her to keep the four dollars change.

"Hey Holden!" Larry Fisher called. "Guys, this is Babs Clark's son. You all had her as a teacher for at least one year." The other policemen nodded.

"No kidding? I thought you moved out east," one of them said. His nameplate read Byrd.

"I did. When my dad passed, I sold my home and came back," Holden replied.

"Sorry about your father. Steve was a good guy," a policeman with the name 'Wirth' stated.

"Thanks." He had a decade or two on all the cops besides Larry, so he wouldn't have recognized them even if twenty-plus years hadn't passed. "This is my daughter, Amanda."

"Good morning officers." Amanda smiled as the younger policemen sat up straight.

"When I got into town last night, I found a crowd hassling my mother and her neighbors. A few of them had armbands like those guys at the checkpoint," Holden said, sitting at an adjacent table but angling his chair toward the policemen. "Can you shed any light?"

Byrd rolled his eyes, while Wirth muttered something under his breath. Higgins, the youngest at the table, sat stone-faced. "The Citizens' Committee sticking their noses in someone else's business," Larry remarked. "Troy Winkle started teaching about the same time your mother retired. He was keen on knocking capitalism as evil and exploitive."

Higgins broke his silence. "Well, in some cases, he's right. Before Y2K, the rich got richer while everyone else fought over crumbs. The top ten percent had two-thirds of the wealth."

"You can't eat stock shares," Holden quipped and took a sip of his lukewarm coffee. How many more Higgins wore a badge?

Larry ignored Higgins' outburst. "As more kids came back from Monmouth, Winkle gained a bigger following. They started pushing for the government to provide more entitlements, as opposed to people to fending for themselves."

"If you have more, you need to hand some over to those who have less," Wirth added.

"So, this Committee is some sort of socialist movement? Holden asked.

"More or less, but they don't have any real authority...yet." Larry's eyes flicked toward Higgins. "Rumor has it Winkle will run for mayor. He already spends enough time browbeating the town council."

"Dad, if you don't want your donut, I'll take it," Amanda remarked.

"Hands off." Holden bit off a large chunk of the pastry. He washed the bite down with coffee. "Sounds as though I have some homework. When is the next council meeting?"

"Two nights from now," Larry replied.

"I know you just came off the road yesterday, but you don't need to walk around town strapped with iron," Wirth remarked.

"We lived in a small community; you always kept your weapons handy. You never knew when pillagers from Pittsburgh or cannibals from Cleveland would come knocking. Unless it's against the law here?" Holden asked between the remaining bites of donut.

"Not yet," Higgins admitted.

Holden downed the remainder of his coffee. "Good. Galesburg is just ten miles up the road, and I'll be damned if I'm going to rely on the Committee to hold the line. I'll see you guys around."

"Goodbye, officers," Amanda added sweetly.

"What do you think?" Holden asked. The parking lot gravel crunched under their boots.

"Higgins will run to tell his armband-wearing buddies all about us first chance he gets," Amanda replied, piling her hair on top of her head and donning her helmet. "What now? Track down this Winkle?"

Holden swung onto his motorcycle. "Time to visit an old friend."

* * *

They roared out the north gate and swung east on DeLong Road. For a few miles of country road, it was almost as though Y2K never happened. Once Holden spotted the first fortified farmstead, the illusion vanished.

Holden led them onto a gravel road following Brush Creek and slowed when he caught sight of the burnt shell of a house. A gravel drive led to a short, stout bridge across the creek. Berms flanked the drive on the other side of the creek, and dogs barked beyond the gate spanning the drive.

"Don't make any sudden moves." Holden dropped the kickstand and went to the post that supported a metal triangle. A steel rod dangled from a rope, and Holden rapped it against all three sides of the triangle.

"Who are you?" a male voice shouted from behind the berm.

"Tell Jared Haynes that Holden Clark is at the gate."

A man peered over the top of the berm and squinted at Holden. "Stay there." A horn sounded a long note followed by two short ones. After a moment, the call was repeated from the distant farmhouse nestled behind a layer of fortifications. Two men strode from the house, rifles or shotguns slung over their shoulders.

Holden remained in the open, his hands in view. At first, he thought his childhood friend had escaped the ravages of time but then Holden realized the younger man must be Jared's oldest son, Toby. The elder of the pair smiled broadly, and Holden recognized his friend under the years.

"Holden! What the hell are you doing back here?" Jared gestured for someone to open the gate. With a clank and metallic groan, the gate crept open behind the berm.

Holden met Jared halfway across the bridge and hugged him. "My father passed away, and I didn't want to leave Mom on her own."

"My condolences. I wish you had a happy reason to come home, but it's still good to see you. I feared you'd gotten caught in the east coast blight."

"We lived in Ohio. Life wasn't easy, but we hunkered down and made it through," Holden said. "This is my daughter, Amanda."

"A pleasure to meet you." Jared shook Amanda's hand. He gestured to the man who accompanied him. "This is my oldest, Toby, and my nephew Josh is manning the gate."

"Toby? When I last saw you, you were four," Holden said.

"Hard to believe it has been 25 years. Come on up to the house."

* * *

"Why do people let these Committee assholes get away with shit?" Holden asked. After two hours of catching up, local politics, and lunch, they moved to the shady side of the porch with cold beers. Everyone pretended not to notice Toby pretending not to watch Amanda.

"They're a small group compared to the rest of the town, but when they all shout at once, it makes them seem larger," Jared replied. "Jack worries they'll convince the town council to raise taxes again to cover their newest social program."

"What program?" Amanda asked.

Jared shrugged. "It's hard to keep up."

"Can you make it to the town council meeting? Better yet, can you get as many people as possible there?" Holden asked.

"I can try, but Jack has more pull with the people in town," Jared replied. "I don't think you'll have any trouble motivating him. The

Citizen's Committee made noise about requiring his butcher shop to provide free food to those they deemed *in need.*"

"It sounds as though their definition of 'need' and your definition differs," Amanda remarked.

"Charity isn't charity at gunpoint," Jared replied. "Some of these kids come back from Monmouth with no useful skills, and they believe they're too educated for manual labor. If your artistic baskets don't sell, find a real job."

"Where's the best place to find Jack besides his house? I heard he married Debbie Wood, and she hated me." Holden set aside his empty beer bottle.

"Probably because..." Jared's eyes went from Holden to Amanda. "That's a story for another time. Either his shop or the Martin Tavern would be a good bet."

"Perfect. The tavern is a few blocks from the house," Holden said.

"Toby, do you know people our age who haven't fallen for the Committee's tactics?" Amanda asked.

Toby blinked. "What? Sure, plenty, but since they don't yell and wave signs, folks don't see the majority."

"In two nights, we need to see them. Can you convince them to come to the meeting?" Amanda favored him with a smile.

Toby nodded. "What should I tell them?"

"It's time to speak for themselves, or this Committee will speak for them," Amanda replied.

* * *

"**I** think Toby has taken a shine to you," Holden remarked as they mounted their motorcycles.

"I noticed."

"So, did you smile at him to get his help or to encourage him?" Holden asked.

Amanda grinned again as she pulled on her helmet. "Maybe a little of both."

Holden led them around the eastern side of Abingdon. Earthen berms blocked off the country roads leading to town. By the time they reached Route 41 south of town, gravel dust coated them and their motorcycles.

Holden didn't spot Larry Fisher among the guard contingent, but Higgins approached, followed by a pair of Committee members. Holden recognized one from the crowd last night.

"Hey, Officer Higgins!" Holden called, loud enough that another cop Holden didn't recognize turned. "Can you do me a favor?"

Caught off guard, Higgins halted.

"I'd appreciate it if you could tell Larry I'm going to be at the Martin Tavern tonight. I'll buy him a beer. Can you do that for me?"

"Um, well, I guess—"

"Thanks! Have a good one." Holden waved as he hit the gas before they could get in front of him and Amanda.

"Why do they have a separate butcher shop and grocery store?" Amanda asked as they parked the bikes.

"I'd guess so the Haynes can sell meat to whoever runs the Buy-Lo at a discount or sell it themselves at market prices."

A bell jingled as Holden pushed the door open. A chalkboard with current prices covered one wall. People clutching numbered wooden tiles waited their turn. Neither of the men behind the counter was old enough to be Jack, but one bore a family resemblance.

"Excuse me, I'm looking for Jack Haynes." Holden drew glares from half the waiting patrons. "I'm not trying to cut in line; I'm an old friend of Jack and his brother."

"Dad went to London Mills for some hogs," one of the butchers replied. "I don't expect him back for a couple hours."

"Please tell him Holden Clark stopped by. I'll be at the Martin Tavern tonight if he wants a beer."

The butcher nodded. "You're related to Babs Clark, right? I'll tell him."

"Is the plan to announce to the whole town where to find you tonight?" Amanda asked once they returned to the motorcycles.

"We've still got a couple more hours to spread the word," Holden replied.

* * *

"Jack!" Holden clapped his old friend on the back. "This is my daughter, Amanda. Let's grab a table, and I'll buy the next round."

"My son said you dropped by the shop. How long have you been back?" Jack collected his beer and followed them.

Holden signaled the waitress for three beers. "Yesterday evening. Almost had to run over some rabble rousers in front of my folks' place."

"So, you met the Citizens' Committee. Millennial pain-in-the-asses—no offense to your daughter," Jack said, draining his beer.

"None taken. I was too young to learn about participation trophies when Y2K hit," Amanda said. "We didn't have time for me to go to college, even if there'd been one around us."

"She's a better electrician than I am, and she can even fix some electronics." Holden pulled out the money to pay for the arriving beers.

"As long as they're dumb enough," Amanda added.

Larry Fisher entered the tavern and scanned the tap room. An older man followed at Larry's heels. Holden waved them over and scooted his chair over to give them room.

Larry nodded to the group. "Holden, this is Cecil Whitaker. He runs the Buy-Lo."

Holden grabbed a chair from an empty table. "Have a seat. Do you know Jack Haynes?"

"I know Haynes, all right." Cecil paused before taking a seat.

Holden ordered beers for the new arrivals. "I know I'm new in town—but I can see we're at a precipice. A small minority of people have bullied themselves into positions as opinion leaders."

"Winkle and those damned college kids," Cecil grumbled.

Larry leaned forward. "I hear Winkle is going to call for a no confidence vote in the council. He has a list of measures he wants passed, and if the council blows him off again, he'll rile everyone up and call for a vote."

"How many people show up for the meetings?" Holden asked.

Larry shrugged. "No more than three or four dozen. You need at least 50 to call a no confidence, and it requires two-thirds to pass. It goes to another meeting within 30 days, but that vote requires a simple majority."

Holden shook his head. Politics—he already longed for the small community back in Ohio. "I have a thought."

* * *

"You stayed quiet," Holden remarked as they walked along Main Street. The night was cool, but not chill.

"I felt out of place. Most of the troublemakers come from my generation," Amanda replied.

"I hope they would judge you by your words and deeds, not your age," Holden replied.

Amanda scoffed. "I don't have any deeds under my belt as far as these people know. Your buddy, Jack, was more interested in whether I was a match for one of his sons."

"I take it neither of them sparked your fancy. You're not getting any younger," Holden remarked, earning a slug in the shoulder.

"I can't see calling me a spinster at 25."

"So how many do you think?" Holden asked. Two blocks remained between them and the homestead.

"Four behind and two in front," Amanda replied. "I wish you hadn't talked me out of bringing my sword."

"They might not muster the nerve if faced by steel," Holden replied. "Also, I spotted another pair lurking across the street."

Amanda snorted. "Four on one? What are they waiting for?"

"The dark patch ahead," Holden replied. On cue, two men emerged from the shadows of a shed while two more cross the street.

"You need to leave town," the biggest man said. He strained the buttons on his shirt from equal parts muscle and good living. "Take your ma with you and go back where you came from."

"I came from two blocks from here," Holden retorted. "Now get out of my way, Biggun."

It took a moment for the nickname to register. "I guess we need to do this the hard way. Grab her."

Holden whistled and a truck engine roared. Biggun turned toward the noise, and Holden slugged him squarely in the jaw. Biggun's wingman gaped long enough for Holden to plant a sidekick in the man's gut and send him staggering back into a hedge.

Amanda charged the group approaching from the rear and felled the closest with a spin kick. Holden didn't have time to chide her before the remaining pair in the front rushed him. He twisted out of the path of one, using him as cover against his partner. Both recovered their bearings and moved to flank Holden. One pulled a buck knife and grinned.

Tires squealed on the pavement as a truck screeched to a halt. Jared tossed Holden his sword-spear while Toby jumped from the bed of the truck with a baseball bat in one hand and Amanda's sheathed sword in the other.

Holden caught his weapon, spun it, and aimed the two-foot blade squarely at the knife wielder. "Mine's bigger."

Amanda whipped her sword out of the sheath. Holden couldn't spare enough attention to track her fight as he whirled his weapon and closed on his opponents. With the reach his weapon provided, he could drive the blade through either man's ribs, but a body count could complicate matters.

The knife wielder fled, but his buddy reached for a holstered pistol. Holden flicked his blade across the man's arm, sending him scrambling while trying to staunch the bleeding. Biggun recovered his wits in time for Holden to crack him across the jaw with the haft of his weapon. Holden spun the sword-spear and sliced away the belt holding Biggun's holster. Based on the scream, the blade traced a furrow through Biggun's flesh.

The man Holden had kicked emerged from the bushes, his shirt ripped by brambles. He took one look at the state of his fellows, uttered a defeated, "*Fuck no,*" and fled into the night.

Holden switched his attention to Amanda's fight. One man lay on the ground, clutching his side, another lay sprawled on the ground, and the remaining two were backing away from Amanda and Toby. One drew a pistol.

A gunshot pierced the night as a bullet *spanged* off the sidewalk in front of the pistol wielding man. "You've had enough fun," Jared announced from behind the pickup. "The next shot won't be a warning."

The ambushers slunk into the night, dragging their wounded along.

"Thanks for having our backs," Holden said after the Committee goons disappeared.

"Yeah, thanks," Amanda added, saying her words directed to Toby.

"About time someone bloodied those bullies' noses," Jared said, watching north along Main Street. Toby grinned sheepishly.

* * *

April 23, 2019

"Order!" Mayor Hastings called. An extra 30 minutes had been allowed since the meeting had been moved to the Disciples of Christ Church to accommodate the burgeoning crowd. People continued to fill the pews. "Sergeant-at-arms, continue tracking attendance, but we need to get the meeting under way."

Arbitrary minutiae dominated the first 15 minutes, including a vote to waive the reading of the last meeting's minutes. As the topic turned to new business, a large man with a bushy beard stood.

Mayor Hastings repressed a sigh. "Mr. Winkle, you have something to say?"

Winkle tugged at the lapels of his sport jacket. "Yes. The council still hasn't addressed the slate of reforms presented two months ago."

"Mr. Winkle, what you suggested is quite…ambitious." The council woman pushed up her glasses. "Not only do we not possess sufficient funds to enact reforms of this scope, some of them trod upon the rights of other citizens."

"Councilor, what you call rights are status quo meant to protect the fortunate," Winkle objected, accompanied by a rising chorus of affirmation. "We are blessed with bounty in an age of scarcity. My reforms merely establish basic rights for all citizens."

Another council member leaned forward. His nameplate read Murphy. "At the cost of other citizens' rights. We do not have the right to seize the property of some citizens to hand over to others."

"Of course, you do," Winkle retorted. "It's called taxation, but our current council lacks the resolve to tell a handful of rich people to share their wealth."

"Rich? Y2K ensured there are no more rich," Mayor Hastings stated. "You're not talking about pieces of paper or entries in computers. You want to seize property and labor."

"I can see our current council lacks the spine to make the hard decisions," Winkle said. "I call for a vote of no confidence against the sitting council. Let's put people in charge who are willing to change the status quo for the better of the masses."

"I second!" a voice cried from the crowd.

Mayor Hastings' shoulders sagged. "A vote of no confidence has been called."

Holden stood. "I wish to address the council."

"You have no standing here!" Winkle shouted. "Go back to Ohio, outsider." A chorus of voices affirmed Winkle's statement.

"If you check the rolls of this church, you'll find me listed— Holden Clark."

"Mr. Clark, please proceed," Hastings said.

"It's no secret I've been away, but I've come home to a vocal minority, shouting themselves into authority. They believe, because they've had book learning, they know how to run our lives. They know better than people who grow crops, who raise livestock, and who work in factories.

"Do you want a handful of people telling you how to live, what to grow, what to make?" Holden asked, sweeping his gaze across the room. The pews were crammed with people, and more filed into the balcony. "Y2K broke the world, but we're rebuilding. Mr. Winkle and his adherents claim they are the few who know better than the people working the soil and sweating on the line. We're doing fine

WE DARE: SEMPER PARATUS | 211

without their 'guidance.' Mr. Whitaker—do you want the council telling you to hand over goods for free?"

"Hell no!" Cecil shouted from the packed pews.

"Vaughn, do you want the council, or should I say the *Committee*, telling you what to charge for fuel?"

"No!"

"Alice and Myra, do you want the Committee telling you who to marry because we need to grow our population?"

"No!" the women cried.

"When you surrender liberties to a so-called collective, you're handing a few absolute power. We have enough struggles in the post Y2K world—we don't need to repeat the mistakes of the Soviet Union or North Korea by putting a small committee of loud bullies in charge. If you remain silent, you cede power to them!"

An angry murmur swept the crowd.

"I move to amend the rules regarding no confidence votes to require a quorum of 25 percent of the *voting* population," Holden shouted. "Don't let these assholes slip in and take your rights behind your backs!"

"I second!" Cecil Whitaker shouted.

"A motion has been brought to the floor," Mayor Hastings stated. "Sergeant-at-arms, do we have a quorum under existing rules?"

"Yes, Mayor!"

"How do the assembled citizens vote?" Hastings called. A chorus of ayes roared across the crowd.

"So noted. Per the rules, this will have to be permanently affirmed at a general election, but until then, the floor vote stands.' Mayor Hastings smiled as he sought Winkle in the crowded chapel. "Mr. Winkle, do you wish to continue your motion?"

The man tugged on his jacket and stormed out.

* * *

"**H**olden, maybe you should run next election," Jared suggested. The meeting had finished shortly after Winkle's coup-by-committee failed. It had been a long time since that many from town had gathered, and the after-meeting had become a much larger social affair.

"Hell no," Holden snapped. "I'd rather face someone mano-a-mano over this political crap. I'm going to reopen my father's shop and do honest work."

Toby wedged his way into the throng around Holden. "Amanda, since you're going to stay a while, I was wondering if I could show you around?"

Amanda smiled. "Sure. Don't wait up for me, Dad."

A warmth kindled in Holden's chest. Maybe they could finally move on from the past?

"Holden!" His mother waved for his attention. "Do you remember the Sandovals? I taught with Jane Sandoval. This is her daughter, Gina."

Holden remembered the family but couldn't place the name. Not surprising, since Gina appeared to be about 40, putting her ten years behind Holden.

"Nice to meet you, Holden. Your mother has told me a lot about you." Gina favored him with a warm smile.

"I guess I have to live up to her tales," Holden said. Time to leave the past behind.

* * * * *

Jon R. Osborne Bio

At thirteen years old, Jon R. Osborne discovered a passion for two things—writing and telling stories. Instead of doing what a normal author-to-be would do and write stories, Jon wrote for his school newspaper and told stories through running role-playing games.

Journalism helped pay his way through college, and gaming garnered him lifelong friends. After college, journalism didn't pan out as a career, but Jon continued creating worlds and forging stories with his gaming friends.

Thirty years later, Jon became a published author in the Four Horsemen Universe anthology, "A Fistful of Credits," and his first book, "A Reluctant Druid." The sequel, "A Tempered Warrior," was a finalist for Best Fantasy Novel at the 2018 Dragon Awards.

Jon lives in Indianapolis, still games, and continues to write science fiction and fantasy. You can find out more about Jon and sign-up for his mailing list at jonrosborne.com. He's on Facebook and Instagram at @jonrosborne.

# # # # #

The Fallow Fields, Part I
by Jason Cordova
and Christopher L. Smith

Somewhere in the forests of Beylorusia—April 1920

Efraitor Davyd Mikhailovich leaned back in his driver's seat and grimaced as the tank crawled over another large rut created by the spring rains. The modified Mark V was not suited to the rough roads of his native lands, in spite of the advanced British design. Eerily similar to the tractor he had driven around his village, it was not nearly as comfortable. In a tractor, he was alone with his thoughts and an occasional cool breeze in his face. In the Mark V, he shared everything with the other seven men crammed inside, including the stale, stagnant air.

"*Starshina* Popov," Davyd said, shouting. The noisy Ricardo engine was located in the center of the tank and made the warmer months miserable. He was thankful he was up front and not in the middle with the others.

"Yes, *Efraitor*?" the tank's commander replied.

"The roads are bad this spring," Davyd said, peering through the driver's viewport.

Next to him, the commander leaned over and tried to see precisely what he was talking about. The poorly rolled cigarette dangling from *Starshina* Vlaidimir Popov's lips dropped ash and tobacco leaves onto the lapel of Davyd's uniform. If he hadn't already been so grimy from the last five days, he would have been irritated. As it was, what was one more spot of dirt in a vast sea of filth?

"They'll be worse in the summer," Popov reminded him as he leaned back in the forward gunner's chair, puffing away on his cheap cigarette. The rancid burnt tobacco smell overwhelmed the stench of the engine's exhaust fumes, making Davyd slightly dizzy. "Back in Minsk we did not have to deal with this *shit.* We had it better than you country bumpkins. Paved roads everywhere, all courtesy of our glorious revolution!"

Davyd wasn't sure the "glorious revolution" alone was responsible. The Germans were far from communists, and he'd been certain that, even in the ruins of Galicia, he had seen properly paved roads. Popov was right about one thing, though. Winter had been wetter, and warmer, than was typical. Less snow meant more mud, and mud meant ruts. When summer came, the mud disappeared, the ruts remained, and the roads became almost impassable.

However, Davyd was not foolish enough to argue. He'd seen what happened to those who spoke out against the Bolsheviks and their "glorious advancements" within the *Rodina.* One day they would be there—the next, they and their family were gone, whisked away in the night. He simply grunted in agreement and focused on his driving.

"You were on the front, *Efraitor,* correct?" Popov asked him.

"I was," Davyd responded warily. He didn't like talking—or even thinking—about his time on the outskirts of Lviv.

"I'm sad to say I missed most of the action." Popov said, wistfully. "I would have loved to kill some Germans."

WE DARE: SEMPER PARATUS | 217

Considering the horrors Davyd had seen in those three years, the tank commander's comment was almost absurd. To imagine anyone wishing they could be there, much less disappointed about it, was something he really couldn't comprehend. He wondered just how much of the propaganda Popov truly believed.

Probably all of it, he thought.

"I was there when the *zapadniki* tried to take Arkhangelsk from us," Popov continued, referring to the westerners. He seemed oblivious to the fact that Davyd was trying to ignore him. "Ha! Our glorious leaders led from the front lines, fighting off the invaders home to home until we expelled them completely!"

Davyd didn't share the Russian's excitement for fighting off the Americans and British. He and the rest of the tank's crew had been conscripted "for the duration," a typically vague phrase used instead of "until we say so."

Things in Poland were a mess. The Soviet invasion—officially the "Communist War of Liberation"—had stalled as it had run into a wall of...*something* just outside Warsaw. Reports were scattered, and rumors ran rampant. Most of the scuttlebutt agreed it was a new German weapon, but there was nothing conclusive. Nobody believed the more outrageous tales, of course. Germany had been defeated and was now nothing more than a corpse-filled landscape from the Maginot Line to Berlin.

Davyd squinted through the viewport, the encroaching dusk making the narrow dirt road difficult to see. Long shadows from the forest around them stretched forward, slowly but steadily obscuring the deep grooves in their path. He considered shutting the tank down on his own, however, he wasn't the commander, and *Starshina* Popov became very upset if anyone appeared to usurp his authority.

The last time it had happened, the screaming and yelling had gone on for two entire hours, only stopping when the *starshina* needed to go relieve himself in some nearby bushes.

"Halt the tank, *Efraitor*," Popov suddenly yelled in his ear. "It is getting too dark to continue. This is as good a place as any to make camp for the night."

Thank God. Davyd pulled back on the levers, bringing the massive vehicle grinding to a halt. *Starshina* Popov killed the engine—the sudden silence tinged by a persistent ringing in his ears. It was something every member of the crew had learned to deal with in the past four months.

The patrol route for the Mark V was always the same. They would leave the military compound just outside Barysaw and travel southwest, following an old trading route which predated the Romanovs. Outside Minsk, they'd turn off and head toward the village of Petrosky, stopping to refuel near Belaya Luszha. After a day or two with their families, they'd return to the fuel depot, then off to Barysaw. It was designed to avoid engaging the local Poles, while showing their Soviet commanders they were indeed contributing to the war effort.

"Crewmen of the great Soviet tank *Krasnyy D'yavol!*" *Starshina* Popov shouted over his shoulder to the six men behind him. "We are pitching camp here for the evening, and soon you shall return to your hovel of a village to enjoy the bounties of the working proletariat!"

Insult aside, every man was thrilled at the news. Each was looking forward to returning home—even Davyd, who wasn't from the village.

Someone in the back popped open the crew hatch and climbed out. Davyd checked his steering levers and locked them in place. Though he wasn't afraid of someone messing with the controls, doctrine dictated they remain locked when the tank was inoperable, and Davyd was a stickler for doctrine. Being a farmer meant paying attention to the details else you lose a limb, or worse.

I wonder if they're drawing lots yet, he thought as Popov climbed over his seat and moved to the exit. Davyd closed his eyes and sighed, smiling. War was hell, but the camaraderie which forged a unit was something he did miss. He'd made his closest friends while serving in the Great Patriotic War. He reached under his seat and pulled out a small bottle.

It was time for new memories with new comrades, he decided, taking a quick pull. Harsh liquor burned his mouth. He tucked the bottle into his pocket and climbed out of his seat to join the others.

* * *

I n a short time, the crew had their camp set up, including a small cooking fire. No matter how tired the men grew of canned meat and soup, eating it hot somehow made the experience more satisfying. Davyd scraped the last of the gelled pork from his cup with a chunk of biscuit, washed it down with vodka, and leaned against the tank's treads.

The faces of his comrades reflected the dancing firelight, teeth flashing as they laughed, eyes catching the occasional flare of sparks from the crackling branches and brush.

Sometimes, Davyd thought, *it wasn't so bad, really.*

Sure, he'd rather be at home—they all would, except maybe *Starshina* Popov—but compared to fighting on the front, this was a walk in the park. The monotony could be crushing, and there were always minor annoyances to put up with, but he'd learned to ignore them. He'd take Popov's snoring and Zhuk's farts over lice and typhoid any day.

Pyotr Radovanovich always brought extra vodka when they made these drives, and even Popov turned a blind eye when the bottle came out after the tank stopped for the night. The camaraderie was precisely what the new Bolshevik regime demanded in the *Rodina*. Thus, certain allowances were made, all in the name of Bolshevism.

They kept the conversation light. Nobody really wanted to dwell on past battles, though Popov often reminisced about his personal experiences in Arkhangelsk. If Davyd heard him right, outside of one skirmish, the senior sergeant spent most of his time in the local whorehouses. As usual, talk shifted from fishing and hunting to women.

"Only a few more days, and we'll be home," Pyotr said, passing the bottle. "More importantly, I'll be in the arms of Adelina, with a gut full of roast and a face full of bosom."

"Ha! Better take a number, my friend, and hope you don't get the leavings of either," Laszlo Vygotsky said, slapping Pyotr on the shoulder.

"Adelina is not that kind of woman!"

"She's gone round more than the town windmill, Pyotr," Laszlo countered with a belch and a guffaw. Pyotr scowled and took another swig from his bottle, as the gunner continued, "Tell me...are her inner thighs as calloused as I've heard, or do you not notice during your three minutes of passion?"

"Leave him alone, Laszlo," Davyd said, pulling out his bottle and passing it to the gunner. Laszlo eyed him, amused, before accepting. He took a short pull, then gasped.

"Bah!" Laszlo rubbed his lips with his sleeve. "What the hell is that, petrol?"

"This is *true* vodka," Davyd said, taking back the bottle. "You barbarians use grain. My *babushka* made it properly, from horseradish. *Hrenovuha.* The best vodka with the most flavor!"

"Never trust a man who refuses to drink a *babushka's* home vodka recipe," Pyotr said, grinning wryly.

"Fifty years ago, my village would have fought yours had we heard you insulting her vodka." Davyd laughed and handed the bottle to Maksin Chubais, the front gunner. Normally, he would have sat next to Davyd when they were underway. However, Popov enjoyed the seat and the breeze, so poor Maksin had been relegated to sit in the belly with the others. "Times have changed."

"For the better," Shlomo Zadkine said as he shot a wary look at their commander. Fortunately, *Starshina* Popov seemed to be asleep, his head resting against a tree and his cap pulled low. The tank commander had pulled his coat tightly around him to ward off the cool spring evening.

"For the better," Davyd agreed, understanding precisely what the rear gunner meant. It was hard being a Jew in most parts of the world, and even under the new Bolshevik regime, things were still a little tense in spite of the promises of change and equality.

Shlomo had always been an odd duck among the crew. His was the only openly Jewish family in the village, having fled to Petrosky from Odessa after the assassination of Tsar Alexander II Romanov.

Davyd actually liked Shlomo, all things considered. He was a reliable, steady shot with the rifle and had seen many months on the front as a sniper. When it came to the tank's rear mounted machine gun, he was an absolute wizard, scoring higher than anyone else on all test firings. He was the one person Davyd knew he could rely on to make every burst count. Plus, Shlomo wasn't a drinker, which meant more vodka for the rest of them.

"Besides, should we take a tally of just how many have seen dear, sweet Adelina on her back?" Shlomo continued, smiling crookedly at Pyotr. "I know I haven't, but who else can say they haven't?"

Davyd and Jan Sarnoff raised their hands.

"Dog style counts," Shlomo added. Now only Davyd's remained, as laughter erupted around the campfire. Pyotr looked at every other member of the tank crew, frowning.

"All of you?"

Heads nodded in agreement.

"…she told me she was a virgin…"

"You believed her?" Laszlo asked, snorting. "Honestly?"

"All right, enough already," Popov said from beneath his hat. He pushed it back and looked at the others. "It is not right to abuse a comrade in such manner. Once the fire goes out, get some sleep. It sounds like some of you might need your energy…if you can find a blind woman who lacks virtue."

Davyd looked at their *starshina*. Popov, joking? As far as anyone knew, a Bolshevik only had a sense of humor if it was assigned to them by one of their glorious revolutionary leaders.

A stunned silence fell over the group before Shlomo started laughing, grabbing his sides, and sliding off the log he was sitting on. Chuckles cascaded through the group, gradually growing in strength, until each man was again laughing hard, even Pyotr. For a moment, they were able to forget about the prospect of war looming on the horizon.

Yes, the times can be very good, Davyd thought as he took another pull of his *babushka's* vodka. The burn was good, familiar, and a link to home. Shifting down off his log, he settled onto the soft grass and looked up into the sky. He found the North Star with ease, and from there, the Great Bear. With a finger, he traced the two stars on the bottom of the constellation.

"Between them, Davyd," *Babushka* had told him, "lies the path home. Trust them, they will always bring you back to me, *Darahi.*"

This is much better than fighting on the front, he thought, sighing contentedly. *Glory be damned.*

* * *

The morning began grey and quiet—heavy mist obscuring most of the area around the tank and its crew. The sun, climbing above the horizon, promised a warmer day than the previous one, for which Davyd was thankful. He knew this was a false spring, and they were due for one more cold snap before planting began, but he enjoyed the warm weather when it did come early.

"Biadula, why do you always smell like horse shit?" Shlomo yelled, shattering the early morning tranquility. Davyd sighed and walked over to the other side of the tank. If allowed to continue to argue, the two men would eventually come to blows. As skilled as he was with a rifle, Shlomo's lanky form was not well suited for fighting someone as short and broad as Biadula Zhuk.

"Don't you have a child to find and murder for your daily blood libel, *ieudy?*" Biadula shot back. Davyd increased his speed and rounded the front of the tank, where he found Shlomo towering over the shorter Biadula.

"*Privet!*" Davyd barked loudly. Both men stepped back and looked at the driver. Davyd scowled. "We need to get the *Krasnyy D'yavol* started. Why are you two bickering like an old married couple?"

"He said I smell like shit!" Biadula said angrily, his fists clenched.

"You do smell like shit, Biadula." Davyd sighed and pinched the bridge of his nose. He was glad he wasn't in command of the tank. Otherwise he'd make both men walk the rest of the way to the village while holding hands. "Check your boots."

"My boots are fine," the short man grumbled, but he leaned against the tank and lifted each foot to check anyway. He shook his head. "See? Nothing."

"Then bathe when you get home," Davyd told him. He grabbed Shlomo before he could add more insults. "And you? Don't you have babies to eat or something?"

"*Mudak,*" Shlomo grunted, though he was smiling as he cursed the tank driver. Situation defused, Davyd continued around to the back and used the treads of the tank to climb up top. From there it was easy for him to slip into the driver's seat. He checked to ensure the levers were in the neutral position, then he half-turned and watched as the men filed into the tank and split up to crank start the beast.

Starshina Popov moved to the front and waited expectantly. After he saw they were all in position, he barked the order to begin. Rhythmically, as one, they began to turn the Ricardo engine. After only four cranks, it rumbled to life. Davyd nodded and waited for Popov to give the order to proceed.

"Forward," Popov shouted. Davyd put the tank in gear.

An hour later, they rolled into the outskirts of the fuel depot. Davyd frowned and leaned against the viewport, trying to properly line up his entry. Coming into the refueling point was a pain in the ass during the best days, when the road wasn't in such poor condition. Something caught his eye, but the angle was wrong. Ever-so-gently he eased the left lever back, turning the tank slightly for a better look.

Squinting, he watched a strange, yellow cloud roll across the open field and envelop the above-ground tanks and larger buildings. His guts twisted in fear and recognition. This was all wrong, but all too familiar at the same time.

"Gas!" he screamed, hauling back on the drive levers. As the tank jerked to a stop, he reached for the mask he'd hoped to never to put on again. "Gas, gas, gas!"

He checked the filter box and saw it was still good. *Thank God.* He slapped the mask in place, tightened the straps, and seal checked it.

Popov jumped, startled, before digging his gas mask out of the box next to his seat. Technically it was Maksin's, but since he was in the rear, he would have to use Popov's. Davyd hoped the *starshina's* was as meticulously cared for as Maksin's was.

The tank commander dropped his mask twice as he struggled to put it on. Davyd stifled a sigh, then turned to assist the *starshina.* Gas attacks were something one never grew used to, no matter how many times they occurred.

Davyd looked behind him, his vision hampered by the gas mask. It was frustrating, but having seen what mustard gas did to a person, he wouldn't have been caught without it. The others, all veterans of the Great Patriotic War, had their masks on and were checking the seals for one another.

Shit, Davyd thought as he watched the cloud roll closer to the tank. *The air vents!*

"Rags! Block the vents! Block them right now!" he cried, fumbling for something to block his viewport. He found an old oil-soaked rag near his feet, slammed both levers into park, and quickly stuffed it into the opening. *Not perfect, but it'll have to do.*

The engine idled steadily as they sat there waiting—each man alone with his thoughts as the yellow cloud rolled over their tank. The crew had managed to block all the large air vents, as well as the left and right machine gun mounts.

Davyd's head hurt, and he was having a hard time keeping his eyes open, in spite of the early hour. The tank's engine began to sputter as the petrol ran low, and it finally died as he leaned back in his seat. He didn't care too much about the engine, however. Resting his head on the steel beam behind him, he reached up to check the seal on his mask one final time. His hands felt strangely weak. If only the headache would go away.

Just a quick nap…

* * *

ebat!" David swore as he opened his eyes. His head still throbbed, eerily reminiscent of a bad hangover from his youth. He and his friends had learned that sneaking off and drinking a bottle of his father's vodka had more consequences than just getting caught. This was far worse.

He glanced over at Popov and saw that the tank commander was stirring as well. "*Starshina* Popov, are you okay?"

"What the hell was that?" Popov asked, turning to look at the others. They were slumped over in their seats, with Shlomo almost resting on the engine, itself. Had it still been running, it could have grabbed his tunic and done him harm.

Davyd pulled the dirty rag out of his viewport to look around. The yellow cloud seemed to have moved on. He wasn't sure what they'd just been hit with. While it resembled mustard gas in appearance, he'd never seen it so thick before. Generally, gas tended to disperse the higher off the ground it went, yet this had seemed to wash over everything.

"Bad air," a call came from the rear. Davyd looked back and saw Shlomo pointing at the engine and mentally slapped himself.

Of course, they'd passed out. Without ventilation, the idling engine had almost killed them as the exhaust poured inside. If not for the petrol running out, they might have died. Instead, they'd gotten off lightly, with a forced nap and a terrible migraine.

"I'm going up top to check on the area," Popov stated as he climbed into the back. "Keep your masks on!"

"Yes, *Starshina*!" the others chorused.

Davyd grunted and leaned against the small driver's viewport, the foggy lens of his mask obscuring his vision. It wasn't too bad, though, just enough for everything to appear shrouded in early morning haze.

The unnaturally quiet fuel depot sent a chill running down his spine. Usually, there were three men stationed there, and none had

228 | IBSON & KENNEDY

come out to check on them after the gas attack. He feared the worst. Death by mustard gas ranked right up there with being gored by an angry bull in a pasture filled with manure.

Popov called down from his position. "All clear, you can remove your masks."

With a sigh of relief, Davyd tore the gear off. The mask had saved his life once more. It was stifling, but it was possibly the most valuable piece of equipment within the tank. Even more than the ammunition for the machineguns, as many crews on the front had discovered. Some had learned the hard way and were now unable to walk more than a few steps before collapsing from exhaustion. It was just one of the many things the Bolsheviks had promised to fix during the October revolution and hadn't quite gotten around to just yet.

"Crack open the vents," Davyd called into the back.

"I think Biadula shit himself," Pyotr responded, laughing.

"I did n—wait, let me…no, I did not!"

Chuckling, Davyd climbed out of his seat and made his way to the exit hatch. The others were still removing and securing their masks under their benches, so Davyd went out of the hatch next. Surprisingly, Shlomo was right behind him. Davyd helped his Jewish friend out, and they turned to survey the silent fuel depot.

"*Starshina* Popov?" Davyd looked around for any sign of life. The place seemed abandoned.

"You two. Refill the engine with the two spare fuel canisters in the rear," Popov ordered as he climbed down carefully. While the commander was arrogant, he wasn't stupid. Every single tanker knew the dangers of jumping from the top of the tank. Many had suffered broken legs or worse while leaping from such a height. "Get the tank over to the refueling point. I'm going to go find Comrade Kazmer."

"Yes, *Starshina*!" Davyd replied and looked at Shlomo, who heaved a long-suffering sigh as soon as Popov was out of hearing range.

"Every fucking time…" Shlomo complained as he carefully maneuvered his way to the rear. The steep angle made the going slow, and more than once, he slipped on the fine, yellow dust covering the hull. Davyd paused to examine it. Whatever it was, it didn't burn or smell. He wiped his hands on his trousers and shrugged.

Probably just pollen.

"Trust *mat'-priroda* to scare the hell out of us," Davyd told Shlomo as the duo unchained two of the reserve fuel canisters. He passed the first of the five-gallon containers to Shlomo, who grunted from the weight. "The 'gas attack' was probably pollen. I'll never look at trees the same again."

"Never seen pollen like that before," Shlomo pointed out as he sat down on the sloped roof of the tank and checked the seal on the fuel canister. Satisfied, he handed it back to Davyd, who passed him the second. After confirming the seal on this one was good as well, he grabbed it by the handle and began to move slowly further down the sloping rear of the tank. "Besides, you know my allergies…"

This was true, Davyd thought as he grabbed the fuel canister and moved aside for Shlomo.

The refueling point was one of the particularly vulnerable spots on the Mark V. Located in the rear, it was supposed to be well-armored and protected from frontal assault. However, many unfortunate crews had learned about the thinner wall surrounding the fuel tanks when an artillery shell struck close behind.

It was still safer than some of the earlier designs used during the Great Patriotic War. He'd heard horror stories of tanks rolling across the open fields aflame, their crews screaming as they were cooked alive. That was before the munitions inside exploded, of course, destroying the tank completely. Davyd felt some small amount of pity for the Germans who had died in those contraptions. It was one thing to die in battle, but another entirely to meet death in such a manner.

Unscrewing the fuel cap, Davyd fitted the spigot to the canister and began to pour. Ten gallons of petrol might not get them far, but it would ensure they reached the refueling point less than one hundred yards away. It was frustrating they were so close, yet out of reach. Had they not stopped for the "gas attack," they would have made it with no issues. The tank must have sat idling for longer than he'd realized.

"*B'lyad!*" Shlomo swore, fumbling the canister and splashing fuel onto his leg. Surprisingly, the pollen disappeared from his trousers as the petrol soaked through instead of caking on as expected. Davyd raised an eyebrow. He'd never seen that before.

"Hey, at least your ass isn't covered in this shit," Davyd pointed out as the last bit of petrol poured into the fuel tank. He unfastened the spigot and set the now-empty canister aside. Shlomo handed him the second.

"You know I'm going to catch fire the first time I light a cigarette, right?" Shlomo asked, scowling. "My allergies will probably act up, too. That's a very Jewish thing to happen if you think about it. Die while burning and sneezing my head off."

"Now you can guess what Biadula's ass rot feels like," Davyd joked as he continued to pour. Shlomo chuckled, then grimaced. His sleeping arrangement was next to Biadula's.

"You talking shit about me again, Davyd?" Biadula asked as he climbed out of the hatch. The short man was barely thin enough to fit into the tank, meeting the weight limits by just enough. Davyd had joked before about how much range they lost with him on board.

"Of course, I am." Davyd smiled crookedly as he poured the last of the fuel into the tank. "Why are you getting out? We need everyone inside to get the *Krasnyy D'yavol* going again."

"Fresh air," Biadula complained, looking back down. How he saw past his impressive girth, Davyd would never know. "Pyotr's breath is as bad as a horse's."

"You should talk!" came the reply from below. "Something is rotting inside your ass! It's unnatural and unholy, whatever it is! Were I your father, I would have forced you into the river until you froze or the smell went away!"

Davyd rolled his eyes and grabbed both empty canisters. Securing them with the chain once more, he accepted Shlomo's proffered hand and climbed back on top of the tank. David wiped his hands off on his filthy trousers and paused and looked out at Popov. The *starshina* was walking into the small office across from the petrol tanks.

"Does it seem a little quiet today?"

"Bah," Shlomo grunted, shrugging. "Probably just being cautious. We need to get *Krasnyy D'yavol* over to the fuel tanks."

"Just like the *starshina* ordered," Davyd added as they climbed back inside. His nose wrinkled as the stench hit him. *There is something very wrong with that man*, he thought. "Ugh. Biadula!"

"All right, comrades," Shlomo said as the men gathered around the engine's crank lever. Shlomo, Biadula, and Sarnoff were on the left side, while Laszlo, Pyotr, and Maksin gathered on the right. Davyd, as driver, was exempt from this activity, but usually called the cadence for them to get it going.

"One, turn!" Davyd called. The crank began to turn, albeit slowly, and the six cylinders began to move. "Turn! Turn! Turn!"

The Ricardo engine coughed, sputtered slightly, then rumbled to life as the pistons began firing. Nodding, Davyd climbed into the driver's seat, checked to ensure nobody was in front of them, and engaged the drive levers. As the tank lurched forward, he eased the levers back slightly, bringing them to their ideal cruising speed of just under three miles per hour.

"Shlomo!" Davyd shouted, leaning over in his seat. "Up top!"

"*B'lyad!*" Shlomo replied, climbing out of the hatch. Grinning, Davyd focused on getting the tank near the large fuel containers. Due to his position's limited visibility, he needed someone to steer him in when he got close.

Clang! Davyd cut his speed and waited for the next signal. A few more seconds passed before a second *clang!* reverberated through the driver's compartment. Davyd slammed the levers into place and waited for the swearing to start.

"Every fucking time, Davyd!" Shlomo's face appeared in the viewport, upside down. He was not pleased. "You try to dump me off *every fucking time!*"

"I have no idea what you mean, *comrade*," Davyd said as he grinned. Shlomo scoffed and disappeared.

A few moments later, he heard the gunner prepping the reserve canisters, as well as the tank's main fuel containers. The mechanical pump attached to the large petrol containers whirred, and within seconds, the *Krasnyy D'yavol* was drinking greedily.

Bored, with nothing else to do, Davyd climbed back up topside. Everyone else stood several feet away, smoking, while Shlomo did the refueling. Popov emerged from the office, scowling. Davyd turned slowly, scanning the area. A flicker of movement in the corner of his eye caught his attention.

"Is that Kazmer? What's he doing?" Davyd wondered aloud. The fuel depot commander lay on the ground, inching toward them. He was still a little way off, though.

"Let Popov deal with it," Shlomo said. Davyd shrugged.

"*Starshina!*" Davyd called, waving. He pointed down the street, toward the man crawling on his elbows. Popov acknowledged, then started toward the cripple.

"What are you doing out here, Kaz? You get too drunk and try to walk again?" Popov asked. "I brought you some good vodka! Maybe you have something for me?"

Popov always tried to bring something extra for Kazmer. The depot master was notorious for finding the best rare items. The last time, Popov had traded for a bottle of twelve-year-old Macallan; before that, a pouch of genuine American tobacco. Keeping with the spirit of Bolshevism, Popov had shared a bit of each with the rest of the crew.

Oddly, Kazmer didn't respond. The war hero was always talkative and gregarious, sometimes to the point where they found it difficult to leave on time. It was even stranger that Kazmer was already drinking. Sure, the depot commander liked his vodka, but he typically waited until after midday.

Davyd shook his head. Kazmer must have really hit the bottle hard if he'd forgotten he no longer had legs.

"Kaz! What are you doing, comrade?" Popov continued, standing over the depot commander. Kazmer reached up, and Popov knelt next to him. Davyd strained his ears but couldn't hear the *starshina*. Popov grasped the depot commander's arm, trying to situate him. Over his shoulder, he yelled, "*Efraitor!* Run and fetch Comrade Kazmer's—Ow! What the fuck, Kaz?"

Popov jerked his hand away from Kazmer, clutching it to his chest. He began cursing loudly as Kazmer grabbed him by the leg. Showing a surprising amount of strength, Kaz dragged the tank commander to the ground and crawled up his body. Popov's shouts of surprise turned to screams as Kazmer began gnawing on the *starshina's* face.

"*Yob tvoyu mat!*" Davyd yelled and scrambled off the rear of the tank.

"What is it, Davyd?" Maksin asked as Davyd ran past him.

"Kaz attacked Popov!" Davyd shouted, running to where Kaz had taken Popov down.

"How? Did he chew on his ankles or something?" Biadula shouted after him, amused.

Davyd reached the struggling duo but found it was too late. He kicked Kaz in the ribs as hard as he could and managed to dislodge the cripple, flipping him onto his back. Kaz flopped for a moment, rolled onto his belly, and started crawling back toward Popov. Davyd hauled on his commander's harness, dragging him away from the depot commander.

A shadow suddenly blocked out the sun above him. Squinting, Davyd looked up at Biadula. The heavyset tanker held a trench tool.

"*Yobanaya suka!*" Biadula swore. He turned, kicked Kaz in the face, and raised the small spade. With an explosive grunt, he brought it down on the back of Kazmer's head. It didn't faze the depot commander, who continued to crawl toward Davyd and Popov.

Biadula swung a second time, then a third, and a fourth. Each impact of the sharp steel was hard enough to knock out a grown man easily, let alone four. Unfazed, Kazmer kept coming.

"Neck!" Davyd shouted, kicking the cripple. "Aim for his neck!"

Biadula shifted his next swing accordingly, and the flat of the spade struck solidly on the back of Kazmer's neck. The depot officer shuddered slightly but continued his struggle to reach Popov.

"No, you idiot! Sharp edge! *Use the edge!*" Davyd screamed, as Kazmer grabbed hold of his boot.

Understanding dawned on Biadula's face, and the gunner flipped the spade over. He brought the thin steel edge down, nearly decapitating the man. Kazmer quit trying to crawl up Davyd's leg and focused on attacking Biadula. The heavyset gunner wasn't having it, though, and he stepped aside and brought the spade down again and again, each impact sounding wetter than the last.

After what felt like forever, Kazmer's head rolled away from his body. With a disgusted grunt, Biadula kicked it as hard as he could, sending it back the way it had come. The depot commander's corpse twitched a few more times, then quit moving.

Davyd leaned back, breathing heavily, cradling Popov protectively in his arms. The tank commander's hands were slick with blood, which were pressed against the gaping wounds in his neck. Wide eyed, Popov stared up at Davyd, struggling to speak through burbling, frothy gasps.

"It's all right, *Starshina*, you'll be fine," Davyd lied, trying to comfort him.

The artery that ran up the commander's neck had been chewed through and torn open completely. There was nothing any of them could do.

A last gasp of air rattled in Popov's chest before he exhaled one last time. His eyes stared up at the sky, vacant and empty.

"Is he...?" Biadula's voice trailed off. He looked down at them, a horrified expression on his face. "Why?"

"I don't know," Davyd said softly, gently laying their commander on the ground. He gave Kazmer a pointed glance as he crawled to his feet. "He just lost his mind."

"Maybe he was gassed? I once saw a man claw his own eyes out at Bolimov. If not for the cold, he would have bled out right there."

It was entirely possible, Davyd reasoned. Gas did strange things to people. Depending on the kind, it could make a rational man go insane from pain. Turning, he saw the others had stopped not too far away. They were staring at the dead bodies with mixed expressions of horror and curiosity.

"We need to cable the army base," Davyd said after a few moments of silence.

"What about them?" Biadula asked, motioning toward the dead.

"We can't carry Kazmer back with us," Davyd decided after a moment. "If he was gassed, it still might be trapped in his body, and if that spoils, we could all suffer."

"Bury them both here then," Biadula suggested. Davyd nodded.

"What about the others?" Shlomo asked, cautiously edging closer. "You know, the idiots who say they work here but never actually do anything?"

"I'm not searching for them," Davyd answered. "The only reason Kazmer didn't get me was because he doesn't have legs. Those two...they might be lazy and stupid, but they're rather large." All the others nodded in agreement. There was no sense in looking for more trouble. Davyd continued after a moment, "We bury them, mark their graves, then head back to base."

"Or we can bury them, mark their graves, and continue to Petrosky. Hear me out," Pyotr said, raising his palms. "We spend a few days with our families as planned, then when we come back, we send a message. Except we say it happened two days from now. Army command won't know any better, and we don't have to face an inquiry now."

"I like this plan," Shlomo said, nodding. At Davyd's scowl, he continued, "Davyd, comrade, my friend...we're going to face a Bolshevik inquisition when we return. We're going to have to tell them what happened, explain the gas attack, everything. We might never get to do this patrol route again. Let's have one final weekend with our families as a crew before we return."

"He's right," Maksin chimed in. "If they don't shoot us when we return, we will probably never be together again. Besides, they might just execute poor Shlomo before he gets his dick wet in a *nochnaya babochka*. Would you do that to your friend?"

"Plus, think of our families," Biadula reminded him. "What's the point of fighting, if not for a full belly and someone to warm the bed?"

238 | IBSON & KENNEDY

Davyd nodded, reluctantly. They were right. No matter which Bolshevik commissar they faced, this was the last ride of the *Krasnyy D'yavol* and her motley crew. "Burial detail. Look in the office and find lime. Check for any rifles and ammunition as well, just in case. Cover the bodies in the lime so nothing will dig them up. Once all that is done, we continue on to Petrosky."

* * *

We should have turned around, Davyd thought, as his eyes drank in the surreal scene greeting them.

He stopped the tank just outside the village, near a slightly elevated—and relatively dry—patch of grass above the road. It wasn't their usual parking spot, but with the mud as bad as it was, Davyd didn't want to risk getting closer to the village. Out here, in sight of the largest corral, it would be easier to hitch up a train of horses, should they become stuck.

"Kill the engine!" Davyd shouted. In the sudden silence, he rubbed his face with grimy hands, then glanced over at the empty seat beside him. He reached under his seat, pulled out the bottle of vodka from the night before, and took a short pull from it.

"*Dosvedanya, Starshina* Popov," Davyd muttered and drank another swallow of the spiced vodka before sliding the empty bottle back into its hiding place. He would refill it the next time he made it home.

He climbed out of his seat and saw he was alone. That suited Davyd just fine. If he couldn't find somewhere to sleep later, he could always stretch out on the back bench. It was warmer there than some of the homes of Petrosky, and he'd slept on the bench enough to know precisely how to get comfortable on it.

Once topside, he looked around. It was eerily quiet. Normally, whenever the tank rolled into town, a dozen or so children would climb all over it once it was parked. The families of his fellow tankers would greet them and then there would be drinking. Lots and lots of drinking. Afterward they'd eat, go to their homes—or visit the young, attractive women in some of the haylofts—and spend the rest of the night simply celebrating their return. They'd done it so often, it felt automatic.

That didn't happen this time.

Some of the chimneys had smoke rising lazily from the stone stacks, but no one was walking around the village. Even the pasture was empty, which was very unusual. Perhaps the horses had been left in the stables? The other tankers were already heading into town, their typical excitement replaced with silence. Davyd slid down the rear of the tank, getting more of the unusual pollen on his hands. Davyd grimaced and cleaned off his hands on his trousers before following the others.

"What do you think?" Shlomo asked him as he caught up with the group.

"I don't know," Davyd admitted as he glanced down at his filthy trousers. "This isn't pollen, but if it's residue from the gas, then why isn't it affecting us? The wind wasn't right...there's so much going on I don't understand."

When the group arrived in the village center, they stopped and stared. Gathered around four large tables lay almost every single person in town, their bodies covered in the unusual yellow dust. Every single man, woman, and child had apparently succumbed to the same gas which had hit them at the fuel depot earlier. There would be no feasting or celebrations this afternoon.

The crew stood, blank faced and silent. Ever since Popov had died and they'd executed—Davyd couldn't really call it anything else—Commander Kazmer, worry had gnawed away inside him, but he'd refused to dwell on the possibility. Instead, he'd let hope slip in and push the growing sense of dread aside. He should have known better. Hope was always squashed by harsh reality.

"Gas," Pyotr confirmed as he eyed the tables. It had to be. Though the food had clearly been left sitting out for many hours, not a single insect could be seen. If the yellow cloud had been pollen, the bugs would have been feasting.

"See...see if anyone survived," Davyd said. The men slowly spread out, eyeing the dead, while trying to see inside some of the darkened hovels.

It was quickly apparent everybody had been outside and away from their homes when the gas hit. The sight was terrifying to behold, yet every man remained stoic as possible as he looked for his family. Davyd's dark thoughts turned to his village.

Randomly, an anguished cry would echo through the square as one of the men discovered their family. Shlomo appeared, eyes rimmed red and cheeks streaked with tears. Davyd's heart went out to the man. His family had survived so much only to be destroyed while "safe" at home. In a life filled with unfairness, the Fates being so cruel to the man was overkill.

"I've got a survivor!" Laszlo suddenly cried out. Davyd spun in time to see the man emerge from a nearby house, followed by a little girl. It was Elga, Laszlo's niece. Clutching hands, the duo walked over to where Davyd stood waiting.

She must have been inside when the cloud rolled through, Davyd thought.

"Hello, Elga," he said as he knelt down to inspect her. She was almost devoid of the strange yellow dust, he noticed. There was a smudge near her right ear and another on one knee, but otherwise, she was clean. He smiled as he found a little comfort in the horror of the situation. The gas had to be inhaled, unlike mustard gas, and the residue didn't appear to have any lingering effects. It was welcome news in the face of everything else.

A scream rippled through the village, only to be abruptly cut off by a wet, gurgling noise. All heads snapped up and looked around as they tried to identify the source. Shlomo blinked and pointed toward one of the closest houses in the square.

"It came from Jan's house," Shlomo said. He paused, glanced around, then started to walk toward the sound.

"I know what it was," Davyd said, grabbing his hand. Shlomo turned and looked at him.

Davyd thought back to all the times he had to sit through Jan's tales of his younger siblings. The family bond was strong, especially with his father. The patriarch was a rock, the anchor who had held everything in place, and Jan was content to live in the man's shadow.

Had been, he mentally corrected. Davyd gave Shlomo a hard look. "You don't want to investigate. Just…leave him be. He's with his family now."

Shlomo looked back at the house for a moment, frowning. Slowly, however, that expression faded to be replaced with wide-eyed understanding. Covering his mouth with the back of his hand, Shlomo walked a few feet away, stopped, and bent over. Davyd turned, focused on the horizon, and tried to ignore the sounds behind him.

"We should leave," Elga declared, looking up at Davyd. He offered her a comforting smile and patted her head twice. The little girl persisted. "We should get somewhere safe where we can find help."

"Do we burn them?" Biadula asked as he approached. He waved a hand at a particularly large cluster of bodies. "We can't bury them all."

"We can't leave them out to rot either," Davyd countered, as he tried to think of something that would satisfy everyone. Unfortunately, nothing came to mind. He sighed heavily. "No, we need to go back to the depot, refuel the *Krasnyy D'yavol,* and return to base as soon as possible."

"It's almost dark, Davyd," Shlomo pointed out, his anxiety apparently under control once more. "You're a good driver, but nobody's that good."

"The sooner we leave, the better," Laszlo snapped. "I don't care if it's only a little way down the road. I don't want to stay here one minute longer than we need to."

"Okay, calm down," Davyd said. Biadula and Laszlo both looked frightened, while Shlomo appeared determined, if a bit agitated. Pyotr and Maksin were looking at him expectantly. It slowly sank in—with Popov dead, he was the highest ranked man. His decision would be the final word on the matter.

Staying put was an option, but not a *viable* option. Without knowing what the yellow dust was, they couldn't assume it was safe to stay outside. Davyd had no issues with sleeping in the vehicle, though Biadula's ass might end up killing them. The problem was food and, more importantly, water. Anything in the village had to be considered contaminated, which meant using what they had in the tank. Eventually, the supplies would run out.

Nobody had thought to grab extra rations from the depot, since they knew they would have to return. Even Davyd had simply assumed they would grab what they needed on their way back to base. They usually stocked up on water from the village well before leaving, but that option was no longer available. They had to go back.

"Laszlo has a point. We should leave as soon as possible. I can get us one-third of the way to the depot before it gets dark if we leave now."

"Davyd?" Pyotr nudged him with an elbow.

"What?"

"Look, over there, that one," Pyotr said, pointing toward a small body cluster.

"I see, Pyotr. I see them all," Davyd replied tiredly.

"No, Davyd. Look closer...she's *moving*." Davyd blinked, then really *looked*. Pyotr's voice grew hopeful. "Adelina! Is she...is she alive? I should check."

It was clearly Adelina's body. Even in death, the woman had a very distinguished look about her. Plus, her bright, yellow dress stood out among the drab colors of the village. She lay on her stomach, arms splayed in front of her. If not for the oozing blisters on her exposed skin, Davyd would have sworn she was sleeping. Her back rose and fell, giving the impression she was still breathing...

It wasn't regular. The movement wasn't a uniform expansion of her ribs; it was erratic, as if there were small animals moving under the cloth. Laszlo placed a hand on Davyd's shoulder to hold him back. It was a useless gesture, since Davyd had no intention of getting any closer. Pyotr, however, continued his cautious approach.

"Adelina?" Pyotr called out. There was a deep longing in his voice which bordered on the edge of hysterics. "It's me, Pyotr. Your *silny lev.*"

Suddenly, Adelina's clothing expanded, held for a moment, then fell. A cloud of yellow smoke erupted from the short sleeves of her dress, drifting slowly to the ground around her. A slight breeze kicked up just then, stirring the particles into the air.

"Pyotr," Davyd said, taking a step back, "I think we should get in the tank. Now."

"Adelina?" The gunner ignored him, moving closer to the now still figure. Kneeling in the soft dirt, he reached out hesitantly.

"Now, Pyotr," Davyd said, louder. "That's an order, comrade."

Pyotr ignored him, gingerly touching his beloved. She moved slightly, and Pyotr looked back over his shoulder, grinning, eyes brimming. "I think she's alive!"

Adelina suddenly rolled onto her back. The gunner felt her move, his grin spreading as he turned to face her. He wrapped his arms around her lacerated, blistered body, burying his face in her hair.

"I knew you were alive!" he cried. Her arms tentatively encircled him, squeezing him tightly. "I knew it! I knew you wouldn't be taken from me!"

Davyd looked on, shocked and horrified. It was clear to him something was wrong, but Pyotr was blinded by love and grief. Adelina might be moving, but she was definitely not alive. She was...something else.

"*Rusalki*," Maksin whispered, horrified. "She walks again."

"Adelina, my love, too tight," Pyotr gasped. The gunner tried to pry her arms off him but was unable. She had strength born of something otherworldly. "Beloved, please...it's...the pain..."

Held still as if by some unseen force, they all watched in horror as Adelina continued to squeeze. Each pistol shot of Pyotr's cracking ribs was punctuated by a cry of pain.

"Back to the tank," Davyd ordered.

"But what about Pyotr?" Biadula asked, taking a step toward his crewman and Adelina. He stopped, however, when the young woman seemed to realize they were watching. She stared at them with empty, milky-white eyes. The beautiful cornflower blue was gone. They were the eyes of the damned; the eyes of *Rusalki*.

"*Zaebis!*" Shlomo swore, pointing. "Look! The others are moving now!"

"Get to the tank, now!" Davyd shouted.

The men ran across the muddy road toward the *Krasnyy D'yavol*. Laszlo had enough sense to stop and scoop up Elga in his arms before following the rest. Davyd cast one final look back and saw the dead villagers, friends he had known for months, struggling to stand up. Pyotr was lying on the ground, frothy blood flowing from his mouth. He was staring at Davyd, mouthing something. Adelina released her hold and slowly rose to her feet. Davyd ran.

Last to arrive at the tank, Davyd stopped and helped Laszlo clamber up the rear, Elga clinging tightly to Laszlo's chest. For a split second, fear's icy claw gripped Davyd's heart, the image of Pyotr's last gasp flashing through his mind. Elga's bright green eyes, filled with fear and life, stared into his, and the feeling passed.

"Up you go," Laszlo said to her. "Just climb down through that hole there. Yes, good. Someone will catch you."

As she disappeared into the tank, Laszlo stood upright and looked back toward the village. He raised a hand and pointed. "Davyd, look."

The driver half-turned and saw what seemed like every villager from the square coming toward them. It reminded him of toddlers learning how to walk for the first time. Cursing under his breath, Davyd climbed up the back of the tank and waited as Laszlo dropped into the hatch. With one final look at the approaching horde, Davyd slipped into the tank and sealed the hatch. Even if they did manage to climb on top of the vehicle, there was no way for the villagers to get in. They were safe.

Unfortunately, that safety had a time limit.

"On the crank!" Davyd shouted as soon as his eyes adjusted to the dim light. Every man reached for the crank and grasped it with both hands, Davyd included. "And one! Turn! And two! Turn! And three! TURN!"

The engine coughed, sputtered, and died. Davyd cursed loudly and then looked over at Elga, mildly ashamed. He hadn't meant for the young girl to hear his swearing. It wasn't polite.

"Again!" Davyd yelled, and the men prepared for another try. "And one! Turn! And two! Turn! And th—"

This time the Ricardo engine rumbled to life. The men immediately turned and began prepping their weapons. They knew something bad was coming, and like all veterans of the Great Patriotic War, the best way to prepare was to lock and load. Davyd looked around and found Pyotr's mask with the ventilator box safely stored next to it.

"*Solnechnyy svet!*" he yelled, handing it to Elga. It was probably too big, but it was better than nothing. "If anyone starts shouting 'gas,' put this on. Laszlo will help you if you need it. Don't be afraid. All right?"

Elga nodded, and Davyd maneuvered to the back, where Shlomo was loading the first round from the ammo belt into his Vickers machine gun. Next to the weapon was a large box, containing almost one thousand rounds. Davyd put his arm on Shlomo's shoulder to get his attention before pointing at the ammo.

"Save half," he ordered. Shlomo looked at him curiously for a moment, then nodded. Reaching into the box, Shlomo felt his way through the loops of the belt before estimating where the middle was. The sniper pulled out his knife and cut the link.

Satisfied, Davyd went back to the front, passing Maksin and Laszlo. Elga had climbed up onto the bench to stay out of the way, her eyes shiny in the dim light as she watched them work. It was clear to Davyd the little girl was confused by everything she was seeing. He couldn't blame her, really. A tank in combat was something to be seen and not told about.

He made it to the front and sat down in the driver's seat. He held the right lever forward, pulled the left lever all the way back, and spun the tank in a tight circle.

At the apex of the turn, someone opened fire. Another gunner quickly joined in. He couldn't be certain if they were shooting because the villagers had gotten close or simply out of fear. He couldn't blame them either way. He'd probably do the same in their position.

Those people were dead, I know they were, Davyd thought as he brought the tank out of the turn. He threw the left lever forward, and the *Krasnyy D'yavol* rumbled slowly down the muddy road.

Normally, he'd be worried about conserving fuel, but that concern had been replaced with getting out of there as fast as they could. His mind drifted back to the sight of Adelina somehow crushing poor Pyotr with her arms. *I've never seen anything like that before. She's too skinny. She shouldn't have been able to do that!*

Davyd shivered as a childhood memory bubbled to the surface: a story his *babushka* told him about the *Rusalki.*

Beautiful beings—women wronged in their past, who had died tragically—would return to life to seek vengeance upon those who had done them harm. His *babushka* always implored him to treat women well, because the *Rusalki* would come for him if he didn't. While it hadn't been on his mind at the time, he'd rejected Adelina's advances, but looking back now, it seemed the fairy tale had left a lasting impression.

What if the stories weren't used to ensure little children behaved, he wondered, thinking of Adelina's milky white eyes and the villagers' odd gait. *What if they were warnings? Could all the stories my* babushka *told me as a child be true? Wolves that walked like men, creatures of the night who drink the blood of the innocent...where does the fable end and reality begin?*

The machine gun fire soon stopped. The tank had enough ammunition for a small-scale engagement, true. Popov, however, had reasoned they would get better mileage on what little fuel they could carry with a lighter load, so instead of carrying almost ten thousand rounds, there was just under half that. It was likely Laszlo and Maksin had fired off all the ammo in their boxes, leaving only Shlomo and Biadula with full loads.

Davyd glanced over at the front gunner position but didn't see the ammo can which was supposed to be there. He fervently hoped Maksin had thought ahead and taken it to the back. Otherwise, they had even less ammo than Davyd had guessed.

Those might not be the same sort of monsters my babushka spoke of, but Rusalki seems to fit the description, he thought some time later. The late afternoon sun was beginning to slip behind the tall pine trees. Soon it would be too dark to continue.

Davyd leaned on the control levers, as though that would squeeze just a bit more speed out of the *Krasnyy D'yavol*. The *Rusalki* had fallen behind but hadn't appeared to tire or change pace. They simply kept plodding along, pursuing the metal monster in front of them, as though they knew it would have to stop at some point.

That point was rapidly approaching, as the sun inched toward the horizon. It was a problem Davyd had been chewing on for the last several minutes—one with no simple answer.

The road was treacherous in the dark—trying to navigate after sundown could leave them stuck. Stopping for the night was safer, however, it would eliminate the lead they'd gained. Any delay could mean rolling into the depot in the middle of the horde. Trying to refuel while fighting off attackers was not something he wanted to try.

By his estimate, they needed another two hours to reach the depot, but they only had about thirty minutes of daylight left. At top speed, and with a lot of luck, they could buy themselves most of an hour to refuel and restock in the morning. He stopped the tank and killed the engine.

"Davyd," Lazlo said in the sudden silence, "what do you think you're doing?"

"We have to stop before it gets dark," Davyd replied.

"And let those things catch up? Hell no." The others nodded in silent agreement.

"I can't go full speed in the dark. They'll catch up to us anyway."

"It's worth the risk," Lazlo snarled. "You saw what happened to Pyotr; hell, you watched Popov die!"

"If we damage *Krasnyy D'yavol*, we'll be in worse shape," Davyd said calmly. "You've seen the roads here. How far do you think we could make it on foot?"

Biadula's face darkened as the others glanced his way.

"We could leave the engine running," Maksin said, "that way we could leave faster." Davyd shook his head.

"We ran out of fuel and almost suffocated the last time. We can't take that chance."

"Idiot," someone whispered. Davyd ignored it.

"No, we stop tonight. I can drive faster if I can see what I'm doing. We'll get ahead again in the morning."

This time, no one argued, even Lazlo. Davyd could tell he wasn't happy about the decision, but he couldn't find fault with the reasoning. He prayed silently that he was right.

* * *

Davyd started, snapped out of his light doze by something slapping against the hull under him.

A quick look showed the others still slept, spread out on the floor and benches surrounding the engine. He turned back to his viewport, getting as close as he could in the tight space. Nothing. He settled back and closed his eyes again.

Just as sleep enveloped him, the sound came again, this time from the rear. Lazlo sat up sharply.

"They're here," he said, eyes wide. As if in response, more impacts thudded against the metal hull. Lazlo jumped at each.

"But out there," Davyd said. "No matter what, they're still flesh. They can't break through steel."

The other men stirred, as the sounds became more frequent. Davyd looked through his viewport and could see, now, there were several figures congregating in front of them. Most of the noise seemed focused on the back of the tank, though.

"Try to ignore them and get some sleep. We're safe in here." The words rang hollow in his ears, even as he made a show of closing his eyes. A wet slap in front of him made them snap open again.

A hand, bloated and covered in oozing sores, gripped the edge of the small window. Davyd pulled his knees to his chest and kicked hard, smashing his foot into the thing's fingers as forcefully as possible. To his relief, the grip relaxed, and the hand disappeared. Davyd quickly leaned forward, yanking the hatch closed and dogging it. Before another *Rusalki* could do the same, he secured the gunner's viewport as well.

"See? Safe."

The hours crawled by.

Davyd was able to catch some sleep, mostly by force of will and by pulling his jacket collar up to his ears. The others seemed to do the same. Except Elga. Several times during the long night, Davyd had caught her staring at him, expressionless, even as the muffled sound of blows reverberated through the compartment.

The sounds were the worst, as the tireless horde outside pawed at the tank's unyielding skin. Countless bodies pressed against the machine formed a nightmare orchestra from the bowels of Hell. Hundreds of hands beat on the hull, their staccato rhythm interspersed with the screech of fingernails and teeth scraping the metal—a demonic bow drawn across the strings of Satan's violin.

Davyd woke from one nap and looked over at Maksin, now huddled next to him. At some point while Davyd slept, the front gunner had taken his rightful seat, capitalizing on the elevated position for reprieve from the noise below. Even so, the smaller man twitched in his sleep with each impact. Davyd checked his watch. Still hours until dawn. He hunched into his jacket and closed his eyes.

Whether from stress, sheer exhaustion, or the combination of both, he fell into a deeper sleep, only to be woken by a loud clang above him. He was halfway out of his seat before he realized Maksin wasn't next to him. Davyd looked up and found the hatch over his head unlatched.

"What the fuck was that?" Lazlo asked, appearing behind him. The man's eyes were wide, bloodshot, and twitching back and forth.

Davyd ignored him and stood up to ease the heavy metal door open enough to see out.

Maksin stood a few feet away, staring toward the rear.

"Maksin," Davyd said, quietly. "What are you doing, comrade?"

"They're clustered around the back and sides," the other man whispered. "I could make it."

"Make it?"

The gunner turned to face him, an insane grin plastered on his face.

"I was the fastest in the village, you know," he said. "Every year, we'd run races in the spring, right about this time. I always won."

"You're tired and not thinking straight," Davyd said. He checked his watch. "It's only an hour or so until sunrise."

Maksin didn't seem to hear him as he looked out at the road ahead.

"It's not far."

"Don't be foolish. Come back inside where it's safe."

"Safe? This isn't safe, comrade." Maksin's chuckle sent chills through Davyd's spine. "This is waiting to die." With two long strides, Maksin passed the hatch before Davyd could react. Davyd pushed the heavy door open and saw the gunner's head disappear over the side.

"Shit!"

"What happened?" Lazlo met him as he retreated into the driver's seat. He pushed the other man aside and opened his viewport.

"Maksin jumped," Davyd said, straining to catch sight of the small crewman. "There! He's out in front and making a break for it!"

The others crowded around, trying to see through the front viewports. Maksin was running hard, barely visible as he distanced himself from the tank. A small crowd of *Rusalki* plodded after him.

"My God," Biadula said. "He's going to make it!"

Davyd had to agree. The *Rusalki* wouldn't, or couldn't, run. Maksin had a good head start and seemed to be keeping his lead as he disappeared into the night. If he could keep it up for long enough…

Davyd's thought was cut off by a cry of pain, followed by cursing. Maksin's voice carried back to them.

"Comrades, help! I…I think I've broken my ankle!"

"Out of my way!" Shlomo started for the hatch, only to be held back by Lazlo. Shlomo stared at him incredulously. "What are you doing?"

"You can't help him." Lazlo's whisper carried steel. "If you go out there, we will lose you too."

"But you saw how far he made it!"

"Lazlo's correct," Davyd said. "There's no way to get to him before the *Rusalki* do."

As if in response, Maksin's pleas changed to curses, then screams. The monsters had caught up to him. His final cries trailed off into gurgled choking, then silence.

Davyd crossed himself, silently praying for his comrade's soul.

* * * * *

Jason Cordova Bio

A 2019 Dragon Award finalist, Jason Cordova is best known for his popular "Kin Wars Saga" military SF series published by Theogony Books. He is a kaiju enthusiast and currently lives in Virginia. You can find him at http://www.jasoncordova.com.

\# \# \# \# \#

The Fallow Fields, Part II
by Christopher L. Smith
and Jason Cordova

Daylight.

Davyd rubbed his grimy eyes and sat upright, the nightmare replay of the last day fading as he woke. He focused, forcing the scratching outside the tank to replace Maksin's final, pleading cries in his head.

The *Rusalki* hadn't gone anywhere. For whatever reason, they were focused on the people inside the Mark V. He cracked his viewport and looked ahead to where Maksin had disappeared the night before.

No sign of him or the monsters that got him, he thought. *Poor bastard.*

Davyd sat back and concentrated. Maksin had proven they could, in fact, outrun the *Rusalki* on foot if they kept moving. The question was how long? With no supplies or ammo, he reasoned, long enough to make it to the depot or further. But what lay waiting for them there? Not to mention the risk of a wrong step. Maksin had proven that, as well.

Poor bastard, he thought again.

No, the tank was their best bet. At full speed, it was slower than a man running unencumbered, but faster than the things chasing them. Getting the big bitch moving, though...

He rolled out of his seat and moved to the back. The scratching and banging were louder here, as though the *Rusalki* could smell the men and child trapped inside. He looked around and saw Shlomo, feet propped up on the ammo can, dozing fitfully, a bullet in each ear.

Davyd stared dumbly. It was a simple, yet brilliant, solution, and one he should have thought of. A quick look at Laszlo and Biadula showed they'd followed Shlomo's example. Elga's ears were exposed, but her peaceful features and deep breathing proved she could sleep through just about anything.

They probably slept more than I did, Davyd grumbled, silently. He reached out and nudged Shlomo. The sniper blinked and yawned.

"Did you sleep?" Shlomo asked without preamble. "Because you look like shit."

"Not really and thanks," Davyd replied. "When I decided to shut down last night, I didn't think Maksin would try and run. I'm not sure the four of us can start the engine."

"Just have Biadula lean his fat ass on it," Shlomo said, with another yawn. "Ugh. What time is it?"

"Sunrise was a few hours ago, so probably close to nine," Davyd answered, pulling out a small pocket watch. He snapped it open, then nodded. "Close enough."

"In all seriousness, I think we can get it going," Shlomo said as he lowered his boots to the steel floor. He stood and stretched out the best he could within the cramped confines. "It'll be tough, though. I heard a crew of three got one started, once. Of course, you know how rumors are."

"Some *starshina* glared at it in the name of the *Rodina*?" Davyd asked, a slight smile on his greasy face. "I've heard that one before."

One of the *Rusalki* slapped the hull where Davyd was standing, killing what little joviality he felt. The creatures had managed to get fully under the tank. Never in his life had Davyd wanted to run something over with the massive metal beast as much as he did at the moment. He kept his calm, however, and looked over at the other bench. Elga was sitting up and watching them with a curious expression on her face.

"Good morning," Davyd said. "You slept well."

"We need to hurry," she said. Outside, the clawing and banging grew more frequent. "Time is running out."

"Let's wake the *Krasnyy D'yavol*," Davyd said and kicked Biadula's boot with his. "Hey! Time to get to work!"

"Damn it, Davyd," Biadula complained as he shifted on the bench. "I just got comfortable."

"We need to start the tank," Davyd told him.

"Can't do it with only four people," Laszlo said, sullenly, as he stared at the Ricardo engine. "Might as well do what Maksin did."

"What, die horribly?" Davyd looked at Laszlo, amazed. "We just need to outrun them to the depot and refuel. Eventually, they'll get tired of chasing us. Once we make it back to Barysaw, we're safe, and we've saved the *Rodina* from something worse than the Germans."

"So then what?" Laszlo asked.

"We worry about that then. For now, we crank this thing up and get out of here," Davyd said. "And comrade? I am not asking."

Laszlo started to say something but stopped as both Biadula and Shlomo stood up behind him. He looked back at the odd duo and shook his head.

"Fine." The man was stubborn but, apparently, not so blind he couldn't read the writing on the wall. "We get the tank started."

* * *

With the *Krasnyy D'yavol* rolling, it quickly became apparent to Davyd that he'd seriously misjudged their travel time. The road, just as muddy as the day before, now had deeper ruts and grooves from the tank's passage, forcing Davyd to adjust the throttle constantly to maintain traction. Moving off the road was worse. The one time he'd tried, the tank had come disastrously close to sinking into the soft tilled earth.

All of this meant that, instead of their top speed of five miles per hour, they barely made three. The *Rusalki* easily kept pace—regularly slapping the hull as though reminding the crew inside they were not alone.

This wasn't without risk for the monsters, however. The occasional telltale bump, followed by loss of traction as one of the cursed villagers became stuck in the treads, gave Davyd a sick flash of glee, followed by nausea. He tried not to envision the body becoming a gory, bloodied pulp as it was ripped open and crushed beneath the weight of the massive tank.

Shlomo, at some point, had elected himself lookout and moved to the front gunner's seat. As they lumbered along, he kept track of the *Rusalki*, monitoring their relative positions and speed. After a particularly rough stretch where Davyd had been forced to slow their progress drastically, Shlomo got up.

"Shlomo?" Davyd felt more than heard the sniper rummaging around just behind his seat. Half-turning, he looked back and saw Shlomo digging into the sea bag filled with ammunition they had pilfered from the fuel depot. The Mosin dragoon carbine rested across his bent knees. There was a look in the Jew's eyes that made Davyd very uncomfortable.

"We haven't pulled ahead far enough, and we can't let them keep harassing us," Shlomo said, grabbing fistfuls of rounds and stuffing them in his pockets. "I'm going to thin the herd."

After a moment, the sniper looked down and noticed how obscene his trousers looked. He muttered a curse under his breath and simply shouldered the repurposed sea bag. He almost lost his balance as he stood upright carefully and kept the barrel of the Mosin dragoon carbine pointed down.

"Shlomo…"

"I know, I know," Shlomo said, cutting him off. "This tank does not stop."

"…be careful," Davyd finished.

Shlomo stared, eyes seemingly focused on something over the horizon. Davyd recognized the look—he'd seen it on others' faces at the front just before a major action. The things following them, that had been friends and loved ones, were now twisted caricatures of their former selves. After a moment, Shlomo smirked, his mask slipping.

"Don't slam on the brakes this time," he said and climbed through the hatch.

Davyd's thoughts churned as he studied the road, comparing it to the map in his head. After a few seconds, he nodded.

"Biadula!" he shouted, looking over his shoulder.

Laszlo and Biadula sat as close to the engine as they could without burning themselves. The portly tanker looked up at him, confused. Davyd motioned for him, pointed to the driver's seat, and slipped into the front gunner's position. Scowling, Biadula did as instructed. Davyd looked out of the viewport, then leaned close and yelled in Biadula's ear.

"The road looks fairly clear here and doesn't turn for another mile or so. Watch closely, and if anything changes, signal me. Otherwise, sit here and don't touch anything!"

"What are you going to do?"

"I'm going to help Shlomo." Davyd clapped Biadula on the shoulder and climbed out.

Up top, Shlomo balanced himself on one knee and set the sea bag to his right. It was safe there, nowhere near the exposed treads of the *Krasnyy D'yavol*. He raised the ladder sight of the Mosin carbine and adjusted the distance. It was no more than fifty yards to the furthest *Rusalki*.

Davyd scrambled out of the hatch and crouched near the sea bag. He began to arrange the rounds in groups of five in his own pockets. It would make reloading the Mosin carbine easier. Shlomo eyed him warily.

"Who's driving?"

"Biadula," Davyd replied. Shlomo chuckled.

"You're never going to get the smell out of your seat."

"If we live through this, I'll worry about it then," Davyd said. "As long as he doesn't touch anything, we'll be fine. You shoot. I'll feed."

"I hope this carbine is in better shape than Comrade Kazmer," Shlomo said. "Watch your ears."

Davyd nodded, covering his ears as Shlomo brought the Model 1907 carbine to his shoulder and picked out his first target. From Davyd's perspective, the villager bore a resemblance to Adelina. For all he knew, it could have been the poor girl's mother. If Shlomo knew, he wasn't showing it. The sniper's eyes were distant again as he lined up his shot. Shlomo squeezed the trigger, and the rifle bucked against his shoulder.

Davyd saw the round strike where the woman's heart should have been. The shot *should* have killed her instantly, yet all it did was cause her to hesitate as she followed along behind the tank. After a few stumbling steps, she regained her balance and continued on. Davyd glanced over at the frowning Shlomo.

"You should be dead," Shlomo muttered, practiced hands working the rifle's bolt. Davyd shook his head, trying to clear his ringing ears. The first shot was always rough. After a while, however, the noise faded away. Shlomo shifted his sights slightly and fired again. This time, the woman's head rocked back as the round split it open. She staggered, fell to her knees, tried crawling a little further, then lay still.

"Yes! Nice shot, comrade!" Davyd pumped his fist, grinning, as hope and elation rushed through him. With Shlomo's skill and their remaining rounds, they could whittle the horde down to a manageable level.

Any joy he felt evaporated when the corpse twitched, then slowly rose to its feet once more. In mere seconds, it had resumed its plodding gait, no slower for the damage. It was clear that not even a headshot would put these abominations down.

"Keep shooting," Davyd said, silently cursing *Starshina* Popov. His policy of scrimping on ammunition to stretch fuel might kill them.

"*Jebać jaho*," Shlomo muttered and began firing. His next three rounds tore into the woman's lower body, leaving one leg ruined and the other simply *gone*. The *Rusalki* fell to the ground and struggled to follow the tank, dragging her remaining leg by a few shreds of skin and sinew. Even at the relatively slow speed the *Krasnyy D'yavol* was going, they quickly lost sight of the seemingly-possessed woman.

"Thank you, Comrade Kazmer," Davyd said, realizing what had inspired Shlomo's shots. If not for Popov's complete and utter idiocy, they could have easily stayed away from the *Rusalki* when the *Krasnyy D'yavol* had first arrived at the fuel depot. Shlomo ejected the empty magazine, accepted the next handful of rounds, and readjusted his aim.

"Can't walk without knees, can you?" Shlomo asked the closest *Rusalki*. After feeding ammo into the tube, he began firing at a quicker pace. One by one, the *Rusalki* fell, all missing at least one of their legs from the knee down, and some, both. It became a routine for the duo—Shlomo would fire five shots, five legs would be ruined. He would open the bolt action, and Davyd would pass him five more rounds. Lather, rinse, repeat.

As good of a shot as Shlomo was, however, the Mosin carbine only had limited ammunition. What had felt like a lot quickly turned into very little as more *Rusalki* fell. The sniper continued his grisly work, until Davyd had no more ammunition to offer him.

"Well…now what?" Shlomo asked as he looked at the Mosin in his hands. He lovingly stroked the wooden butt.

"The tank doesn't stop," Davyd reaffirmed. "You lowered their numbers."

"In a way." Shlomo shrugged as he looked down at the carbine in his hands. "This is a fine weapon. I'm surprised by how well it fired."

"Comrade Mosin made a good rifle," Davyd agreed.

Suddenly, the tank lurched down and to the left. Davyd managed to grab one of the railing bars next to the treads and kept from sliding into Shlomo. The sniper, however, was standing upright and stumbled when the tank shifted. He tried to use his foot to balance himself on the opposite rail bar but missed, snagging it on a tread. Horrified, Davyd reached out to grab Shlomo as his friend continued to slide sideways. The Mosin clattered against the hull as Shlomo reached for Davyd's outstretched hands.

Davyd's heart stopped as he clutched at empty space before snagging the cloth of Shlomo's sleeve. He blinked, surprised he had managed to save his friend. Shlomo coughed, laughed, and extended the butt of the carbine.

That was too close, Davyd thought as he reached for the rifle.

The tank lurched again.

Fireworks erupted before Davyd's eyes as his face slammed into the steel deck. Momentarily stunned, he could do nothing as his hand relaxed, allowing Shlomo to slip from his grasp. He lunged forward and reached out…

...and felt his friend's fingertips slide across his. Davyd stared in horror as Shlomo disappeared over the edge, carbine still in hand.

Davyd rose to his knees, stomach heaving. He bit down hard on the urge to vomit, forcing himself to take several deep, slow breaths.

Rise above it, detached, he thought. *Just like the front.*

He'd seen many horrible things in the war, often in the middle of a dangerous situation. Where other men had frozen, petrified by what was going on around them, he'd been able to do his duty by pulling back within himself. He felt it happening now as though he were a passenger in his own body.

Where is the current objective? Close. The fuel depot was just up the road.

How do we reach the objective? Keep moving forward.

What is the mission? Save the *Rodina*.

What is the value of life? Insignificant. Be it Shlomo, Maksin, Jan, Pyotr...hell, even Davyd, himself. No cost was too great for the Motherland.

"Davyd!" a panicked scream from inside the tank drew his attention. The heavyset tanker continued yelling for him. "Davyd! I do not know how to drive this fucking thing!"

"*Navoz*," Davyd growled. He crawled over to the rear hatch, slid in headfirst, flipped right-side up, and landed on the raised bench near Elga and Laszlo.

"Shlomo?" Laszlo looked up at him with a vacant expression. Davyd shook his head.

"He's in a better place now," Elga said, gently.

I'm losing my damn mind, Davyd thought, pinching the bridge of his nose.

There was no way he should have been able to hear what the little girl said, yet her words were as clear as a bell. He recalled times on the front when he'd been able to hear whispers just as loudly while in the middle of an artillery bombardment.

"Davyd!" Biadula shouted. "We're going to hit a tree!"

Davyd hurried forward and found Biadula staring at the levers, his face a mixture of confusion and terror. Pushing the other tanker aside, he looked out the viewport and saw a rather large pine tree, directly in their path. The tank's left tread had rolled through and over an overgrown ditch on the side of the road, pulling them off course—and causing Shlomo's death.

Davyd pulled the right lever back while keeping the left fully forward and turned sharply back onto the road. Once clear of the rut, he pushed both levers forward again. He watched carefully and waited until he was just past the center of the road before adjusting again and straightening out properly. He eased both levers ahead full, and the Mark V chugged onward.

Davyd took a deep breath and almost gagged.

"Christ Almighty, man," he said, glaring at Biadula. "I'd swear you shit yourself."

"Sorry," the gunner said sheepishly. "That time I did."

Davyd silently gave thanks for the early afternoon sun—not to mention the breeze—as he looked ahead. The mud had dried some, allowing him to run the *Krasnyy D'yavol* at full speed. They should be arriving...

"There! We made it!" Davyd called over his shoulder. In the distance, the depot's buildings crawled into view. He looked over at

Biadula. "Fuel depot coming up. I need you and Laszlo to prepare for refueling."

"But...those *things* are back there!" the tanker whined. Davyd smacked the other man across the face with the back of his hand, shutting him up.

"We have to escape, and the only way to do that is to refuel," Davyd reminded him. "Otherwise, we don't make it to the city. Do you want to take your chances on foot or in here?"

"Is it safe to refuel while the engine is on?" Biadula asked. Davyd shook his head.

"Probably not," he answered. "But since there's only three of us, there is no way we can get the engine cranked if we turn it off. Refueling takes two people, and we've seen you drive."

"But what if those things catch up to us?"

"Go in the back and check all of our ammunition for the machine guns," Davyd told him.

"One crate left," Biadula answered immediately.

"You certain?"

"You're good at your job; I'm good at mine."

"How many of those are tracers?"

"Uh..."

"Go check," Davyd told him as he focused on the road ahead. He slowed the tank a little to buy Biadula more time as a wretched, horrid plan began to take shape in his mind. The heavyset gunner hurried to the back to check. Davyd began muttering under his breath. "Just lure them in closer...like baiting a bear."

"About five hundred rounds left," Biadula said as he returned. He leaned against Davyd's seat so he wouldn't need to yell as loud.

"Shlomo didn't fire all of his. Every fifth round is a tracer, so one hundred or so?"

"That should be enough," Davyd acknowledged, glad he'd told Shlomo to conserve his ammunition. It might save them after all. "Did you tell Laszlo about the refueling?"

"He didn't look happy," Biadula admitted. "But he didn't say no."

"Good enough for me," Davyd said. "We're getting close. Be careful when filling the petrol tanks."

"I've done this once or twice," Biadula reminded him.

"When you first became a tanker," Davyd corrected. "You haven't done it since then because Popov always made Shlomo do it."

Biadula smirked but didn't argue the point. Instead, the portly tanker went back to prepare for the refueling process. Davyd carefully steered the tank as close to the refueling station as he could. Without Shlomo to guide him, however, he had to be extra careful lest he blow them all up by crashing into the above-ground storage container. Guessing where the proper spot was, he eased the levers back until the tank was no longer moving. Tricky part complete, it was now time to get down to the hard part—not getting them all killed.

"All right, go!" Davyd shouted over the steady idling of the engine. "Laszlo! Once you're finished, keep the petrol flowing! Don't shut off the fuel pump!"

"Are you insane?" Laszlo shouted back. "That could—"

"I know!"

"*I* don't know how you survived on the front!" Laszlo screamed as he climbed out. Davyd secured the levers before climbing out of his seat and hurrying to the rear. He peered out the gun slit but saw no sign of the *Rusalki*.

I hope Biadula was right about these tracer rounds, Davyd thought as he worked the remaining ammunition belt into place. He pulled back the charging handle and fed the cloth strap into the mechanism. He pulled it back a second time and chambered a round. The machine gun was ready.

Biadula and Laszlo worked to refuel the tank. Over the din of the engine Davyd could hear them arguing, but since they were not screaming about the *Rusalki* and the tank hadn't blown up yet, his plan was working. So far, at least.

Don't worry, Babushka, I'm not counting those chickens yet.

Davyd lined up the barrel of the gun on the above-ground storage container. It was large, possibly one of the biggest in Byelorussia, and contained somewhere close to fifty thousand gallons of petrol. Everyone knew the risks of such a large storage container. It was why smoking within one hundred feet was prohibited. Even Kazmer, who had violated every other rule in the book, had obeyed that one.

Now...where are those Rusalki?

Shlomo had put a dent in them, true, but for every one he'd slowed, four more had joined from the smaller, nearby villages, drawn to the sound of the large tank moving through the area. He needed them to be as close to the storage container as possible.

"Here they come!" Laszlo shouted. "We're done! Coming in!"

"Leaving the petrol flowing!" Biadula said. "Let's go!"

Davyd scrambled out of the rear gunner's position and moved to the front, passing by a very confused-looking Elga.

"Stay calm, little one." He tussled her hair as he passed. "And cover your ears. Things are about to get very noisy."

Biadula slid into the tank first, his boots landing heavily on the steel floor. Davyd grabbed him and turned him toward the rear gunner position.

"When I give the order, shoot the fuel container!" Davyd told him. Biadula's face paled.

"*What?!*"

"Just do it!"

"It'll kill us all!" Biadula protested.

"Maybe," Davyd acknowledged. "But we'll take them with us."

"You didn't see how many are after us, did you?" Biadula asked, before heading toward the rear gunner position. He stopped and looked back. "There are a lot of them."

Davyd moved aside as Laszlo came in next. The skinny tanker, reeking of petrol, glared at Davyd.

"We lived!"

"I noticed."

"Now what?"

"I need you to tell me when they're all gathered around us," Davyd told him. "I want to bring them in closer."

"Closer!?" Laszlo's eyes bugged out slightly. "You really are mad!"

"Yes, I am!" Davyd's grin felt borderline maniacal. "Tell me when they're all around us!"

"You should be able to tell yourself," Laszlo responded. "There must be thousands of them out there!"

"Thousands?" Davyd asked, horrified. He knew there were many small towns around the area, but he really hadn't known just how many people lived in his district. If the German gas had caused everyone around to become *Rusalki*, then the fuel containers and his plan might not be enough.

No, he decided, firmly. *It had to be enough.*

Davyd quickly secured the top hatch—which Laszlo had forgotten to do—before moving forward into his driver's seat. A quick glance out of his viewport told him all he needed to know. Laszlo had not been exaggerating when he said there were thousands swarming the *Krasnyy D'yavol*. It appeared that every single human being within one hundred miles was outside their tank, with more crowding into the fuel depot by the moment. They didn't move very fast but then neither did the *Krasnyy D'yavol*.

"They're all around us!" Laszlo screamed from the back. "We need to leave, NOW!"

It was as good a time as any. Davyd carefully shifted the tank into gear. The *Krasnyy D'yavol* moved forward, running over a few of the unfortunate souls who did not get out of the way. The pungent stench of petrol filled the tank. Davyd knew the fuel had spilled onto the back. He knew it would be pointless to hope it didn't catch fire, but there was the possibility the heat wouldn't get high enough to blow up the tank's internal fuel storage.

One hundred yards, then two hundred. They were still too close to the depot's fuel storage containers, but all the *Rusalki* were following the tank. None were in front, which meant—

"*Fire!*" Davyd screamed over his shoulder. Biadula let off a long burst into the smallest container. The rounds impacted, and petrol began to spill onto the ground. As the firing continued, a small flame erupted near the pooling fuel when one of the tracer rounds caught. The fire leapt to another puddle, and the flames quickly grew higher. The fire spread rapidly, and soon, a long flame was shooting out of the small container, very much like one of the hated German flamethrowers the men had feared so much.

A low rumbling sound could be heard as the fire grew. An unusual howling noise joined it off in the distance. Even over the roar of the engine and the treads outside, Davyd could hear it. Not knowing what it was, he instinctively continued to drive forward.

"Are we far enough away?" Davyd could barely hear Laszlo's high-pitched shout over the noise.

"I don't know!"

"Will we be caught in the explosion?"

"I don't know!"

"Are we going to make it?"

"I DON'T KNOW!"

"What if—"

"We keep driving, Laszlo! The tank does not stop!"

The tank does not stop, he repeated the mantra silently over and over again. *The tank does not stop.*

The howling sound grew louder. It was as though the earth, itself, was screaming in agony and pain from the damage being wrought upon it. Davyd had no idea what was making the noise, but he presumed it wasn't good. He threw the tank's levers forward all the way, and the speed slowly increased. The heat from the fire expanded. The howling, rumbling sound grew even louder until it was all Davyd could hear. It even drowned out the beating of his heart.

There was a bright flash, then the world exploded. The concussive blast wave rapidly caught up to the *Krasnyy D'yavol.* Davyd felt it through the thick armor of the tank.

Years before, his unit had taken fire from the German artillery. He'd huddled with the others, fearing the next explosion, and praying they'd be alive when another came. He found himself looking back on that experience fondly.

A secondary explosion rocked the rear of the tank, and for a moment, Davyd thought the main fuel tank had gone. Since he was still alive, he presumed it had not. But then what, precisely, had the second explosion come from?

The reserve tanks, he realized.

Chained to the back of the tank where the armor was thinnest, the reserve fuel tanks were filled with fifty gallons of highly flammable petrol. The tank had actually lifted a few inches off the ground as the force from the secondary explosion rippled through the armor. The 28-ton tank crashed back down to the ground, sending everyone in the back sprawling. Surprised, Davyd could only wait and see if they had thrown a track. If it had happened, the odds of their survival dipped from slim to zero. There was no way the three of them could change a tread track in the middle of nowhere without a team to assist.

Elga screamed loudly as the hot air washed through the tank. Davyd was protected up in the front, but he could hear the others cry out in alarm as the massive, expanding fireball from the fuel explosion heated the interior.

No, he realized. *Those aren't cries of pain from Biadula and Laszlo. Only Elga. Well, she is a child…it could be a cry of fear.*

"The heat hurts!" Elga cried out. Davyd turned in his seat and saw the young girl had covered her face and begun to weep. Either the child was hurt because of the heat wave which had crashed over them, or she'd injured herself when the tank had been lifted off the ground. Davyd couldn't help her, though. Not at the moment. Once they rounded the bend three miles north, it would be a straight shot to the base. Until then, he had to stay in his seat.

He needed to drive and keep driving.

The tank does not stop.

Davyd remained focused on the viewport in front of him, his world defined by the narrow slit. Nothing else mattered.

The tank does not stop.

Time passed—how much, he didn't know. Or care. As long as the machine continued moving. Miles disappeared beneath their treads. Night fell. Day broke. Davyd's eyes burned. The luxury of sleep was a distant memory. His sole purpose was driving.

The tank. Does not. Stop.

"Laszlo! What are you doing?" Davyd heard a loud cry from the back. It was Biadula yelling at Laszlo again. He ignored it. Their petty bickering didn't matter, only progress.

The. Tank. Does. Not. Stop.

"Davyd! Come back here and help me! Laszlo's trying to kill Elga!"

"Fuck." Davyd slipped the levers into neutral.

The tank stopped.

His atrophied muscles protesting, Davyd clambered from his seat and almost fell over. He was dizzy, but he managed to stay upright as he moved into the back. Sure enough, he found Laszlo holding Popov's small caliber pistol to Elga's head. The little girl had tears running down her face but otherwise was holding absolutely still. Laszlo's hand was steady, but his eyes were wild, crazy.

After everything they had seen and done the past few days, he could not blame his fellow tanker one bit. To lose it now, though, was the worst thing Davyd could think of. They'd survived against all odds. They had lived through an explosion bigger than anything he'd seen during the Great Patriotic War.

"Laszlo," Davyd said as softly as he could over the loud idling of the engine, "put down the pistol. Please *tovarisch*, it's not worth it. We're almost to Barysaw; this is almost over."

"I can't take it, Davyd." Laszlo's hand didn't waver, the pistol's muzzle pointing steadily at Elga's blonde head. "She's a *Rusalki*, the reason behind all this. You didn't see what happened when the heat hit the tank. I did. She can't hide it forever. If I kill her, it's over."

"Think about what you're saying, Laszlo. Are you really willing to kill her? She's no monster, just a scared little girl. You said yourself, she's your sister's daughter. How many times have you held her hand, swung her around, or bounced her on your knee? Look at her—really look at her," Davyd pleaded. "Tell me she isn't your niece."

Elga's eyes, brimming with fresh tears, never left Laszlo's face. To her credit, she faced him, though fear was written plainly on her features.

"Please, *dziadzka*, it's me…it's Elga. I'm scared."

Laszlo's jaw clenched, his finger tightening on the trigger. Davyd didn't breathe, couldn't move. He couldn't risk startling his friend.

"Please *dziadzka*…" Elga begged.

Laszlo's arm dropped, lowering the gun. He sank to the floor, tears rolling down his cheeks. His shoulders heaved as he began to sob.

"*Boishe moi*…what have I become?"

Elga crossed the distance between them and wrapped her arms around Laszlo's chest, snuggling in close. She wiped a tear from his cheek, smearing the days' old grime with her tiny thumb.

Laszlo stroked her hair with his left hand and softly kissed her forehead.

"Do you really think I'm a monster, *dziadźka*?"

"No little *sviaty*, you are no monster." Laszlo raised the pistol to his chin. "I am."

Davyd's ears rang with the sound of the shot. He stood in stunned silence as Laszlo's body toppled, seemingly in slow motion. Slowly, the ringing in his ears subsided and was replaced with Elga's screaming sobs. He lunged forward, scooping the little girl into his arms and pressing her face into his chest, and turned her away from the blood and brains sliding down the metal of the hatch. It took everything he had to choke back his rising gorge.

"How could he…she's his niece!" Biadula turned away to hide his tears. Davyd's chin rested on his chest. They had come so far only to fall so short.

No, Davyd thought. *Laszlo failed. We have not. We will not. The* Rodina *needs us.*

"*Samoubiystva*…he just…I don't know."

"*Chert*," Biadula's head bowed ever so slightly. 'May God have mercy on us. What do we do?"

"We drive," Davyd said, climbing into his seat. "This tank doesn't stop until we get to Barysaw."

"With his body just lying there? In the dark?" Biadula sounded terrified. "Why can't we stop and, I don't know, let him out?"

"This tank doesn't stop." Davyd threw the levers forward. The engine roared in response. *Krasnyy D'yavol* lurched forward, their destination awaiting them.

* * *

The day's waning tendrils of light showed them the way as they reached the main road into Barysaw.

"We're almost there, comrade! Not long now!" Biadula's face split into a toothy grin. Davyd felt his own smile forming but tried to stifle the elation bubbling up inside him. They were so close...

Then he saw it—the yellow cloud rolling across the field to his right.

"Masks on! Now! Seal the tank!"

He throttled back as much as he dared as Biadula poured the last of the vodka onto a rag before stuffing it into the driver's viewport. If there were any dead behind them, they would have a better chance of catching up, but it was a risk he had to take for the few seconds needed to cover the slit. As soon as Biadula finished, Davyd slammed the throttles forward.

Driving by feel was risky, however, less so on the road than in the fields. This section was relatively straight. He should be able to navigate the gentle turns at full speed by the texture under the treads.

"Come on *vozlyublennaya*, we can do this," Davyd murmured to the *Krasnyy D'yavol.* He took a quick look and saw Biadula helping Elga with her mask in between jamming more rags into every gap in the hull. There would be no way of knowing when the cloud had passed, not without compromising the seals. He prayed the cloud would pass them quickly, before they reached the guard station at the edge of town.

Time crawled, made worse by the narrow field of vision afforded by his mask. He checked his pocket watch—an hour had gone by. If his memory served, they were close to the gate. Davyd eased back on the levers.

"I need to check our location," he said. "I'll take a quick look from here and see if the gas is gone."

Carefully, slowly, so as not to dislodge the rag, Davyd pulled one corner free, opening his viewport slightly. He pressed a lens to the gap and tried to focus.

The unmanned guard station stood in front of them, approximately five yards from the idling machine, barrier raised. Behind it, the streets of Barysaw lay empty. Sunlight flared from distant windows, unhindered by anything in the air. The sun had almost completely disappeared beyond the horizon. Darkness loomed, but in the city, there were a few gaslights showing the way.

"I think we're through it," Davyd said, grinning behind his mask. "We're in Barysaw."

The tank's engine, as though in relief, sputtered into silence. What fuel they'd had, had just run out. Davyd turned to look at his comrade. Biadula was slumped on the bench, apparently sleeping, his mask pulled down around his double chin. His skin was coated with the yellow filth from the cloud. Davyd looked around and saw one of the rags had come loose and let the gas in. Horrified, he glanced down. The yellow filmy substance from the gas was on his exposed skin as well. He was completely covered, yet he hadn't noticed anything. He felt fine, however.

Was it the same as the stuff from the village? He couldn't be sure.

Something behind Davyd moved and caught his eye. Laszlo's clothing pulsed slowly in erratic yet familiar patterns. He had seen this before.

No, he thought, horrified. *We won! We escaped! How...?*

"We're where we need to be now?" Elga's voice was clear in the sudden silence. Davyd looked at the young girl. Her mask dangled from one small hand, spinning on its straps. Her arms and neck were coated with the remnants of the gas cloud. Like him, she appeared to be in good health. "Thank you for bringing us so far, Comrade. You saved us."

"Everyone is dead, little one. I haven't saved sh—anything. You, me—we touched the yellow gas. It's all over us. We did not turn into the mindless things, the *Rusalki*. Why? Where do we go from here? I don't understand any of this."

"I don't either," Elga said. The child-like innocence of her tone trembled slightly with fear. Bravely, she pushed on. "What's over that hill? The worst is surely behind us."

"The only thing behind us are those creatures," Davyd muttered softly, his eyes gazing distantly into the empty town. "Probably what's in front as well. Maybe...maybe Laszlo had the right idea. How can we survive in this sort of world?"

A tiny, warm hand slipped into his. Looking down, Davyd saw Elga looking up at him. She was smiling. Timid, yet there. It wasn't much, but it was enough to remind him there was much to fight for. Lives could still be saved. The *Rodina* could still fight this new, mysterious enemy. The cloud was dangerous. However, not to all. Elga was alive, as was he. Plus, they could fight those who had succumbed to the cloud. The *Rusalki* hadn't been able to survive the explosion at the fuel depot. The heat and flames had been too much. Why though?

He didn't have an answer. Not yet, at least. However, he did have one idea. One which could help keep them alive longer while they tried to contact central command.

"The weapons depot isn't too far, Elga," Davyd murmured as he gently squeezed the little girl's hand. "We'll find something there that could help."

"Something can help?" Elga asked, her voice hopeful. "What is it?"

"You probably never heard of them before, but we call them 'flamethrowers' in the army…"

"Then what?"

"Then we hide and stay alive until the army comes to save us. Fight when we have to but mainly just…wait. Survive."

"You think they will come? The army?"

"Yes," Davyd answered with complete honesty. "I believe they will. And when they come, there will be a reckoning on these fallow fields."

* * * * *

Christopher L. Smith Bio

A native Texan by birth (if not geography), Chris moved 'home' as soon as he could.

He attended Texas A+M where he learned quickly that there was more to college than beer and football games. He relocated to San Antonio and attended SAC and UTSA, graduating in late 2000 with a BA in Lit. While there, he met a wonderful lady who somehow found him to be funny, charming, and worth marrying. (She has since changed her mind on the funny and charming).

Christopher began writing fiction in 2012. His short stories can be found in multiple anthologies, including John Ringo and Gary Poole's Black Tide Rising, Mike Williamson's Forged In Blood, Larry Correia and Kacey Ezell's Noir Fatale, and Tom Kratman's Terra Nova.

Christopher has co-written two novels, Kraken Mare with Jason Cordova, and Gunpowder & Embers with Kacey Ezell and John Ringo.

His cats allow his family and their dogs to reside with them outside of San Antonio.

# # # # #

The Reservoir by Kevin Fritz Fotovich

"I don't wanna be here today any more than you do!"

"It's Sunday! I don't care if we get extra pay!" Jerry exclaimed from the passenger seat. Jack parked his truck in the foreman's parking lot of the Dodge City Reservoir Dam construction site on an early, already too-warm, July morning. "Shit, dude! How did we get roped into this?"

"Um...they asked who wanted to work for extra pay on their off day, and we raised our hands?" Jack replied and laughed while he unbuckled his seatbelt.

"Don't remind me," Jerry responded. He drew a resigned breath, undid his seatbelt, and exited the truck. His head was pounding, and he grumped as they made their way inside. "Remind me not to drink with you and Taylor again on a work night, especially the night before one of the hottest days of the year."

"Oh, c'mon now. It's not that bad. I wouldn't call walking around the reservoir perimeter physically taxing labor," Jack said. He turned toward the construction site and pointed to the edge of the reservoir while tracing its shape in the air. "We walk the perimeter, double-check the berm and embankments, make sure the 'rete is setting as expected, and sign off that all is well. We'll be done before it hits 100 degrees. Beer by two."

Jerry plugged both fingers in his ears and scrunched up his eyes. "Just! Shut! Up!" They both laughed, and he followed Jack into the site. When they approached the security booth, Jerry was surprised to see his friend working. "Good morning, Officer Solgeo," he said, smiling. They approached the booth and presented their badges to the pretty brunette to inspect. "What are you doing here? You're not one for working on off days. Explains why we missed you at Jack's place last night."

"Good morning, troublemakers," Stacy replied with a grin. "And you can call me Captain Solgeo, thank you very much," she said with a smile. The security gate clicked and started to open. "Sorry I couldn't make it last night. Unlike you young'ns," she said sarcastically, "I actually need sleep before spending all day sitting in a shack on what is promising to be a very unbusy day." She was only a couple years older, but age had become the kind of thing friends teased each other about. She paused as she leaned out the window to look at the clear, blue, morning sky. "It is supposed to be a very hot off day. To answer your question, though, none of my officers volunteered to work today. So, I'm here because I won't force somebody to do what I won't do myself."

"Fair enough," Jack said. "Next time then, which is next Saturday night. The game is not the same without you."

"I'll be there," she said. "You two stay safe and hydrated. It's gonna be a hot one today."

"Yes ma'am, Captain ma'am," Jerry responded with a chuckle and a lazy salute with his right hand as he quickly passed through the gate. They walked to the equipment shed to put on their safety gear, grabbed a couple of digipads, and headed to the project site.

Both men, who were in their late twenties and single, had been lured to the Dodge City settlement by the promise of work. Jack Chapman was tall, lanky, and physically fit. He was black and hailed from the southeast sector of the North American Region. Jerry Morgan was white with brown hair, shorter than Jack but just as strong. He'd grown up outside Dodge City in a ruined 'burb not too far out from the city, itself.

Sixty-five years earlier, Earth had suffered the catastrophic Trimmudian rock-slaught after first contact went horribly wrong. *That* war ended when the Trimmudians and the Terrans signed the Bernard's Star Intragalactic Peace Treaty. The catastrophic damage done by the asteroid-based kinetic weapons was widespread, but even then, some regions fared better than others. With peace declared, grievances over resources and where to rebuild led to the twenty-year-long Global Civil War. With the conclusion of hostilities, the United Earth government started rebuilding in earnest.

Finally, four years ago, the United Earth had officially announced that Dodge City was one of the final 100 2BES—To Build a Better Earth for its Survivors—Projects. It had been a long slog as Terrans everywhere rebuilt. But there was plenty of work, and Jack and Jerry had joined the new project as manual laborers. They had both been promoted to team leads with crews, responsibilities, and first crack at overtime.

As they approached the edge of the three-kilometer-long berm, Jerry said, "Ya know, I just don't get the need for a complete 'Human Eyes' inspection for this work. I mean, really, the drones are out checking this stuff at least once a week. And they do it faster than we can. Can't we just check the video footage and inspect any possible problem areas? It's not like our teams are slackers and shit."

"Yeah. True. I see what you're sayin,'" Jack responded as he kicked a pebble toward the edge of the berm. It bounced over the rim and rolled down the steep, fifty-meter embankment. "But them's the rules. It's in the contract. A lead has to do it, so it might as well be us; especially since we both wanted the overtime. Anyway, I heard you in the other room last night talking about finishing your grandad's porch. I missed the story, but everyone was laughing. What was so funny?"

"Ohhh…" Jerry replied with a small laugh. "So, you know I finished rebuilding Grandad's porch a few weeks ago. I showed up last week to paint it, and he was waiting on me with these two old ass cans of paint he wanted to use. I don't know what Grandad was thinking, but I painted the porch the way he wanted it, and he was very happy when I was done. I sent my Mom a pic of the new porch. Not even a minute later, she called, screaming at me, 'Oh, my God, Jerry! Do not leave the deck that color!' To which I responded, as calmly as I could without laughing, 'It's the color Grandad wanted, Mom.' She replied, a little bit calmer, 'You have got to paint it a different color. You can't leave it like that!'

"I told her, 'Mom…Grandad is 80 plus years old. He's a child of the rock-slaught, he survived the hunger era. He fought in the Global Civil War, he stormed the Sands of the Western Front in the very first wave! He was a Southern Baptist who fell in love with an east coast Catholic and changed his religion to marry his love. They moved into and survived the Overlord Badlands, raised four kids, and had lots of grandkids and countless greats. He's done his duty, rebuilding and repopulating this poor, tortured planet, and if he wants his back porch to be hot pink, then by God I will paint his back porch hot pink!'"

"You did not!"

"Yes, I did! And hot pink it stayed. For three days—until Grannie made me paint it brown."

"Oh, my God, I bet your Mom was pissed!" Jack said, laughing hard. "Holy shit, Dude. That's rich."

The ground beneath his feet buzzed, and he froze.

"Did you feel—?" he asked, but Jerry's wide eyes told him he'd detected the tremors too. They rushed to the edge of the unfinished berm as the buzzing grew into a distinct rumble. They were, perhaps, a quarter way across the dam. Farther out, toward the center of the fifty-meter tall berm, the earthworks were obscured by a cloud of dust.

The cloud was getting…closer?

Though obscured by the dust cloud, Jack could see the structure released a 'rete boulder the size of Jack's truck, which tumbled into the open air below the dam and plummeted. It could only mean one thing.

"Run!" Jack shouted and fled. Jerry was slower to react. Jack's long legs drove him far ahead of his friend as he raced to escape the collapsing berm. The rumble became a roar. Jack's heart hammered in his ears, and his feet pounded like pistons. He was halfway back to the safety of the bank when he glanced over his shoulder and caught one last glimpse of Jerry as the dust cloud swallowed him. Then Jack tripped, bashed his chin on the hard 'rete surface, and saw stars. In the few seconds it took him to regain his feet, the dust swarmed around him, blinding him and filling his ears, nose, and throat. Then the ground disappeared.

* * *

Search and rescue found Jack Chapman's and Jerry Morgan's shattered bodies days later, still wearing their high-vis safety vests. Dr. Kurk Daniel and his second, Dr. Neil DuCote, notified the next of kin.

* * *

Neil sat on one of the long pews close to the door in the back of the gallery of the Midwest Sector Senate hearing room.

I should have gotten here earlier. I should have known this was going to be a media circus. The netlinks are flooded with articles about this cluster grope. Still, I didn't think so many reporters, and whoever the rest of these people are, would be here for this.

He didn't have the best view of the hearing. He could only see Kurk's shock of white hair over the heads of the people sitting in front of him. The hearing chamber, with its tall ceilings, had horrible acoustics that amplified the cacophony of nearly one hundred people quietly chattering and typing notes on their digipads. The slight hum of three video drones floating above the forum, combined with the noise of the journalists, grew to a dull roar.

They are going to eat Kurk alive. I should be by his side. Neil rubbed his bearded chin. He knew the first day of the tribunal was going to be hell. As far as he was concerned, they'd designed the hearings to find a fall guy for the accident.

Bahm! Bahm! Bahm!

The room fell silent, except for the soft buzzing of the floating video drones. The tribunal chairman, Senator Greg Bissel, set the gavel down. Senator Bissel represented the North American Region's

Senate for the Midwest, and he was Chairman of the Ministry of Environment and Rural Affairs.

Considering the Midwest was North America's breadbasket and grew sixty-four percent of the food that kept the rest of the continent alive, he was a very important person. He sat behind a raised, ornate, wooden desk and was flanked on each side by pairs of well-dressed men and women. The five of them imperiously gazed down at Kurk and his lawyers.

As the clamor died down, Senator Bissel began speaking. "Today, at the eighth hour of the twentieth day of September in the year 2417, I do hereby bring to order these proceedings. We will hear from Dr. Kurk Daniel, the engineering manager of the Dodge City 2BES Project. We are hoping his testimony will help shed light on the cause of the catastrophic events at the Dodge City Reservoir Dam. This catastrophe, sadly, claimed the lives of two people. Welcome, Dr. Daniel."

"Thank you," Kurk said. His voice was a deep baritone and carried the confidence of a man who'd been in charge of some very important projects for most of his sixty-eight years. Neil had worked for Kurk for a decade on two earlier 2BES Projects. The senior engineer was a laconic man who wasted nothing, words included. *I just hope the words he uses today get him out of this mess.*

"Dr. Daniel, you are the Chief Engineering Director of the North American Region for the United Earth's Civil Engineer Corp, commonly referred to as the C-E-C. You were promoted to this position due to your extensive experience and knowledge of civil engineering design and practices. You are also the Chief Engineer for the UE's Dodge City 2BES Project. You have worked with the CEC for thirty-four years and were the chief engineer on two other 2BES Projects before the current one. Is that correct?"

"Yes."

Just yes? Really? Come on, boss. You could have at least followed with Mr. Chairman. This thing just started. Show them the respect they deserve, just like we practiced.

"You graduated with an engineering degree from the University of New Huntsville at the age of twenty, received a Master's Degree in civil engineering three years later from Albany University, and went on to earn multiple doctorates in civil and engineering mechanics. You helped found the study of applied xenotechnology in the civil, mechanical, and electrical engineering fields. You helped develop courses in these fields that are now taught in universities and institutions around the globe. You have personally championed the blending of Trimmudian and Terran technology for three decades. Is this also correct?"

"No."

"No?"

"I began studying Trimmudian engineering practices while still working on my undergrad degree, shortly after the Trimmudian and Terran Intragalactic Peace Treaty was signed, and what I learned upended everything I'd been taught about civil engineering. I published my first peer-reviewed paper on Trimmudian xenotechnology's possibilities in 2376. It's therefore been forty-one years, not thirty."

"Uh…right." Bissel stumbled, reviewed his notes, and forged on. "Would you say the techniques and technologies you used in your engineering designs, throughout your many years of service, are higher quality than the industry standard?"

"Yes."

"Can you expand on this?"

"Yes."

His answer was followed by silence. Three seconds later, someone in the gallery cleared their throat, and everyone heard it.

"Dr. Daniel," Bissel said, a touch annoyed, "Please do so now."

"Gladly, Senator Bissel." Neil knew that tone. Kurk most definitely was not glad. "The Trimmudian construction techniques and technologies we have infused with our own have allowed us to build stronger structures in a much quicker timeframe…"

"I didn't ask you about the timeframe, Dr. Daniel," Bissel interrupted. "I asked you to expand on the quality of the product. Please expand on the difference of the quality of product you employ now versus what you used at the beginning of your career."

Neil knew Kurk hated being interrupted, and this questioning tactic was the reason Neil had insisted on spending plenty of time preparing for this hearing. Neil moved a little closer to the edge of his seat and attempted to get a better view of Kurk. *You got this, Kurk. We practiced this.*

After a momentary lull, Kurk calmly responded, "Yes. Without fifteen years of studying molecular physics, metallurgy, chemical processing, and the xenotechnology courses I drafted, the easiest way to sum it up is: Terran technology is akin to a horse and trolley, while Trimmudian tech is like a hover jet. The Trimmudians rebuilt in record time after *our* rock-slaught attack on their homeworld because of how they manufacture their construction materials. They grow their building materials at the molecular level using chemical soups that do not, can not, exist on Earth, except in very tightly controlled laboratory conditions. Very expensive laboratory conditions. But it's worth it because the Terran alternative is welded rebar and poured concrete. On this scale, projects like the Dam take decades to dry deep within their core structure. The first project I managed is still drying, even today, while the surface is pitted, weathered, and crumbling, because of the limitations of human materials. Infused Trimmudian tech is stronger, lighter, more durable, more easily handled on-site, and generally superior in every way that matters. Is that clear enough for you, Mr. Chairman?"

The gallery, including Neil, busted out laughing. Bissel banged his gavel and brought the laughter under control. He and the other four committee members were not pleased with the outburst from the gallery.

"If the audience is unable to control themselves, we will clear the room and continue these proceedings behind closed doors," Bissel declared sternly. He looked down at Kurk and continued, "Now...Dr. Daniel." He paused for a moment. "You're saying this infused technology is far superior to anything that was available on Earth just a few short decades ago."

"Absolutely."

"These are technologies and techniques you have championed and used for most of your career and have implemented in the 2BES Projects you have managed."

"Once the 'authorities' accepted that I understood the processes and material better than they did, yes. Until I received that approval, I was compelled to stick with all-Terran tech."

"How do you explain, then, how a five-point-three magnitude earthquake leveled a dam that didn't have any water behind it yet?"

"I can't. Yet."

Raising his voice, the chairman shot back, "That's your answer? You can't?"

"Yet."

In a calmer voice, the chairman replied, "Of course." He paused, then picked up and shuffled a small stack of papers in front of him. He continued, "The investigation is still incomplete, but I have read some preliminary results. You have built two other dams using these hybrid technologies that are supposed to withstand magnitude ten-point-oh earthquakes but have never been tested. Neither dam has been hit by any type of earthquake to date. Dodge City's location in the Midwest Sector isn't any more earthquake-prone than the European Region's Northern Sector or the North American Region's East Coast Sector where you built those megastructures. What do you suppose might happen, Dr. Daniel, to the city settlements of Passau and Wilmington that use those dams to hold back massive amounts of water when, not if, their dams are tested by an earthquake, and your technology fails?"

"They won't fail."

"Really, Dr. Daniel? Are you really sure about that? Or are you refusing to accept that nearly a million lives are at risk because of the construction technologies and techniques you chose to use? Technologies and techniques that have already claimed two lives. How many more lives need to be lost before you're ready to admit the technology isn't quite up to the Trimmudian 'hover jet' standard you claim it is?"

Neil sank back into his hard, wooden seat as he heard the questions and saw the faces of the five committee members staring down at Kurk. The real point of these hearings suddenly hit him. *How the hell did we not see this coming? They don't care about the loss of life. Shit. This isn't even about the technology. They're gonna screw him to try to challenge our alliance with the Trimmu.*

* * *

The following morning, Neil caught the first air transport from Colorado Springs to Dodge City. Ninety minutes later, his flight landed, and twenty minutes after that, he was in his office at the DC 2BES Project headquarters.

A daunting row of double-stacked boxes, containing years of paperwork, lined the base of the wall next to his desk. As he pondered where to start, there was a knock at the door.

"Captain Solgeo?"

"Morning, sir. I—" The security officer looked embarrassed for a second, then composed herself. "Jack and Jerry were friends of mine. I saw the broadcast of the hearing. Dr. Daniel called me earlier and told me why you were heading home this morning. If you're hunting for whoever killed them, I want to help."

He thought about her offer for a moment, and glanced at the boxes representing the gargantuan task before him. The math on the infused Trimmudian tech was solid. The dam couldn't have failed without being sabotaged. The safety investigation still hadn't revealed the cause of the failure and having a suspicious security officer with investigative training could be quite helpful in identifying evidence supporting the saboteur theory. Obviously, Kurk trusted her, which settled the issue for Neil. He had to trust her, not to mention he was thankful to have an extra set of eyes on the team.

"Welcome." He gestured to a second desk and picked up the first of several boxes labeled 'Employees.' Together, they began reviewing the background checks of all employees hired from day one.

* * *

It was well into the evening before they finished reading all the files in the box. By the time dinner was over, they had flagged six files. The one on top was labeled 'Nathan Hill.' His employment history indicated he had worked with the CEC for many years. Prior to the Dodge City 2BES Project, he had been a laborer on the Phase Two land reclamations.

Neil reached for his desk phone, hit the speaker button, and dialed Kurk's number.

Before the second ring, Kurk picked up and said, "Hello, Neil."

"Good evening, boss." He knew his boss liked to keep things brief, so he cut to the chase. "Solgeo is here helping me review personnel files. There are six we have questions about. The first belongs to a foreman named Nathan Hill. Nothing in his file indicates he had the experience, let alone the expertise, to be hired as foreman. However, his record shows you hired him. Do you know something about his previous work experience that is not in his records?"

"The short answer is 'no.'"

"What's the long answer, Kurk? Why'd you hire the guy?"

"I didn't have much choice, Neil. After I took on the project, I was told to bring him on board as, at least, junior management. He wasn't hired for his skills. He was hired for his…contacts, or rather, his uncle's contacts."

"What?" Neil got up from his chair, walked around his desk, and started pacing. "You're just now letting me know this, Kurk?" Frustration quickly boiled up inside him as he continued, "Don't you think you should have brought this up last night?"

After a momentary pause, Kurk continued, "I didn't bring up Nathan earlier because he couldn't have been responsible. I kept extremely close tabs on him. Everything he ordered, jobs he completed, and anything he did or touched were scrutinized by me."

Stacy cut in. "What? How much scrutiny are we talking about?"

"A lot. This isn't the first time I've had to deal with nepotism. You're right. Mr. Hill and, I suspect, the other five you identified, absolutely did not have the skills needed for the jobs they were hired to do. But I ensured they had the proper training to excel in their work. They all exceeded my expectations. Since Nathan was a lead, I paid special attention to him. I double-checked all orders and shipments, incoming and outgoing, he touched. I inspected and signed off on all work completed by him and his crew until I was thoroughly comfortable with his working without supervision. I didn't let up on the reins until early this year. Until then, there was nothing he did that I didn't sign off on."

"You did this for over three years?" Neil asked.

"Yes. Hiring him was beyond my control but training him was well within my authority. It's not his fault he was a pawn in the political game of ineptotism."

"What?" Stacy laughed. "Did you say inept-otism?"

"Yes. It's what I call having to hire a worker who is totally inept for the job they're hired to do. The only real qualification they have is being related to somebody who has the local contacts and means to help make a project a success. In Mr. Hill's case, it was his uncle, a former warlord from the Overland Badlands. They were hammered in the rock-slaught but came out on the other side somewhat intact and sided with the winners in the civil war."

Neil sank back in his chair, letting the information Kurk had just given him sink in. He looked at the files on his desk, then the box of files he'd spent the day reading, and said, "Well, shit. That brings us back to square one. We spent the entire day going through personnel jackets, every single one of them. Nothing raised a flag except these guys."

"Keep at it, Neil. You'll find something. I assure you Nathan is a good kid. And a good foreman. If he was a problem on the site, you would have noticed. You sign the assessments, you authorize promotions. Now that I think about it, I believe you recommended one of his team members for a promotion six months after you arrived. Who he's related to is not Nathan's fault. He may have some sketchy blood in his veins, but he's his own man. He's no saboteur. If I had thought, even for a moment, he was, I assure you, I would have said something."

"Alright." Neil eyeballed the row of boxes and gave a long, heavy sigh. "If you say so. We've got lots more work to do, so I'm going to let you go. If we find anything, I'll contact you in the morning. Speaking of which, good luck tomorrow."

"And good luck to you two as well." The phone speaker clicked as the call ended.

Neil silently stared at the open box of folders on his desk for a minute. "Alright, fine. You and your cronies have been given the all-clear, Mr. Nathan Hill. The boss says so." *Wait. Your cronies.* He flipped through the folders and found the one for Daniel Whitehead. He looked at Stacy. "I recommended Daniel Whitehead for promotion but did Kurk give him the same special attention he gave Nathan? Leads are responsible for certain jobs and signing off on work as it's completed." Neil located the boxes labelled 'Shipping and Receiving,' and Stacy helped him move them to the middle of the office.

* * *

298 | IBSON & KENNEDY

By one a.m., they'd searched through the contents of seven boxes of paperwork, covering four years of material deliveries, and set aside all the records for materials ordered and received by Nathan and Daniel. Nathan's stack was taller than Daniel's. Every single one of Nathan's orders had Kurk's initials on it.

Daniel's receipts, on the other hand, did not.

"Alright, that's all of them," Stacy said as she closed the last box. "Should we go through them individually?"

"Yes. But first," Neil said as he picked up an empty mug, "more coffee." They were both three mugs in when Neil noticed something odd.

Dates, fine...foundation materials from CEC ReteWorks, fine...delivered from UE 2BES Materials, fine...received by Daniel Whitehead, fine...transit distribution, NettWorks Transport, typo..." Neil stared at the sheet for a moment. "Huh..."

"What's that?" Stacy asked.

"NettWorks Transport. This was signed by Rich Doty, the Yard Materials Manager. Rich doesn't normally make typos, but he spelled NettWorks with two Ts."

"I spotted a couple like that too," Stacy said. She rifled through the stack of receipts she'd just reviewed and found two order slips with the same typo: *NettWorks*, not *NetWorks*. "Typo, huh?" Neil scanned the remaining stack and found one more receipt with the same error.

"Let's see..." he said as he set the four pieces of paper side-by-side in front of him on his desk station. He compared the materials manager's signature on the receipts with typos to a randomly selected sample without typos and determined the signatures matched. He set the random receipts aside and focused on the four questionable ones.

"Looks like Rich wrote these up. Of course, he did. I don't think he's ever missed a day of work." He scanned each sheet and said, "Alright, then, what else? Let's see, the signatures all match…all four orders were for foundation supplies…they were all received back in…hmmm…" he said as he checked the dates. "Each of these shipments was a week apart."

He turned to his desk and pulled up a calendar from two years earlier. He checked the dates and said, "And those dates were Fridays. So, Mr. Up-n-Up," he said in a snarky voice referring to Daniel, "this typo regarding transports not listed as NetWorks delivering foundation supplies on the days before overtime weekends is awfully consistent."

Stacy, who covered gate access, pulled up her duty rosters from that month on her portable workstation. "Let's see…Daniel Whitehead…of course, you volunteered for overtime that weekend…that weekend…that weekend…and…that weekend too! And look who volunteered to work with you on the same weekends—Mr. Hill."

Neil had Stacy review Daniel and Nathan's access logs while he pulled up their overtime claims. After a quick review, he smiled and said, "Really, gentlemen, you both seem to like overtime. Well, work-week overtime anyway." He paused as ran his finger down the screen to double-check the records. A few minutes later, he said with confidence, "But the two of you only volunteered to work weekend overtime these four times. How convenient, gentlemen."

He pulled up the material yard's manifest records for those weekends. "OK, let's see. We know who actually received these shipments and loaded them into the yard. Let's find out who scanned these particular materials for use." Less than a minute later, he said, "As expected. Still, coincidences happen, so let's see how often Friday shipments actually get used the day after they arrive." A minute later, he grinned at Stacy. "Answer: pretty much never."

"And that," Stacy said, "is what we in the biz call a clue."

* * *

Neil opened his eyes as he raised his head up from his desktop and straightened himself up in his chair. He forced several hard blinks and shook his head. "Damn. Whoooh. Wake up, Neil!" He continued shaking his head. He looked at the clock on the wall across from him. It read: 9:06 a.m. *I think...* He paused as he tried to figure out how long he had slept. *Uuuumm... about four hours? Nine o'clock...that's...*

"Damnit!" *The hearings had already started!*

He placed his hands on the edge of his desk and pushed his chair back far enough to give himself room to stand. He picked up his jacket from the back of his chair and retrieved his personal mobile from the inside pocket. He held the device in front of him and saw the green message indicator light blinking. "Notifications," he said, instructing the mobile to open the message center. *Three missed calls from Kurk. All within the last hour.* "Great. Just great." He checked his desk phone and saw that he had missed a call at 7:55 a.m. *I slept through them all.* He checked both devices for audiomail. *He didn't leave a voice-rec.* But he'd received a digitext from Kurk on his mobile at 8:58 a.m. "Open message from Kurk." The message read: "Day 2 is about to begin. I hope your day is more productive than mine will be. Stay safe." *Will do boss. And thanks for waking me up.*

He called Captain Solgeo, who answered on the third ring. "Be there in five."

She sounded more chipper than he felt, but she worked security and investigations. This kind of sleuthing was squarely in her wheelhouse. She'd looked positively giddy when she'd headed home at 4 a.m.

The coffee had just finished brewing when Solgeo barged in. She had a double espresso in one hand and a box of coffee in the other. She chuckled when she saw him pouring his first cup. "Keep the pot on; we're gonna need a lot of fuel today. What's first?"

"Let's check the video logs from the dates Mister Whitehead received these mystery NettWorks shipments and see who made the deliveries. It's not like Rich to misspell the delivery trucks' company names."

Solgeo logged into her security system and pulled up the video archive for the material yard's loading zone. They searched for the date and time of delivery from the first delivery receipt, queued up the footage, and pressed play.

"Son. Of. A. Holy shit..." he slowly said as he felt a rush of adrenalin. The screen displayed a transport with a long white container that had a NetWorks logo on the side but was spelled NettWorks. As Stacy saved a print of the screen, Neil smiled and said, "Thank you, Mr. Rich Doty! Your most excellent attention to detail has been noted!"

The three remaining video files included the same bogus truck with the same bogus logo. The captain captured screen prints for each of the deliveries. Neil asked aloud, "So, what was delivered?" *Whatever was unloaded had to appear legit; anything out of place would have been immediately flagged.*

He backed his chair away from his desk, started gently spinning it around with his feet, and let his head tilt back. As he stared at the revolving ceiling, he reviewed their investigation thus far. "Whitehead and Hill don't work weekends. But these four weekends, they did. On four Fridays in a row, they received bogus shipments from NettWorks who was supposed to deliver infused Semigrow Starter foundation materials. *Nice job on the logo, by the way.* Whitehead received the material, and both he and Hill used the same material the very next day. These four weekends are the only four times on record where the material was delivered and used one day apart. Suspicious."

Solgeo grinned. "Very suspicious."

He stopped spinning his chair. "Mobile, write DigiText to Kurk Daniel: I know you're busy. But go use the bathroom or something. I need to talk to you! Now! End. Send."

Four minutes later, his mobile rang. "Accept call. Speaker."

"Good Morning, Neil. I've got very limited time, so make this quick."

"You said you inspected and signed off on all work Nathan completed. We've discovered significant irregularities in the work he and Daniel Whitehead did on weekend overtime. I know exactly when, but I need to know what and where. I know you kept records. Where are they, and how can I access them?"

After a few seconds of silence, Kurk let out a long breath. "You'll find everything at my desk station." Stacy nodded and flashed him a thumbs up. "You'll need my security codes, but I'm not sending them by text. Write these down, and don't use a digi." He gave Neil the security codes and information needed to access his personal security drives on his office's desk station.

"Got it. And thank you. I'll send you a summary as soon as I can."

"Neil, are you sure?" Kurk asked. After a brief pause, he continued, "About him? Them?"

"Yes," Neil answered confidently. "They knew you were keeping tabs on Nathan. I promoted Whitehead; he was their workaround. They planned for it."

After a few seconds of silence, Kurk said, "I've got to go, Neil. Good work. And thank you."

"You're welcome, boss."

* * *

As he suspected, the work Hill and Whitehead had done those four weekends had created the epicenter of the collapse. Whatever they'd used wasn't the infused Trimmudian Semigrow material the dam called for. A call to the demolition administrator confirmed their examination of the shattered material was out of a facility in Great Bend. The investigation teams were effectively rebuilding the structure but laid out on the ground instead of upright. Stacy had used her credentials to demand transponder tracking data for the transports hauling rubble, and he'd co-signed the authorization. Seven of the transports hauling away remnants of the ruined dam had deviated from the standard path and stopped at the Kinsley Fuel Hub for ten to twelve minutes, then continued to Great Bend. Those seven were hauling debris from the quadrants corresponding to the location of the foundation work Whitehead and Hill had done.

"Another clue." Stacy grinned. With two leads, they'd split up. Stacy would investigate NettWorks' bogus transports and try to identify the loads and where they had been picked up. Neil would go to the only fuel hub in the township of Kinsley. The pair locked down their workstations, reloaded their coffee cups, and headed out.

Forty minutes later, Neil slowed and pulled his transit into the Kinsley Fuel Hub. *So, this is it. This is where you covered your tracks.* He drove around the property, getting the lay of the land. The fuel hub consisted of the main store building located in the front, center of the multi-acre lot, four covered personal transit fueling stations out front, two much taller fuel stations for commercial and freight transports behind. An additional building with three large bay doors sat at the back of the lot, apart from the much busier fuel hub. A sign mounted above the three bay doors read, "Kinsley Transport Repair." *Looks like the DC project has been good for them.* The station was in good shape, with lots of recent upgrades and refurbishments.

After circling the lot, he brought his transit back to the front of the hub center. He parked in an available spot located on the west side of the building where he could see the repair shop as well as through the windows in into the building in front of him. He turned off the vehicle, let go of the steering wheel, set his hands on his lap, and paused for a few moments and took a few deep relaxing breaths.

Here, at this location, this hub, in a few quick minutes, those materials were offloaded. They had to go somewhere. I have no hard proof of sabotage. All I have is circumstantial evidence. If I present my case with the little information I have, they'll just see a guy trying to save Kurk's bacon. He picked up his mobile and checked for any new messages from Stacy. There were none. *Apparently, she hasn't found anything yet.*

"Gotta start somewhere," he said and exited the transit. Neil entered the hub and perused the aisles. He picked up two packages of nuts and a cold citrus fizzy, then went to pay. Outside, a transport rig chuffed as it pulled into the hub and drove straight to the transport-sized fuel islands. As the attendant scanned his provisions, Neil asked, "Does the repair shop only service freight transports or will they look at personal transits too?"

"They mostly work on the big ones, but they'll give your transit a look. If they can fix it, they will." He glanced at the scanner screen and said, "That'll be nine fifty-eight."

"I don't think it's a major issue, but it is something I would like to have looked at," Neil said as he placed his mobile in front of the scanner to pay for his items. "I bet you get plenty of traffic in here from Dodge City, especially transports hauling rubble from the DC Death Dam."

"Nah, those things don't stop. They just drive on by and turn north toward Great Bend."

"Really? I could have sworn I saw a CEC transport stopped here a few weeks ago when I passed by."

"I dunno. I mean, maybe. But I don't recall ever seeing one stop. I work here nearly every day. Those transports have been driving by several times a day for the last two months. I'm pretty sure I'd remember seeing a CEC transport pull in. It's not like you can mistake them for other transports. Anyway, yeah. The repair shop should be able to hook you up. Do you need a bag for these?"

"No, thank you. Have a good day."

Neil moved his vehicle from the hub to the front entrance of the repair shop next to three, large, bay doors. *They could easily have pulled into one of those bays and shut the door. But unload the mystery rubble inside a building in ten minutes, then drive on?*

He entered the building's small lobby which was adjacent to the cavernous work bay. An attendant asked, "How can I help you today, sir?"

"I've got a slight issue with my transit. There's a thumping sound coming from the right, front wheel. It started about halfway between here and Dodge City. I'm hoping you guys can look at it."

"Can do, sir. If you'll bring'er into Bay Three, we'll get her on a lift and take a look."

Neil exited the lobby, got into his transit, and brought it over to the right bay as the door was opening. A mechanic, whose coveralls bore a nametag emblazoned with "Mack," waved him in. He pulled forward and, once the transit was fully inside, the mechanic held up his hand, signaling him to stop. As Neil exited the vehicle, he was taken aback by how loud it was inside the shop. The bay doors closing filled the cavernous service area with a raucous clatter. As soon as the door shut, the mechanic apologized for the noise. "Sam says you're having problems with the right, front tire?"

"Yes, sir. I'm not sure what it is. It started making a repetitive thumping sound about fifteen kilometers outside Dodge."

"Let's get her up on the lift and take a look, shall we? If you'll stand outside the work zone, in the safety area over there," he said as he pointed toward an open area marked with yellow lines painted on the ground, "I'll get'er up."

As soon as Neil was in the safety zone, the mechanic nodded and pressed a button on one of the pillars between the bays. The hissing sound of hydraulic compression filled the room. A few moments later, the hydraulic lift hoisted the transit, suspending it two meters in the air.

"Let's see what we've got," the mechanic said as he picked up a long, metal, light stick from the tool bench next to him and walked under the transit. He bent his head slightly and looked up into the transit's undercarriage, then he turned on the light and began to inspect the area around the passenger side, front wheel. "Hmmm…" He checked the axle, the brake assembly, and the wheel well. "I don't know…" he said as he slowly spun the tire. "Huh. You say it's making a thumping sound?"

"Yeah."

"Does the rhythm of the thump change depending on how fast you're going?" he asked as he spun the tire a little faster. "Does it thump faster if you go faster?" he asked.

"Well…yeah." *He's not going to find anything wrong with this wheel. I better come up with something else.* "But…it quit making the noise when I slowed down to pull into the lot. Do you think it could be a speed issue?"

Mack stopped the tire, stepped out from underneath the transit, and tapped the wheel's rim with the light stick. He spun the tire again and leaned closer to listen. "I'm listening, but I'm just not hearing anything." He stepped out of the work area and joined Neil in the safety zone. "I'm not sure the thumping is your problem, Dr. DuCote."

"Excuse me?"

The mechanic clocked Neil across the side of his head with the light stick, and Neil saw stars. He collapsed. It felt like his entire body was spinning out of control. He blinked and opened his eyes, but the flurry of yellow shooting stars didn't go anywhere. "Your problem is poking your nose in where it don't belong." Neil felt the sharp pain of another blow to the back of his head, and everything went black.

* * *

Stacy hung up her mobile after the eighth ring. *He should have answered by now.* Stacy turned her attention back to the road. She kept her eyes mostly on the freeway, but she quickly glanced at the portable station screen set up in the passenger seat. It displayed a terrain map with a blinking, red light at the coordinates of the Kinsley Fuel Hub. *And, he hasn't moved in thirty minutes.* She was concerned. She checked her estimated arrival time. *Just five more minutes. Almost there.*

A minute before she reached the hub, Neil's location beacon started to move on the screen. She called him again, but he didn't pick up. As she neared the hub, she saw Neil's transit waiting to pull onto the highway, but there wasn't a driver behind the wheel. "What the hell?" she said aloud as she quickly processed what she was seeing. She watched the transit turn left at the crossroads to head toward Great Bend.

She accelerated, followed the transit's course, and said, "Mobile: Call CEC Dispatch." As the mobile connected, she glanced at her display. Neil's beacon continued moving along the map, in sync with the vehicle she was tailing.

"CEC Security Dispatch."

"This is Captain Stacy Solgeo. I need a remote shutdown of the CEC vehicle registered to Dr. Neil DuCote." She looked at the transit's tag and quickly followed with, "CEC transit number Omega-Indigo-812. I need this done NOW!"

"Yes, ma'am."

Moments later, Neil's vehicle began to slow and then it stopped on the road. She stopped her transit, exited, and drew her sidearm. As she approached the vehicle, she heard a banging noise from inside the trunk. "Hold on! I'm gonna get you out." She opened the driver's door, accessed the trunk release, and flipped the switch. As she did so, she saw a remote driver override mounted on the steering column.

She raced back to the trunk to help Neil. "Oh, my God!" She gasped at his bloodied face. "Let me get these for you," she said as she pulled out a knife and cut the restraints binding his hands and feet. He removed the tape across his mouth and said, "We need to go back! Nathan and Daniel are there."

"Let's get you out of here first."

Moments later, with sirens blaring, they raced back to the repair shop. In the sixty-eight seconds it took them to arrive, she called for backup and toggled on her body cam. She blasted through the crossroads and whipped her vehicle into the fuel hub's lot. She headed straight to the repair shop and saw three men run inside the open, right bay door. She sped across the lot as the bay door was closing. Her vehicle screeched as she stopped it with the front inside the bay, blocking the overhead door. She and Neil quickly exited the transit. As they did, Stacy drew her weapon, then they entered the shop. *It was empty.*

Stacy scanned the space, then said, "There's no place to hide." She quickly moved to the back door and opened it, but she saw nothing between her and the horizon. "If they didn't make a run for it, they're in the bathroom or behind that door." She walked over to an unmarked door near the refrigerator in the break area.

She flung the door open and revealed a set of stairs going down.

She looked at Neil and said, "You need to stay back, Doctor."

"I don't think so," he said. He picked up a light stick from a nearby workbench. "What are you gonna do, arrest me? Let's go."

They ran down two short flights of stairs that led to an enormous underground facility directly beneath Bay One and saw a full-sized CEC Transport Truck. Across the space was an opening to a long tunnel. Three men were running toward the entrance.

Stacy and Neil ran after them. "Freeze!" Stacy screamed, her voice echoing through the underground bay. The men did not freeze. She fired a shot, and one fell, clutching his leg. As she ran by, she scanned the screaming man for a weapon but saw none.

"That's Daniel Whitehead! Stay with him while I go after the other two!"

"No way!" Neil hollered back while doing his best to keep up with Stacy. They followed the other two men down the tunnel and saw them turn left.

Stacy was leading by several strides when Neil saw her slow down and peer around the corner. She ducked as Mack appeared, swinging a light stick. In the few seconds it took Neil to catch up, Stacy had her opponent disarmed and doubled over. "I'm going after the other one!" he yelled as he ran past her.

"I'm right behind you!" she yelled back as she whipped out her cuffs.

Neil ran as fast as he could down the tunnel, but he didn't see anyone in front of him. *There's only one way to go.* Fifty meters ahead, the tunnel appeared to open into a much larger space. Neil slowed as he reached the end of the tunnel and cautiously entered the cavern. He looked around, but his fleeing suspect was nowhere to be found. The enormous space had a dim orange glow. It was illuminated by lights hanging from the ceiling, spaced about three meters apart. One entire wall was dominated by piles of rubble. He turned on his light stick and pointed it at the rubble. It was raw concrete that wasn't infused with Semigrow. Had they somehow swapped shipments headed for the investigation site? Neil slowly walked forward, searching the gloom for the third conspirator.

"AAAAIIEEE!" Neil spun around just as Nathan rammed him, slamming him into the rubble behind him. Neil dropped his light, and it clattered to the ground. The single blow had knocked the wind out of him. Nathan bashed him in the abdomen with a light stick, then brought the weapon above his head for another blow. A blur—Captain Solgeo—tackled Nathan at the knees.

She yanked his arms behind him and handcuffed him, then she rose and prodded him with the toe of her boot to get him to sit upright. "Mr. Nathan Hill, you are under arrest!"

"Fuck off, Copper!" he said and spit at her. "Do you know who I am? My uncle is gonna be pissed! You don't EVEN know how much shit you're in!"

Neil stood up, holding his side. *Damn, on top of everything else, I think he broke some ribs.* He picked up the light stick he dropped, moved in front of Nathan, and said, "The same uncle who funded half of the DC 2BES Project?" He shined the light on the rubble in front of him, "The same uncle whose dam you sabotaged?"

Nathan laughed hysterically. "God damn, you're a dumbass. Whose idea do you think this was? The Trimmu killed thousands—tens of thousands—of my people! You want to use their fucking tech to fix our land? What the fuck? My uncle owns this land. This ends now!"

"Yes, it does," Stacy said as she forced him to his feet and dragged him back down the tunnel. Neil took one last look at the tainted rubble filling the room and followed.

* * *

They emerged from the subterranean cavern in the hub which was swarming with CEC Security personnel. They'd taped off the lot, and a medic was tending to Whitehead's wound. He'd live. It took a few minutes for Captain Solgeo to upload her body cam footage to her transit's workstation, then she selected vital bits for transmission. She uploaded the footage directly to Dr. Daniel's mobile, with a message: *URGENT. REVIEW THIS IMMEDIATELY—Solgeo/DuCote*

* * *

Kurk received Stacy's message and asked for a short recess. He didn't know what to expect, but he immediately shared the message with his legal team. The team motioned for a closed-door consultation with the tribunal panel, stating that their request was due to new, sensitive evidence they had just received that was extraordinarily relevant to the proceedings. An hour later, after everyone had reconvened in the hearing room, Senator Bissel banged his gavel.

"Good afternoon, everyone," Bissel began as he set his gavel to the side, then folded his hands in front him. "Welcome back. This has been a long two days, so I'm going to keep this short. This panel has just reviewed some rather interesting findings from the ongoing DC Dam disaster investigation." He gestured toward his fellow committee members sitting at the tribunal bench. "We need time to consider these findings. As such, we have no further questions for Dr. Daniel at this time. These hearings will resume in seven days." He picked up his gavel, whacked the wooden stop in front of him, and said, "Today's hearing is adjourned."

* * *

Epilogue

Three years later, on a chilly, sunny October morning with only a few clouds in the sky, Kurk Daniel stood on top of the newly constructed DC 2BES Project dam and looked out across the great, manmade valley that would become the Dodge City Reservoir. Water had started flowing into it two weeks earlier, and it was already a meter deep.

At least this project is done.

"Kurk!" Neil called from the dam crest on the south side. Kurk waved and then returned his attention to the landscape before him. Neil crossed the long walkway, and as he got closer, Kurk noticed the clipboard in his right hand.

Always paperwork. In an age where digipads are the norm, we still have to sign paper copies in triplicate. Though, in this case, unalterable, paper records proved vital.

"Good morning, boss." Neil held up the clipboard as he continued toward Kurk, "I've got the document you wanted to sign." He handed over the clipboard and joined Kurk in looking over the landscape and project. "It's beautiful, Kurk. You done good."

"You're only saying that to make me feel better," Kurk said with a smile. His smile disappeared. With a bit of resignation in his voice, he said, "It should have been done a long time ago."

Neil replied, "How many times do we have to tell you it wasn't your fault, Kurk?"

"You weren't the one who was duped, Neil. I signed off on the work that caused the collapse. I thought I was being careful and diligent. I wasn't."

"They knew you were watching him and his work. They planned accordingly and hid it well. The tribunal found you weren't at fault. Nathan, Daniel, Uncle Warlord, the entire outfit—the whole lot of them—were sent off to the prison colonies."

"I know. Still, I had hoped to see the end of xenophobia in my lifetime." He let out a heavy sigh. "I thought we were getting there." Kurk turned his attention to the clipboard in his hand. "You got a pen?"

"It's hard to fight xenophobia," Neil said as he fished a pen out of his inside jacket pocket and handed it to Kurk. "But it's a fight worth fighting."

"True that," Kurk replied. He nodded and read the documents on the clipboard. "Maybe it'll end in your lifetime, Neil." After he finished reading the formal request to change the name of the structure he was standing on from the Dodge City Dam to the Chapman-Morgan Memorial Dam, he signed on the dotted line and said, "I hope this will help people remember how bad it can be."

* * * * *

Kevin Fritz Fotovich Bio

"Colonel" Kevin Fritz Fotovich is a non-starving artist, masquerading as a logistics engineer, contracting for the United States Government. He has extensive experience creating multimedia training for engineers and soldiers. He was awarded the title Honorary Colonel by the Governor of Alabama in 2017. He is an award-winning artist whose artwork graces the covers of many books, including all the covers of the Curse of the Dullahan series by Taylor S Hoch. He has quite a love and passion for science fiction and fantasy and is a sitting member of the Board of Directors for LibertyCon. "The Reservoir" is Fritz's first published work of fiction.

# # # # #

Warlord by Christopher Woods

A Fallen World Universe Short Story

Chapter One

I sat atop a rundown scraper and looked down at the city that had been known as Philadelphia. No one called it that anymore. It had become part of the huge urban sprawl that had been Obsidian. Then it had become the urban wreckage I looked at today. The bombs had taken most of the east coast and left a ruin of the old Philadelphia where I made my home.

Our home. I chuckled as Stephen Gaunt's voice echoed inside my head.

"True enough," I muttered. "I guess there's no reason to perch on top of a building like Batman."

I actually understood that reference, William Childers said.

"Sadly, I can remember something like that, but I can't remember the stuff I should know about my past."

I haven't heard you talk about that issue much, Mathew. The voice in my head was female.

"Hey, Doc."

Would you like to talk about it?

317

"Tryin' to head shrink me, Doc?"

It's what I do Mathew, she said. *What else is a psychologist supposed to do in a place like this? Our situation is completely unprecedented. Even when we were in a world of imprints and Agents.*

"I would have been a head case then," I said. "Just like I'm a head case now."

I'm pretty sure they couldn't have used an imprinter to pull us out of your head once the whole database was loaded into it. Frankly, I don't understand how we are able to survive. It was thought impossible for something like this to happen, she said.

"I have little pieces of memories about someplace else I was, maybe, a mayor... or something like it." I shook my head. "I even remember being there with some of you guys. I remember meeting Gaunt in a garden..."

If only you could remember all of it, Childers said.

"Yep, it would be nice to remember who I was before I became an Agent. Or even remember all the time I was an Agent. There are so many fragments that seem like they would be interesting, but I can't remember enough to really see them."

Perhaps, if you hadn't kept all of us... Angela Richards, my resident psychologist let the comment drop.

"What would give me the right to purge any of you? This isn't my body either. Every one of us has the right to live in it."

"You are a much better man than many of us," Gaunt said aloud. "I'm fairly certain things would not be the same if one of us had become the dominant personality. Seventeen years ago, I wouldn't have given a second thought to purging this mind of everyone but me."

And you would now? Childers asked.

I have grown quite fond of our little family, William, he answered. *It would pain me to do it now. Perhaps I have gotten soft.*

Perhaps we all have, Childers said.

"It's not a bad thing," I said as I stood and slipped back from the edge of the roof toward the access. "What say we go inside and get this job done so Lucy can work on the garden tomorrow?"

She does like the garden, Angela said.

"We all like the food she produces," I said.

Much better for us than those blasted tacos you are so enamored with, Gaunt said.

"Leave my tacos alone," I said and entered the door.

The warlords always live at the top of the scrapers. They think the top is the safest place. Not from someone who can scale the outside of an immense building, though. I only had one floor of the warlord's people to deal with if I came in from the top.

"Alright, Stephen," I muttered, turning control over to the former Corporate assassin.

"Thank you, Mathew."

I slipped through the shadowy hall like a ghost. Stephen is a master at what he does. He can move in ways most people can't even imagine, and his imprint is one of the few originals that makes full use of an Agent's body. It wasn't that I couldn't fully use the body, but Gaunt had the imprinted training, along with the skills, to be a master assassin. Whereas I would have had to concentrate to do what he did, he did it out of habit.

There was a guard at the far end of the hall. I'm fairly certain he wasn't supposed to be sitting in the chair with his head lolled back, snoring lightly. It was a mistake he would never get to acknowledge.

I could feel the aversion from Angela.

It's bloody work, I said. *He works for a guy who buys pretty little boys and girls for his perverse pleasure.*

It doesn't mean I have to like it, she said.

"Ah, but I do," muttered Gaunt.

I pushed the door inward and slipped into the room.

Something was wrong. Instead of the sleeping warlord I expected, I found him standing in the center of the room. Several naked women were huddled near the wall.

"Kade, I presume," he said in a deep voice. I had a flashback to a movie in the depths of my mind about a giant black man who had been in prison for a murder he hadn't committed.

Only I knew this giant had murdered plenty.

"I've been waiting for you," he said. "Right now, forty of my toughest men are on their way up those stairs. But they aren't who you have to worry about. His hand flashed, and I caught the handle of the knife he had thrown.

"Which imprint are you?" I asked with a savage grin. "I can let you talk it out with yourself."

"What are you yammering about? I'm no Agent. All natural here, baby. Teledyne's finest."

I could hear running footsteps coming from the stairwell.

His other hand flashed, and I caught the second knife.

"Oh my, I haven't had a Specialist in ages," I said in Gaunt's voice. "They're so much fun."

"Shit!" I said in my own voice.

"What the hell is the matter with you?" The giant Specialist looked confused.

"He just realized the gravity of the situation," I said in Gaunt's voice. "I am going to get blood on his coat. Alas, sacrifices must be made in this Fallen World."

* * * * *

Chapter Two

Hart, the warlord in question, charged forward with another blade in his right hand. He was incredibly fast, but Gaunt really was the best at what he does. I slipped to my left and sliced the muscle along the back of the arm holding the knife, using one of the blades he had thrown at me.

Hart grunted, and the arm fell in toward his body.

"Quick little bastard,"

I looked at the blade. "This is very nice. Do you mind if I keep it?"

"I'll be taking it from your corpse, Agent." The big man moved his already-healing right arm. "You got no idea what you're messing with."

"Enhanced healing nanites," Gaunt said. "Those are lovely."

I glanced past the Specialist and saw the door at the end of the hall bang open. Guards erupted into the hallway. Then I looked down at my coat and saw several small splotches of blood on the sleeve. I shrugged and sighed.

Hart grinned and charged again.

This time I dodged to his right and sank the other blade to the hilt in the warlord's left ear. I turned back to look at the big man as he swept by me and toppled face first to the floor.

"You were saying?" I asked. I smiled at the women, who were staring with wide eyes at the former warlord, and grasped both sides of his head. "Get behind the bed."

The men were about halfway down the hall when Hart's head rolled to the leader's feet.

"Perhaps you should have stayed just a bit closer to your boss, my good fellows."

A second later, I was in the hallway and moving fast. The first knife Hart had thrown at me was a wonderful blade, and I used it to sever arteries and tendons as Gaunt danced between the men in the hallway.

Angela had receded into the back of my mind so she wouldn't have to watch. The hallway was too small to worry about blood, and Gaunt had already gotten Hart's blood on the sleeve of my coat.

"If I'd known you were gonna mess it up three days after leaving the Bastion, I would have let you keep it on when you went to talk with the Phobes."

"Shush, Mathew. This is a thing of beauty. Don't ruin the moment."

"Psycho."

"Yes. Isn't it glorious?" Gaunt has way too much fun in situations like this.

The fight down the hallway was short and brutal. The last ten or so men started firing weapons at me since it was pretty obvious that those who got close to me were faring badly. I dropped and rolled to the side and rose with a pistol. I only had one magazine left, but it held sixteen shots. More than enough to clear the rest of the hallway.

One of their shots had grazed my side, but the bleeding was already slowing because of the healing nanites.

"I would like to have some of those healing nanites," I said as Stephen stepped back from the forefront.

They would be very nice, Childers said. *I would say you were getting sloppy, Stephen, but I doubt I could have dodged ten shooters in such a small area.*

"Gonna have to agree," I said. "Very well done, Stephen."

Probably would have gone better if you would lay off the tacos, Mathew.

"I told you to leave my tacos out of it."

I could feel their amusement.

"May as well head down the stairs and let everyone know the place is under new management."

By the time I reached the ground floor, I was not alone. There was a line of children, teens, and adults, who had been freed from the rooms they were being held in, following me. There was more than one dead guard along the way as well. After seeing the faces of the prisoners at the sight of the guards, I didn't spare any. Outside, in the street, were the forms of the erstwhile captors, lying where they had fallen from almost every floor of the scraper.

My left eye was twitching as I watched the line of women and children I had freed exit the scraper. If I could have brought Hart back, I would have killed him again. Some monsters have no business living in any world, whether a Fallen World or not.

* * * * *

Chapter Three

The streets of Hart were filled with people who looked worn out. An air of doom seemed to lay heavily on their shoulders. These were people who had been under the thumb of someone they couldn't do anything about, even if they had wanted to. They looked about as defeated as any I had seen in this city.

I raised the wrapped bundle I had carried down the stairs. I figured they wouldn't take my word, so I tossed the Specialist's head into the street right in front of them.

"Hart is dead," I said. I pointed at the crumpled forms who had fallen from the scraper as I descended. "Most of his lieutenants are lying in the street where they landed. You have a chance to make something better of this place. Representatives of the Society of the Sword will be here in a few days. If you are smart, you'll listen to what they have to say. Teresa Manora is good people."

"What about us?" a young girl, perhaps fifteen, asked. She had been one of the captives. "I don't have anyone in this city except my sister who was taken at the same time I was."

"Where are you from?"

"My family was living on an island down south until pirates raided us. My sister and I were kept because…well I guess you can figure that out after seeing what was inside."

"I would suggest the Society. They can help you learn to protect yourself. Where's your sister?"

"I don't know. We were sold to different buyers at the waterfront. I, for one, don't think I can stay here. Many of us are from different places and know very little about this city."

"Then I will make sure you make it safely to the Society," I said. "It's several zones to the west of here."

"Thank you. I thought all the people in this awful place were animals."

"Not all of us," I said. "There are some good people left here, but it's hard to find them among the awfulness. We're trying to do better over to the west."

"Thank you again," she said and turned to the others. "This man is going to take us to a safe place if we want to go."

I hadn't really planned on escorting them, but it was on my way home. The job at the Bastion had been interesting, but I wanted some down time.

Well deserved, Tim Bolgeo said inside my head. *Thank you for letting me spend the time with my daughter.*

"Family is important, Timmy," I said.

The girl turned back to me. "What?"

"Nothin'. Just talkin' to my selves."

She shook her head and went back to directing the other former slaves.

She is a natural leader, Angela said.

"She'll do well with Teresa," I muttered. "And speaking of Teresa, I guess I should send her a warning."

I touched the girl's shoulder, and she tensed. "If I was gonna hurt you, I would have already done it."

She took a deep breath. "I'm still up there in my head." She pointed back at the scraper with a thumb.

I nodded. "Understandable. I'm going to drop down in the Tees and send a message to Teresa. She needs to know I'm bringing fifty-three people to her."

The girl looked scared.

"I'm not leavin'," I said. "You can come with me if you need to, but you seem to be the person they need right now."

She looked back at the others, all of whom were looking to her for direction. "How did that happen? I'm fifteen years old. Who looks to a fifteen-year-old for leadership?"

"Teresa wasn't much older when she started the Society."

"They told us stories about her at night. They needed to give us hope."

"Who?"

"The older slaves. They weren't as appealing to the animals as we were, so they worked as cleaners and cooks. They told us that one day she cut off the head of the man who had held her captive for three years. She was fifteen years old."

"She did," I said. "He was called the General, and he was a bastard. She left his head mounted on one of his bedposts and escaped with a small group of people. I met one of them recently in a place called the Bastion. The others stayed with her and, later, became Knights of the Sword."

"They say she learned to fight from a master swordsman and founded the Society to help the innocent."

I chuckled.

"What?"

"Not exactly a master swordsman."

"Then who was he?"

"He was an old Corporate Agent with too many voices in his damned head." I turned toward the nearest entrance to the Tees. "I'll be back in a few. Get your people ready to make the trip."

I stopped and pointed at a man wearing a red armband that resembled those of the guards I had thrown out of the scraper. "Gather food and enough clothing for these folks to wear. Not this thin see-through shit, either. They are not to be bothered by anyone, or you can join your friends. If you're wearing that red armband when I get back, I just might feed it to you."

He swallowed and glanced toward one of the crumpled forms who had impacted the pavement. "Y...yes, sir."

I walked toward the Tees shaking my head. What people will do with no one to keep them in check makes my skin crawl. I understood some of the reasons behind these people. The Specialist, Teledyne's version of an Agent, was someone who could easily dominate. No one with the ability to stop him lived here. I had no doubt some of the Knights who had disappeared over the years had done so here, in Hart, or the zone that used to be called Hart.

I opened the door centered in an otherwise blank brick wall under one of the buildings and stepped inside.

"Hello, Mister Kade."

"Portus," I said, "it's almost like you were waiting for me."

Portus was the Mardin who led us through the Tees during one of the cases I was involved in last year.

"Perhaps we have discovered that a Mardin should be available in any zone you have been active in, sir. We do watch topside to keep apprised of any violence."

"Really?"

He laughed. "Actually, pure chance had me here. When bodies began falling from the scraper, I thought I should investigate. There aren't many people who have your flair for the dramatic. The Farmers used to, but they haven't let Zee and Jimmy back into the city for some time."

"I heard a little about them from a vendor some time back. The Steadholder's sons?"

"Yes," Portus said. "They were a force to be reckoned with until the Accords were signed, forbidding them to return to the city. Zee's daughter runs one of the major caravans into the city now."

"I've met a couple of the Caravan Masters," I said. "Not sure if I met her."

"She just began her term as a Master recently. Allie Pratt is much like her father. She brooks no nonsense. Do not provoke the Pratts."

"I don't plan to," I said. "Who did she replace as a Master? It wasn't that old bastard, Kalet, was it?"

He chuckled. "No, Kalet will run his caravan until he dies of old age. No one has been able to kill him, but many have tried. It was Reynard."

"Reynard?" I asked. "I thought he was happy where he was."

"They said something about a new posting that was much sought after."

"He's good people," I said. "Glad he got a promotion."

"Agreed," he said. "But I seriously doubt you came into the Tees to talk about the Farmers. What can we do for you?"

"I need a message relayed to Teresa. I just freed fifty-three women and children from Hart and will be bringing them to her."

"I will send it on the short wave."

"Thanks, Portus."

"Thank you, Mister Kade. Without you, we would have been quickly overrun by Derris's savages last year."

"One of these days, I need to have a discussion with Derris."

"His people have stayed out of the Tees since their confrontation with you and the two Squires."

"Speaking of Squires, you might also tell Teresa that Hart is in need of new management."

He chuckled again. "I assumed as much when the bodies began falling from the sky."

Some days, the rain isn't the worst thing falling from the sky in this Fallen World.

* * * * *

Chapter Four

I stopped just past the corner of the building and watched as a fifteen-year-old girl wrangled fifty people into a group. She was handing each one a small package of food from the supply the guard was carrying along behind her. His red armband was gone, and he was following any order the girl was giving.

"Natural leader, indeed."

Reminds me of another young woman, Angela said. *A certain woman you took in and trained.*

"She has some of the qualities," I said. "Teresa will make a good Knight out of her."

Perhaps we could find her sister for her, Childers said.

"It's not out of the question," I said. "We get them to the Society, then we can put out some feelers."

Looks like they are as ready as they are ever going to be, Gaunt said. *Some of those chaps look like they might want to try our patience.*

He was right. Several of the men were talking among themselves. Occasionally, one of the men looked hungrily in the direction of the girl and her charges.

I slipped around the corner, rounded a building, and stepped out of the shadows directly behind the man who seemed to be the ringleader. I tapped the knife I had planted in Hart's brain lightly against the side of his neck, just a fraction of an inch from his jugular.

He froze.

"If you were to try what you're thinking about, I would let a friend of mine skin you alive. These people have been through enough. You will turn to your right and start walking. If you stop before you are completely out of this zone, your head will join your former warlord's. Do you understand?"

He swallowed and nodded.

"Good. Now walk." I looked at the four who had been talking with the man. "That is your only warning. If you're still standing here in five minutes, well, you can figure out from the condition of Hart's guards what will happen to you. These people are off limits."

They scattered. They wanted no part of the man who had killed their leader and tossed most of his thugs out of the windows of his scraper.

Should have just killed them, Gaunt said.

"If we kill them, they won't learn anything."

I could hear Gaunt chuckling in my head.

As the thugs fled down the alley, I stepped back into the square in front of the scraper where the girl was gathering her people.

"I wasn't sure you would come back," she said.

"Understandable," I said. "This place hasn't done much to instill trust, has it?"

"You've done more in an hour than anyone has done in the two years I have been away from the island."

"There are good people left," I said. "Not as many as there should be, but more than what you might expect. There are probably some right here, in this street, who have been afraid to step forward. A guy like Hart is enhanced and would be hard to take down without special skills."

"But you did," she said. "Mister…?"

"Kade," I said. "Mathew Kade. Most of the time, anyway."

"I'm Lynx," she said. "Lynn Xavier. My sister and I called each other Lynx and Jynx. Her name is Jennifer. She started calling herself Jynx after the accident."

"Accident?" My eyes narrowed.

"She lost an arm and a leg when the boat crashed. Dad was an engineer before the world went crazy, and mom was a surgeon. Between the two, they saved her."

"This is crazy," I said. "Teresa has an assistant named Jynx. You say she lost an arm and a leg? Did they build cybernetic prosthetics?"

"What?" She was staring at me with her mouth hanging open. "Yes! They built her an arm and a leg! Is she already there?"

"I doubt there is more than one girl named Jynx with cybernetic prosthetics in the city. I am fairly certain she's already at the Society. I haven't talked to her much. I got her some parts to tune up the leg up some time back."

"That has to be her!" The girl was bouncing with excitement. I was amazed she could be as exuberant as she was after the time she had spent in the scraper. Perhaps it was why her people followed her lead when they were freed. What she had gone through hadn't destroyed her as it had many.

Her excitement was contagious. I grinned. Sometimes, there is a ray of sunshine in the dark, even in this Fallen World.

* * * * *

Chapter Five

The zone to the west of Hart was called Gord. The warlord held his territory through the help of some ex-military types he had pulled together after the fall. He had been in charge of his territory for all the years since. Anyone who had been around for that length of time was there for a reason. Gord wasn't as bad as some, but his men were standing in the street as my group of refugees entered the zone.

"I understand there was a ruckus next door," the leader of the guards said as I approached.

I motioned to Lynx to hold back. "Not particularly happy with the notion of slavery. Seems like this area is a little better than most. But there was this blight to an otherwise decent area."

"Hart," the man said. "The man's an Agent. Not much we can do with him except stay out of his zone. The guy before him was a little better to deal with."

"The next guy should be a little better," I said.

"He's gone?"

"Yep."

"Who the hell are you?"

"I'm the guy who removed Hart from his position. I intend to take these folks west to Stiner. They've been treated pretty rough by Hart and his men. They'll be taken care of there. You gonna have a problem with us crossing through here?"

"You took out Hart and his men by yourself, and you're heading to Stiner. My guess is you're Mathew Kade. I'd rather wrap myself in razor wire and roll down the street than cause you any problems. My boys will provide you with an escort through our zone just to be on the safe side. Some people are idiots, and I'd rather make sure none of them interfere."

"That would be greatly appreciated...?" I let the statement trail off into a question.

"Avery Foiler," he said. "I'm Gord's head of security. I'm very familiar with what an Agent can do, and I understand you are one of the best."

"Maybe," I said. "It's hard to say."

"I'd rather go with it and offer you any help I can."

"Thank you, Foiler. I'm sure these folks have seen enough violence to last them a while."

"Undoubtedly."

I motioned for Lynx to bring her people forward. "If you don't mind, I would like to get underway."

"Do you mind if I walk along with you?"

"Not at all," I said. I looked at Lynx. "Lynx, this is Avery Foiler. He's decided he is going to escort us through this zone so there won't be any trouble."

"Thank you, Mister Foiler." She went over to help one of the kids that followed.

"She's pretty young."

"Hart was a right bastard," I said.

"He was that," Foiler said. "Saw him take apart a whole squad of men about five years ago. We've stayed out of his zone since then. I had my suspicions about what was going on, but what could we do?"

"It's not my place to say, but a sniper shot to the brain would have ended it."

"And if the sniper missed, he'd have signed the death warrant for a whole zone. You know what an Agent can do."

"You're right. He deserved an Agent. And he got a bunch."

"What?"

"Inside joke," I said. "Sometimes I wish all of the enhanced had died with the Corporations."

"That would include you, Mister Kade."

"Yep."

"I see."

"World would be a better place without the nanites, the genetic mutations, and the damned imprint tech. Teledyne, Obsidian...they were two sides of the same coin."

"Agreed. I worked for Obsidian, but they weren't any better than Teledyne. Ran into a squad of Teledyne guys just before the end and took them prisoner. They were just guys like us, and the time we spent guarding them was more of an eye opener than any other part of the war. Guess you didn't spend much time talking to anyone else. Agents always seemed to be on a mission."

"You'd be surprised how many."

"Really? I didn't think they let you guys out unless you were on a mission."

"They kept more than the Agent programs in the database," I said.

"That makes sense," he said. "Guess you got one of those."

"You could say that."

"We're getting close to Fandi," he said. "I sent word ahead. You should be clear for the next two zones, and the Farmers are in Jeffrey, so there shouldn't be any trouble. Just leaves a few zones between them and Jeffrey."

"Normally, I would go around Jeffrey but, with the Farmers there, I agree. He shouldn't cause trouble. Antilles and Payne shouldn't be too bad. They know me. Thanks for sending word. It was good to meet you, Foiler."

"Good to actually meet you, too, Kade. My boss might be interested in this thing you've got going with the Society and a certain group of warlords. If you think your people might have an interest, I can talk to him and see what we can work out."

"There would definitely be interest," I said. "And there will be a Society presence right next door in the near future."

"I'm glad." He slowed his pace as we neared the boundary of his zone. "Be nice to see some stability in that area."

I nodded as he raised his hand and the guards dropped back from the flanks of our group.

"He seems to be a lot better than the guys who worked for Hart," Lynx said as she walked over to Kade.

I saw how she kept a wary eye on the man as he walked away. She was a strong girl, but I knew she had been treated badly by most of the men she had met in the last year. How badly, I might never know, and I'm not sure I wanted to. Most of those who had been behind the mistreatment had taken a dive from various floors of the scraper.

We walked down the street toward the scraper Seamus Fandi held. He was somewhat new to his position since Darvis had crossed someone he shouldn't have. You didn't try to screw over the Circus. I heard three Clowns had walked into Darvis and had left the zone freshly renamed Fandi. Kelly Darvis has never been seen again that I am aware of.

Gaunt chuckled inside my head. *It doesn't pay to make that kind of enemy.*

"True."

"What?" Lynx asked.

"Nothin, just talking to my selves."

"You are a strange man, Mister Kade."

"It's not like we haven't heard that before," I said with a grin.

"We?"

"A little schizophrenic humor." I laughed. "There is a good side to my situation. I may be a schizophrenic, but I'll always have each other."

She shook her head and walked silently beside me as I chuckled.

That was rather horrid, Mathew, Gaunt said.

"It wasn't that bad," I muttered.

Lynx glanced at me sideways with an eyebrow raised.

"Hmpf," I grunted.

Everyone seems to be a critic in this Fallen World.

* * * * *

Chapter Six

"I thought there would be more people here," Lynx said. "I haven't been out of the scraper in close to a year, but there were more people around when they brought me in from the waterfront."

"Waterfront is the other direction," I said. "But I think Fandi took Foiler's warning to heart."

"Does he have that much power?" she asked. "I admit, I don't know a lot about the city."

A man who wore makeshift armor darted into an alley, muttering, "It's him…"

"Or is it you they're afraid of?"

"Maybe."

"I think it is," she said. "I saw you throw men around as if they weighed nothing."

"They deserved what they got," I said. "You can't deny that."

"Considering where you found me," she said, "I don't deny it at all."

I remained silent.

"I just wonder who you are," she said. "You showed up like some hero of old."

"I'm no hero," I said.

"Then why did you do it? You had no reason to save us. Even if you had reason to kill Hart, you had no reason to save us. No reason to be leading us through several zones where we would have been taken as soon as we crossed into them. That hungry look I see on those men over there is one I know quite well. If you aren't a hero, you would have left us behind and gone about your business. We would be back there in a scraper serving someone else. Maybe someone that isn't as bad as Hart was, but there is always someone."

"Pretty young to be that cynical," I said.

"From the moment my parents were slaughtered, all I have seen is one evil person after another. There weren't any good among them. The only good people I found were those who were being held in that scraper, just like me. Then you arrived like one of the old Greek heroes my father used to tell me about. Whether you want me to or not, I see you as a hero, just like these people who are following us do."

Never been called a bloody hero, Mathew. She doesn't know me very well.

I chuckled. *More of a hero than you think, Stephen. We all saw your moment back at the Bastion. Unexpected, but welcome.*

Momentary lapse, I assure you, he said.

I could hear the others snickering in my mind.

Have your fun, Gaunt said.

I chuckled again and walked onward through Fandi's zone. The street was fairly clean, which spoke well of Fandi on some level. Many of the zones throughout the city were piled with refuse. It was kept to a certain level, though, or the Farmers would bypass the zone. Even the savages throughout the city were on their best behavior when the Farmers came through.

The next zone was Rollins, and the people there were preparing for the arrival of the Farmers. They were three zones away in Jeffrey, but they would be in Rollins in the next few days. The Farmers tended to stay in a zone for a day and then move to the next. In the early days, they ran through many zones each day, but they were working to save a city.

Sometimes, I wondered if it had been worth it. There were days I wanted to walk away and leave the city behind. Then I would think about Teresa and the Society trying to make a difference and know that I couldn't leave. I owed too much for the things I had done.

"Oh…Hello," I said as my eyes were drawn to a vendor on the left side of the street. "I haven't seen that in a long time."

"What?" Lynx asked.

"That's denim." I approached the vendor who was a woman of about fifty years or so. "I haven't seen that in some time."

"You like what you see?" the lady asked with an accent I'd heard somewhere before.

Romanian, Angela said.

"I do. If you have some of those pants in my size, I'd like to buy some."

"You look like about a thirty-four-inch waist."

"Yes, and a thirty-two inseam."

"I have four pairs that would fit you, sir."

"I'll take them."

"You didn't ask for the price," she said.

"I think this will cover it." I laid a coin on her table that she quickly covered with her hand.

"Not many of these around," she said. "Amazing what you can buy with a silver dollar. I remember when you could buy a drink with it. Now, there are places where you could buy a person for this coin. I don't have enough scrip to give you the necessary change."

"The coin is yours." I pointed to the pants. "Consider it an order for some more if you still have access to denim. I would like ten more pairs. Have them delivered to the Society in Stiner. If you agree to the delivery, I'll add another coin."

"Placing a lot of trust in a stranger," she said.

"I know where to find you if you don't follow through," I said, and she recoiled just a little as she detected the change in my demeanor.

"Not many would cross you," she said. "The coat, the blades, and I believe there is a certain straight razor in one of your pockets. You are known, Mister Kade. There are stories of warlords that fear your coming. Conveniently, our own brave warlord, Rollins, is up in his tower with the majority of his men. I like thinking of him up there quaking in his boots as Mathew Kade walks down his street. Your pants will arrive within two weeks, Mister Kade."

I smiled and drew another coin from my pocket and placed it near her hand where she could easily cover it.

"If you would step around here, I will get a few measurements, and I can make them to fit you precisely. I was a tailor before the fall and managed to acquire the denim from the Farmers this year."

"That would be great," I said. "What other sorts of fabric do you have? You see, I need a new coat. This one is taking a beating."

"Perhaps a darker color?"

"Dark colors make me look pale. Better stick with light."

"As you wish." She smiled. "It takes all kinds to make a world, Mister Kade."

I nodded. "Even in this Fallen World."

* * * * *

WE DARE: SEMPER PARATUS | 343

Chapter Seven

Antilles' zone was much like Rollins'. People were preparing for the Farmers to come their way.

"Who are the Farmers?" Lynx asked.

"I don't hear that question very often," I said.

"I never saw them when they came through Hart," she said. "We were always locked in our rooms when they came through. They were the only people I ever saw who frightened Hart."

"They're a force no one wants to be on the wrong side of," I said. "Pretty sure they are the reason this city survived right after the Fall, not that it deserved to."

"What did they do? Hart forbade us to even speak about them. There were whispers, but most of us were terrified of him."

"When the bombs fell, farms to our west banded together and sent caravans of food into the city. They brought some order with them, and they were well on the way to dragging this place back into the light. Then something happened, and they changed. I'm not sure what it was, but I have my suspicions after I met some Clowns last year. The Accords were signed, and the Farmers became merchants instead of benefactors."

"Clowns? I love the books my mother gave me about them."

"These Clowns are different. You definitely don't want to contemplate ending up at the Circus."

"I like the tigers."

"You've never seen a circus like this. Those you saw in books were shows to entertain children. This one is a twisted perversion of the old ones. Anything a twisted soul wants to see or do can be found at the Circus. The Clowns are the guards."

"That's horrible," she said. "Why do you let them continue?"

"I'm tough, girl. I've never hesitated to face anything this shitty city has thrown at me, but I need help to take down the Circus."

"They are that strong? I thought Hart was the strongest person I had ever seen. But Lydia said you killed him so fast, she barely saw you move. I saw you throw men, who weighed hundreds of pounds, as if they were toys."

"They are," I said looking to the southwest. "One day, I may have to do something about them, but how is the question."

"You'll do it," she said matter-of-factly.

I shook my head and continued walking down the street. None of the bravos who normally loitered along the sidewalks were there. Apparently, Antilles didn't want to provoke anyone. Most of the zones around the area knew the Society and wouldn't provoke Teresa for all the scrip in the city.

"Do you really think the girl you know is my sister?"

"Odds are really good. Jynx is not a common name, and cybernetics are very rare. Most of them don't work anymore."

"Jynx had a catch in her leg," she said.

"It's her, girl. That catch got fixed using the part I got for her from my guy in Dana's zone."

"I can't wait to see her again," Lynx said looking west. "I hope she's been treated better than I was. I'm not sure she could have…"

The statement trailed off.

"I think she's been at the Society for about eight months," I said.

I was thinking about what had been done to this girl and wishing I could kill Hart and his thugs again. This had been the first job I had done that hadn't coincided with a case I had been hired to do or asked to do by Teresa.

Perhaps you can see what you've been doing, now, Tim Bolgeo said. *I think our path to redemption demands that we do something.*

"Nothing out of you for years," I muttered. "Now you're preaching redemption."

I could feel Bolgeo laughing inside my head.

"What?" Lynx asked.

"Nothing," I answered. I tapped the side of my head. "Voices are getting restless."

You gave me back my daughter, Bolgeo said. *Now, you're stuck with me. I do know some useful tidbits about defensive tactics.*

"Do you really have voices in your head?"

"Yep. Some of them yap a lot."

"I've read some of my mom's books. Schizophrenia is serious."

"That's what the doc says." I tapped my head again.

"Doc?"

"She's a psychologist."

"So, I guess you could say you're already in therapy," she said and grinned. "That's one of the first steps in the book."

I chuckled. "I guess you could say that."

Her smile was infectious. How did someone live in Hell for two years and come out smiling?

She is refusing to be a victim, Angela said. *She will face her demons on her own terms, Mathew. Once she is somewhere safe where she can do so. She is a strong one. Reminds me of Teresa.*

"Yep," I muttered as we crossed into Payne's zone.

Jonas Payne and a large group of his guards were waiting a short distance inside his zone.

"Payne." I nodded at him. "We have a problem here?'

"Absolutely not," he said. "I heard you had a problem with Randall Hart and ended it in a rather permanent fashion. No, I do not have any problem with you or your little band of refugees. I came out to meet you and warn you about what happened in Overton yesterday. Last year, a group of representatives of the Circus were robbed and killed."

"I remember a little bit about that." I chuckled.

"I figured you would," he said. "Yesterday, three Clowns walked into Overton. When they left, there wasn't a single person alive in the zone."

"Damn," I said. "None?"

"Every man, woman, and child."

"There were a lot of people there who had no choice, Jonas."

"I know. That's why I'm here. I don't know about you, but I'm scared. The only thing I can think to do is look for allies. If you will give Manora a message for me, I'd like to talk about this consortium you, Teresa, and the others are building around here."

"I can do that," I said. "There are rules, and they are enforced. I know you skirt the edge on many of them. You need to keep that in mind if you want to move forward. Jeffrey won't like it. He makes his scrip as a slaver, and I understand many of his caravans come through here."

"I understand the price of admission. He can find another route."

"Then I'll relay the message with my endorsement. Something has to change in this city. These are the first steps."

"Agreed."

"I'll go through Jeffrey's zone and bypass Overton's by using Xeno's. Somehow, I don't think these folks need to see what the Clowns left there."

"I wish I hadn't seen it. Manora is there with her folks, cleaning up the mess."

"I'll go back after I get these folks to the Society in Stiner."

"I was about to go back to Overton's to talk to Manora, but I think it might be better if it came from you. I'll send men to help her clean out the area."

"That will say more about your intentions than any amount of talk," I said. "Would show more if you go with them. Talk to her. I'll add my endorsement when I get there. Not that it will make a difference in her decision. Teresa does what she thinks is right whether I say anything or not."

"Then I'll go, too."

"I think it's be a better approach."

"Thank you, Mister Kade."

"A few more like you, Jonas, and we may actually make a difference in this Fallen World."

* * * * *

Chapter Eight

We heard the noise from the streets ahead long before we could see the wagons. The Farmers were lined up along the street throughout Jeffrey's zone.

"These are the Farmers?" Lynx asked when she saw the colorful canopies.

"Yep," I said. "If you've never met them, it's a sight to see."

A woman was close behind us, and I recognized her as one of the women from Hart's chambers.

"I saw them years ago," she said. "Before I was…"

There was still a haunted look in her eyes. It was hard to think about what they had been through when I talked to Lynx.

"The Society is a safe place," I said. "You won't have to worry about that sort of thing anymore…?"

"Lydia," she said. "Lydia Savrill."

"Teresa can show you how to fight, Lydia."

"Like you?"

"I'm a little different. I've been enhanced like Hart was. We don't have the technology to do that anymore, and that's not a bad thing. But being a full Knight of the Society is about as close as you can come."

"How long does it take to become a Knight?"

"It takes years to reach Knighthood," I said. "Some never reach that skill level, but the strength of the Society isn't her Knights. They are like family. If you attack one of them, you attack them all. They will come from all corners of this city if the call goes out."

"They sound too good to be true."

"In a city like this, that doesn't surprise me. It's not hard to sound too good to be true."

"If there was a way to just leave this city…" she said wistfully.

"There is," I said. "We're about to walk through a zone full of a way out of the city. The Farmers are always willing to hire workers. Farming requires a lot of work, and they have a lot of farmland."

"They would let us go with them?"

"The only way to know is to ask them. We'll take our time through here." I was watching Lynx getting further ahead of us, looking at the wagons with a wonder I wouldn't have expected from someone who had been through what she had in the last couple of years.

"You like the girl."

"She reminded me of a friend when I first met her."

"She is one of the pretty ones, so they limited the places they left scars."

My eye twitched.

"They were not gentle people, Mister Kade."

"They are now."

She smiled for the first time since I saw her in the penthouse. "Yes…yes, they are."

We followed Lynx down the row of wagons. She was looking into each one as she passed, but she wouldn't spend much time at any. She had no scrip, but she wanted to see everything.

"She kept me going when I wanted to end it," Lydia said. "She was the only brightness in our dreary lives. Every time she came back to the cells, she would wipe away the tears and lie down. When she woke, it was like the sun rising in our dark rooms."

"Teresa was like that when she came out of that place on the waterfront. I was in a dark place, and she walked into my camp like the morning sun. She didn't speak much about what she had been through, but she came out the other side forged into something different."

"The Matron?"

"Yes."

"Everyone knows the story of the Matron. She cut off the General's head and left it impaled on his bedpost and escaped with her friends. Then she found a master swordsman who trained her to be the greatest fighter ever..."

Her words trailed off as she looked at me and my smile.

"She found you, didn't she?"

"Yeah," I said. "She saved me from myself, and I taught her some things about the swords she carried. Don't know about that Master Swordsman thing though."

"I saw what you did with a small blade, Mister Kade."

I shrugged. "I don't use a sword very often, but there's a time for it, and it pays to know how to use one."

"Who would I speak to about joining these Farmers, Mister Kade?"

"It's Mathew," I said and turned toward a stall.

The guy working it raised his head in acknowledgement. "What can I do for you?"

"Looking for the Master. Is this one under Kalet?"

"Nope, this is the first run for Allie," he said, pointing toward a woman who held the reins of a massive, black horse.

"Thanks."

He nodded.

I strode over to the woman. She was tall and fit, with black hair. When she looked up at my approach, I noticed her striking, silver eyes.

The horse stepped toward me.

"Now, Shank," she said and patted his chest. "Back up."

The horse snorted.

"I know," she said and stepped between me and the horse.

"He looks like a handful."

"He's overprotective, but I would trust him with my life. He sees you like I do. You walk like my uncle. Enhanced can hide it, but not to those who know what to look for."

"I heard some things a little while back about your uncle. If he is who I think he is, I owe him my life."

"Uncle Jimmy has saved a lot of people."

"I don't doubt it." I motioned toward the refugees. "I have some people who would love to leave this place behind. I was wondering if—"

I spun and held a blade in both hands as a commotion interrupted my question. A pale man was sprinting straight toward me.

I stepped toward him, and he skidded to a halt in front of me.

"Mister Kade! Derris hit a group of our people and dragged them into his zone! They were meeting with Manora's people! I have to find the Matron!"

"Slow down. When?"

"It's been an hour and a half, sir."

"How many people were taken?"

"Four Mardins and the Matron's assistant, the girl with the prosthetic."

"What?"

"The novice was setting up a meeting for the Matron," he said. "They dragged all five of them into Derris's zone! We don't have the forces to go in after them, sir."

I heard a sob behind me and turned. Lynx had dropped to her knees.

My whole body was trembling with rage when I turned back around to face Pratt. I pulled a handful of coins and held them out to her. "I need you to guarantee their safety. I'll pay whatever it takes."

She looked at the sobbing girl and said, "They'll be safe. What are you going to do?"

"I'm going after them." I pointed toward one of her guards who wore two short swords on his back. "I need those."

"Not selling my—"

"Give him the swords, Allen," Pratt said. "I'll get you another set when we get home.

Allen unbuckled the harness. I removed my coat and slung the harness over my shoulders. "Teresa is in Overton's. Can you send a runner to tell her what is happening?"

"Absolutely."

I turned and laid my coat across Lynx's shoulders. "If she's alive, I'll bring her back. You understand?"

She looked up with tear filled eyes that made my chest hurt and nodded. I turned toward the street that led to the west into Xeno.

The world seemed to slow as I leapt forward into a sprint. An Agent can attain speeds a normal person only dreams of, and I was running at my enhanced body's highest output.

"Guards! Mount up!" Allie Pratt yelled as I turned the corner.

All I could see was the face of a despairing girl, and fury filled me. Not just my own fury. Everyone in my head had been affected by her brightness. I was feeling the fury of a thousand souls, and there's not many things that drive a person like rage in this Fallen World.

* * * * *

Chapter Nine

*S*he could be alive, Angela said.

Not likely, Gaunt said. *Derris's people have never been much more than savages.*

I growled as I leapt a pavilion along the street entering Xeno's zone. I turned north and poured on the speed again and dodged several people who didn't have time to notice me before I passed them.

Have to find out, Bolgeo said. *This could break that girl. All she went through just to have this happen. It could.*

"Not if I can help it," I said between breaths.

Moments later, I turned left inside Stiner and charged straight toward Derris's zone. The Society headquarters flew by on my right, and I heard yells from the guards at the front gate.

I ran past the old bank building I called home, and the twin swords leapt to my hands.

"Derris!"

My voice echoed from the buildings. The streets ahead of me were already full of his people. They were unclean and wore whatever they could find as armor or clothing. Some didn't bother with clothing at all. But they all carried weapons, and they all charged into the street to meet me.

My swords were moving faster than the eye could see, and body parts sailed through the air. I wasn't using anything but brute force to slice through them. There is a beautiful dance that can be done with a sword that is filled with grace and skill. I didn't do that. I charged straight into the crowd of screaming savages. All that were left in my wake were dead or dying. My rage seemed bottomless as I thought of a girl's tears.

I found one of the Mardins, still alive, near the largest scraper in the zone.

"Jynx?" I asked the woman. "The Matron's assistant?"

She looked back at the street full of dead, and her face became even paler than it already was. "Th…they dragged her inside there."

She was pointing at the scraper, and I was moving again. There was nothing living that could hurt her behind me. I heard the noises, chanting of some sort, coming from inside the scraper.

The door was made of steel, but I kicked it completely off its hinges, and it slammed to the floor inside. I was met by three men who screamed and charged right into my swords. I kicked one in the chest with a pleasant *crunch* as the other two fell, headless, to the floor. I heard the chanting getting louder behind a pair of double doors that lead to some sort of auditorium. I slammed a shoulder into the doors. They exploded inward. Inside were fifty or so of the savages. At the front of the room was a stage, and on the stage, I saw a large man holding a small girl by her arm. Her other arm was held near his side. He had torn the cybernetic arm from her shoulder with his bare hands.

He tossed the screaming girl to the side, pulled a piece from the arm, and placed it in a spot on his wrist.

Then he turned toward me. His eyes glowed red, and I recognized him for what he was.

"War Borg," I said.

"Are you the one making such a racket out there?" Derris asked in a deep voice that didn't sound completely human. "What are you? Agent? Specialist?"

"I'm the guy who's gonna kill you," I said.

"We'll see," he said and glanced at the girl in the corner. "I'll be back in a minute darlin'. You got somethin' else I want, but I gotta kill me a little Agent first."

Over where Jynx was struggling to her feet, there was a pile of prosthetics and cybernetics.

"I thought the cyborgs had stopped working over the years," I said. "How long have you been harvesting them for parts?"

"Since the beginning," he said and looked at the group of followers between him and me. "Kill him."

"Alright then," I said. "Let's see what you got, you bag of bolts."

Fifty savages and JalCom's answer to the Agent program charged toward me. I grinned and met them halfway.

* * *

I staggered as I tried to climb one of the steps in the auditorium. I felt someone slip in under my arm on the right side. My right eye was swollen shut, and I could feel the nanites already working. My stomach felt like a hollow pit.

"You're heavy, Mister Kade," Jynx said.

"Thanks, girl," I grunted.

"You just saved my life," she said. "The least I can do is help you up the steps. I don't know how you survived that. I've never seen anything like that before."

"I'd like to say I haven't either, but…"

I looked down at the object I carried under my left arm, "How 'bout you?"

"Are you really talking to that?"

I chuckled and grunted. "That hurts."

As she helped me step over the door, I heard a yell and saw someone running toward us with a large axe. Then an arrow was protruding from his chest. He tumbled and landed on his face.

I chuckled again and almost fell.

With my left eye I could see a group of people approaching. Teresa was in the lead, but the person beside her held the bow loaded with an arrow, ready to fly.

"Lynx!?" I almost fell as Jynx was suddenly gone.

She was running toward her sister. I staggered again and smiled a red-toothed grin. I could still taste the blood in my mouth. Then Teresa was there and caught me before I could fall.

"What did they do to you?" she asked.

"I'm okay," I muttered. "They're not."

I grinned again and swayed drunkenly.

"Dammit, Kade."

She helped me step forward. "You know you're not bringing that home, right?"

"Really?"

"Really," she said. "Drop the head."

I sighed, and it hurt.

Derris's head thudded as it landed in the street.

"I guess you just can't get a head in this Fallen World."

Teresa snorted.

* * * * *

Chapter Ten

"I thought you were supposed to let me help," Wilson Poe said from the door of the infirmary.

"You were too slow, buddy."

"I hadn't even been back from the Bastion for a day when someone at the gate said they saw you running toward Derris like a bat out of hell."

"Had things to do, people to kill," I said. "If you can call that bunch people."

"We spent the day clearing out the stragglers. Can I ask you a question?"

"Sure."

"Why did you pick who you did to be the warlord of that zone?"

"She'll do better than you think."

"How do you expect a fifteen-year-old girl to hold it?"

"If anyone has a problem with her, they can deal with me."

"Okay," he shrugged. "I was just curious."

"Did you guys gather all the cybernetics?"

"Yeah," he said. "What do you want us to do with them?"

"I know a guy over in Dana who can put Jynx's arm back together. He owes me a favor."

"That makes sense."

"I thought it did."

"Yeah. Your choices are just a bit suspect. Seems like you spend a lot of time in the infirmary."

"A lot of my decisions are suspect, but that one? Nope. That one is solid. Have you met the girl?"

He laughed. "Yes, I did, and I know why you did it. I would have made the same choice in your shoes."

"Keep your big feet out of my shoes."

Poe laughed and walked back out the door.

Teresa stepped in, and her smile lit up the room like the morning sun.

Some things are worth fighting for in this Fallen World.

* * * * *

Christopher Woods Bio

Christopher Woods, teller of tales, writer of fiction, and professional liar, is the author of multiple series: his popular Soulguard series, the Legend series in the Four Horsemen Universe, The Fallen World, and Traitor's Moon in Kevin Steverson's Salvage Universe. He has written nine novels and been featured in several anthologies. As a carpenter of thirty years, he spends his time building, whether it be homes or worlds. He lives in Woodbury, TN with his wonderful wife and daughter. To see what he is doing just go to www.theprofessionalliar.com.

# # # # #

Ten Breaths by Marisa Wolf

Sahna stood at the edge of town and stared west. The pool of black, shot through with neon violet, had grown in the weeks since her husband had left, climbing nearly halfway up the dome of the world.

The Anadae had prophesized for decades that their Lady of Shadows, the Noctura, would cover the whole of the sky in darkness and ruin, but at the time, no one had had any cause to believe the slithery priests. The sky had then been a peerless blue and gold roof to the world, without a hint of the knotted threads that grew from the horizon where the suns normally set.

She allowed herself ten breaths and rested her hands on her growing stomach, until the smaller sun disappeared behind the growing tumor of the Noctura's power.

Night found them earlier every day, which was disconcerting in the middle of summer. The farmers who lived outside town muttered about it on market days, and there was no telling how the longer night would affect the full fall harvest. She supposed, if the shadows continued unchecked, the fall harvest would be, perhaps, the third most-pressing of their worries.

She let out the last of her allotted breaths and dropped her hand from her stomach. Arvik would return. He would win, the sky would ebb back to normal, and he would return. He was the Chosen One. There could be no other outcome.

She had known him before he became one of the deadliest swordfighters in the land. She'd handed him his first sword. She knew he would never let the world fall to shadow and the final darkness.

Sahna took one more steadying breath and turned back toward Parrington and the mountains. Their town nestled in the long, fertile crescent between the tallest mountain range she'd ever seen and the broad sweep of the roiling sea. Long ago, a boy had crossed the mountains in search of his fate and found it.

Found *her*.

She'd lived across that sea, long ago, until a search for adventure had taken her sailing over its depths. Lived as a sailor, traveler, pirate, merchant, until she fell in love with a town by the sea. And then, far more surprisingly, with a wet-behind-the-ears farm boy from beyond the mountains.

"Sahna!"

"Zunel." She quickened her pace, stepping carefully on the dirt path. The larger sun hung lower in the sky, nearing the shadows, but still leaving them some light. Zunel leaned against the broken old cottage that marked the border between the half-wild road outside of town and the cobblestones that led to the heart of their sprawling village. "I'm on my way back; I don't need a guard."

"You say that every night." The ancient water nymph pushed back her long braids of green-blue hair and bared her teeth. "And every night, I ignore you. And then every night you say—"

"I've been protecting myself for longer than I've known you," Sahna answered dutifully, a smile pulling at the corners of her lips.

"And then, *chechna*, I remind you your balance will be off while you continue to grow your child, so, for as long as the darkness spreads, you will not be left unattended."

Ten breaths. Ten breaths she gave herself every day, away from the pressures of her people. Time to think only of herself and her love before picking back up the needs of others.

"Not unattended. Such a nice way to say smothered. As though the rangers don't have eyes on all the outskirts." Sahna grinned briefly to show she was—mostly—teasing and continued toward town. "It is still spreading, isn't it?"

Zunel made a noise deep in her throat and fell into step beside her.

"He might not have reached Noctura's stronghold yet. It's a long way to travel. They might have had to stop somewhere to save someone or recover."

"Over the mountains, through the Aronset Plains, through the Unsettled Marsh." Sahna willed her thoughts away from the dangers of each long stretch.

"Through Ingarad City, or around, into the Sinoch steppes." Zunel spun the words in a singsong, likely quoting some new ballad drummed up by one of the wandering musicians. "The lava pits, the faerie forests, the quest to find the path through the Labyrinth. There are only so many magic horses to help."

At that, Sahna pictured the tireless Jynx, her husband's most high-tempered companion, and laughed. It made for a far better thought than considering the dangers her husband, their friends, and his horse would endure.

"Maybe one more month, before we know he's reached her." *Before she truly needed to worry.* "I always thought she'd come to find him, to set the battle where she wanted. It wouldn't have been any easier for our heroes, but at least it would have been over sooner." A cold breath swept from the back of her neck down her spine, and she shook herself to dispel it. "Another month?"

"The skies always darken before the next dawn." Zunel reached over and tugged at Sahna's sensible braid. "That's why we have the songs, to remind us it's not the end."

"We have songs so you can decide which singers to take home from the tavern," Sahna replied, allowing herself to be pulled back toward hope. The sky would darken until her husband and his trio of companions met the shadow daemon and defeated her. "Isn't that why you invented sea shanties, a thousand years ago?"

"Sea shanties are as old as the water itself, youngling, and even *I* haven't lived that long." As always, Zunel avoided confirming or denying her age.

Nymphs tended to live for several human generations—perhaps that influenced why one or another of them used their inborn magics to unite or conquer the continent every few hundred years. According to the stories, water nymphs had either the shortest or longest lifespans, but that meant little when measured against millennia. Besides, Sahna had learned to question even the most reliable tales after her life entwined with that of a Chosen One.

"Sahna!" A small figure raced down the cobblestones toward them, heedless of his footing. "There's a ship docking! Nobody recognizes it! Will you come?" Riggs slid to a halt in front of them, shifting his weight as though poised to take flight again.

Sahna blinked. Not at the news—their calm harbor was a common stop for all sorts of travelers, especially with the increase in shadows roaming unchecked—but at the silvered outline that coated

Riggs for the span of a breath. The half-grown human, orphaned on the winding streets of Ingarad City, had been a fixture in her life for a handful of years. Never once had she seen him glow.

"Zunel?" she asked, blinking after the sheen disappeared.

"Of course, I will go to the harbor with you." The water nymph snorted and clapped Riggs on his normal, non-shining shoulder as she passed him. "I'm your protector. Breaking my word to you is as good as breaking my connection to my magic."

"No, I meant—" Perhaps it had been a trick of the remaining sun. Perhaps Zunel was right, and she needed more sleep. "Tell them we're coming, Riggs."

He grinned and took off, immediately passing Zunel, who continued on at a much more sedate pace, and Riggs disappeared around the bend.

"Hello, Sahna!"

"Greetings, Zunel!"

Various voices chorused from inside the cottages they passed, from grandmothers on the stoops stripping herbs to children running between houses on errands or small adventures. Shutters and windows had been thrown open to make the most of the late afternoon breeze, and the rising scents of a dozen different dinners purled around them. The normalcy of it was undercut by multiple glances cast to the west and the near constant gesture of warding against evil that flashed from every set of hands.

In the center of town, rough stone cottages shifted into smoothed-faced row homes, with flowers bursting from windowsills in a riot of colors that matched the activity in the streets.

There were less shouted greetings here—a quick nod, an anxious smile, people of various species going quickly about their respective businesses. Sahna's breath shortened, and with dismay, she realized Zunel's measured pace was not for the nymph's benefit.

She pressed a hand to the growing curve of her abdomen and allowed herself a small wince. If a walk through Parrington winded her, she'd better hope nothing more exciting than merchants awaited them at the docks.

"Told you," Zunel muttered as they rounded the last curve where the lines of houses ended as the road angled down the cliff to the harbor.

"Two members of the Council are already on the docks, Sahna." Nendarre, spotted and silky like many of her kind from the far north, tilted her enormous hat as she continued up toward town. "Three of the tyaga swam out to inspect the ship and guide it in."

"Thanks, Darry. You on your way to the Seat?"

"Yes, ma'am. I'll let the rest of the Council know as they arrive."

"If Eckard is there, tell him I'm collecting my winnings tonight, and he might want to double them," Zunel called, her eyes fixed on the curve of sparkling water ahead. She could leave the ocean for as long as she liked and travel along any waterway in the known world, but the daemon was always most comfortable within reach of the sea.

"I'll do no such thing, *Najana*, and you know it." Nendarre had been raised in the constrictive, disciplined culture of the long-faced, long-furred therians of the north. Therians who demanded utter respect for the ruling water nymphs of her region—but Zunel had rejected such reverence. Over time, they had compromised—Nendarre happily sassed Zunel when the nymph asked for outrageous things, and Zunel allowed the one formal address. They held onto the routine as the world grew messier, which Sahna appreciated.

"Then he'll be surprised when I interrupt his dinner, and I'll be sure he knows who to blame!"

Nendarre made a rude noise, and Zunel grunted quietly in satisfaction. Sahna shook her head; her attention was on the activity below. Most of the fishing ships floated above their shadows, safely moored ahead of nightfall. The last of the catches had been cleaned and transported or stored in one of the ice houses nestled under the cliff. The long strip of dark, gray sand shone in the ebbing sunshine, dotted with an occasional canoe or citizen. Most of the people moved about on the boardwalks between the rough cliffside buildings and the large dock that stretched out into the harbor.

Three large, familiar ships remained tied alongside the dock. A fourth ship, mid-sized and double-sailed, angled through the harbor, escorted by three dark shapes under the water.

The lead tyaga sped up, breeched the water, and signaled the all clear with a spinning, airborne twist. Sahna blew her breath out and watched the buzz of activity among the people below them shift. A softening of postures, a shift of attention—the main focus remained on the harbor, but hands moved further from weapons, the weave of magic shifted, and normal end of day business resumed.

On the beach side of the dock, two people stood with their heads close together, and all who passed gave them a respectful wide berth. Zunel grunted.

"No wonder Nendarre didn't tell you which Council members were down here."

Sahna's lips twisted before she smoothed her expression. She touched Zunel's elbow with her own and stepped from the end of the cliff's zigzag path down to the boardwalk.

"Councilmembers," she said, dipping her chin. "The tyaga have cleared our unexpected visitors of malicious intent. Do you still wish to wait, or shall I see you at dinner?"

"Sahna, my darling!" The taller of the two whirled, hands reaching out from her flaring cloak. "As though we would leave you here alone with strangers in your condition."

Zunel made a noise so low in her throat, it might have been mistaken for a growl. Sahna bit the inside of her cheek, and the salty sting of copper lit the top of her tongue. She took Celedarn's hands and squeezed, knowing the older woman's hands would have otherwise ended up pressed to her midsection, feeling for the baby.

"My condition remains unchanged, Councilmember. As it will for the next few months, may the suns and moons be willing." She set a look of polite interest on her face and turned slightly toward the other older individual.

Archemody inclined his head, keeping his hands clasped and tucked into his drooping sleeves. "May they will it so," he murmured in answer. "Do let the young Councilmember go, Celedarn, you know very well humans can operate perfectly normally while breeding." He winked one of his luminous yellow eyes at Sahna, and between that and Zunel's low growl of a laugh, she nearly lost her composure.

"Oh, stuff it, Archemody." Celedarn released Sahna and touched the younger woman's cheek. "She is so very precious; we must not risk her. What would the great Hero of Tarteron say if we let his wife and unborn child come to harm while he strove to save our lands?"

"He'd say we should have gotten out of her way so she could protect herself," Zunel interjected, her tone innocent. Sahna didn't miss the gentle lap of water that reached over the edge of the dock, and she stared hard at Zunel until the water smoothed again.

"Do we have any guesses as to who might be coming to visit, Councilmembers? I know you each keep up some measure of lively correspondence with other townships." If she could shift the conversation back to the matter at hand, she wouldn't need to hear a long, detailed description of the many joys and bodily realities that faced her during her pregnancy and the resulting birth.

"Oh, my darling, you know my sea jellies have been going astray, and the winds have been so unreliable I haven't had a bird in weeks." Celedarn put a hand to her neatly pinned white hair and opened her mouth to continue talking, but Archemody smoothly stepped in.

"I have not received a new message through my pools in over a week." Despite the calm of his tone, Archemody's tufted ears twitched until his hood slid off his furred head. "None from the string of villages along the coast before that, either. This ship may have stopped elsewhere, or perhaps they've come from across the sea."

"It moves well on the water," Zunel said approvingly.

The lead tyaga saved the trio from a long delivery of human breeding practicalities from Celedarn or a lecture on how you could tell the build of a ship by the method of its water displacement from Zunel. The sleek shadow formed silver-grey ripples, then broke the water in a sudden burst. With a neat leap and minimum splashing, the tyaga landed on a free side of the dock, shifting from sleek, aquatic mammal to sleek, walking humanoid.

"Councilmembers," he said in the lilting cadence of his kind. "The ship is from the far reaches of Gerahi. They are priests, carrying a message they will share only with you." He bowed slightly, the dying sun sparkling off the even smoothness of his hide.

"Gerahi." Sahna racked her memories and considered all she'd heard in her travels. After a moment, she had it. "Gerahi, the far side of Harborscine. Famous for their oceanside caves."

"Quite a long way. Thank you, Eeaali'i." Celedarn tilted her head forward and made a flowing gesture with her arms. "Please pass on our gratitude to your compatriots."

"Of course. They will wait with the ship until it is docked." With nearly as much grace as the tyaga showed in the water, Eeaali'i sat on the edge of the dock, the tips of his feet touching the water. Unlike water nymphs, tyaga could not leave the sea for long. Staying in contact with the water could be for his comfort or could indicate he wasn't quite as sanguine about the intentions of their guests and wanted to remain lubricated in case he needed to shift rapidly. They all leaned toward caution these days.

Or, Sahna told herself in an attempt to ease her own tension, he'd been drawn into one of Celedarn's well-meaning, deeply enthusiastic, incredibly detailed conversations before and had chosen to stay a healthy distance away.

The Councilmembers kept the conversation light and free of horrifying details while the ship angled into the dock. A handful of the dockmaster's staff sprang into action, and the ship was properly secured at roughly the same time as other workers finished lifting bioluminescent torches from the water. The blue and green lights lined the boardwalk and dock, and their glow intensified as the larger sun disappeared into the creeping darkness.

The mix of fading golden sunlight and growing algae-fed radiance set their visitors in clear relief as they disembarked. Two appeared human, dressed in belted robes and adorned with spiraling tattoos that seemed one piece from skin to cloth. Three others were smaller and squatter—gnomes kitted in practical gear.

Others moved around on the boat, but made no move toward the ramp, so Sahna left them to the watchful attention of the tyaga. She arranged herself with Celedarn and Archemody so they stood in a welcoming line, shoulder to shoulder, knowing Zunel would set herself most advantageously for defense or attack, were either to become necessary.

"Welcome to Parrington," Celedarn said once the five visitors were close enough to hear over the sound of the waves and dock activity. "The dockmaster will see to your captain and any goods you wish to declare. I am Councilmember Celedarn, and these are my fellow councilors, Archemody and Sahna."

One of the gnomes blanched, and the other two stared hard at Sahna's midsection. She raised her eyebrows, wondering at the reaction. Rumor had it, gnomes grew out of well-mined mineral seams, so perhaps, they found a living creature growing inside another's body disturbing. There had been plenty of days lately where Sahna would have agreed with them.

"I am Heru, Preceptor of the Uluvian Order. We have been at sea for nearly two months, and I regret that we have not arrived sooner." The priest raised both hands toward them, palms up, then placed a hand on their heart and one against their bare, tattooed temple. "We have come to speak with you, Sahna of the Deeps."

Sahna permitted herself one deep breath before responding. Zunel's magic radiated behind her, and Sahna placed two fingers on the back of her neck. *Wait.*

"I am Sahna of Parrington now, honored guest. Our Council room is in the town." She pointed with the hand she had used to signal Zunel, then folded both hands in front of her. "We also have a smaller space set aside, against the cliff, if you are unable to travel too far from your ship."

So many peoples of the known lands had restrictions of belief or survival, or some combination thereof, and it behooved a trading town to have options for such circumstances.

"Let us stay close to the docks for now, shall we?" Celedarn beamed warmth upon all of them. "After such an unexpectedly long journey, we do not want to keep you from your message any longer. Once we have had a chance to talk, we will see to accommodations and rest."

Not for the first time, Sahna reminded herself Celedarn was quite good at her job. All the other woman projected cheery daftness and considered all personal matters occasions for public conversation, but Celedarn had been a key member of the Council for nearly fifty years, and for good cause. In a handful of lovingly delivered sentences, she had informed the priest and his companions that they would not speak to Sahna alone and would remain poised for a quick exit were their actions not to the Council's liking.

Archemody pivoted, sweeping his tail low, and led the way. Heru nodded and gestured at the other priest as they walked. "This is Nona, a Watcher of our order. Fellix, Jerden, and Arsiddy are three of our most talented cultivators."

"An important skill," Celedarn replied. "Are you all from Gerahi?"

The older Councilmember kept the conversation to small talk for the short walk, neatly avoiding introducing Zunel. The water nymph trailed behind the procession, pausing to talk to passersby and taking little apparent interest in the conversation.

"You do not build into the cliffs?" Fellix asked, peering at the structures ahead.

"Some of our ancient predecessors did, but the tides are uncertain in the winter, and being inside the earth can lead to quite a bit of trouble should the sea charge in unexpectedly." Celedarn gestured to the row of single-story structures. "Each roof is a woven mat that rolls back in case of flooding. If needed, we are able to lower ladders, ropes, and platforms with the pulley system we use to lift the daily catches and trade goods. It's all very efficient for normal days and bad days, in ways living inside the cliff did not allow our ancestors."

Fellix tilted his head up to stare harder at the pulley system as they entered a building roughly in the middle of the long sweep of the cliff. The smell of fresh-caught fish faded once they were inside, and cool bioluminescent light filled the small space.

A heavy stone table was centered in the room, surrounded by simple chairs with bright cushions. The long back wall displayed a newly freshened mural of waves made of paint, shells, and coral. The gnome, Jerden, crossed over to examine it more closely.

Archemody strode directly to the stone cistern in the back corner, then murmured and stirred the water until it emitted the low, blue light of an open channel.

"The rest of the Councilmembers will join us through the pool. We do not want to keep you waiting for their physical arrival." The older Councilmember gestured for them to sit, indicating he would stay by the pool to monitor the connection.

The other back corner held a stone cabinet, and as the youngest Councilmember present, Sahna took out a tray loaded with cups, a carafe of water, and a jug of wine. As she placed the tray carefully on the table, Riggs ran in with two large bowls, precariously balanced. Fruit and fresh biscuits safely delivered, he bowed in the general direction of the gathered beings and ran out to a chorus of gratitude.

Sahna cocked her head but knew she'd never hear him climb up to the roof to eavesdrop—he'd gotten far too talented at sneaking over the years.

"Preceptor Heru, please, what is it that has brought you all this way?" Celedarn waved toward the bowls and cups, indicating they should all help themselves, then sat and leaned forward in polite attention.

"The light is failing, and the time for our teachings has come." Heru sat board-straight, turning their head to meet every pair of eyes at the table, their gaze pulling back to Sahna's. "We come to you, Sahna of the Deeps, because your face came to our Oracle, deep in the caves of Gerahi."

"Preceptors, Watchers, and Cultivators have been sent to many corners of the known lands, but the Oracle tasked us specifically with coming to you." Nona's voice, hushed where Heru's was bold, did not match their broad-shouldered appearance. "Our ship is filled with soil and cuttings and seeds. We meant to arrive before Arvik left, to warn…" Their words faltered, and under the table, Sahna curled her fingers tight against her legs.

"I understand there are many mysteries in the known lands I will never learn, honored guests, but if you know of Arvik, you know we knew the light was failing. It's why he left—to bring the fight to the Noctura, to stop the spread of her shadows." Sahna spaced her words with deliberation, monitoring her tone. So many times, strangers had come to her, trying to influence her husband's path. It had started before she loved him, when he was but a lad, blindly swinging a sword with moons-eyes for her. She'd told herself she'd gotten used to it, but now, with the weight of her worry for him in every bone, it grated. Would they never be done asking of her?

"My lady—ah, Councilmember—forgive me. I see we must speak more plainly—the light will fail, because Arvik will fail. We raced to this town, to you, to warn you before he left. To try and change the path, but…" Heru spread their hands in an encompassing gesture, their black eyes intent on hers. "The path will not be changed. Storms and attacks from the Noctura's Anadae and yet more storms pushed us off course."

"He will not—" Sahna interrupted herself to breathe and steady her tone. A whisper of Zunel's presence reminded her what and *who* she was. She trusted herself to continue. "Paths and prophecies are all well and good, Preceptor. They are what set Arvik on this journey to begin with. I am not surprised they conflict with each other, knowing any could apply to this generation or another. What is the message you wished to share, and will it help us now?"

Heru looked down, a dark flush climbing their neck, following the lines of their tattoos.

"The shadows have won before, Sahna. When it is light, we Uluvians know that it will be dark again. When the dark comes, we know it will not always be so. Our order is charged with seeing survival through one period to the next."

"And that is your message?" She spoke with crisp politeness and forgot to look to Archemody and Celedarn to see if the other Councilmembers had a more effective approach to drive the priests toward clarity. "My husband will die, and the dark will come?"

"My lady…you would think extended time on the ship would have made me perfectly clear, but I'm afraid I am…" Heru stared at the woven ceiling for a moment, then sighed. "I have imagined this conversation too much to allow it its own reality, I fear. Let me try again."

Heru met her eyes, and she inclined her head fractionally. Unseen, her nails dug into the thick cloth of her pants. Zunel's magic, carried by the salt-heavy air, brushed reassuringly around her neck.

"Old dwellings have root cellars, town centers are often built around large, underground caverns or large cellars supported under the earth. That is because our many peoples live in cycles—the shadows, the light, the shadows again. As our two suns spin, so does the light wane and wax. Every few generations, a nymph rises, determined to save or punish, another cycle. Sometimes they combine, shadow nymph, the time of darkness…when that happens, no hero, no matter how prepared and prophesized, can stop it."

"We didn't know," Nona interjected, eyes wide. "Our charts were wrong. We didn't know until recently what part of the cycle we were in. We came to warn you and to help you survive."

"We can do the latter, at least." Fellix slammed a small fist on the table and thrust a finger against his chest. "We settle near cellars and caves because it was dark before, but it will be light again. *We* might not see it. But our children, our children's children? They might. We'll preserve your seeds through the darkness, and we bring you seeds we kept through the light."

"Mushrooms, mostly, and night-bloomers," Arsiddy offered, touching the ragged edge of her long, drooping ear. "I know three that will like the algae you use so well." She cast an admiring gaze at the streaks of blue and green that threaded across the walls around them.

Nerves fired along Sahna's arms, urging her to move, to do, to *fight*. The calm priests presented no obvious threat, but their words, their sorrow, their preparation…something thick and heavy sloshed in her stomach, and she stood. With a hand on her abdomen as a silent excuse, she met Celedarn's eyes.

"I will leave our more experienced Councilmembers to determine what aid is most needed by Parrington," she said. "Thank you for your concern for our town."

"Yes, dear holy priests, please tell us of your requirements, and we will see what accommodation we can agree to." Celedarn dove in immediately, before any protest could be registered, and Sahna strode out of the room, reminding herself to never roll her eyes at the old woman again.

Zunel pushed off the exterior wall she'd been leaning against and matched Sahna's pace without question.

"Zunel."

"*Chechna?*"

"Can you make me something? Something I can stab?"

* * *

Sleep avoided her. Even after pushing her limits, sparring with Zunel, and eating a late dinner, energy buzzed through her veins. Her thoughts crowded against the backs of her eyelids, so she tried pacing. When that only sent twinges of pain running from her back down her legs, she leaned out the window and studied the sky.

When her eyes adjusted enough to the darkness to note the threads cutting across the view of the familiar stars, she attempted lying very still on top of her bed.

Snacks, reading close by the lantern, more blankets, no blankets...none of them were of any use.

There was no magic that would allow her to reach her husband, to assure herself the Gerahi priests had been wrong. Which, of course, they were.

A faery had claimed Arvik in the forest the day the boy turned fifteen. Other signs of his chosen-one fate followed. He met a wise, old hermit who taught him how to use his body as a weapon. He attached himself to a land caravan full of honest-leaning merchants who showed him the value and skill of haggling and surviving off the land. He met a dashing pirate girl who threw him a sword and stole his heart.

He saved a kingdom, a forest, and a herd of wild, magical horses. He fulfilled prophecies and built a crew of loyal, like-minded heroes who joined him in rescuing orphans and diverting magical explosions.

When the shadow nymph rose in Ingarad City and claimed a new title, the Noctura, he had dedicated himself to opposing her. The known lands operated best as independent entities—long-lived magic users with god complexes had never been the answer.

But she should have gone with them. Her husband set off with their friends who had become family, united in their mission, and she had stayed behind. A mistake. So, what if she was growing a person? Women had borne children and managed what had to be managed for millennia. She could have...she should have...

"Sahna?"

She sat up, startled that she had missed Riggs' telltale step outside her door.

"Riggs? Why are you…?" She shook her head and remembered he'd been eavesdropping. She was well out of sorts, not to have checked in on him. "Go to the kitchen and heat some water, we'll have some tea."

Arvik was the one who loved tea. Riggs and Sahna tolerated it, but drinking it together made it seem more like he was there and had just stepped outside for a moment. She shrugged on her house robe and looped it closed over her rumpled sleeping clothes, then padded out of her room on bare feet.

Riggs had set the kettle on the wood stove, and he stared at it in the same unseeing way she'd been studying the ceiling of her room. She passed by to ruffle his hair, then dropped a kiss on the top of his head.

Though Riggs had doubled in height since they'd found him roaming the alleyways like a feral cat, most times she couldn't help seeing him as the small ragamuffin he'd been. They'd had no business taking a child on their adventures, but he hadn't left them much choice. He found them every time they left him somewhere safe. Arvik had sworn he'd been meant for the famed trackers of the Idlehaunt Forests and simply been misplaced in Ingarad City.

"He's coming back," Riggs declared, blinking out of his fugue and glaring at a spot somewhere between her and the stove.

"We don't know these priests, Riggs. There's no reason to trust them over anyone else."

"Right." The boy sat across from her at the table, though he fidgeted so much he might as well have been pacing. "Right. What's a shadow nymph after we defeated the Ravened Beast tamer of Idlehaunt? Or the cyclone witch of the Far Shore?" His eyes shone for a moment, then he slumped. "But we were there for those."

"Arvik has fought plenty of monsters and trials without us, remember?" Hearing her own mental loop from a teenage boy should have put her worries into perspective, but she only felt them more acutely.

"I know Zunel couldn't go, so she wouldn't be corrupted by the Noctura. And I know you said you needed me here to protect you. I also know you only stayed so I wouldn't follow the group. But we should be there. We should be with him."

"We should." She rested one hand on her abdomen and reached for his with her other one. "But what we're doing here is important too. The Noctura has attacked the homes of her enemies before, and it doesn't take an evil demigoddess to know how important Parrington is to all of us."

The quietest two years of their lives had been when they'd chosen to stay, when they'd finally had their wedding and celebration, when they had rested and believed they might stay in one place, after all. Until the Noctura had risen.

Riggs nodded, then shook his head and jumped to his feet, crossing to the window and unhooking the glass to open it fully. She joined him to look out at the town they loved, then squinted to bring the mix of natural shadows and biolume torches into better focus. Over the low shine of the midnight lighting, something shimmered. A coating of silver...but the algae they used for lighting came in blue and green. What...?

"Do you see—" The words dropped midsentence, as her eyes came into better focus. Nothing silvery at all.

"I understand, Sahna, I do," Riggs replied, misunderstanding her half-asked question. "Arvik and Sapsy and Alnero and Jynx and Yarrow will win, and we'll keep everything safe for them to come home to." He sounded no more convinced then she was.

"Speaking of keeping the town safe, I've missed patrols for the last week. What say you—should we join them tomorrow to make sure all's well on the outskirts?" She bumped him with her shoulder and turned back to the stove to check on their water.

He spun around, and she saw joy mix with worry, as he glanced at her stomach.

"If you say one word about this baby," she added pleasantly, bending to pull out mugs, "I'll ensure you have primary nappy-changing duty for the entire first year of your sibling's life."

Riggs covered his horror by fetching the tin with the tea leaves. "I don't know what you're talking about," he said, rushing his words in his eagerness. "Patrol in the morning sounds great!"

* * *

Zunel, though less enthusiastic, took one look at her Sahna's expression and shrugged. "Patrol it is."

They walked to the Council Seat to select their assignments, and Sahna glanced up at the sickly gleam of the suns. Dawn had been a late and not entirely successful affair, the Noctura's reach having grown further during the night. Endless black bit through with blinding purple made the sky hard to look at.

The other six Council members were arranged throughout the Seat when Sahna, Zunel, and Riggs arrived.

"There will be plenty of dried and pickled fish, regardless of the harvest." Archemody pointed at the meticulous ledgers he kept.

Sahna saw a series of worried faces, from both the Councilmembers and their aides, but no one demanded proof.

"Dried seaweed at the worst," the ancient Dussian put in while he rocked his chair.

"That can carry us a long way. And if we take these Gerahi priests at their word, by then, we will be accustomed to the nightblooms." Terahi, tall and dapple-skinned, waved to the incoming group and gestured for them to sit. "All that balances one late dawn and a slow day of fishing."

"You know, it's more than one late dawn," Gorlav said, drumming his three long fingers on the table. "The priests—"

"Ah, Sahna." Celedarn crossed the room, arms out, her voice drowning out whatever else the marshclomp was saying. "Have you eaten? We expected you at the docks today, not the Seat."

"We're overdue to join a patrol, Celedarn, and we came to see what routes need to be covered."

"A patrol!" Celedarn dropped Sahna's hands and pressed the younger woman's cheeks. "Why, under the moons, would we force you to patrol?"

"Because every member of Parrington serves, and I've seen how exhausted the rangers look." Sahna placed her hands over Celedarn's, squeezed them, and gently pulled them from her face. "And I am of better use in the fields than on the docks."

Celedarn looked to Zunel for support, but the water nymph was intently studying the fresco ceiling. Riggs had already slipped away to look at the patrol lists. The old Councilmember sighed, tsked, then nodded.

"Oh, very well. The patrols have been quiet, other than a small shadow-wraith here and there. With market day tomorrow, some of the farmers will arrive throughout the day if they've other business to attend to."

"And the weather is determined not to clear," Archemody added, sliding in next to Celedarn. "In normal times, it would not be enough for the shadows to provide a threat during the day, but as it is…" His wide eyes showed he knew the moment he misspoke, even without the tightening of Sahna's jaw. They were all so careful not to speak of the possibility of failure that even this glancing reference stung.

"Just so. Then we will take a well-traveled, clear route for ease of motion," Sahna said firmly. She bowed to the two Councilmembers and strode purposefully toward Riggs.

"The rangers marked the path through the fields as a top need. They expect the Atherrons and Sithuans to send wagons from their farms before midday."

"Perfect. Mark it ours. Zunel?"

"A bit far from the river for my taste, but there's rain on the wind." She shook her ropes of hair back and bared her teeth. "We've done worse."

The first two hours were uneventful. Their prairie horses swished their tails and lapped lazily at the tall grasses, and two of the Atherrons' grown children passed safely with the wagon for market.

Sahna had just remembered the cheese and dried fruit in her saddlebag when something caught her eye. She turned her prairie horse and stood up taller, squinting. Motion. Dust?

"Zunel."

The water nymph closed her eyes and wriggled her fingers. "A party. Moving fast."

"That's not the Sithuans," Riggs said as his hand twitched toward his bow. "Wrong direction."

"Well." It wasn't satisfaction in Sahna's tone, given the circumstances. But there was something grounding in having a direction for all her nervous energy. "Be ready for a fight."

The dust resolved into figures within minutes. Lathered horses and panicked herdbeasts, and riders—human, therian, and sylvan. Behind them...

This was no individual shadow-wraith. It was a low wave of darkness, stabbing out with tentacles and claws, and claws that sprouted tentacles. Before they were in range, something lunged out of the roiling mass of darkness, lassoed one of the human riders, and yanked it faster than thought back into the shadowed mass.

Sahna cursed under her breath. "Fire-tipped arrows, Riggs!"

He knew his business. She was grateful he'd had so many quiet afternoons to dip arrowheads into the two sun temples' fires. Zunel guided her prairie horse with her legs, hands raised as she pulled the burgeoning rain from the gathered clouds and lashed the newly formed ropes into the shadows.

The riders ducked under the loose spray of water but were smart—or desperate—enough to keep driving forward. Riggs fired, his aim unerring. As each arrow connected with the churning mess, sparks flew, and shadows thinned. The fluid darkness was too spread out to form any offensive weapons. The beast writhed and reformed with slightly less spread to its mass.

Sahna whispered encouragement to her mount and pulled out her whip. Her short swords, effective against a single wraith, would do nothing that close to a spreading mass. Prairie horses, lower-slung than their larger cousins and double-legged, were nimble and cor-

WE DARE: SEMPER PARATUS | 385

nered well, but they would fail against the writhing of a shadow beast.

"Try to angle it back," she shouted to Zunel, gesturing wildly to catch the attention of the oncoming escapees. "We'll cut hard for the stone edge."

There was nothing holy about Riggs' arrows or her whip, but they'd been treated with magic to keep the effects of fire close at hand. They sparked into life on contact with the malicious shadow, lessening its power and reach little by little. They wouldn't be enough to fully destroy that much pooling darkness, but they could hurt it.

She hoped.

The fight erupted in complete chaos. Sahna hoped the incoming people had understood the directions she'd gestured, but the air around them darkened, and nothing was certain.

Darkness solidified around her, and she lashed back, her prairie horse kicking as many legs as it could while it ran. She cut in and around, trying to find the edges of the beast, but it flowed too fast around her. Each strike missed her by the barest margin. Her's and her steed's reflexes were all that stood between her and grievous injury.

The mounts of the escaping party screamed, as did their riders, and only the occasional flares of fire from her whip or Riggs' arrows making contact lightened the pressing gloom around her. Every motion was suspect, and she nearly sliced a panicked human when he charged past, a hairsbreadth from crashing into her.

"Don't throw me," she whispered, letting go of her reins to grab her short sword. She kept her whip weaving above them in an old training pattern, knowing she would tire soon were she to put more into it.

A coil of shadow darted toward her face and avoided the arc of the whip, but she managed to cut across it at the last moment, and the motion nearly toppled her from the prairie horse.

Zunel was right. My balance is for crap.

Sweat dripped down her back, and her whip hand began to cramp. She had neglected practice for too long and could barely keep the enchanted length moving between her and the bulk of the shadow beast.

"GET CLEAR!" Zunel's bellow rocketed through her, and Sahna had a moment to appreciate Zunel's faith in her, that she might have an idea which direction 'clear' was, before she cast up a perfunctory prayer and kicked her mount.

Eight powerful legs could jump a long way, and she trusted the prairie horse's instincts to jump *away* from the monster's main mass.

She didn't look back to see what mess Zunel had made of the shadowbeast but focused, instead, on the stone break ahead. They'd be in reach of the rangers' bows, now, if they'd aimed right…

The air lightened as her prairie horse launched over the line of stone that had marked the town's borders for generations. Whatever Zunel and the rangers had done had worked.

She let her steed run and turned to ensure Riggs and Zunel were there and to take a quick count of the new arrivals.

There were ten, perhaps twelve, if some of those bulges tied to riders were tightly wrapped younglings rather than possessions.

"Thank you," one gasped, riding close to her.

Two long horn calls sounded, signaling the all clear. She pulled up, motioning for the others to stop. It took a few minutes and some shouting, but exhaustion won out, and everyone staggered to a halt.

"The rangers will meet us," Sahna said as she dismounted. "You have wounded, and your mounts need to rest. You've made it to Parrington," she added, in case that was where they were headed.

"We'd been riding to the east, away from the shadows," a tall human man, supporting a drooping Therian, said. The bundle strapped to his chest wailed, confirming that it was some sort of living creature. "We thought the light would last longer, stay further away, but every day…" He ran out of breath, or energy, and stalled.

"We've lost…about half of our number," a woman continued, wavering on her feet. Riggs eased toward her, unthreatening, alert in case she fell. "A few chose to stay in towns we found along the way. The rest…"

"We've been chased before, but never like…like this," a sylvan said. She was graceful and green, with strings of leaves waving behind her head. "It came out of the last mountain pass and took Leese before…" Like the others, she trailed off, her eyes staring past them at a remembered horror.

Sahna took water out of her saddlebag and passed it around, while Zunel made the rounds of the creatures they'd brought. None of them seemed shadow-touched, but the water nymph was best positioned to feel another daemon's influence.

"Parrington." One of the men stepped forward, staring at Riggs, then turned disbelieving eyes on Sahna. "Parrington. Where Arvik of Tarteron, Sahna of the Deeps, Alnero the Bold, Yarrow the Fae, and Sapsy the—Sahna?" He staggered, focusing on her, sweat streaking his dusty face.

"Rilvin?" The name rose from the depths of her memory, recalling the taste of fresh bread in the back of her throat. The inn they'd hidden in for weeks, the innkeeper who lied and bartered to save them and snuck rolls into the crawlspace under the stairs to tide them over.

"We're safe, friends, we're safe." He smiled so brightly she couldn't help but respond, then he took a step forward—and collapsed.

Riggs was there first, followed by two rangers not long after, but it was hours before everyone was treated, settled, and sorted.

Sahna bore several lectures from Celedarn while debriefing the Council. She only took a break to send Riggs to convert her and Arvik's study into a temporary bedroom for Rilvin and his wife once they'd determined who would be staying where.

"Should we expect more people to flee toward the ocean, following the light?" Dussian asked, glaring at Archemody's ledgers. "We'll need to harvest something more than mushrooms, if so."

"The Sithuans didn't come in today," Tarmillo of the rangers interjected when no one answered the ancient Councilmember. "We'll send a pair of rangers to check on them as soon as the suns come through in the morning."

"The priests have found their planting grounds?" Sahna asked, keeping her tone neutral with effort.

"Yes. Unfortunately, they settled on the cave system in the foothills. It has large stretches of harvestable areas, and they decided it would be best for a large-scale effort. Until the attack today, we thought it close enough to protect." Terahi shook her head. "Even if we put all the rangers on that path, if a shadow beast of that size were to return or any of the Noctura's other creatures were to come, the caves are too far out for us to easily protect."

"I'll draw up a few rotation plans tonight so we can discuss what's possible, Councilmembers." Tarmillo bowed his head. "Councilmember Sahna, may I include you, Riggs, and Zunel?"

"Yes," Sahna and Zunel answered before Celedarn could do more than lean forward to protest.

"Very good. I'll ask the dockmaster for volunteers as well." Tarmillo stepped away from the table, which served as the Council Seat, to confer with the other rangers in the room.

Sahna listened to the continuing conversation with half her attention, nodding at appropriate intervals and tracing the carvings on the great wooden table. Other Parrington residents stepped up to speak to the Council. The large space remained busy, but not crowded, until late into the evening. Sahna's sense of time was warped by the early nightfall. Zunel, who was leaning against the refreshment table across the room, began to list to one side.

After her mind insisted for the fourth time that an enormous shadow beast encroaching upon Parrington meant the Noctura still considered Arvik a threat, Sahna raised her hand to suggest a closing to Council matters for the night.

She'd missed her chance to stand on the edge of town, take her ten breaths, and watch for Arvik. The realization landed like a blow.

* * *

Every day, the darkness swelled across the sky, relieved only by the flickering, pulsing, purple lightening. A near perfect oval remained open almost directly above them that allowed a few hours of sunlight each day.

More shadow creatures prowled outside the boundaries of the town, shying away from the circle of pure sky, even at night.

"Perhaps the Noctura doesn't want all light-needing creatures to die," Nona said to the Council one evening. The wind was howling outside the Seat's long, low building. "She knows there is a cycle to life just as we do."

"Our records tell us the shadows will settle as time passes. They are stretching after so many years underground. It's almost understandable," Heru hastily continued before anyone moved to interrupt. There had been news of Cerra Village's destruction just that afternoon. "There is no cause for wholesale slaughter and devastation. It will lessen, as time goes on."

"How much time, good priest?" Sahna asked, aggressively neutral. "Days? Weeks? Years?"

"Uh, years, perhaps. But it will not always be so."

"And, perhaps, the circle above us is meant to drive survivors to us, so we are gathered in one place, before the Noctura wipes us out?" Terahi lifted her voice as though asking a question, but Sahna knew the other woman neither wanted nor expected an answer. She simply spoke the unspoken worry aloud.

Celedarn shook her head. "We must survive as we can and let go of the worries we cannot control. Tarmillo, what was recovered from Cerra Village?"

* * *

More attacks came, and Sahna fought until her body became too unwieldy. She insisted pregnancy made her a stronger fighter, and it certainly seemed so. Despite endless close calls, she took no wounds. She and Riggs were invincible. For a few weeks after she left the field, she stood atop a ranger's lookout with a bow, but that had never been her strength.

She spent more time in the Council Seat, listening to the stories of the survivors who arrived and working closely with her fellow Councilmembers to shift resources and space as best they could. As Terahi had suggested, the open circle of sky attracted the desperate and the lost—those who could not bear to live under the Noctura's near-permanent night.

They came in ships, on foot, and in wagons, but there were never enough to overwhelm the town. The shadows saw to that, winnowing the travelers and leaving only bits of evidence behind for the rangers to find.

Sahna missed her time on the edge of town more days than she made it, but she told herself it was all right. She would know Arvik was on his way back when the sky lightened and the space above them widened until they could see both suns at once. Every day, she tilted her head up to study the opening. Surely, as her body swelled around her, that space grew as well, meaning her husband would come home to her, and their world would return to normal.

She leaned on Zunel, more for warmth than support, as they walked to the Council Seat in what passed for morning. Despite their layers, despite it being no more than early fall, the wind bit and held, fierce as midwinter.

"Fellix said all the mushrooms are flourishing, and so far, only the zetroot has failed." Zunel, who had helped arrange the proper irrigation alongside the gnomes, had taken some small interest in the Cultivators' results. "I'll take Riggs with me tonight so we can start learning which to harvest when."

Sahna nodded. Most of her focus was on keeping her pace steady. Her legs had started giving out unexpectedly, one and then the other, and given the size of her belly, regaining her balance was a dicey matter. If she fell again, Celedarn would start demanding that Council meetings relocate to Sahna's house, so she didn't need to walk anywhere.

They arrived safely at the Seat, and the suns came and went before Sahna had a chance to step back outside. As she was considering whether the bright circle of sky had grown bigger during the one day she hadn't looked at it, Riggs burst into the room, arms clutched tightly to his chest.

Cold wind swept in around him before Zunel shut the door. Sahna half stood from her chair, knowing the look on his face was fear.

"Sahna," he gasped. She meant to run to him, but her leg went out from under her, and she fell back into her chair. He hurried across the room, and she reassured herself he wasn't injured. He carried a woven sling, piled high with scraps of fabric, and as he got closer, something in it stirred.

"Riggs?"

"Riggsy Riggs, got so big, silver sailors in the harbor," a tiny voice said from the sling. A familiar voice, so familiar, an ache traveled up her spine.

Impossibly familiar. Faeries never parted from those they claimed. Never.

"Y-Yarrow?" Her back cramped, and she tightened her fingers on the edge of the table. *No!*

"Sahna, Lady of the Deeps. Sahna, pirate for keeps. Sahna, are you all silver too?" The fabric shifted, and a face emerged. Fragile, perfect, and smaller than the palm of her hand, the face that appeared was shaded in pinks, blues, and greens, mottled like a spray of flowers.

"Yarrow," Sahna said again, her voice breaking. Faeries could not be parted from their chosen partner, not by any power in the known lands. No power but death.

"Silver here and silver there, my lady-lou, my lady-la. All of a piece, my lady Sahna."

Riggs stared at the faery, then lifted his eyes to Sahna, pleading. "A boat came into the harbor. They found her wandering Ingarad City, setting things on fire. She…she—"

Pain split Sahna to her core, but she pushed it away, grasping for her composure, for her breath.

"Let's take her home. Maybe the distance has…" They both knew it wasn't the distance. There could be no distance if Arvik still lived. "Yarrow, what *happened?*"

Yarrow's eyes, crystalline prisms of light, traced the designs on the ceiling. Sparks jumped from the tips of her ears but faded before catching anything on fire.

"Made a deal. Cracked the world. You're cracking, Sahnamygirl, Sahnamylove. You're cracking just like the moons, pulling the sea away." Yarrow slipped deeper into her blankets.

Sahna tried to push up from the table and stand, but both legs wobbled this time. Another flaring bolt of pain tore through her middle, and she gasped, understanding.

The baby.

Of course.

* * *

Far too many people leaped into action, but Celedarn cut across them all and managed the chaos with an iron hand and flagrant use of the word 'dear.' Sahna had lost all sense of time, but she recognized the healer's cottage. They were taking no chances after Yarrow's appearance.

Zunel and Celedarn stayed by her side. Now and then, she heard Riggs in the outside room, Yarrow singing, and people inquiring about her health, but they were disconnected moments.

The baby's arrival was meant to be *hope*—she'd always known, to her core, that Arvik would be back before their baby arrived. Her thoughts were jumbled by all the things her baby was meant to be— the child who would see the light return, the child of a Chosen One and the one he chose, the child of heroes born into a world she wouldn't have to save. It was wrong now, and soured, and all pain and pain and pain—

And Zunel, murmuring encouragement.

Celedarn, demanding Sahna handle her business the way she handled the Council.

The healer, pushing and prodding.

The smell of fresh-baked bread, and Rilvin's loud voice reassuring Riggs.

Riggs, pacing with his too-big feet.

Parrington, and all its people, centered under a circle of blue in a black and purple sky.

The piercing cry, indignant and unafraid, of the baby Arvik would never meet.

$$* * *$$

The baby was swaddled and tucked against her, and slept as hard as Riggs in the chair next to the bed. Sahna looked from one to the other, smiling through her exhaustion.

"Yarrow," she whispered, and the bundle on Riggs' chest stirred.

"Sahna-of-the-silver," the faery replied, pushing into view.

"Tell me. Please."

"The Noctura swirled into the Labyrinth. Shadows to the left and darkness to the right, nowhere to turn."

Sahna wanted to close her eyes, but she'd asked for it. She extended her free hand, and, after a moment, Yarrow struggled free and half-jumped, half-flapped into it. The faery curled up like a tiny cat, wrapping her arms around Sahna's fingers.

"We should have gone around, not through. The Labyrinth was hers, everything in it was hers. We couldn't..."

"He made a deal," Sahna prompted.

"And broke the world." The words were faint, and Yarrow's now-ragged wings fluttered with each one in mild protest. "The light had to go. He bottled it though. Some for me and some for you, for Riggsy and Jynx-ie and Parrington too..."

"The sky?" Why else would it have stayed clear, just a bit, just above them?

"Everyone he loved, she wouldn't hurt. Everyone he pictured, she couldn't touch. Harm could still come, but not by her orders, not by her hand, not by those she owned. She made a deal."

"He...gave up?" Riggs had opened his eyes, and betrayal was thick in his voice.

"No," Sahna said, exhaustion and sorrow weighing her down. "He saved us."

"And broke the world!" Riggs kept his voice low, remembering the baby, but the raw hurt and anger came across clear as day.

"No," she said again, tucking Yarrow between her shoulder and neck, trusting the mad faery to contain her flames. "The light had to pass, like the priests said. But they didn't say how long it had to be gone."

"Sahna—"

"He made a deal. She's tied to it. She'll break over it."

He wanted to argue; she saw it written all over his face. But her surety gave him pause, and her eyes closed before he recovered.

* * *

Ten breaths. Ten breaths at the end of their world. They were ready. They would finish Arvik's quest. A warrior, a teenager, a mad faery, and an innkeeper. A handful of loved ones protected from the Noctura's power by her own words.

Ten breaths, then Sahna took another step west. Out of Parrington. Into the darkness that yielded before her.

Breathe. And step.

* * * * *

Marisa Wolf Bio

Marisa Wolf was born in New England and raised on Boston sports teams, Star Wars, Star Trek, and the longest books in the library (usually fantasy). Over the years, she majored in English, in part to get credits for reading (this only partly worked), taught middle school, was headbutted by an alligator, built a career in education, earned a black belt in Tae Kwon Do, and finally decided to finish all those half-started stories in her head.

She currently lives in Texas with three absurd rescue dogs, one deeply understanding husband, and more books than seems sensible. Learn more at www.marisawolf.net.

# # # # #

Moments by Kevin Ikenberry

The last deader fell as the bright red sun rose over the eastern horizon. Tendrils of fog crept over the long, unkempt grass around them, adding to the macabre scene and its sudden, eerie silence. Pistol in hand, a solitary man swept the immediate area one last time before holstering his pistol and turning inward to the remains of their perimeter. Everything they'd been trying to avoid had happened in one, awful night. Exhausted, they'd entered the college campus, trying to find a place to shelter from the dead. They'd tried the stadium and climbing to the high press box only to find the place crawling with dead. Cut off from their escape route on the highway, they moved south through the campus. Surrounded, they made their final stand in a quadrangle between burned out husks of academia as the dead surged toward them. The survivor's defensive perimeter had collapsed, leaving only two of them alive.

Matt wiped his face, grimaced at the bloody gobbets between his fingers, and turned. Only Sonny remained alive. The older man knelt over his backpack. "Dude! What the fuck?"

His shock of white hair disheveled and flecked with blood and tissue, Sonny replied, "I got that last one before it ate your fucking face, Matt. Got a little close, huh? It ain't that damn gross."

Laughing, Sonny broke down the twelve-gauge shotgun, ejecting two smoking rounds onto the gory ground at their feet. He shook out a soggy cigarette and poked it between his lips. "We got 'em all, pard. Good thing the sun's up, or them fuckers woulda just kept on coming."

Matt nodded. Fourteen of them had left North Carolina three months ago. They'd lost seven between Charlotte and Birmingham. Now, only two remained. They hadn't seen another living soul since Georgia. Crossing Alabama, there'd been nothing but deaders everywhere they looked. The whole damned state. Might as well be the whole damned country. The six of them believed they were going to make it to the Mississippi and get across to civilization. They'd pushed hard since Tuscaloosa, but it hadn't mattered. Only two remained.

Vanessa and James, the newlyweds, lay in torn pieces fifty meters away. James could have made it. Vanessa's broken ankle wouldn't let her go any further, and James refused to leave her, making sure they died together. Sally didn't make it to the makeshift perimeter. The deaders caught her, but not before she got eight with her shotgun. Damned tough chick. She didn't scream when they killed her. Unlike Derrick, the big, muscular, ex-Auburn football player. He wailed while the deaders tore his legs off. He might have called for his mommy, but it was hard to remember exactly what had happened.

The last hour before sunrise had been a cycle of shoot, reload, shoot, reload. Three hundred dead lay around them. Under a hazy sunrise the color of blood, it was fitting. The thick, Mississippi air was redolent with rotten flesh and the metallic smell of spilt blood.

Matt wiped his brow with a forearm and grimaced at what came off on his skin. "We gotta move, Sonny."

"Yeah, about that…" The older man lit the cigarette with shaking hands.

"They're gonna come at sundown. When they get out of the shadows, and the sun don't burn 'em. We gotta get far away from here and find shelter." Matt picked up an empty rifle from the ground, checked the magazine, and discarded it. They'd been short on 5.56-millimeter ammunition, and he knew there wasn't any in the packs of his fallen friends. He walked over to Sally's body and picked up her shotgun. They had plenty of 12-gauge rounds. Matt walked back toward Sonny and picked up Derrick's forty-five pistol. He ejected the magazine and snorted. The bastard had never fired a shot. He rifled through Derrick's gear and grabbed more ammunition and a plastic bag for the second pistol.

"Gonna be a long night 'less we find more survivors."

Sonny laughed with scorn. "You don't get it, do you, boy?"

Matt squinted. "I told you not to call me that."

"Yeah, yeah." Sonny sucked a drag from the cigarette and exhaled in a spasmodic cough. The wet sounds had grown worse over the last few weeks. Cancer. Sonny wouldn't make it two more months without treatment. The kind of treatment that only Arizona had, if the shortwave was to be believed. "We gotta find transportation again. That's the thing."

"We tried that." Matt shoved the pistol and ammunition inside and then shouldered his pack, an olive drab Army one he'd found at the remains of Fort Gordon two months ago. "All the gas is bad. No car is going to get us across the big river. Maybe we can find a couple of bikes or something."

"Finding bikes cost us time and lives, boy. Or don't you remember Atlanta? Nah. They's gotta be some good gas somewheres." Sonny shook his head. "Make getting to Arizona a helluva lot faster. Maybe on the other side, huh?"

"A car would only last until we got there. Still have to swim across."

Sonny coughed. "Yeah. Can you even swim?"

"Lifeguarded at the pool every summer since I was fourteen." Matt turned back to the older man and frowned. "Yeah, I can swim."

"Will wonders never cease?" Sonny laughed and shook his head. He'd once felt anger at Sonny's mocking, but Matt simply sighed. They didn't have time for this, and he'd heard enough.

"Yeah. Let's get moving. There's a town about fifteen miles or so up the road. We can make it by dark if we move now. Find us a good place to hole up for the night," Matt said. The part about praying that the dead were not plentiful there, he left out. There shouldn't have been this many deaders on a college campus, but there were. "Get some of that stink on you, Sonny. We'll make a noise bomb and be off like the wind."

His face clean, mostly, Matt looked over his tee-shirt and dirty jeans. The deaders couldn't see very well, but they could smell human flesh. They'd discovered in South Carolina, completely by accident, that the tissue and fluids from a deader weren't dangerously contaminated, and they could be used to mask a normal human being's scent. There was enough fresh matter on him to last a day or so. He'd have to replenish, but that was part of their routine. He turned northwest, back toward the highway, and started walking. He'd gone twenty steps before he turned around.

He stared hard at Sonny. "Hey, man. You coming?"

Sonny smoked for a moment, looking over what had once been a quiet, inviting plaza between academic buildings. A broken statue of a long dead educator lay across the long, lush grass. "Fuck it. I ain't going."

"What?"

"I'm tired of running, Matt."

Matt shook his head. "Come on. We gonna make it together."

"You really think that?" Sonny coughed again. "We ain't even gonna make the big river."

"It's a couple days away. On the other side, there's fewer dead, Sonny. All we gotta do is get to the heat and the sun, man." Matt started walking. "Grab your shit and come on."

"I'm not coming."

"Then you're a dead man." Matt said.

"So are you, Matt. Big, athlete hero gonna be a dead motherfucker like the rest of us. You ain't gonna come near the Miss'ippi." Sonny laughed. "You remind me of my lieutenant in 'Nam. All hopeful and shit. Like Charlie could be reasoned with. I seen what them bastards did, just like these dead fuckers. We fightin' a losing war."

"Bullshit." Matt spat on the ground between them. A deader screeched in the distance. "We can make it, Sonny."

Truth was, the old man's worsening condition slowed them down. They'd once made up to thirty miles a day as a group. Anymore, ten was all they could handle.

The older man turned away and sat down. "I'm staying right fucking here. Let those bastards come and get me. I ain't gonna make it with this lung sickness no how."

Matt stepped across Derrick's body and held out the big pistol. "Take it."

"You'll need it more than I will. I got my shotgun, so I'll keep 'em off ya. Shoot a round every hour or so. Them bastards will come soon as it gets dark," Sonny said. He looked up and smiled, the corners of his scruffy, white beard twitching in the afternoon breeze. "Get on out of here, Matt. Maybe you'll make the big river."

"Or die tryin'," Matt said with a smile. Their old joke. It had been funny until somebody had actually died. Marissa had killed herself trying to cook them dinner. She had been a chef, and when they had tried to hole up in a hotel for a night, she'd tried to cook them dinner on a propane grill she found. Blew herself up in a gas explosion that drew in every dead motherfucker within twenty miles.

Matt stuck out his hand. "Bye, Sonny."

"Yeah," Sonny said, but he didn't move to shake his hand. "Get the fuck out of here."

Matt turned and walked west. A few deaders screeched from the darkened, broken windows of the academic buildings, but he avoided them. They couldn't really see, but all the dead listened. They could hear an engine at ten miles, and a gunshot at twenty, maybe more. They hated sunlight, and they hated heat. Water stopped them, too. The heat and light in the lower corner of Arizona called to him. The shortwave sounded promising. There was life out west. Anything was better than the trail of dead towns he'd left behind.

By himself, ten miles would be easy. Depending on how fast he walked, he might even make the next big town another fifty miles down the highway. He wouldn't be waiting on anyone anymore, so why couldn't he go faster? It was all up to him. This should have inspired a confidence, a swagger, but it didn't. When night came, he'd be alone. If he chose the wrong place to sleep, he wouldn't wake up in the morning. If he didn't find more supplies, he'd starve or die of thirst. The tattered atlas in his pack said it was a hundred and six miles from the campus to the river. He could make it in four days. There was enough food in his pack for six people for three days. It would be more than enough. Losing folks paid off in some ways. They weren't gonna need it anymore.

For a second, Matt wondered if he'd hear Sonny take his own life. Nah, that hard sumbitch would take a few with him when he went. It's all any of them hoped to do when their moment came.

* * *

WE DARE: SEMPER PARATUS | 405

Should've been his moment. The score was tied. With two seconds remaining in the game, Central Carolina College had the ball and could upset the defending national champion in the big dance. An upset like that had only happened once before. Central Carolina had never made it this far in the tournament. This would be their best chance, and, improbably, it would be his moment.

During the timeout, coach Winchester told them bluntly, "Everybody in the building thinks Calvin's going to get the ball. We will set it up that way, but Matt's going to take the last shot from the corner."

He felt his teammates' eyes on him. Some trusted him. Some were unsure of him. But Calvin was mad. He was their best player and undoubtedly wanted the last shot. A chance to be part of the national highlights for at least one evening. But no one said anything. Everyone trusted coach Winchester. His decisions all season long had gotten them not only into the end-of-year tournament for the first time, but had given them a realistic chance of pulling off one of the biggest upsets in sports history. Nobody would disagree. He said a few other things, the standard motivational tripe, and they put their hands together in the circle, yelled 'team,' and headed back onto the floor.

Rudy, the big center from Iowa, put the ball in play from the sideline. Just like Coach had told them, everyone focused on Calvin. They left Matt virtually undefended in the corner, just inside the three-point line. Rudy faked the ball toward Calvin and then flung it downcourt to Matt like a soccer player.

In the millisecond the ball traveled through the air, Matt heard a gasp of surprise from the 40,000 spectators. He saw the shocked faces of the players on the other bench as they realized their mistake. The other coach, red-faced and pointing at Matt, tried in vain to get his players' attention. Matt caught the ball, squared to the basket, and released the shot. He watched it travel through the air with a perfect shooter's backspin in a perfect arc toward the hoop. Time clicked to zero. Red lights on the backboard indicated time had run out and the game was over. But his shot was still in the air. Everything slowed. He glanced at the referee to make sure the ball was still live. It was. The ref's hand was up in the air. All it had to do was go in. He looked back at the ball. The shot looked good.

It looked damn good.

The ball caught the rim on the far side and rebounded immediately toward the near side before bouncing straight up into the air. Everyone in the building held their breath. And then the ball fell away from the goal. Half of the crowd was stunned and the other half relieved. Matt's shoulders slumped forward, and he jogged to the bench where Coach Winchester talked about how they were going to win the overtime. But Matt wasn't listening because his moment was over.

He lasted only a couple of minutes into overtime. Unable to focus, detached from the game around him, he left no other recourse for the coaching staff. Matt sat on the bench despondently. He had let it get away from him. The one moment where his life could have been bigger than it was, and he let it go. He sat, head in hands, for the rest of the game. When they won, with an outstanding play from Calvin no less, Matt could not take any joy in the celebration. He smiled and hugged his teammates, but his stomach continued to knot inward upon itself. He was the last out of the shower and the last on the bus. No one said anything, but he knew they could see it in his face.

When the time came for the team to celebrate the victory with a meal, Matt feigned illness and remained behind at the hotel. He turned off the lights in his room, put on his headphones, and fell asleep. When he woke the next morning, the sun was bright and shining on a day that would be unlike any other in human history. He pulled back the curtains and saw smoke rising from dozens of fires across the city. He realized it couldn't have been disgruntled fans from the game, though those things happened occasionally. Something much larger was in play. Smoke even appeared to be rising from his hotel.

Matt grabbed his cell phone and saw that there was no service. There were no messages of any type, nor could he connect to the Internet. He grabbed the hotel phone and found it was dead. At that moment, he also realized the power was out. The smoke from the building spurred him to action, and he quickly dressed and threw on his shoes before making his way into the hallway. The dark corridor was only lit by emergency lights, but Matt found the staircase and raced down the four flights of stairs to the lobby.

He burst into the sunlit space and immediately froze in shock and revulsion. Lying on the floor were two bodies. The woman and her young child appeared to have been partially eaten. Blood splatters covered the floor and walls. There was no one else in sight.

What the fuck?

Matt raced across the foyer and tried not to look at the carnage in the lobby. He walked to the door and immediately heard a cacophony of sirens and alarms and an unearthly screeching sound echoing among the downtown buildings. In the parking lot, he caught sight of more bodies on the sidewalk and even more lying in the deserted street. Several cars appeared to be on fire. At the intersection, there appeared to be more than thirty bodies. There was not a first responder in sight.

Movement to his left caught Matt's eye. A young man with long, dark hair moved among the bodies as if he were injured and trying to sit up. Inside his shocked mind, Matt's adolescent first-aid training suddenly surfaced. He made his way toward the man.

"Hey, man, you all right?

The man stood, and his head snapped toward Matt. In that moment, Matt knew everything had gone wrong. Skin hung from the young man's face, and Matt could see his exposed jaw and cervical column. His eyes seemed opaque and bloodshot at the same time. He regarded Matt with a feral grin that sent icy rivers of terror down Matt's spine. The impossibly loud honking of a truck horn came from behind him. As the engine roared, Matt could tell the truck was moving up the main street in his direction.

A voice augmented by a bullhorn screamed at him. "Get away from that man! Get over here! Get in the truck before he eats you!"

In that moment, Matt realized the injured man wasn't injured at all. He was dead and, somehow, still alive, too. Matt sprinted for the truck. It was one of those tractor-trailer wreckers; they looked like a big rig in the front and had a wide, high rail deck on the back that sloped down to a truck hitch. He could see three people in the truck's cab and at least four in the back. The ones in the rear were all holding rifles of some type. One of them fired several shots over Matt's head, presumably at the dead man he had left in the parking lot. Matt wasn't going to turn around to make sure.

As Matt closed the distance to the truck, he could see that it had mostly been white at one time but was covered in dark red blood and some sort of black matter across its front and sides. None of that mattered. It was a safe spot, and everything around him was crazy as fuck. He scrambled aboard the truck, and it tore through downtown Charlotte and headed west. Matt crawled to a spot with his back against the cab next to an older man smoking a cigarette. The white-haired man looked at him with a wry smile on his face.

"My name's Sonny. Who're you?"

"Matt." He glanced back over the rear deck of the truck as they left downtown behind. "What the fuck happened, man?"

"End of the world, boy." Sonny chuckled. "End of the fucking world."

* * *

Matt reached a gas station outside of Mathiston, Mississippi, late that afternoon. Pistol drawn, he looked inside the dirty glass windows of the store for any signs of deaders. He saw nothing out of the ordinary, except for some partially stocked shelves. One wide pane of glass had been shattered; the bricks he believed responsible for the carnage lay across the bottom shelves which were full of overpriced school supplies. He stepped through the opening and quickly made his way through the shattered aisles. He found several cans of soup and a box of chocolate bars tucked behind a broken shelf. Snickers weren't his favorite, but he took them anyway. To his surprise, there were two gallon jugs of distilled water on another shelf. He took them, too, and made his way out of the store and into the summer heat.

He stood under the gasoline pump awning, consulted his atlas on the hood of a burned-out car, and drank from one of the gallon jugs. Eupora was another twelve miles down the road, and he could likely make it there before sunset. The challenge would be finding a good place to sleep. While deaders possessed incredible hearing and could sniff out a normal human being, there were limitations to their abilities. Stairs slowed them down considerably. Ladders or anything requiring climbing almost paralyzed them. Problem solving was beyond their capability. Survivors used that to their advantage and, when possible, shared their methods with others.

As he made his way into Mathiston, Matt saw a water tower with a wide platform ringing the lower portion of the tank more than thirty feet off the ground. The built-in ladder was about ten feet off the ground, which would make it impossible for the deaders to get to him. On the tower, someone had painted a red pound sign near the ladder and the small porch where it connected to the tank structure. They'd heard about codes on the shortwave, and the pound sign indicated a good place to sleep. Matt figured he'd need to find a ladder to get up there. The sky looked clear enough. Sleeping on a water tower during a thunderstorm wasn't a smart idea, but it beat the alternative.

No, he had to keep moving. If survivors had been through here, there would be another sign further down the road. Humans taking care of humans for a change. Matt had to smile. Carrying a jug of water in each hand, he stepped out onto the highway and walked west.

He made it to the road junction south of Eupora about an hour before sunset. Several herds of deer crossed the highway, and he smiled, remembering Sonny and Derrick talking about going deer hunting. How the deer were loving all the humans being gone. No one was around to shoot them. A gunshot would bring the dead in droves. At the junction of US Highway 82 and Highway 9, there were several red painted signs. On the road toward Eupora were three X's. Too many dead up that way. Don't even try.

On the far side of the junction sat a gas station. This one appeared to be completely intact. On it were a painted pound sign and a cross. Sleep here. Supplies. Out of options in the failing light, Matt jogged toward the station. The glass windows were covered with boards, and the doors were chained shut. He wondered how in the hell he was supposed to get inside. He walked around the back and found a ladder lying in the weeds about ten feet from the building's foundation. The upper half of it appeared to have been cut off. Where the upper supports ended, someone had welded a sturdy hook on the inside of the top rung. Matt spun to look at the building and saw the other half of the ladder hanging over the lip of the roof by about three feet. Indentations in the lowest rung gave him his answer. Matt reached down for the ladder in the weeds, and a black snake roiled and shot into the thick grass. His heart leapt in his chest, and he froze for a moment, but regained his composure and grabbed the lower ladder and raised it up to its mate. They fit together perfectly. Without a second thought, he climbed the ladder to the roof and then reached over to pull it up. A square hatch sat about six feet from him. It was closed and appeared watertight. All good signs.

Matt doffed his pack and dug for the flashlight in one of the three outside pockets. With it in one hand, he drew his pistol and opened the hatch. A small ladder dropped into the dark space below. He took a deep breath and descended the ladder. The small storage and janitorial area was eerily clean and quiet. The sole door was ajar and led past the restrooms and into the store. Both restroom doors were open, and he quickly cleared them. Nothing. Nobody inside.

"Anybody here?" he whispered. He heard no response. The deaders would've screeched. He stepped out of the hallway.

Inside the store, several shelves had candles on them. He found a book of matches, too. With the candles lit, he barely needed the flashlight. He quickly looked through the store. No water, but plenty of knock-off sodas and junk food. More importantly, there was an area cleared out with several old Army blankets lying folded on the ground. Matt walked back to the storage area and climbed the ladder. Retrieving his pack took only a second, and as he hauled it down, he realized the roof hatch could be locked from the inside.

Almost too good to be true. He closed the hatch and flicked the internal bolt lock shut before dropping into the store. His sleep that night was better than any since Charlotte. In his dream, that final shot went through the basket, but there was no one in the stands—no

412 | IBSON & KENNEDY

crowds, no television cameras, no teammates. Just him and an empty stadium. No one saw his moment.

* * *

He woke the next morning to another bright, sunny day. The light coming through the cracks along the window frames was enough to illuminate the space without the candles or his flashlight. There were several cans of food and first aid supplies on a shelf near the sleeping area. He looked through them and decided he didn't need any—maybe someone after him might need them more. The feeling of hope was familiar and something he tried not to latch onto. But seeing the markings and finding this place had given him hope for humanity. He drank one of the orange sodas, wincing at the room temperature fizz burning his throat, and ate a can of soup for breakfast. Satisfied, he stood up and folded the blankets, packed his backpack, and ensured the rest station was in as good a shape as it had been when he arrived.

Leave it better than you found it, Matthew.

His father's mantra from their Boy Scout camping days. He'd grown up making his bed every day, even in hotels, because of the same philosophy. To that end, he left the second gallon jug of water on the shelf near the matches and made his way to the roof. Matt unlocked and carefully opened the hatch, being as silent as he could. The rooftop was empty and already warm. He climbed through the hatch and hauled his pack through before slipping it onto his shoulders.

Matt grabbed the ladder and lowered it over the side of the building under the access area. He climbed down, and the ladder banged once, sharply, against the wall. With a jump, Matt got off the ladder, picked it up, and set it aside in the tall grass. He rose in time to see a deader dressed in torn and ragged camouflage overalls come around the shaded side of the gas station and shamble toward him.

"Fuck!"

Surprised, Matt drew the pistol, sighted on the deader's skull, and pulled the trigger twice. As it fell to the ground, Matt was already running toward the highway, his eyes sweeping the surrounding area for any more of the awful things. A half mile down the road, he stopped running and caught his breath, scolding himself. Sunlight burned the dead, but it hurt them, too. Their pain turned to aggression, and he'd seen them burn to death chasing flesh. He shouldn't have been surprised.

"Should've grabbed some stink at least, man. Shit."

Matt looked up into the sky. To the west were far more puffy clouds than the day before. Rain was coming. Maybe as early as lunchtime. With no good stink, he considered returning to the station and waiting it out. But he was so close to the big river now.

So close.

* * *

Matt unthinkably made Kilmichael before noon and pressed west. The bike helped. Three miles west of his overnight stop south of Eupora, about the time his heart rate and panic level came down and the morning sun's heat began roasting his back, Matt came upon an abandoned Subaru with Colorado plates. He'd seen thousands of empty, discarded cars, but this was the first time he'd found one with an intact bicycle rack carrying two identical mountain bikes. The big padlock didn't stop a .45 round. The pistol's report echoed off the kudzu-covered trees on both sides of the highway. He had the deader's attention now, which was fine as long as he could get a bike moving and put some distance between him and this place.

Once he got the bikes off the rack, Matt quickly stripped one frame of the wheels, chain, and everything else he could think of. By the time he pushed off down the road, the overloaded bike looked like something out of a cartoon with him and his big pack astride it. The pedals were some funky shit that required special shoes, but he didn't have them. It made the going slow at first, but once he was moving, it became easier. The first mile took him only three minutes of steady pedaling. The twenty miles to Kilmichael flew past. Thrilled at the speed, Matt kept pushing, reaching Winona, another twelve miles beyond, before the sun reached its zenith. After a quick lunch in the shelter of an overpass, Matt pedaled up the ramp to the highway and made for Greenwood as the western skies turned a dull, slate gray. Rain was coming.

The still, humid day turned breezy within an hour. He pedaled harder into the headwind and the gear on his back, which had been light and easy, bore down on his shoulders. Sweating hard, Matt pushed until his thighs burned from the effort. The farther he pedaled, the darker the clouds grew. Thunderstorms.

Come on. Give me a fuckin' break, man.

He heard the first rumble of thunder when he passed a sign reading, 'Greenwood 12 miles.' The deep forests pressed in on both sides of the highway. As the sun dove behind the thick clouds, the heat relented somewhat, and the breeze felt good against his sweat-slicked skin. Without the sun, the screeching of the deaders rose like an ear shattering swarm of cicadas from the trees. As the storm closed in and the sky darkened further, Matt pedaled faster. One of the extra wheels came away from the handlebars where he'd secured them. He watched it clatter to the pavement and skid into the weeds at the roadside.

When he looked up, he could see the rain. An opaque sheet hid the road ahead, and the trees bounced as the gusty front tore down on him. Within seconds, the first great, cold drops of rain slammed into his chest and face. Matt slowed the bike and put his feet down on the asphalt to come to a complete stop as the brunt of the storm slammed him. Lightning flashed somewhere off to the north as the deluge immediately soaked his shirt and jeans through. He pitched forward, his head and arms across the handlebars, and the pack kept the stinging cold drops from hitting his skin, but it didn't stop the icy rivers of rainfall running across his body. Thunder and rain blotted out the sounds of the deaders in the woods, but Matt knew it was only a matter of time.

Storms drove the dead crazy. The noise of the rain, wind, and thunder overloaded their hyped-up senses. The first time he'd seen it, they'd been moving through a late afternoon thunderstorm outside of Birmingham. They'd still had the truck at that point, but the choked lanes of Interstate 20 made going slow. As the storm broke, they'd attempted to pass a snarl of traffic on the shoulder where the trees were only a few yards from the road. Matt had been in the cab, in the far-right seat, when he saw the first deader emerge from the forest like a swimmer fighting for air. In the torrential rain, with the wind thrashing the trees and throwing branches across the road, the dead came out. Every blast of thunder changed their path. The flashes of lightning made them screech hideously. Water, which rotted them and drove them to their final death, coursed through the remnants of their clothes and flesh. The deaders didn't care, though. They kept coming.

The rain slackened ever-so-slightly, and Matt rose and saw a swarm of dead making their way toward him. Matt raised one foot to the pedal and blinked away the rain. In their aimless swarm, the dead wandered across the road. There were two choices: sit and let them swarm and hope they wandered away from him before the rain stopped and they could smell him or ride.

Matt pushed off and pedaled. The rain-slicked pedals, not built for his shoes, made it difficult, and he swerved violently to maintain his balance, but he stayed upright. There wasn't a single thought in his head. Every moment and every shred of concentration were about driving the bike forward and swerving between the wandering deaders. He picked up speed. Rain blinded him, but he dared not wipe his face. Once, he came a little too close to a deader, one who looked like a farmer wearing a tattered beer company shirt, and actually clipped its arm. The deader spun violently toward him, but Matt bore down on the pedals hard, and a lightning strike, much too close for comfort, made the dead around him wail.

Fuck!

He pedaled into the maelstrom, and the dead farther to the west thinned out considerably. The center of the storm was somewhere just north of the highway, and the west side of the road and shoulder swarmed with them. The far side, the eastbound side, was clear. Ahead was a patch of gravel connecting them—one of the ones marked for authorized vehicles only. Matt smiled.

Nobody gonna stop me these days.

He steered onto the loose surface and moved the handlebars to miss a puddle that might have concealed a deep pool. The bike slid out from under him, and he slammed to the ground.

Shit! Shit! Shit!

The impact stunned him, and his left shoulder and hip took the brunt of the fall. The remaining extra wheel bounced away, and his stuffed pack burst. Cans of food and his only other clothes fell into the mud. Sally's shotgun clattered to the ground and discharged to the east.

Motherfucker!

Matt scrambled up and saw every deader in the immediate area looking in his direction. As one, they started for him in the pouring rain. Several of them hissed. A sudden gust of wind tore at them. Thunder erupted at the exact instant a lightning strike hit immediately to the north of the highway. Pressure and noise threatened to burst his eardrums. The dead flinched and lurched in that direction. Matt stood and dragged the bike up and mounted it. The remnants of his pack against his back, Matt pedaled hard to the west.

As the rain slackened to a fine shower and then a mist, the deaders continued their shamble after it. There were breaks in the clouds ahead, and he descended a long hill as the road turned to the southwest and fell toward the Mississippi Delta. Matt coasted and leaned back and tried to enjoy the feeling of the speed and the crushing relief before sudden loneliness returned. Matt shook it off and focused on the ride. The hill bottomed out and gave way to flat farmland as far as he could see. There were still trees, likely following the creeks feeding the big river, but the sheer, flat openness of the delta took his breath away. He'd dreamed for weeks of wide open, warm spaces. The kind he'd find in Arizona. They were closer now than ever. All he had to do was—

There was a soft popping sound. He felt the bike lurch and saw the front tire shedding rubber as it went flat. He slowed to a stop, swung a leg over the bike's frame and then pushed it ceremonially into the weeds. Survivors discarded things without a purpose. Yeah, he could fix it, but dragging it would slow him down.

Fuck it.

Greenwood was still five miles ahead, and the hour was getting late. He'd need to find a good place to sleep and dress the stinging scrapes on his shoulder and hip. Maybe find some new clothes, too. The big river would have to wait a day or two.

Matt laughed. "Recovery is everything, right, Sonny?"

He shook his head and took off his pack. He'd lost almost everything in the wreck. Fresh anger flashed through him, and he almost threw the pack away before stopping himself. He could find another pack. There was enough food for a day or so, and he could find something to drink. He still had two pistols and ammunition for them. He could make it.

Suddenly tired, the last thing he wanted to do was walk another five miles before sunset, but there was nothing else he could do. Matt turned west, felt the sun poke through a break in the clouds over the horizon, and walked.

* * *

For the next two days, Matt rested in Greenwood. Sore from the wreck, he found another marked sleeping place much like the one outside Eupora. Finding supplies in the somewhat larger town had been easy. A new backpack, bottled water, clean clothes from a thrift store, and even some newer Army packaged rations were strange, but welcome, finds in the deserted town. Stranger yet, he hadn't seen a single deader since the storm. Matt didn't mind. All of it made his hope soar. He'd crawled into the secured hardware store and collapsed in exhaustion. When he woke, he'd taken Tylenol, drank water, and eaten as much as he could stomach before sleeping again. He set out on the morning of the third day before the sun had fully risen.

He made Leland at sunset of the second day and found a walk-in freezer in the ruins of a restaurant, marked with a red pound sign. It stank, but he reasoned the smell covered his own scent, which helped keep the deaders away. Plus, given the insulation, he could make noise without their swarming him. It was a damned good place to hole up and rest. In the morning, he'd make the eighteen-mile run for the big river. He smiled, thinking about walking into it. The Army had destroyed all the bridges to keep the deaders on the east side of the continent. He had heard no news about whether it was successful or not, but he knew the deaders couldn't swim, and that brought a chuckle from his throat as sleep overtook him.

Fuckers ain't gonna follow me across the river. I'm a good swimmer, and they ain't gonna catch me.

Matt walked into fierce sunlight and a heap of trouble. Some damned fool was making enough noise to draw every deader within fifty miles. They were already converging on the town, though he couldn't see them. Damned things would keep to shadows and sewers to get close to anything they heard and make their move at night. Metal on metal, struck purposefully, with a beat that would bring them by the hundreds.

The person making the noise two blocks away either didn't know that or no longer cared. Matt gathered his backpack, water jug, and weapons and ran down the street toward the highway. He'd wanted a break, and here it was. They'd swarm the town, and he'd be long gone.

Yeah, just run on by. Cross the river by sundown. Hell, yeah.

The downy-haired girl banging on a picnic table leg looked to be about four or five. She'd made it, somehow, unlike the dozens of rotted corpses lying in the street. She looked up at him with wide, blue eyes as he jogged by.

Damned if you think I'm gonna stop and help—

"Hungry," she said and brushed a lock of hair away from her filthy face. "Hungry, mister."

Her face stopped him cold. Damned if she didn't have his niece's eyes. Or something in them was the same. All innocent and shit.

Leave it better than you found it, Matthew.

Matt dug in his pack for an Army ration to give her, but he'd have to give her his can opener, too. "You alone, baby?"

"Yeah." The skinny girl's eyes welled up with tears. "Nobody but me now. Mommy died the other day." He waited for sobs, but they didn't come. The girl was tough. Matt thought his life had been hard, but this little one and her kin had made it months down here. Likely alone.

She picked up the metal bar and swung it toward the leg. Matt grabbed it. "No, baby. They gonna come."

"Them dead people?" she asked. "Gonna eat us?"

Matt wanted to stand, to run, and never look back.

Don't need no damned kid. Shit.

She can't stay here.

"We gotta go, baby."

"Okay. Hungry." She smiled. Matt opened a ration and gave her his spoon from his back pocket. The air was a little cooler. Rain clouds speckled the western sky. The little girl wore dirty shorts and a too small t-shirt. Matt looked into the town square and spotted a consignment store.

"You stay here, baby." Matt dropped everything but his pistol. "I'll be right back."

The storefront said, 'Re-Do's Consignment Store: You Outgrow It, We Sell It.' Matt pushed open the shattered glass door. The store faced east, so the early morning sun streamed in. He leveled the pistol and walked in. It took a few minutes to search the store, but he found no deaders. He grabbed a purple unicorn backpack and guessed at her sizes for clothes—some shirts, shorts, jeans, and a jacket. After he stuffed them into the backpack, he realized it was light for him, but she couldn't carry it.

Damn it, man. He walked back into the street and found her demolishing his last chocolate bar. Junk food couldn't be found anymore. Everybody ate it when the end came. He scooped out his brand new extra sets of clothes and a few cans of food. With a sigh, he stuffed her backpack into his. The damned thing weighed as much as the one he'd lost outside Winona, and he was gonna have to carry it across the big river. "Let's go, baby."

They passed the courthouse and old town square. The girl flinched as a deader hissed from nearby shattered basement windows. "Go faster."

Matt scooped the girl into his arms and tried to run, but he wound up jogging. The slow, shuffling pace made him grin against the strain. His father would have loved it—his son doing the slow and steady airborne shuffle like a paratrooper running all loaded down. Twenty-two years of jumping had left Daddy in a wheelchair at fifty-six, except his mind went first. PTSD and all that shit. Matt knew the truth. The Vietnam War never ended for the man. Even before he died, all knotted up in the Veteran's Home, Daddy screamed orders to men long dead.

Just run.

The first mile was easy, same for the second. By the third, his legs burned. He found a rhythm, humming nothing new or popular. The best songs were the gospel hymns his momma sang. Mile four came and went, leaving him covered in a thick sheen of sweat. He stopped and put the girl down.

"Gotta walk fast, baby girl."

The little girl said nothing as they walked. Matt felt her tiny fingers in his hand, and he held hers tight. By noon, they'd gone more than eight miles, though he'd carried her for most of it. In the shade of an overturned tractor-trailer, they shared a can of pork and beans, taking turns with Matt's spoon.

He studied her for a moment. "What's your name?"

She dug the spoon into the can. "Molly."

"I'm Matt."

She smiled around a mouthful of beans. "Where we go?"

"Across the big river," Matt said. "By sundown, if we go fast."

The girl nodded, then yawned. "I'm tired."

Matt grunted. He would sleep for days when they got to Texas. Maybe even a full night if the rumors about Arizona held up. "We gotta go, baby."

"Mo' water?"

Matt shook his head. "Can't, baby. We'll find some up ahead, okay?"

"Okay."

Matt put on his backpack and lifted the girl to his shoulders. He was probably carrying a hundred pounds total, give or take, but it didn't feel so bad. They hit the outskirts of Greenville at five-thirty. The smell of the river filled Matt's nose. Markings on the road told him to turn south and go around the town. A red circle around a CRX told him to follow the arrows to the best place to cross, so they went. A mile later, he stopped. His well-worn feet were aching in his boots, and he lifted the girl off his shoulders.

"You 'sleep, Molly?"

"Yeah." She wiped her mouth with the back of her hand. "Walk fast?"

"Yeah. We'll walk fast."

A screech pierced the fading twilight an hour later in the middle of town. Matt looked into the orange sunset. The river was still a half-mile away. Two more screeches shattered the air. The hunt was on.

Matt scooped up the girl and ran into the setting sun. On the long, muddy bank of the river, the taste of freedom on his tongue, Matt sank to mid-calf, and the girl tumbled out of his arms. His knee buckled and twisted. He fell hard on his left side. The backpack hit the back of his head with a thud. He shrugged off the straps and rolled over to his stomach.

"Okay?" the little girl asked. "Okay?"

"Yeah," Matt lied. Twisting and turning his leg to free it from the mud made his knee scream. Teeth bared, he pulled hard and left his boot in the mud, freeing his leg. He worked the other boot off quickly. The sun settled on the horizon. Matt thrust the purple backpack at the girl.

"Take this, baby," he said. She didn't reach for it. He looked at her. "I said, take it!"

Tears appeared in the girl's eyes. Matt followed her gaze back toward Greenville and felt his gut twist. From buildings and across rotten docks, deaders poured by the hundreds. Matt pulled his pistol from his waistband. The barrel looked clogged with mud. The other pistol was in his backpack.

The dead screeched in harmony, and Matt jumped to his feet. He dumped his backpack in the mud and found the trash bag-wrapped forty-five he had tried to give to Sonny. He unwrapped the pistol and looked at the little girl. "Go out into the water, baby. They ain't gonna come an' get you. Get out as far as you can and still touch bottom! Go!"

"No!" The girl screamed and clutched his leg. "No!"

Matt brushed her away. "No, baby. You gotta go! Molly! Go!"

The dead screeched again, now a couple hundred yards away. The breeze picked up behind Matt, and the deaders shuffled faster, smelling his living flesh. Matt worked the pistol's action to chamber a round. Eight shots. He leveled the pistol at the first deader he saw, the tattered remains of a football uniform hanging from its decomposing flesh. He flicked the safety off, and they screamed again. The girl splashed into the river away from him, her steps loud in the muddy water.

"I made it, Sonny. You dumb, sick motherfucker." For the briefest moment, Matt hesitated as the faces of his friends appeared in his mind's eye.

Time to go out like a man.

Matt took aim and pulled the trigger. The head of the football player exploded like a melon. Matt stepped backward. He found the next closest deader, a woman in a gold dress, and dispatched her. A businessman in a black suit jacket was next. Five shots left.

Make every motherfucker count.

"Help!" the girl screamed. Matt turned and saw her thrashing, head back and arms at her sides. A drowning posture. Daddy had taught him all about the war, but Momma had taught him to swim. He'd been a lifeguard so very long ago. Matt jumped in after the girl, grabbed her and held her to his chest, and ran deeper. The dead followed them into the river.

You can't do that! Dead hate water!

He fired again, and another one, his black skin hanging in sheets, fell facedown into the river.

The water rose to Matt's waist and then his chest. As he moved slower in the deeper water, the deaders came faster and faster into the shallows. Four shots to go. A deader with a lot of skin and muscle, a recent convert, lunged closer. Matt wasted two shots on it before it fell. Another one in a string bikini came in, and Matt fired twice as his feet left the bottom.

Matt kicked hard and leaned back into the water. He rolled the girl onto his left hip, grasped her under his left arm, and pushed into deeper water. The pistol seemed to weigh twenty pounds. Swimming hard, Matt dropped it to the muddy bottom. Side-stroking with the little girl on his hip was easier than it should have been. He tried to find a rhythm and swim. They'd taught him the sidestroke was like reaching for apples and putting them in a basket. Reach for an apple. Reach for an apple. Kick hard and glide. Rinse. Repeat.

"They gone," the girl said. She'd sat up on his hip and looked back toward the shattered bridge south of Greenville. Matt kept swimming hard. Arms aching, he reached for yet another imaginary apple and felt mud. And then another handful. He sat on the bottom and clutched the girl to him. She shivered in the cool night air. His big hands stroked the girl's hair.

"We made it, baby. Made it across the big river." Matt laughed.

"We made it." The little girl suddenly sobbed, her face screwed up in happiness and grief.

Matt sat up and hugged her. "It's okay, Molly. Everything's gonna be okay."

"You ain't gonna leave me?" she asked into his neck.

Matt felt a raindrop on his head, followed by another. They washed over him like the sudden truth. "No, baby. I ain't ever gonna leave you."

He moved to shallower water and held the little girl tight. There was no sign of the dead on the western bank. They'd have to move into the darkness soon, but Matt waited. Molly snored against his chest. He'd almost passed her by. The only one he had ever wanted to leave, but he couldn't imagine himself not doing it the same way again. Then again, had he passed her by, neither of them would be headed to Arizona and a chance to live. Maybe fight back against the deaders, too.

To the west, Matt could see a light. An honest to God light. Streetlight or whatever, didn't much matter. If they had power, they were still human. They'd have food and, maybe, some dry clothes for him and Molly. Maybe even a real bed for a change. A motor revved behind him, and headlights swept out over the river. He stood and turned with the sleeping girl still clutching his neck.

Three men carrying rifles climbed out of the Army National Guard truck and walked toward him. Their weapons at the ready, all of them looked as if they'd seen a ghost or worse.

"You swam her across the river?" the leader asked. He had the silver bars of a captain on his hat.

Matt nodded. "Yeah. We made it."

The captain smiled and looked at his counterparts. "That may be the greatest thing I've ever seen, my friend. One of those moments you might never see again."

Matt hugged the girl impossibly tight against his chest and felt tears building in his eyes. He'd come through in the moment that counted, and his life would never be the same.

* * * * *

Kevin Ikenberry Bio

Kevin Ikenberry is a life-long space geek and retired Army officer. As an adult, he managed the U.S. Space Camp program and served as a space operations officer before Space Force was a thing. He's an international bestselling author, award finalist, and a core author in the wildly successful Four Horsemen Universe. His eleven novels include *Sleeper Protocol*, *Vendetta Protocol*, *Runs in the Family*, *Peacemaker*, *Honor the Threat*, *Stand or Fall*, and *Deathangel*. He's co-written several novels with amazing authors. He is an Active Member of SFWA, International Thriller Writers, and SIGMA—the science fiction think tank.

# # # # #

You Have to Go Out
by Philip Wohlrab

New Ptangar, Year 0

Wrengel felt sick as he stared down at the lovely blue and green marble in his display. A marble that was splotched with large, white cloud formations.

"Are you sure?" he asked bitterly.

"Our fears have been confirmed, Commander. This world isn't just inhabited; it is crawling with these creatures."

"The radio signals were bad enough, but this?" Wrengel pointed to a screen. "This is madness."

The image on the screen made no sense to the gathered beings. Row upon row of ground vehicles rolled down a large boulevard. Each vehicle had a turret on top, and a long tube jutted from each turret. One of the creatures stood in a hatch on top of the turret, gesturing with one of its arms. A red flag, its center filled with a white circle and a black, multi-armed symbol, whipped in the breeze behind it. He supposed it could identify a polity or unit. Their observation devices showed similar scenes on several continents.

"Kitchol, turn that off. What are our options?"

Another Theru, her blue skin flushed with passion, interjected, "We must exterminate these creatures! We have nowhere else to go.

Our ships don't have enough fuel to leave this star system. Why would the sacred Ptath allow such a thing?"

Wrengel paused before answering. He, too, questioned why Ptath would allow such a thing. Had not Ptath shown them the way when their own world was in its last years of life?

"Amtul, I don't know why Ptath would allow this. Perhaps this is the work of the Adversary? A final test of our people? Regardless, it is one we will rise to meet!"

"That may be, Commander, but we are not warriors. We have limited weapons on our ships, and based on what we see here"—Kitchol gestured to the blank screen—"these people are warlike. If I am not mistaken, those vehicles are a type of war machine." Kitchol shifted through several more images that showed more Earthers in more war machines displaying numerous flags. One was red with a yellow icon in the corner. Others were red, white, and blue, in different configurations. Still others were multi-colored and equally impossible to identify or understand.

Wrengel reached up with a delicate, four-fingered hand and scratched his brow. His bridge crew knew he was thinking. He gazed around the spacious deck, at the instrument displays, and finally, at the large screen in the center of the bridge which bore the icons for twenty-four world ships and four factory ships. These twenty-eight leviathans were home to all that was left of his people.

"We, Theru, have travelled the stars for twenty-one generations. Our ancestors crafted these ships to cross the depths of interstellar space. We survived the destruction of our home world. We can overcome these creatures as well."

Wrengel walked over to the large screen and punched in a series of commands. The view shifted to the system they called New Ptangar. It showed the nine planets in their orbits and the large asteroid belt between the fourth and fifth worlds. He tapped the asteroid belt with a long, slender digit.

"We will mine these for raw materials. We will convert one of our factory ships to make our own weapons of war, and once we are ready, we will descend on Ptangar Three and take it for ourselves."

"Sir, that will take years!" Amtul protested.

"A few decades, at most, to have the weapons we will need," Wrengel said. "But what are a few more decades after such a journey?"

"I suppose I should scan the ship's libraries to see what we have in the way of weapon designs. We aren't much more advanced in the ways of war than these…these *Earthers*. Earthers, seems a name as good as any given our radio intercepts suggest they speak multiple languages—they call themselves *Mensch*, or *Ningen*, or *Human*," said Kitchol.

* * *

New Ptangar Year 4

Wrengel was aging quickly. Kitchol could see it every time he returned from the factory ship to World Ship One. That didn't stop Wrengel from driving like a possessed Theru toward their eventual goal: conquering Ptangar Three. Wrengel pulled Kitchol into his private office off the bridge to go over the latest intelligence from the human world. They'd listened in on sufficient radio intercepts to roughly understand who the major polities were and who was at war with whom.

"Is it true, Kitchol?"

"Yes. One of the Earther powers has detonated a primitive fission device. The Americans deployed it against Imperial Japan."

"Yield?"

"Twenty kilotons or so. Our scout was over a place called Maine when they observed it."

"We must be more careful when observing these humans. Especially these Americans. We don't have enough scout craft, nor do we have the material to make more. This will complicate our eventual invasion. We need to know where these weapons are stored and disable them before we land. This planet will be no good to us if it is radioactive."

Kitchol nodded. Nuclear devices were a threat. It was time to dust off some of their more esoteric technologies and neutralize any Earther fissile materials.

* * *

New Ptangar Year 6

"We have lost Scout Ship Four," Amtul groaned.

"We what?" asked an astonished Wrengel.

"It was testing the new nuclear degradation device, and something went wrong. We received some data from the vessel, but the ship was damaged and crashed in a place the local Earthers call...New Mexico."

"Kitchol, what are we going to do?"

"Fleet Commander Wrengel, we received enough data to know what happened to the device, and we can correct for that. It is unfortunate the ship crashed, as it will alert the Earthers to our presence. But the weapons programs continue to progress, and we are on schedule to meet our invasion timeline. What I am worried about is the humans' rapid technological development since the cessation of their global conflict. Though a few discoveries in our weapons archives should give us a decisive edge, the invasion will be bloody."

* * *

June 12th, 1966

"Alright, men, I am not going to sugar coat this. We are losing. We are losing badly. The Air Force tried to nuke the invasion site in Iowa last night, and the damn things didn't work. Worse, none of the aircraft survived the mission." The Coast Guard Commander was a portly, stern-faced veteran named Jensen.

"Uh, Commander, what do you mean the nukes didn't work?" one of the assembled officers asked.

"Just that. The damn things never initiated. When the bombs failed, the Air Force tried sending a missile, and it, too, failed to initiate. The Army has collapsed in western North Carolina, and we have an alien force driving through Virginia. Elements of the Virginia Army National Guard are holding a line just west of Newport News and another line just west of Portsmouth and Chesapeake."

"Where's the active Army in all of this?" asked Lieutenant Oscars.

"Still trying to defend Washington, though a few units have been caught up in the Portsmouth pocket. This is where we come in. Most of the civilians escaped overland a week ago, but not all of them. The Navy has scraped together dozens of LSTs and old troop transports plus some commercial liners to evacuate the remaining civilians. They also want to pull whatever forces they can out of the pockets, but the priority is the civilians."

"Commander Jensen, is the Navy sending any support other than those ships?"

"Lieutenant Freece, I don't know yet. What I can tell you is that, in addition to our Mosquito Fleet and the *Ingham*, we have the cutters *Cape Fox*, *Cape Gull*, *Cape Wash*, *Point Grey*, *Point Garnet*, and *Point Thatcher*. All of them have been rigged with extra firepower, but they are still nothing more than big gunboats."

Lieutenant Senior Grade Mickey Freece, USCG(R), sighed. He looked around the crowded briefing room and wondered how many of his friends were going to survive the next couple of days. *We were Auxiliarists just a year ago. Who would have thought this could happen?*

"Ahh, hell, Commander, you know what they say," Chief Gunners Mate Deke Macon cut in. "You gotta go out…" The barrel-chested chief had a big chaw in one cheek and looked as though he were about to spit on the deck but then thought better of it. Unlike most of the assembled officers and crew, he was an Active Duty Coast Guardsman who had been assigned to the Mosquito Fleet. He was there to bring the former Auxies up to speed on their boat's new weapon systems.

Commander Jensen smiled at the chief's reference to the Coast Guard's unofficial motto. "You're right, Chief. Gentlemen, we have a job to do. We will assist the Navy in getting the civilians out. They will be landing the LSTs and other small boats on Virginia Beach. The civilians will board there and then cross load onto the bigger ships that are waiting further out from shore. The Virginia Air Guard is flying top cover for us to keep any alien saucers at bay. Thank God, they don't seem to be using many, or we would truly be in trouble. Lieutenant Freece, you will be in charge of the inshore squadron covering the landing craft. I will support you from the *Ingham*, understood?"

"Yes sir," Freece responded.

* * *

June 14th, 1966

"Ya know, if I had to guess, I would say there's about eight thousand people over there."

Chief Macon pointed to the shoreline where civilians were camped out, waiting for the Navy LSTs to arrive. The wind carried the noise of the large crowd offshore to Freece's boat. Freece glanced over at the chief, who was working on one of the twin .50 mounts. Freece chuckled wryly. His boat, *The Golden Freece,* had started life as *PT-756* before being sold out of service and converted for civilian use. Those conversions were gone now, and a new set had been installed since the Coast Guard had taken her into service as *CG-82039.* The twin .50s had been reinstalled on either side of the pilot house, which had been cut back down to her wartime standard. Forward of the pilot house, they'd installed a strange looking, Frankenstein's monster of a mount that had been designed by Chief Gunners Mate Hicks to punch up the firepower of the smaller cutters in the Coast Guard. The weapon was an 81mm mortar that was adapted to a pedestal mount with an M2 .50 caliber machine gun mounted on its recoil tube. Aft of the pilot house, they'd added a single 40mm Bofors gun and four single mount 20mm Oerlikons.

All of that, and they gave my crew M20 Bazookas as well. What am I supposed to do with those?

"You're probably right, Chief. I wish the Navy would hurry up and get here."

"Yeah, well, the Navy has never been known for being all that punctual." The chief spat a stream of tobacco juice over the side of the boat.

One of the ratings, the one assigned to the forward M2, shouted back at them, "You guys hear that?" The man pointed just beyond the city of Virginia Beach. Freece looked. Billowing, black clouds of smoke rose above the two- and three-story beachfront buildings.

"Contact," Freece said, laconically. Chief Macon spat another stream of tobacco juice over the side.

"The Navy better be here soon, or we are going to have a whole bunch of issues."

The billowing smoke carried the muted sounds of battle. Freece, a WWII veteran, listened intently, trying to judge the scope of the battle by its sound. He heard a mass of tank cannons, some artillery pieces, the crump of mortars, and the rat-a-tat of machine guns. But there was something else mixed in, a sound he didn't recognize, a snap-hiss that sounded like nothing he had ever heard. Even though his PT boat sat nearly a mile from shore, he saw a brilliant explosion light up the sky to the west.

"Something big just went off," Freece said, shading his eyes.

"Yeah," replied Macon and spat more chew overboard.

* * *

Twelve Hours Later

The fighting reached Virginia Beach proper. Freece and his gunboat squadron floated close to shore and provided what fire support they could to the Army. Seaman Jones, his radioman, poked his head out of the fore cabin hatch and shouted up to Freece but couldn't make himself heard. Freece beckoned the man over. Jones leaned in next to Freece's ear and shouted, "Sir, the LST's report they will be here in about a half day!"

Freece nodded, then returned his attention to the shore. He watched a pair of M-60 Patton tanks nose out from side streets to engage something he couldn't see. Both tanks fired. Five seconds later, despite being a mile away, Freece felt the percussive thump in his chest. The two tanks backed up, but an electric, blue beam of light touched one, and it detonated. The tank's turret rocketed into the air, and Freece was horrified to spot the tank commander sailing away, blazing, into the evening sky.

"What, in God's name, did that?" Deke Macon gasped from the twin .50 turret.

"I don't know, but I think we're going to find out."

CRUMP!

The forward gunner fired his 81mm mortar, then his assistant gunner handed him another round. Freece could just make out the streak of the outgoing mortar round with his peripheral vision, but he lost the mortar as it streaked into shore. Freece couldn't tell if it had any effect. The gunner reloaded and fired another round. On the stern, his 40mm Bofors gunner tracked back and forth, looking for a target.

"What in the hell are those things?" the helmsman shrieked.

Freece followed the man's finger to the south end of the beachfront. He could just make out a pair of machines striding onto the beach. One of them fired one of the blue, electric beams from a device at the end of its extended arm. The beam struck a group of soldiers who were dug into a foxhole, and the five men…exploded. The pair of machines turned down the beach, and Freece could hear the panicking civilians over the gunfire. Freece found his binoculars and scanned the beach. The silver and blue bipedal machines were close to twelve feet tall. Their heads looked like grinning, mechanical skulls that were framed on either side by antenna arrays. Behind him, his stern 40mm gun and two of his 20mm Oerlikons opened up on one of the machines.

"Shit, shit, shit, shit, shit!" Chief Macon screamed as he swung his guns onto the new targets and cut loose. They were a mile offshore, which put them at the edge of tracer burnout range, but the stream of bright red tracers kicked up sand around the two machines until the chief walked them into the other guns' target. More gunboats targeted them, and their combined fire made one robot stagger. Both alien walkers swiveled their bodies toward the Coast Guard gunboats, oriented on the *Cape Fox,* and let loose with four of their hellish blue beams. The cutter rocked in the water as the alien weapons intersected its hull. The bridge exploded, and the *Cape Fox* vanished behind a cloud of dense, black smoke.

"What are we supposed to do against those things?" Jones screamed. The answer came from further offshore. The USCGC *Ingham* was a *Treasury*-class high endurance cutter, now armed as well as a WWII destroyer escort. She has a pair of 76mm anti-aircraft guns and a five-inch gun on her foredeck. They'd added another 5-inch gun, a third 76mm AA gun mount, and several 20mm Oerlikons aft of her superstructure. The cutter steamed out of the offshore haze like a wraith, her white hull standing out against the deep blue of the ocean. She turned broadside to the beach, and her 5-inch guns rained fire on the two alien machines. First one, then the other, exploded in showers of small explosions. The *Ingham* didn't let up on her broadsides though; the walkers had merely been the vanguard for more alien infantry.

Freece raised his binoculars again. The powerful Zeiss glasses brought the beach into sharp focus. He could see several humanoid creatures, and he focused on one. He was shocked to see that the creature was definitively female, given the form fitting garment the alien wore. Her blue skin was the hue of cornflowers, and her elfin features would have been pleasing to the eye were she not intent on slaughtering humanity. An explosion lifted her into the air and tossed her away like a ragdoll. Freece lost sight of her.

"Jaysus," Freece muttered as he lowered his glasses.

* * *

WE DARE: SEMPER PARATUS | 439

Field Commander Kitchol was pleased with himself. He sat in his command craft and watched as his "tanks" forced back the original, inferior, Earther versions. Kitchol was proud of his promotion from technician. He hadn't been sure Wrengel would allow the promotion, and Amtul had counselled against it. She had held a grudge for twenty, long, Ptangaran years, unhappy that it had taken so long to land, but Wrengel had finally come around. And now he, as field commander, was driving his forces forward to take out an important American military base cluster.

"Subcommander, bring more of our infantry to bear against this sector." Kitchol tapped a position on the viewscreen.

"Aye, Field Commander, I will make it so. What of the human vessels gathering off the shore?"

"Our attack craft will deal with those."

"Yes, Field Commander, but most of them have been diverted to Zone Commander Amtul's attack on their Capitol region. We only have a single flight of atmospheric craft and one of our scout ships to support this effort."

"Hmm…can we pull any from the attack to the south?"

"I will raise Subcommander Breetai and see if we can."

"Good. In the meantime, let us move up a bit to observe the fighting closer."

The silver, saucer-shaped command craft floated above the destroyed wreckage of the city of Portsmouth. Below it, Kitchol's infantry rooted out the human survivors. Any they found, they shot. The Earthers received no quarter as they were beneath the Theru. Occasionally, Kitchol's infantry would come across a pocket of resistance. Rather than risk taking any more losses, his troops would call in a fire mission from the command craft. The craft would deploy its main beamer array from the bottom of its hull, an electric blue beam would leap from it, and another bit of Portsmouth would disappear in flame and ruin.

Kitchol deployed the main beamer array and aligned the targeting caret over the ruined building the Earthers had taken shelter in. He readied the weapon to fire, but an explosion rocked the command craft.

"What was that?" Kitchol demanded.

"Some kind of rocket, Field Commander," a subaltern answered. He marked the origin of the attack for Kitchol. "The crew are assessing damage now, sir."

"Isn't it remarkable how much these creatures can change in such a short time? It is almost a pity we must destroy them, but we cannot allow them to cohabitate with us. There would be endless friction."

"As you say, Field Commander," the subaltern answered, though it was clear his attention was elsewhere.

Kitchol adjusted his screen to display the area from which the humans had fired. One of the boxy Theru tanks blasted the building where the humans had taken cover, and its beams ignited each area of the building it touched. Three Earthers stumbled from the wreckage; two were fully engulfed, walking torches, and they soon fell over, dead. The third merely smoldered but was dazed, nonetheless. A Theruan infantrywoman shot the Earther with her beamer, and the enemy soldier went up in a puff of smoke. Kitchol was about to focus his viewscreen elsewhere, when he saw something streak past the camera pickup. Though the tank was no longer in the frame, debris rained across his screen. It had just exploded, though he wasn't sure of the cause. He growled to himself. *Why won't these...these shixists give up and die?*

* * *

Six Hours Later

Mickey Freece was exhausted. His gunboat squadron had been in continuous operation for thirty-six hours. He rotated his crew to give them a little rest, but he had only managed an hour nap for himself. The alien forces seemed to have pulled back from Virginia Beach for the moment. Reports suggested they were consolidating around the wreckage of Portsmouth. The dark night was quiet except for the gentle lapping of waves against his boat and a tank occasionally cooking off ammunition on shore. The smell of burning metal and rubber wafted out to the PT boat.

"Thankful they gave us this breather," remarked Chief Macon, his voice betraying how tired he was.

"Yeah, though I'm worried they will mount a more powerful attack once they do whatever it is they're doing."

The chief sighed and looked out to sea as if searching for an answer to this problem. The Navy still hadn't shown up. An offshore storm had blown in during the night, and the LSTs were forced to slow their pace. Just a few of the transports had arrived, but nowhere near enough to lift all the civilians. Lieutenant Freece watched as a transport's whale boat passed on its way to shore to pick up more civilians. Some of the civilians had made their way down to the beach after the fighting pulled back. They were likely stragglers, those who had only thought to run at the last minute.

"It is going to take hours to get everyone offshore."

"Yeah, Chief, but we have a tradition to uphold."

The chief snorted. The story of Signalman First Class Douglas Munro, Medal of Honor recipient, was drummed into every member of the United States Coast Guard. Marines on patrol on Guadalcanal were cut off by Japanese forces, and Munro used his landing craft to shield the Marines as they were evacuated by others. His boat laid down suppressive fire while the other landing craft pulled every Marine off the beach. One of the landing craft got stuck, and Munro shielded the stricken boat with his while under intense fire. The boat was eventually freed, but in the action, Munro was struck in the head by Japanese fire. He briefly regained consciousness and asked if all the Marines were safe. When he was assured they were, he died.

Chief Macon had joined the service not long after Guadalcanal and had fought in WWII with men who had known S1C Munro. He had used that story to teach new recruits at Cape May when he did a brief stint there as an instructor. Now, he and Freece were being asked to do something very similar, but instead of Marines, civilians needed saving.

"Yeah, sir, yeah there is. I wonder what Munro would have made of all this Buck Rogers stuff?"

"Not sure what to think of it myself. It's been a helluva year."

"Yeah, I was serving on the *Taney* when this all started. Got pulled off when she went in for refit, and that's how I ended up with you guys. Last I heard, the *Taney* was back at Pearl Harbor."

"Hell, Chief, I was just getting ready to retire from the Potomac Gas Company when this started. Then the order came to activate the Auxiliary, just like it did back in WWII. Found myself back in the service again, but with the Coasties instead of the Navy. I guess the Navy decided they had no use for an old PT boatman. Since I had *The Golden Freece*, they let me be rather than calling me back to them."

"What I want to know is why they decided to invade Iowa of all places?"

"Makes a certain kind of sense, Chief. Think of it this way: if we could have invaded a location that was lightly defended or had no defenses, how do you think Iwo Jima or Normandy would have gone?"

"I guess that makes sense. What about the Soviets? Do we know what they are up to?"

"They had the same kind of luck we did per the last intel I got, but that was a while back. The aliens landed in out of the way places and consolidated their beachheads before the Soviets knew something was up. And their nukes didn't work any better than ours."

"How did we not see this coming? I mean, these aliens were out there, so why didn't we see them with our telescopes or something?"

"I have no idea, Chief," Freece said, shaking his head.

The two men bantered for a couple more hours, until the sun began to rise in the east. With it came clouds of smoke on the horizon. The LSTs had finally arrived. But to the west, where the sun hadn't yet banished the night, bright flashes lit the sky. There was hell coming, and both men knew it.

* * *

"Kitchol! Why have you not completed the destruction of the shixist Earthers in the—" Amtul paused to check her data pad, "—Virginia Beach area? The troops there are from third-rate formations, and the rest are civilians. Fleet Commander Wrengel should never have put you in charge!"

Kitchol silently counted to eight in his head before answering Amtul's question. He tried desperately to keep the look of annoyance off his face and deny the woman a minor victory in seeing she had angered him.

"The Earther troops have proven to be quite resilient. We estimate they have lost two-thirds of their original force, but they still continue to push back at us. These so-called third-rate troops fight hardest near large civilian populations. Perhaps it is because these

444 | IBSON & KENNEDY

troops are drawn from these population centers, and it is their family units they are fighting for?"

Amtul paused for a moment and thought about Kitchol's question. He went on.

"If that is the case, no wonder they are so fanatical and unwilling to give up! We're just getting a handle on how these Earthers, Americans, whatever, think. Ptath knows their actions are far from uniform. Anyway, what I really need is some of our air power. If I can get some of our attack craft in addition to the squadron I already have, I think I can overwhelm their surface vessels and cut off these humans' escape."

Amtul again looked at her data pad, then back at Kitchol.

"I can spare a pair of squadrons. If you can't do this with thirty attack craft plus your command craft, then Wrengel should relegate you to the asteroid mines with a pick and shovel. This nation's capitol remains the true objective, this... *Washington.*"

"As you say, Zone Commander Amtul, as you say."

"The squadrons will be in your area in two hours. Do not fail me, Kitchol."

* * *

The Golden Freece cruised a half mile back from the LSTs. The massive tank landing ships had beached and were taking on civilian passengers. Lieutenant Freece had napped for an hour while things were quiet, and he was feeling a bit better about life. Morale was particularly high because Seaman Jones had made a fresh batch of coffee for the crew in the small galley.

"Jones, what is it that you do to your coffee to make it taste so good?" asked Freece.

"Well, sir, it's all about how you grind the beans. You see, most people grind the hell out of them, so they get this powdery crap they put in the filter. I don't think that's right, so I don't grind them as much."

"Ahhh, this is a damn good cup of joe. Has everyone who wants it gotten some?"

"Aye, sir, even Adams down in the engine room got some."

The mention of Adams made Freece wince. The engine room on an unmodified PT boat was a hellish place to be given the heat produced by the big engines. When Freece bought his converted boat, he swapped the original engines for a slower, more reliable pair of marine diesels. But when the Coast Guard took the *Freece* and converted it back to a gunboat, they swapped out his diesels for a different pair of engines to give it back some of its original speed. Then, when they installed the guns on her aft deck, they removed some of the ventilators for the engine room. Now, it was unbearably hot down there.

"I'm surprised he wanted any given the heat down there."

"He said he needed the caffeine, sir. You know those Machinist Mates; they are a weird lot."

"True enough."

The radioman ducked back into the forward cabin to return to his radios, while Lieutenant Freece raised his binoculars to watch the loading of the first three LSTs. The Navy didn't want to risk all twenty-four of them being stuck on the beach at the same time, so they were bringing them in in groups of three.

On shore, Navy beachmasters were dividing the civilians up into loading groups and generally organizing the clusters that had formed. The LSTs weren't small vessels. At 350 feet long with beams of 55 feet, they had been designed to drop a company of ten tanks and fifteen supporting vehicles on shore during WWII. They also had some limited air defense capability that would have been modern during WWII but was hopelessly out of date by 1966.

Freece snorted at the AA guns. *Not like ours are much better. Hell, this whole boat was obsolete before that war ended, and here we are using it against ray guns and aliens.*

"What do you think the aliens are up to, sir?"

"I don't know, Chief. Reorganizing? You can still hear some fighting further out, so maybe something is going on in Portsmouth that is keeping them from driving fully on Virginia Beach."

"At least the Army has had time to dig in." The chief nodded toward the fighting positions down the boulevards facing *The Golden Freece*. Mostly, infantry had dug in, but one of the Patton tanks had pulled out from behind a building just enough so its gun could cover the enemy's likely advance. Freece suspected there were others pointing down the other avenues of approach, but communications with the Army were spotty. He turned his binoculars out to sea; a dark smudge on the horizon worried him.

"Hey Jones, call up the *Ingham* and see if Commander Jensen is expecting anything else from the Navy. It appears something is coming from the northeast."

"Aye, sir!"

A dull roar from the west pulled his attention away. The noise didn't sound like jets—it was more like a *buzz* than whining engines. Freece scanned the western horizon with his binos, looking for the source of the sound. Ten black dots began to take shape low on the horizon.

"AIR ACTION PORT!"

Freece jammed the throttles forward and began to pull the boat away from shore. He wanted to give his guns as much room as he could. The dots quickly grew into delta-wing shaped, alien flying machines. They weren't quite airbreathing jets, but not quite rockets either. They moved fast, and their wings were heavily laden with ordnance. As the alien attack craft swept over the city of Virginia

Beach, they dropped clutches of bombs on the Army fighting positions. Freece felt the explosions in his chest even though they were nearly a mile away. The 40mm Bofors spat shells, and the Oerlikons opened up. The .50 gunners held their fire until the aircraft swept over the beach. Tracers streaked into the sky, but most fell short of their targets.

One of the alien flyers staggered after a running into a stream of fire from an LST, then it flew overhead, and there didn't appear to be any damage. A soldier on the distant beach shouldered a Redeye missile launcher and fired a SAM upward. The missile streaked after one of the alien craft, but the craft dumped a blinding, dazzling thing from its aft that confused the missile, and the SAM exploded harmlessly.

"Dammit! We need air support," Freece growled.

One of the enemy craft lined up on Freece's PT boat and stitched the water with bolts of coherent energy. The sizzling beams emerged from the alien flyer's wingtips, but the pilot misjudged the weaving PT boat and missed. Freece was hit with a strong smell of ozone, as if a lightning bolt had hit nearby, and the sea to starboard flashed into steam. The alien was behind the PT boat now. Instead of turning back toward it, the enemy jet lined up on one of the Point-class cutters and fired its energy weapons. The crew of *Point Thatcher* were not as lucky as Freece, and the ship staggered under the hellish beams. The cutter's bridge exploded in flames, the gun crews were washed away by the energy fire, and the hull seemed to…melt. A bomb struck one of the Cape-class cutters, and it disappeared in flame and smoke. The smoke dissipated, leaving the *Cape Gull* burning from stem to stern.

"God damn," Chief Macon whispered, almost prayerfully.

Before Freece could say anything, a second, fresh group of alien attackers appeared. They concentrated on the beached LSTs as they roared overhead to drop their bombs. All three LSTs took hits, and one exploded like a tin can. Flame and smoke burst from the seams of the ship, and Freece could see burning people jumping from the upper works into the water. The other two LSTs were smoking but not destroyed. Even at this distance, they could hear civilians screaming on the beach. The alien flyers wheeled around to come in for another pass.

Several things seemed to happen at the same time.

Plumes of smoke from the beach indicated soldiers had massed together and fired a score of shoulder launched SAMs at the alien fighters.

Two flights of human aircraft screamed overhead, coming from the south.

Most of the SAMs went wide, but three connected with the alien machines. One exploded, and two more were smoking as they barreled off toward the west. The first Navy A-4 Skyhawks, their wings laden with Sidewinder missiles, streaked into the fray and lined up on the fleeing, alien machines. F-5B Tigers dove toward the survivors of the first group of alien attack craft. A short, vicious air battle raged overhead; Freece watched as human and alien fighters shot missiles, guns, and beam weapons at each other. Another fresh wave of alien fighters came in low from the northwest and were met by fire from the humans.

As if this weren't enough, the fighting in the city redoubled as alien tanks, war machines, and infantry swept in on the human defenders.

"Jaysus, all hell is breaking out!"

"You can say that again, Chief!"

The lone, surviving Cape-class cutter burst into flames, and three of the ex-civilian Auxiliary boats disappeared as enemy beam weapons touched them. Freece was randomly zigzagging his PT boat to throw off the alien aircraft and tanks that were coming in from the south end of the beach. It seemed like the whole beachfront was on fire. An alien war machine strode out behind the tanks, lifted one of its arms, and shot a bolt of coherent light at a group of National Guardsmen manning a heavy machine gun. The Army Guardsmen caught fire and the machine gun cooked off its ammo. An M-60 tank rounded the corner of a boulevard and drove onto the beach. It engaged the war machine with its 105mm. The gunner shot true, and the walker flew apart as a high explosive anti-tank round detonated in its chest. The M-60 fired another HEAT round into one of the alien tanks and blew it apart. The human tank's luck ran out, and an alien infantryman scorched it with a rocket, destroying it. More alien infantry poured onto the beach, and Freece screamed for his gunners to engage them.

"We have to hold them for as long as possible. The Navy still has some boats going in to pick up civilians. I don't think we are going to survive very long, but for as long as we've got, we will hold!"

"You know what they say, sir, you gotta go out…"

The PT boat paralleled the shore, its guns blazing. The forward gunner had depressed his 81mm mortar mount, so it was firing almost in the direct role. Fat mortar bombs streaked onto shore and exploded among the alien infantry. Soldiers on shore hurled their defiance, while every boat that wasn't actively engaged in combat raced in to rescue screaming civilians. Overhead, fighters from both sides were engaged in a terrific battle. Machines exploded or fell from the sky, streaming fire and smoke as they plunged into the ocean. A burning A-4 Skyhawk plowed directly into a cluster of alien tanks, and they detonated in a cataclysmic explosion.

"Aye, Chief, that's what they say. Bad enough when nature is trying to kill you, but this is insane!"

450 | IBSON & KENNEDY

The *Ingham* had come in closer to shore and was laying on direct fire with all her guns.

A giant alien saucer lazily floated over the burning city of Virginia Beach, moving unhurriedly toward the battle. To Freece's eyes, the thing moved unnaturally. Nothing that big should have been able to move the way it was moving. The saucer came to rest over the beach, and Freece got the impression it was tracking something. To his horror, he realized that something was the *Ingham*.

A bolt of energy shot out from one of the dishes on the underside of the saucer. It connected with the five-inch gun turret on the stern of the *Ingham*, and the turret blew apart spectacularly. The force of the explosion pushed the *Ingham* down in the water, and she began to turn away. Another bolt found her aft 76mm gun mount and blew it apart, starting a large fire on the *Ingham's* stern.

"GODDAMN YOU TO HELL," Chief Macon screamed as he poured fire from his twin .50s into the saucer, but the puny, half-inch bullets had no effect.

* * *

Kitchol was pleased even though the Earthers had managed to scare up some aircraft to combat his. The two more or less cancelled each other out, but that was okay. His forces had mopped up resistance in the city called 'Portsmouth,' and they had blown through the thin screen of soldiers on the outskirts of Virginia Beach. Even now, his forces were encircling the embattled Earthers, and it was only a matter of time before his foes were destroyed.

"Sir, the technicians are still unable to bring the defensive systems online. The Earther missile did more damage than we thought."

"That's fine, Ship Commander, we have our main gun back! Look at them burn!"

Kitchol pointed to where the *Ingham* lay in the water, fires blazing out of control from her stern to her aft stack. His gunners shifted targets from the helpless *Ingham* and vaporized the *Point Grey* as it moved to assist the larger, stricken cutter. Kitchol could hear rounds pinging off the hull from dozens of machine guns and autocannons that had been turned on his command craft, but he didn't care. They lacked the ability to pierce his ship's tough hide.

"Field Commander Kitchol, we have destroyed most of the small vessels. The largest ship seems to be out of the fight, which only leaves the ones they are using to rescue their civilians."

"Yes, Ship Commander, it appears we have time to finish our victory. Let us burn down this last human war vessel and then we will turn our attention to destroying that fleet of transports. Our ground forces can take the civilians once they finish off the last of the human defenders."

"Aye, Field Commander Kitchol, it will be as you will!"

* * *

"**D**ammit! Dammit, dammit, dammit!" Freece muttered to himself, over and over.

All three LSTs were burning. The civilians on the beach were huddled in sobbing groups. A line of National Guardsmen formed a thin, defensive cordon between the civilians and their alien tormentors, who seemed bent on absolute eradication of all human life. The situation at sea wasn't much better.

The *Ingham* was burning completely, and her crew was abandoning her. Most of the other cutters and small craft had been destroyed. Freece wasn't sure how his boat had survived, but he kept weaving it to keep the enemy saucer from getting a clear shot. The aircraft from both sides were gone—most of the human fighters had been shot down, and the rest had retreated when the last wave of enemy warplanes showed up. But they left once they expended their ordnance.

Mickey Freece, formerly US Navy, US Coast Guard Auxiliary, and now, US Coast Guard Reserve, was out of time and out of hope. "KEEP POURING FIRE INTO THOSE ALIEN TANKS! BUY THE CIVILIANS MORE TIME!" he shouted to the crew.

He had just cut the boat hard to port to bring her back around when an alien beam weapon found his port 20mm Oerlikons. It was a small mercy the shot came from a handheld beam rifle fired by an alien infantryman and not a tank or a war machine. Instead of the whole PT boat exploding, the men clustered around the two autocannons flashed into steam and dust as the guns blew up. Shards of metal lashed out from the destroyed guns, scything down the crew on the aft 40mm gun and cutting the portside twin .50 gunner in half. Fragments tore Freece away from the small ship's wheel.

"SIR? SIR? ARE YOU OKAY SIR?" Chief Macon yelled. Even though he was standing right there, he sounded very far away,

Freece shook himself and stood on shaky legs. He staggered to the wheel before processing that his PT boat was no longer under power. The roar of the battle seemed to have abated, but then he realized he was hearing very little. He could see and vaguely hear what Chief Macon was yelling. He lifted a hand to his head, and it came away bloody.

The world seemed to press in on him for a moment and then his hearing snapped back.

"I'm alright, Chief," Freece responded testily.

"Sir, you are bleeding like a stuck hog. You are not alright."

"Why have we stopped?" Freece asked.

"I don't know, sir."

Freece jumped down through the small hatch into the pilot house. Something tore inside, but he didn't care anymore. He found Jones, the radioman, going over his equipment and shaking his head.

"Jones, are you okay?"

"Yes, sir, but the radios have had it."

Freece climbed back on deck, went through the small cabin behind the bridge, then down the hatchway to the small engine room. He poked his head through and immediately saw why the boat was no longer moving.

The explosions had peppered the engine room with fragments. The deck was awash in oil, diesel, and pieces of Adams. Their engineer had been torn apart, and the smell of oil, burnt insulation, and perforated bowels hit Freece all at once. He violently threw up what little was in his stomach and staggered back on the deck.

"We've had it, Chief. The engine room is toast."

"What do you want to do, sir?"

"Keep shooting until we are out of ammo, or they have destroyed us."

"Aye, aye, sir!"

The gunners on the fore gun let loose with another round, and the surviving Oerlikon gunners turned their weapons so they could fire on any alien in sight.

"You know, Chief, you keep forgetting the other half of the unofficial motto."

"Sir?" asked the distracted chief.

"You *have* to go out, but you don't *have* to come back."

The chief chuckled. "Yeah, sir, you are probably…"

The chief was cut off mid-sentence by something that sounded like freight trains passing overhead.

"What fresh hell is that?"

"That, Chief, is the sound of large caliber gun fire, and if you look to starboard, you might see a heavy cruiser. In fact, given that nest of radars on the back, that has got to be the USS *Boston*!"

Sure enough, the USS *Boston* had steamed past the waiting transports and was firing her 8-inch and 5-inch guns. She swung broadside to the beach, bringing most of her weapons to bear, and blazed away. Rounds from each of her six 8-inch guns fired every fifteen seconds, while her 5-inch guns fired once every five. By swinging broadside, she enabled her tertiary 76-mm AA guns to add their own fury at nearly twenty rounds a minute. The *Boston's* batteries slammed into the alien troops on the beach. Confronted by a monstrosity they couldn't touch, they fell back from where the last handful of National Guardsmen were hunkered down in their defensive positions.

The *Boston's* fire was joined by that of the USS *Newport News* and the USS *Salem*, both of which had been trailing the *Boston*. The ships had retained their all-gun armament, and once they turned broadside, they also blasted away with their 8-inch and 5-inch guns. The aliens' devastation was complete.

* * *

"Field Commander Kitchol! The Earthers!"

"I see them, Ship Commander! Fire on that first ship!"

"Aye, sir!"

The silver, disc-shaped command craft, one of a bare handful left in the invasion fleet, moved away from the stricken PT boat. When it was less than eight miles from the USS *Boston*, it brought its main weapons array to bear. The beam struck the bow of the *Boston*, and its armor flowed like water, superheating and melting under the beam's withering intensity. The bow caught fire, but the *Boston* kept firing her guns while turning ever so slightly in the water to expose her stern.

Her stern featured four rail launchers, and each rail mounted one Terrier surface-to-air missile. Terrier missiles were twenty-seven feet long and capable of reaching Mach three before detonating their 218-pound warheads. Flames backlit the launchers, and all four leapt into the air and streaked toward the saucer.

"Sir, the humans have fired missiles at us!"

"Shoot them down with our defensive weapons!"

"We can't sir! The defensive systems haven't been…"

* * * * *

Philip Wohlrab Bio

Philip Wohlrab spent time in the United States Coast Guard and has served for more than 13 years in the Virginia Army National Guard. As a medic attached to an infantry company, he earned the title "Doc" the hard way while serving two tours in Iraq. He returned home and continued his education, earning a Master of Public Health degree in 2016. He currently works with Booz Allen Hamilton as an Adaptive Wargamer for the United States Air Force.

#

Eight Ounces a Day by Kevin Steverson

Chapter One

Reed Carfton put on his nametag. He straightened his hat while looking at his reflection in the window of his truck. His job as a night custodian at the Center for Disease Control wasn't a glamorous job, but it helped pay for his education at Kennesaw State. Between it and the education benefits from being an honorably discharged member of the Georgia Army National Guard, he would be able to graduate, one day, with no student loan debt.

He nodded at the security guard as he entered the building and headed toward the custodial room at the rear of the building. Tonight was the night he would run the buffer for eight hours, polishing the floors. He didn't mind. It allowed him to put his ear buds in and get lost in one of several of his playlists.

He was scrolling through them trying to decide what Cypress Spring song to start with when he noticed Dr. Greta Jorgensen walking down the hall. She carried a briefcase and was still in her lab coat. She seemed to be in a hurry. "Hey, Greta," Reed said, "I didn't think I would see you tonight. Aren't you supposed to be on vacation?"

"Hi, Reed," she answered with a smile as she glanced up and down the hall. She coughed into a closed fist and said in her slightly accented voice, "My vacation starts tomorrow. We take a redeye flight tonight from Atlanta to Munich. From there, we will spend the next week all over Europe. I can't wait."

"Are you taking your notes home with you?" Reed asked. He grinned. "You know that's not how vacations work?"

She gave him a tight smile and said, "I've worked a long time to achieve my goals. Working a little while on vacation won't...kill me."

"I hear ya," Reed said. "Wait." He was confused. "I thought you were going to Hong Kong, Seoul, or somewhere in the Far East?"

"We are." Greta grinned. "The second week of our vacation, we fly to Tokyo. From there we will go to Hong Kong, Seoul and Bangkok. Afterwards, it is Rio de Janeiro for the last three days. Well, the last three days we will be gone, anyway. We will spend a few days resting from our vacation before I come back to the lab, and Andreas goes back to work."

"With all that travel," Reed said with a grin, "you'll need a vacation to recover from your vacation."

"Yes," she agreed, "but that is why we take it all at once. Last year, we spent two weeks in the Middle East and one in Indonesia."

"Must be nice," Reed teased. "I hope I marry someone oil-rich one day. Thanks for the tickets, by the way. I can't wait to go to my first Major League Soccer game. How was the game last night?"

"Match," Greta said. "It's a match...and it is football, not soccer, in my mind anyway. It was great. We won three to one." She coughed again into her hand. "Excuse me. We spent most of the day with our friends and some new ones who were there to support Toronto. There were seventy thousand people, and I had to get stuck in a private box with someone wearing a perfume that irritated me."

"I hope it's not a cold," Reed said. "It would suck to be sick on vacation. But I guess having a cold is a lot better than some of the stuff you people work with."

WE DARE: SEMPER PARATUS | 459

"Very true," she agreed. "There is always something nasty in the labs here. Samples come in from all over the world. The trick is safety. We follow the guidelines and do not rush."

"That's a relief," Reed said. "Can you imagine what would happen if a couple of the viruses were accidently mutated together to become something new? That would be bad on toast."

She gave Reed a look that indicated he had no idea what he was talking about. "Viruses don't mutate by interacting with other viruses, not directly. The true danger comes when two or more viruses infect the same host, in the same cells. Sometimes, having all this education is not comforting. Viruses infect us at a cellular level, and when multiple viruses attack the same cell at the same time, there's bound to be genetic errors. I know what could happen if the wrong RNA coding is put into the wrong viral coat, or worse, combined."

"Yeah, well, I'm glad I'm a floor guy. The other crew is crazy, if you ask me," Reed said. "Those guys clean the labs. If something ever gets broken and mixed, it won't be on me. Well, I gotta get to work. Tell Andreas I said hello, and thanks again for the tickets."

He put his earbuds in and continued down the hall. He never saw Gretta look down at her metal briefcase or the tear dripping down her cheek as she turned and rushed to the parking lot to meet her husband.

* * *

It was the last time he ever saw Dr. Greta Jorgensen. Reed never discussed it with anyone, but when the Occupy Extinction extremists announced the plague was *not* an accident, there were daily news briefs about hunting down those responsible before time ran out. Andreas Jorgensen, a Norwegian-American oil tycoon, was a "person of interest." OE was an offshoot of the Voluntary Human Extinction Movement, but obviously believed in taking a more active, extreme role. Reed figured Greta had purposely tailored the disease in the labs and traveled the world with her husband as some kind of mad, suicide, plague bomber. By the time he put two and two together, there was no one he could tell.

In the beginning, people got sick, but the plague only killed those with severe underlying conditions much like an extreme strain of the flu. The first sign it was so much more came from animals. They were the first to go. People's pets died in days. The ironic part was that OE's manifesto claimed they were doing it for nature, to put a stop to humanity's crimes, but the plague had jumped species and wound up killing vast swathes of non-human mammals. They'd murdered humanity and accidentally taken "the innocents" too.

It was vicious, carried by the very people who loved them. The virus, dubbed The Planet Killer, killed without remorse. Pets and domesticated livestock died. Wild prey animals died. Predators ate the prey animals and died. Scavengers ate the bodies of both and died. Birds, fish, reptiles and the like were more or less fine, but warm-blooded mammals, humans included, were decidedly *not.*

Reed had no idea how it did it. Something about the virus latching onto blood cells and forcing their way in, rendering them incapable of carrying oxygen. There were lots of biologically wrong, but functionally similar, comparisons to carbon monoxide. In the beginning, he watched the daily news updates and listened to the radio, but the technical stuff was beyond him. Some said it was an Act of God as he decided to punish the world. Offshoot religions popped up everywhere in every country claiming the end was near and people should repent before it was all gone.

They weren't altogether wrong.

* * * * *

WE DARE: SEMPER PARATUS | 461

Chapter Two

For the first month, Reed stayed home like almost everyone else. Every nation ordered their citizens to selfquarantine. There had been something similar years before, called Covid-19, so the governments didn't hesitate to lock things down. Of course, many people didn't listen, which in hindsight, fueled the problem. He only left his apartment for the bare essentials. The smell was offensive in the extreme—Reed thought it couldn't get any worse when people struggled to find places to bury their animals.

He was wrong.

It got to where no one even tried to bury the humans.

Scavengers emptied grocery stores of all types of meat. Canned meat, dried meat, and fresh meat were gone from the shelves. Mobs stormed the warehouses in countries across the world. The markets crashed. All money was worthless, so people simply took what they wanted.

Everyone scrambled to find fishing gear, nets, and fish traps. Not only could you get yourself killed sneaking onto someone's land to fish in their pond, someone would shoot you if they thought you had an eye on their boat. It was only the beginning of the end.

People began dying too. It took longer, but there was nothing the specialists could do. The techniques tried in 2020 didn't help. Social distancing didn't work. Masks didn't work. Complete isolation was nearly impossible. Mosquitoes and other insects spread the plague by feasting on infected people and animal carcasses.

The insects were especially bad. The news reports blamed the infestation on the lack of bats that were victims of the virus, too. The animals the biting insects fed from were no longer there, so humans suffered from the bug's instinct to seek out sustenance. Citronella candles became a desirable commodity for about a week.

The world ground to a halt. The power grids failed, and the world went dark. Trucks no longer delivered food or fuel. No one answered 911 anymore. Inside of three months, half the Earth's population was gone. Yards, parks, and especially rural areas quickly became overgrown. People kept dying in greater numbers. Health care couldn't keep up, so no one tried.

* * *

Six months later

Reed was sick and tired of vegetables. *Sick of them.*

Fishing was terrible on the Chattahoochee River, and you had to keep your head on a swivel. Fishing at night was a little better, once frogs became hard to find in the Atlanta area and no one was out looking for them anymore. They had been hunted down in the first three months before most died.

The problem with fishing was that rival survivors would watch from a hiding spot. If you caught something, you could die for it. There was no other way to get meat, though. He checked all the abandoned grocery stores near him, hoping to find an overlooked can. Every now and then, he saw someone else out doing the same thing. He avoided them.

Leaving his building was a dangerous endeavor. He had once been shot at by two men while he was on a foraging expedition. They kept firing even after he yelled several times from behind the counter that he didn't have any meat. One of the men laughed and said he *was* the meat. He didn't want to, but he had no choice. He used the anti-theft mirrors located in the ceiling and maneuvered down the aisles until he was behind them.

He killed them both with well-placed shots from his AR-15, a Christmas gift from his father the year before. It lacked the giggle switch but was otherwise functionally identical to the weapon he had used during his three-year stint in the National Guard. Even though he was no longer in the military, the training he received the summer after he graduated from high school came in handy.

Reed supposed there was some type of government and military somewhere. He did not doubt for a moment that groups of men and women, led by the new lords, had broken into armories or military installations to get to the weapons, ammunition, and equipment. He knew from the news reports that mobs had stormed them months ago, looking for the field rations and the meat in them. Most soldiers stationed at those bases had gone AWOL or refused to shoot fellow Americans.

There were still some cans of vegetables lying around. They were not easy to find unless one knew where to look. Abandoned homes sometimes had them, but never any meat. Nowadays, most people grew whatever they could so they wouldn't have to encounter any of the roving cannibals or snatch teams. Occasionally, he caught a glimpse of greenery in a window.

Reed considered seeking out someone to trade vegetables with to gain different seeds, but it wasn't worth the risk. Several of the new lords sent teams out to "gather" subjects so they could force them to live in their little kingdoms, gather supplies, guard the chicken farms and ponds, and live under the watchful eyes of the overlords.

The one station he still picked up on the radio referred to them as the Chicken Kings. Even though many of the birds had been killed by desperate people who didn't think of raising them or even cared beyond their next meal, there were some who thought ahead.

The man on the radio said wars were fought over chickens. Reed wondered if anyone would ever have thought birds would be the most valuable commodity on Earth. Almost like the Dodo and passenger pigeon, every type of bird had nearly been hunted to extinction in a matter of months. The same voice said it was truly the Wild West down near the Gulf of Mexico. Reed figured it was that way near any body of water. Fish were in high demand. There was a sort of hierarchy down that way; the haves, who would kill to protect what they had, and the have nots, who would kill to take it.

Reed had his own small garden in several of the abandoned apartments in his building. He wasn't a gardener, but he could read and follow instructions. One of his neighbor-buddies liked to think he was some sort of prepper and had a collection of heirloom seeds. He zealously followed the directions printed on the packages, and grew tomatoes, green peppers, loose-leaf lettuce, squash, and cucumbers. He had a few others but decided to wait on planting them. Watermelon and pumpkins required more room than he wanted to use right now.

He scavenged containers and turned them into tiny gardens in front of the apartment windows. Sheer curtains kept anyone from seeing in but allowed enough sunlight to filter through for the plants. He used buckets, garbage cans, and even a dresser laid on its back with the drawers pulled out. The drawers held his growing lettuce. Watering them was becoming a pain since the water tower had run dry three days ago, and no longer provided water to the few who lived within its system.

One morning, Reed left his apartment building after checking to ensure no one was nearby to see where he came from. The last thing he needed was for someone to find his meager food supplies and take them before he got back. It was time to search a few more stores. As he headed toward the parking lot to his truck of the week, he debated moving north to find somewhere to live near a creek or stream away from others.

He had elected to stay where he was because he was near Kennesaw State University, and therefore, had all manner of stores within walking distance. He thought he had a better chance of finding food. Now, he was not so sure. His own truck, a victim of the riots, no longer ran. But he didn't walk anymore after finding a set of keys in an ignition in a driveway. He could go north now, he just needed to stock up first. He grew up in the mountains so surviving wouldn't be hard for him. The thing he found the hardest was the near-vegan life.

Up near Roswell, he spotted a Kroger's. It was one he had not searched before. He circled the parking lot twice, avoiding the few abandoned cars, looking through the shattered windows for any movement. There was none, so he stopped his truck halfway up the walkway. He rolled up the windows, got out, locked the doors, and went inside.

Most of the shelves were empty. A few were broken and scattered across the floor. He walked past the empty food shelves to check other areas of the store. Sometimes he got lucky in areas that didn't have food for human consumption.

"I'd eat a dang rat if I could catch one," Reed said out loud as he stuck a couple of cans of pinto beans in his backpack. He found them tucked away with cans of dog food on the shelf. The wrapping on the cans was similar. An employee had probably hidden them when it all started, and truth be told, dog food was starting to look pretty good.

At least the beans had protein, but protein wasn't enough. He was looking specifically for meat. The week before, while on another scavenging run, he'd hit the campus library. Reed had grabbed several books, including a copy of a book for vegetarians, and discovered it had a whole chapter on vitamin B12. Apparently, even the most diehard vegans had to take the supplement or suffer all kinds of damage to their body from its deficiency. Weakness, heart problems, digestive issues, mental issues, and vision loss were bound to happen to someone if they did not take in B12.

The only way to get it was by eating meat. From what he could tell, an adult needed eight ounces of meat a day. Sure, it was in chicken but not at the levels needed, unless someone ate a huge portion. That wasn't happening for most folks. It was too hard to come by.

Supplements could supply it, and every time Reed scoured an abandoned pharmacy, he searched for it. The shelves were empty; like any type of vitamin, iron pill, or protein powder, it was long gone.

He realized he was a latecomer to the knowledge. People had killed over supplements, too, during the first month or so of the pandemic.

A rat, he thought. He stopped in his tracks. Bobby, one of the guys on the lab cleaning crew, told him about an experiment with rats in the basement of one of the CDC buildings. They were in a lab in separate cages with automated waterers and feeders. The CDC went through a lot of rats. *What are the odds any survived the planet killer?*

He walked toward the front of the grocery store and passed more empty shelves. He remembered the first ones to empty. *Toilet paper. Why did everyone hoard toilet paper when it all started? Meat was what disappeared.* He shook his head. He adjusted the sling on his rifle and carefully moved through the plate glass frame out onto the sidewalk. He stepped over the remains and bones of some poor victim of the virus or the fight for food.

Glass crunched beneath his boots as he walked to his truck. Well, it wasn't really his, but it was the one he drove these days. He checked his gas gauge and looked over on the floorboard of the passenger side and counted. He still had three bottles of fuel additive from a find at a parts store. Like a lot of things, fuel was finite, and they weren't making any more. It would go bad, eventually, but the additive extended its life. It would be time to siphon more fuel soon, and he always added some in case it was old before all this started. It wasn't like there weren't plenty of vehicles to choose from.

* * * * *

Chapter Three

Twelve miles away

The CDC complex was the same as he remembered it, except for the overgrown grass and shrubbery. There were a few abandoned cars in the parking lot. Most of their license plates showed they belong to what was once the government.

He was surprised the buildings had intact windows, or still stood, for that matter. Then again, nobody trusted the CDC not to be a hot zone. No one in their right mind would go into these buildings scavenging, for fear there were vials of active virus or whatever containers they kept it in to study. Reed had to admit to himself he was nervous, even though he'd worked here.

He listened to a radio station that broadcast for an hour every Sunday at noon. He had no idea whether they were reliable, but a few weeks ago, they'd announced the virus had mutated and was harmless. Maybe it was true, maybe not. It may have been the guesswork of the old DJ, who made his way to a small station in a town east of Atlanta and ran it with power from a generator in his truck. His decision made, he turned to go to the building housing the labs where the rats were supposedly kept.

Reed slipped his knife between the building's sliding doors. It was easy to wedge them open. The electronic looks had long since disengaged with lack of power. No one ever bothered to physically lock them with a key. He suspected the internal locks would be open too. Most buildings had the safety feature in case a fire killed the power so people would not be locked in.

He walked to the stairway on one end of the building, wedged the door open, turned on his flashlight, and made his way down. He propped the door open with a fire extinguisher. The sign on the third door down the hallway indicated live animals were kept inside. He opened the door and looked inside.

Two walls were lined with rows of cages, and the room smelled strongly of rat feces, urine, and…something else. He gagged. It was so bad, he propped the door open with a stool from the nearest counter and gave the room a few minutes to air out. He pulled a bandana out of his backpack and covered his nose and mouth, tying it off behind his head.

He moved the beam of his flashlight around the room and discovered the main source of the smell. A decomposing body sat in the chair behind the desk in the corner. The body had…liquefied, but the process hadn't been helped along by the usual insects since they were in a "clean" part of the CDC's facility. The skull was leaned back, part of it missing. The arms extended down, and a pistol lay on the floor, stuck in the dried blood and matter. In front of the man were the dried remains of a rat on a plate and an empty bottle of Jack Daniels. Apparently, Reed was not the only one with the idea of eating rats.

On closer examination, he recognized his friend, Bobby, from the pointy toed boots. Reed wondered how long he had been coming here. There were twenty empty cages along one wall. He had a decent little setup, with a frying pan and hot plate on a counter and a garbage can full of tiny bones.

The first few cages on another wall held dead rats, their bodies dried out. There was no food in the small chute at the back of the cages. There was water in the automated watering containers. They were fed by gravity from the huge tanks on the roof of the building. Many of the experiments in this building needed a water supply even if the power went out. The generators on top probably ran for weeks until their fuel supply ran out, too.

The next five cages had movement in them. Whatever the scientists had used to try and find a cure for The Planet Killer must have prevented these from catching it. Or at least allowed them to fight it off. The first cage had a skinny rat that shied away from the light of his flashlight. Its water container was full, but there were no food pellets in its feeding shoot. There was one rat in the second cage and two in each of the others. He looked closely and found bones in the single. The rats had fought; the strongest had survived. It was a little bit like humanity outside. The next four cages had food. Reed looked around and noticed a large stainless-steel hopper above the numbered cages. Tubes ran to each of them.

Reed tapped on the big hopper, and it sounded hollow. Whatever was still in the tubes running to the four cages was all there was left. These rats would starve in the next few weeks. He poked around in the cabinets and drawers but didn't find anything useful. In a small closet on one side, he found three boxes of rat treats. He dropped a handful into the cage of the first rat. Fear of the light gone, it scrambled to eat the food.

On a counter was a large, three-ring notebook. The last entry was two months ago. Bobby's entries hinted that he'd become a reclusive alcoholic who had decided to check out when his booze ran out. He scanned the pages and found the number system for the cages. The last three held breeding females. The skinny, grey rat was a male, according to the number on the cage. So was the large brown one in the next cage. They had not been used to produce the females. If he was going to farm rats, he wanted to avoid inbreeding. Nothing but the best for him.

A book title on a shelf caught his eye. "A Manual on Breeding and Maintaining Laboratory Rodents."

Perfect.

He flipped through the pages. If Bobby, or whoever had maintained this book, was accurate, Reed figured he should be able to breed the males with the females. *The average person probably doesn't know books like this exist. I wonder why Bobby didn't try and breed them? Maybe he did and ate those?*

He checked other rooms in the basement but didn't find much of interest until he discovered the break room. One of the cabinets held two cans of ravioli and one can of chicken noodle soup hidden behind a pack of napkins. The best find in the room was a four-pack of tuna. He put all seven cans in his backpack with the beans. If nothing else, the find was worth the trip. He decided to thoroughly check the other buildings, every desk and every break room, to see what else he could find. People's fear of this building was turning into his lucky day.

As he searched the rest of the day, he filled his original backpack and another one he found under a desk with cans of food, candy, gum, stale crackers, and anything else he could find. Most of it was hidden in drawers. *Must have been a no eating at your desk rule.* In the building he used to work in, he searched the custodial room and was rewarded with the cans of Vienna sausage and Beanie Weenies his boss always kept in a drawer. The man would buy them once a month and stock up for his lunches. Reed found half a month's supply.

On the first floor of another building, he discovered that the vending machines were still full. He broke the glass on the one filled with snacks. Many would be spoiled and stale, but some he could eat. He eyed the drink machines and decided he would tackle those with his crowbar when he came back tomorrow. He now had a plan.

* * * * *

Chapter Four

R eed looked around one last time before he started loading the small wire fence into the delivery truck. When he was sure no one was around, he put ten rolls in it along with the pieces of stainless steel he got from the hardware store. Next, he threw in automated water bottles, bedding, and bags of dried dog food. One of the places left untouched had been a pet supply store he discovered near his home. When the animals died, the owner closed it, boarded up the windows and doors, and left it.

He filled the back of the rental truck. The last things he put in the seat were handsaws and, on the floorboard, a toolbox full of hammers, nails, pliers, wire cutters, crimps, and wire ties. He threw in five boxes of large nails for good measure.

He loaded a chainsaw and two of the boxed windmill kits into the bed of his truck, drove it up on the dolly hooked to the back of the rental, and drove north up I-85. The highway was eerily empty. Occasionally, he saw someone, but he ignored them the same way they chose to ignore him. It was still too soon for most people to trust others. As he went farther north and turned up toward the mountains, he didn't see anyone else.

He drove for two hours until he reached his grandfather's land in Rabun County, Georgia. It was above Clayton and Tiger, east of Dillard. It was tucked away in the back of a holler in the northeast corner of the state down Warwoman Road. Even when the world was normal, it was considered secluded.

The cabin was as empty as the old barn, except for the old tractor with the bucket on its front. His grandfather bought it years ago to dig out a small pond in the back of his fields. It was a simple task to route a section of the stream to and from it, ensuring it never dried out.

What once was the garden was overgrown like the rest of the yard and the field on the side with the pecan trees scattered in it. Reed remembered climbing them as a child. The three apple trees and the fig tree looked the same.

Along with the small spring-fed creek running through the property, there was a well with a small pump house. He planned to hook a windmill to a bank of batteries and power the pump. On his next trip up, he would bring two generators and a small solar panel kit he found in the hardware store.

He pulled the truck into the barn and unloaded it. He then hooked the dolly to his truck and drove back to Kennesaw. It was late when he got home, so he went to bed. The next two weeks would be a busy.

* * *

Two weeks later, Reed backed the hotwired bus up until he only had enough room to open the back door. He had taken all the seats out of this one too. Working quickly, he loaded the cages with the eight rats. There was barely enough room. The rest of the space was taken up with everything he felt he would need on the farm. There were buckets and containers, shovels, hoes, rakes, ropes, boxes of nails, screw guns, spare batteries to charge with his generators, and many cans of gas and diesel. He also had several hand operated siphons, stacks of car batteries, two inverters, and a hand-cranked generator.

When he got to the farm that afternoon, he unloaded everything except the rats, stacked the dried dog food high behind the driver's seat, and backed the second bus down into the hole against the first. Digging out the deep trench had taken several days using the old tractor and its bucket. Half of the first day had been spent draining the tank and the fuel lines before he could use it. It sputtered occasionally, but the diesel Reed siphoned from the first school bus was still ok to use. With both doors open, he screwed the framework for the sheet metal to the buses and connected them. He now had two buses, one stacked full of cages with removable waste trays beneath them, in a long hole. It had driven him half crazy, trying to do the math; it was a word problem from hell. *If Reed needs to maintain a stable breeding population, and a single, full-grown rat provides four ounces of meat, how many cages and how many rats does Reed need to get his eight ounces per day and not die of malnutrition?*

Once he connected the stainless-steel ventilation ducts, he pushed the dirt over them. He spread the excess dirt over the site of the old garden. When he was done, he moved his grandfather's beehive on top of it. It was still active, so he had to don the netted suit to do it. He put the other three hives in a row with it and connected the duct to a small fan inside the third one. It didn't use much power, so its solar panel provided enough for it to run.

Three weeks later, he had visitors. It wasn't a pleasant visit. He heard them coming long before they came around the bend in the dirt road at the beginning of the holler. He was waiting for them with his rifle behind his truck.

Three men and a woman got out of the jeep with weapons. Two had shotguns while the woman and the driver held hunting rifles. They stayed near the jeep, looking around. He knew they saw the smoke from his fire pit. He had a pot of vegetable soup cooking. He still maintained his little garden in its containers. He'd planted his remaining heirloom seeds, but they would take months to come to fruition.

The driver shouted at the farm. "Hey! Come on out! We saw the smoke! You need to come on out now. This land belongs to me. You can't just move here. You got to pay your respects and your taxes.

We can start with that pot of soup and those tomato plants in the buckets. Hey! You hear me?"

"I hear you," Reed said. "This land belonged to my granddaddy. Its mine now, and I don't pay taxes. You can leave."

"That ain't how it works around here," the man said. "We came up from down around Commerce and laid claim to all this."

"Commerce?" Reed shouted. "That's an easy hour or more south of here. Hell, it's below I85."

"I'm beginning to think you're hiding something back here," the man said. "You got a cow, or a goat, or something? Chickens? You got chickens?"

"You know good and well, I don't," Reed shouted. "There probably ain't none in the entire state of Georgia."

"Yeah, well, Greg Morton has some livestock down near Gainesville. I aim to find some of my own. He already took over down where we are from. If I can get some of my own, I'll have more than these three following me. Might even pay him back what I took from him. Why don't you come on out, and we can discuss it? You need protection."

"I don't need anything you got," Reed said. "And I'm not paying any kind of taxes for my own land, especially since it's been in my family for over seventy years. How 'bout you respect that and get the hell off my land? You know what? I'm tired of talking." Reed eased his rifle off safe. He didn't want to kill them, but like the other times, he had no choice. He aimed at the man on the far left and started to squeeze the trigger.

The man ducked and said something quietly to one of those with him. The other man took off at a run toward the barn. The woman spotted Reed behind the truck, raised her rifle, and fired a shot. The round hit the truck bed, went through, and whistled by Reed. He had no choice, so he fired back, killing her instantly. The two with her unloaded on the truck, toward him.

Reed crouched low and moved toward the front of the truck to put the engine between him and them. He dropped low and shot the driver in his leg. When the man fell to the ground, Reed finished him. The windshield on his truck shattered when one of them came around the barn, firing his shotgun. Two rounds took him out.

The last one threw his empty shotgun down and drew a pistol. Before he could fire it, Reed emptied his magazine of its last three rounds, ending the fight. Less than two minutes after the first shot was fired, it was over. Reed sat against the tire, breathing heavily from the adrenaline rush. It was like his drill sergeant had told him when he was only eighteen; combat is usually more than twenty-three and a half hours of boredom and minutes of engagement.

He took the weapons, loaded up the bodies in the bed of his truck, and left his farm. At the end of Warwoman Road, he turned south. He drove down to the edge of Gainesville and rode around until he saw a feminine figure dart between the houses. He held his hands out the window to show he had no weapon in them and shouted out the window at her, "Hey, can you tell me where Greg Morton is?"

The woman reached behind her, pulled a pistol, and aimed it at him. She looked around nervously and stepped into the street. He didn't move his hands, so she lowered her pistol. "Why?" she asked. "Are you going to tell him you saw me? I told him I'm not interested in joining his little harem. Why can't you people just leave me alone?" She started crying and raised her pistol in shaky hands.

"Hey, easy...easy," Reed said. "I'm not looking for you. I don't know the guy. I live an hour away from here. I'm only here to deliver these bodies and tell him to stay away from my place."

She stepped closer and looked into the back of the truck. She grimaced when she saw the bodies. Now that she was closer, Reed could see she was about his age, maybe a little older. Her clothes were dirty, and she could use a bath. She was also a little on the thin side which was not unusual these days.

"You don't live in Gainesville?" she asked. "Can you take me with you? I can cook. I will work as long as you don't expect anything more." She put her hand on the handle of the knife tucked in her belt while still holding her pistol at her side. "I'll tell you how to find him if you'll come back and get me. I don't want to go near him again. I don't think he'll let me leave next time."

Reed studied her for a moment. "What's your name?" he asked.

"Jennie," she said. 'I'm not from here originally. I'm from Savannah and was going to school here to be a nurse. I only needed one more year before it all happened."

Reed looked around and spotted a house with a raised garage door. He pointed at it. "My name is Reed. Tell me where to find him and wait in the garage. I doubt anyone is home. I'll come back for you in a little while. See what you can find in there while you wait."

She brightened. "Ok," she said, "I'll be waiting. You better come back for me! He lives in the big house on Old Cornelia Hwy. It's off White Sulfur road. I can draw a map for you. I had to walk from there."

* * * * *

Chapter Five

Reed climbed out of his truck. He left his rifle in the front seat and waited. His pistol was tucked in his waistband under his shirt. Two men walked over with rifles in their hands. One glanced at the bullet holes and raised an eyebrow. "What do you want?" he asked.

"I brought something for Greg," Reed answered. He tilted his head sideways toward the bed of his truck.

The man stepped over, looked in, and grinned. "That's Pete Tarnel. You sure did a number on them. All by yourself? Oh yeah, the boss is gonna like you. Come on. I'll take you to him."

The man led Reed into the giant house. They walked past the kitchen and out the opened sliding glass doors. Reed stopped and stared. A man was sitting in the shade of an umbrella while three women swam in a pool. Reed wasn't looking at them. He was looking beyond into a field with four goats eating grass! Off in the distance, four men with weapons watched over them. To one side, he heard the sound of chickens in a pen. The chickens he expected, but the goats were amazing.

"Mr. Morton," the man said. "This man is here to see you. He brought a gift."

Greg Morton looked up, took his sunglasses off, and said, "You're not from around here. What did you bring me? Tell me it's livestock, and I might let you leave without putting you to work here, in my kingdom."

"The name is Reed," answered Reed. "First of all, you're not making me do anything. Let's go ahead and put that on the table right now. I came, bringing a gift, and you treat me this way? I can leave. Don't think your guys will stop me either."

Greg looked up at his guard with a raised eyebrow. The man shifted a little away from Reed but didn't point his rifle at him and said, "You might want to hear what he brought you, boss, before you tell me to try and take him. 'Cause…I don't know."

Greg interlaced his fingers on his stomach and said, "You make Jimmy nervous. I haven't seen that before. He's armed. You don't look armed unless you have something hidden?" He glanced at his man. The look on Jimmy's face let him know he never searched Reed. "What do you have for me?"

"I brought you…what did you say his name was, Jimmy?" Reed looked over at the man.

"Pete Tarnel," Jimmy answered.

"Pete Tarnel," Reed repeated. "I brought you his body and those of the three lackeys with him. Hated to kill them, but they left me no choice. There's not very many of us left. We should be growing the population, not ending it."

Greg sat forward in his chair. "Yeah? You took out Pete and the others? Great. Good riddance to them. The idiot stole a chicken from me, killed it, and ate it. I'm trying to breed them, you know. I heard he ran north. Is that where you're from? Tell me? What do I owe you for this?"

"Nothing," Reed answered. "Except I expect you to recognize that I own my family land. Me. I own it. I don't care how far you expand your little kingdom. My land won't be part of it."

"I see," Greg said. "Just where is this land?"

"Up near Pine Mountain off Warwoman road," Reed answered. "I'm telling you this for a couple of reasons. One, I'm an honest guy. Two, if you send anyone my way with plans to take what I have? They will never make it back to you. And three, I tend to hold grudges."

"That's way up in the corner of the state," Greg said. "I don't think I'll expand that far. We'll leave you alone. Unless...Unless I hear you have livestock. I find out you have any, it's on. You try and defend it, and we'll try and take it. That's the way it is these days."

"Fine," Reed said. "I'll kill your guys and then I'll come take yours. You have some good ol' boys. I have the training."

"Training?" Jimmy asked. He took another step away from Reed.

"Meh, you know," Reed answered nonchalantly. He stepped closer to Greg. He did his best to act like the heroes in the movies. He figured if he showed no fear, it might scare the bad guys. They didn't need to know his military job was "carpenter," assigned to the engineering unit in Toccoa. "It was a need to know thing in the Army. You don't need to know."

"Shit," Jimmy muttered.

"Calm down," Greg said. Reed could hear the nerves in his voice. "Reed just came by to bring us a gift, that's all. We don't need to make more of this than we have to. He lives well outside of my kingdom. We can keep it that way. If we're in the area, we'll just stop by every now and then all neighborly like. You know, to see if he spotted any deer or squirrels or whatever. I'm sure he'll be happy to tell us."

"Maybe," Reed said. "We'll see. I will tell you this; I raise bees. I even brought two jars of honey to sweeten the gift. I got stung eight times collecting it. Have your boys unload my truck, and I'll leave them with you."

"Eight times?" Jimmy asked. He shook his head slowly. "That would kill me. I'm allergic. We'll get them unloaded, boss."

Reed followed Jimmy through the house and out to his truck. They unloaded the bodies, and he handed the jars to Jimmy. "Be seeing you, Jimmy. Oh, if I were you, I would blow my horn before coming down the road into my holler. Otherwise, you might not make it back out. I didn't even break a sweat with these four."

* * *

Reed pulled into the driveway and up to the open garage. Jennie stepped out of the door going into the house and waved. Stacked against the back wall of the garage were towels, sheets, pillows, and blankets. There were two baskets of clothes.

"I wasn't sure if you were coming back," Jennie said. "To be honest, I half thought you wouldn't. I was ready to go find a car and see if I could get it to run."

"I said, I would," Reed answered. He shrugged his shoulders. "I'm an honest guy."

She grinned. Reed liked her crooked smile. "The woman who lived here was only a little bigger than me," she said. "I can wear the jeans with a belt. Do you need a mattress? There is a set of bunk beds in one room, and the plastic is still on the mattresses. We could put them in your truck. Do you know how to take them apart?"

"Also, I found this box." She pointed to a small, plastic lockbox. "It has packs of seeds in it. A lot of them. Mostly corn, squash, and lima beans. A few beets. I never liked beets. Not sure if you want those. There are some potatoes on the counter in the kitchen. They have sprouts growing on them, so I don't think we can eat them. Maybe we can plant them."

* * * * *

Chapter Six

They were driving through Clayton when Reed saw something that amazed him. In the street, right before the turn to take him to Warwoman Road, a truck and a car were sitting in the intersection. The car was blocking the truck. Several young people were gathered, arguing. Reed slowed and stopped. He listened for a minute and then got out with his rifle in hand.

The teenagers stopped arguing and looked at him, eyes wide. "What's the problem?" Reed asked.

"It's him, Mister," a girl said. "He wants to keep going to Gainesville and join some kingdom. "We don't want to go." The three with her nodded in agreement.

Reed was dumbfounded. Not only was he surprised to see this many people at once, he couldn't believe none of them were armed. Didn't they know it was the Wild West out here? "So, let him go," Reed suggested. "You go where you want and let him go where he wants."

"We can't," she argued. "He has our food in those boxes. We found it, not him."

"We don't have time for this," the older boy shouted. "They're chasing us, and you know it!"

"Only because you told them where we were going!" the girl shouted.

"Hold on," Reed said. "Who is chasing you?"

"One of them used to be a deputy. I don't know the other one's name," the girl said. "He is kind of creepy. I think he was in jail when it all happened, and the deputy let him out."

"Where did you come from?" Reed asked.

"We were boarding at the private school," she explained. "We waited for our parents to come get us...but they never came. We have been living off the food in storage at our school and what we could find elsewhere. A lot of the farms around us had vegetables scattered in their fields. I think they came up from last year's crops."

Reed knew the school they were referring to. It was an expensive one. "How many more of you are there?" he asked.

"Five of us," she answered. "And the two men chasing us. They said we couldn't leave. I don't like the way the deputy keeps brushing against me when he walks by."

"The other one said some stuff to me," the other girl explained. Her face turned beet red. The boy with her balled his fists, obviously angry. "He said things to Trudy too, but they have guns, so I didn't say anything. It's why we left today."

Before Reed could say anything, a police car came skidding to a halt behind the truck. Two men got out. One was wearing a disheveled uniform shirt unbuttoned like a light jacket over his t-shirt. The other wore regular clothes and carried a shotgun. The man with the deputy had his hair pulled back in a ponytail. The deputy's hair wasn't in a ponytail, but it was much longer than regulation, making him look like an imposter in his half-uniform.

"What seems to be the problem?" the deputy asked.

"Nothing, officer," Reed answered. "These kids were telling me they decided to leave where they've been staying."

"They're not going anywhere," the deputy said. His hand strayed near his pistol. "They're gonna stay with us, so we can keep them safe."

"That's not what I'm hearing," Reed said. He eased his finger up and took his rifle off safe.

"Tell you what," the man with the ponytail said. "Why don't you let the boys go with you, and we'll take the girls back to the school. They don't need to go anywhere with a stranger. It ain't safe."

Jennie whispered through the window to Reed, "That guy sets my threat radar off like Greg did. Those girls aren't safe around him."

Reed nodded but didn't say a word. Right then, the older boy turned and ran toward his truck. Before he could get in the open door, the man with the ponytail shot him with the shotgun. The girls screamed, and the deputy fumbled as he tried to draw his pistol.

In what seemed to Reed to be in slow motion, the shotgun turned toward Reed. He fired first. Two shots, center mass, and then he spun toward the deputy. Both fired at the same time. The deputy went down, and Reed felt a burning sensation in his arm. He looked down and saw that he had been shot in his forearm. Time started flowing again, and he stumbled.

Jennie pulled out her knife and cut the bottom two inches of her shirt off to use as a bandage. She wrapped Reed's arm to slow the bleeding. Reed tried, but failed, to avert his eyes from her bare midriff. He snapped his eyes up to avoid leering; he knew these girls were going through hell and vowed that he would remain a gentleman.

"I'm going to have to take the bullet out. It doesn't look like it's going to keep bleeding this bad, but it may have hit the bone. I won't know until we can get somewhere for me to see."

Jennie turned to the four. "There's nothing I can do for your friend. I'm sorry, but he's gone. Two of you get in his truck and follow us. First, get their guns and ammunition. Now. Move."

* * * * *

Chapter Seven

Years later...

The men walked back to their rusted truck, loaded up, and drove off in a cloud of blue smoke and billowing red clay dust. After fifteen years of no gasoline production, the vehicles all smoked these days, running off a mix of moonshine and a little of the old gas pumped from storage tanks and abandoned gas stations. It wasn't as if a lot of vehicles were still in operation, so there was plenty of the old stuff to use. Reed sat back down on his favorite stump and watched them go. Once again, they didn't find what they hoped to find. He smiled to himself, picked up his spoon and stirred the pot of cabbage, hanging over the open fire.

Every now and then, they turned off the crumbling, overgrown highway and followed what remained of the dirt road up the holler to his land and the small cluster of cabins. It didn't happen very often these days. Reed figured, eventually, they would quit coming. It wasn't as if he didn't have what they were looking for. He had it, but they would never find it.

Trudy and her son, Neal, walked over to the fire and sat down on a rough wood bench. The boy still had the stick Reed had carved, shaped into a toy gun. At five years old, he was like most children and full of questions.

"Mr. Reed," Neal asked, "will they come back today?"

"No," Reed answered, "I don't reckon they will. It's been five months since the last visit."

"They're afraid of the bees, huh?" Neal asked. "They could get stung. Stings hurt."

"Yeah," Reed answered, "stings hurt. That's why we don't mess with the bees or play by them." He glanced over to the row of four beehives sitting in edge of the shade under a huge oak tree. He smiled to himself. *Ol' Jimmy still won't go near the hives. Allergies.*

Of the four, the three hives actually in use were a pain to keep up. Removing honey, yet leaving enough for the bees, checking for mites, cleaning, and everything else that went along with it were probably worth the honey he collected. Maybe. What was concealed below the hives was the real reward. They'd added more cages over the years, of course. More mouths to feed and all. They were worth more than money used to be.

Money was no longer used, so it probably wasn't a good comparison. He and those living on his land in the back of the holler were healthy. Not very many of the few people left elsewhere could make the same claim.

Reed reached up, ran his hand over his moustache, and slid it down the length of his beard. He gave it a slight tug as he straightened it. He often debated with himself whether he should shave or not. *Maybe just a trim*, he thought, his usual compromise.

He glanced down at his feet, pursed his lips, and decided to swap boots tomorrow when he got dressed. He had worn a hole in the sole of one of the ones he was wearing, and the other was threatening to follow suit. He had gotten two years out of this pair. They hadn't lasted as long as the last pair. He saved those like he would save these. One day, he would run out of the boots stacked in his back closet that fit him. When it happened, he would cut the sole out of a larger pair and take the time to trim and hand sew the soles on. He had several saved for that purpose.

It wouldn't be perfect, but it beat making the trip out of the mountains to where civilization used to be. Down near Atlanta, he was sure he could find some. There were stacks of them in the back rooms of stores, the buildings crumbling around them. He would rather repair his own than deal with the trip.

Not that he would run into very many people, but if he did come across any, they might attack him on sight. If that happened, he would be forced to kill them. He didn't want to do that. It had been years since he had to. The world needed every human left, even if the individuals didn't know it. He glanced over at the boy, happily playing next to his pregnant mother.

About a hundred yards away, a couple sat on their porch watching Annie play. Annie was four now, and her sister, in her mother's arms, was just six months old. Reed did the math in his head and came up with fifteen years. *It would be about fifteen years or so when Annie would have her own child to watch. Maybe it would be Neal's?*

Fifteen years, he thought. It seemed like a long time, but it really wasn't. It was a little over that long ago when the world had come to a screeching halt, and he still remembered it like it was yesterday. The surprise visit from the closest lord's lackeys reminded him of it all. He and the people living near him didn't fall under Greg Morton's claimed lands, but they still came. If they saw signs of what they were after, they wouldn't have hesitated to try and take it and kill whoever tried to hide it, like people did when it all started.

He looked up and saw a man and a group of teenagers walking out of the trees. He smiled. The five of them came over to the fire. They were all armed with scoped deer rifles.

"Well?" Reed asked.

"We saw them," Randolf confirmed. He sat down beside his wife, Trudy; they'd been together since they attended the private school. "We pulled back from the cliffs after those men left, and we saw them. Two gobblers and at least six hens. They're staying around the draw and the hillside like you said they would."

"Good. We'll keep feeding them," Reed said, "and let this flock grow for a few more years before we kill one or two from it. It's not like they have to worry about coyotes, foxes, or bobcats."

"True," Bobby said. He was the oldest teenager of the group. The others turned to go to the house with the porch and one other further down the holler. "What are you cooking? What's for dinner?"

"Cabbage," Reed answered. "Potatoes, too. Your mom made me cook this out here. She says they stink up the house."

"They do, Dad," he agreed. "They smell like someone has stomach issues."

"They might stink a little," Reed agreed. He stared off into the distance. "But I've smelled worse."

Jennie stepped out of the cabin and called out to their oldest son, named after Reed's friend from his old life. "Bobby! Come help me clean and peel these potatoes. I'm going to fry them in the same grease as the meat."

Before she could shut the door, Janie and Leah, his twin girls, poked their heads out of the door and giggled at their brother. They both knew he would chase them and act like he was going to tickle them.

"Coming, Mom," Bobby said. He tussled young Neal's hair and walked away.

"I'm not eating cabbage," Neal declared.

Trudy shook her head and said, "You can't live off rat, Neal."

"Sure, I can," the boy said with a grin. "I like rat on a stick. I can live off rat, can't I Mr. Reed."

"I don't see why not," Reed teased. "It's good eating."

"See, Mom," Neal said with his hands on his hips. "Eight ounces a day. That's what Mr. Reed says. Eight ounces a day."

* * * * *

Kevin Steverson Bio

Kevin Steverson is a retired veteran of the U.S. Army. He is a best-selling author and published songwriter. When he is not on the road as the tour manager for the band Cypress Spring, he can be found in the foothills of the NE Georgia mountains, writing in one form or another.

# # # # #

Wraith by
Marie Whittaker

In 2027 Sleepy Eye, Minnesota, few things were a commodity, but salt was at the top of the list.

It all started with a seemingly harmless crack in a sidewalk down in the Tenderloin District of San Francisco. That crack was a little deeper than most thought. It was a fissure that ran deep below the city into the volatile earth. What the world mistakenly thought was some kind of methane gas escaping was actually the beginning of The End. Patient Zero was an undeserving homeless woman who'd been asleep in a big cardboard box. She'd taken the blast of dark mist straight in the face, tried to run, and dropped like a brick.

Enter Wraith One.

The following weeks went by like cinema as I watched my species perish to near extinction. I was only fourteen when people started dropping like bricks and rising like kites, Vantablack in the shadows like the shades they were.

And then the world crumbled in on itself. The world fell. Three years had gone by like molasses in Minnesota pond water since then.

People died fast, and wraiths appeared from the piles of bodies like sheets of black death clawing their way out of an oil spill. I'd watched a few of them being born, if I could call it that. Spawned was more like it. They were predators who hunted humans.

First, there was the buzzing, humming sound to let a victim know they would soon be dead. Then there was the dark mist that sprayed from the wraith's face hole. It was sort of like a spider paralyzing its prey. The human would go down hard, and the wraith would go to lunch, devouring the person's soul and fluids as their body died, shriveling into nothing more than a leathery husk that drifted on the wind, skittering down deserted streets like crumpled, yellow newspaper. From that husk, just after the wraith finished its meal, would emerge a new wraith, what was left of the person who had been killed.

Most times.

Other times, the wraith would eat the human, and no new wraith would spawn from the mess. I still didn't know why. Was it that the human was sick with something? Would some disease like cancer stop a new wraith from being born?

And it wasn't just a physical or biological thing. Wraiths were supernatural. Nothing natural or pure could exist and gut the world the way they did. Wraiths were oozing, cloaked evil in a physical form. Deadly and ravenous.

The dominant predator at the top of the food chain.

Three years later, the world was full of starving wraiths. I was a commodity for them just like protein powder was for me. The root cellar in Sleepy Eye at my family home was my safe haven. Three years is a long time for a young woman to exist inside a hole in the ground with no contact with the outside world. Skin hunger began to drive me insane. Humans are social creatures by nature. I wanted someone to talk to. To touch. It wasn't a sexual thing by any means. I was lonely and wanted to find my tribe.

I wanted a hug and a back rub and a reassuring pat on the shoulder. All the things I got from my dad and my friends at school before the fall. Thinking about my dad hurt really bad at first, before my heart was hardened.

As close as I could figure, it was my seventeenth birthday. My dad named me June "Bug" Dempsey on June thirteenth, about seven hours after my mom died. "June" had fallen away quickly, thank God, and "Bug" stuck around. These days, I scarcely remembered my last name.

So, I crafted a plan to leave the root cellar and Sleepy Eye, Minnesota, to see who was left. Maybe I'd make it to the west coast someday. I figured I might as well check out the Golden Gate Bridge and Ground Zero at the same time.

Who knew Dad's Mossberg pistol-grip 20 gauge, loaded with rock salt, would be my salvation? Like me, Dad didn't like to kill anything. It was summer, and the coyotes wouldn't leave the hen house alone, so he used rock salt to make believers out of them. The shotgun was loaded and leaning next to the door as we worked in the shop. Dad was teaching me welding, which was the next step in my survival education. I loved working with him. We were partners. I looked just like him, with black hair and pale skin, with ice blue eyes that came from my grandmother. I wanted to be an underwater welder when I grew up. They got to travel to the ocean, and they made bank at the same time, but we'd learned about the wraiths a few days before. Dad had known back then, three years ago, that they were coming for us. He taught me how to use that shotgun for self-defense. Wraiths were coming for everyone that drew breath.

We were both at the workbench, and I was the one welding while he coached me. We were nearly finished. I finished the bead and was really happy with the job I'd done. I looked up at my Dad, and that's when I saw the dark mist blast him in the face. He dropped at my feet, and I instinctively skittered back against the shop wall by the door. I couldn't see well through the welding helmet, so I lifted it up just in time to see my first wraith as it murdered my father. I didn't know what to do, frantically looking for a way to help my dad as he clawed at the floor to get away. That's when my fingertip brushed the barrel of the shotgun where it leaned behind me.

I palmed the grip with my left and pumped up a shell with my right, then put a hole through the wraith right at what would have been a human's chest. The thing shrieked as it was blown backward off my dad, where it plastered itself against the shop wall like a greasy poster. The hole in its chest grew as rock salt ate through it, gradually disintegrating the entire thing. It took four excruciatingly long seconds of listening to it scream before it faded to black dust.

It took longer than that for my dad to die. I turned and dropped to the floor beside him. His body seized over and over again. The wraith had begun draining him before I shot it. Dad's face was withered. His eyes were flat in the sockets, like they were cardboard cutouts. His hands were bone with thin hide stretched over them. One rested on my forearm as he stopped moving. I didn't know it at the time, but I had stopped a new wraith from spawning from the remains of my father.

After that day, I raided the house, barn, tool shed, and shop, loading everything I found useful into the root cellar and went into survival mode. Shotgun shells were easy to reload with rounds of chunky salt and crimp closed again. Dad had taught me that, how to weld, vegetable gardening, and basic self-defense since I was little. In middle school, we turned our attention to rebuilding a 289 gas motor into a recycled biofuel engine for my science fair project. I'd taken first place with that engine. To celebrate, Dad and I dropped the motor into a modified dune buggy frame and tore around the back forty like it was a racetrack.

They were the good days.

I observed wraiths as they took over my world and recorded their activity in my journals. I shot the ones that came to the farm, at first trying standard scattershot, but learning quickly that didn't kill them. It had to be rock salt for some reason. I enjoyed hunting them, but it still squicked me out to hear them scream at death.

They skimmed the place a lot. I hunted them. I hid silently until I could get back to the root cellar if I got scared, but I learned all about them. Wraiths were faint hearted, giving up quickly. They had the heart of a mushroom and the attention span of a peanut. They didn't bother animals. I'd set our stock loose after dad died. The chickens stuck around for a few months and so did two of the horses. The rest were lost to the wide open. Wraiths didn't look twice at anything breathing besides humans.

I wasn't so full of myself to think that other people, somewhere out there, hadn't survived, too. I wondered about them.

If there were any survivors who hadn't considered holing up at the salt mines in Utah, I would have been surprised. I caught onto the fact that salt kills wraiths just a little too late to save anyone else from what authorities thought was a medical pandemic before the fall. It wasn't. They weren't zombies. I'd seen clean through a wraith before. Depending on the lighting, they were transparent. Besides, why would anyone listen to a fourteen-year-old kid talking about a shotgun full of rock salt?

If only people had stopped trying to retain their normal way of life and listened to the warnings of other, I wouldn't have been that lonely. People simply disregarded the news of mass death back when the Internet still worked. It was mind boggling. My aunt Janice would have said they "poo-pooed" the warnings. Though other people had suffered—and that meant every bit of depth the word could harbor—from denial during that first week, heeding the warnings had never been a problem for me and Dad. From the first time a video of a wraith spawning hit YouTube, I was a believer. While others claimed it was an Internet hoax and attempted to hold onto life as they preferred, the smart ones, like my dad and me, hunkered down at home and tried to prepare. Our mistake was thinking our rural map dot would shield us somewhat. That video circled the globe in about four minutes. It circled my mind almost daily.

One should never poo-poo a wraith.

It had taken under a week for things like the Internet to go down. Power and running water went after that. People dropped from other things like heat strokes in the south if they survived the wraiths. My root cellar didn't freeze or overheat. It got chilly, but it stayed livable in both winter and summer.

I hadn't seen a wraith in over a month. My plan was to make it from home to Salt Lake City, Utah, as I searched for other survivors. Dad's old Ford had a paper atlas tucked into the glove box. There weren't many people left as far as I knew. Smoke pillars occasionally drifted into the sky, which I decided were like neon fast food signs to wraiths. Only someone who was suicidal would start a fire. They were beacons that wraiths followed to their next meal.

My buggy was loaded with everything I could strap to it, including the filter mechanism I'd created for producing fuel for my science project. Dried apples from the orchard and some vegetables from the greenhouse kept me healthy and packed well. I filled tanks from the water well and took as much as I dared carry. I left the farm, armed and mobile, after sunup.

I did my best not to look inside cars as I wove through piles of ruin on the highway. That was an easy mistake to make, as I'd learned during my first outing a couple years back. Some people refused to let themselves be killed and eaten, and I'd happened on a family in a car that took the matter into their own hands. One of the parents had used a handgun to save them all from what seemed inevitable at the time.

I wouldn't make that mistake again. I skirted Sleepy Eye and was onto the freeway in minutes.

But my mind was tormented as I glanced behind me at Sleepy Eye as it grew smaller, where deserted buildings stood bastion at the edge of my current reality and the only safety I knew. Seeing the city without people kept my world fairly small. I stopped at well-lit, deserted convenience stores when I felt it was safe. It was all so eerie. So quiet. I moved on quickly, dodging husks of human remains blowing along the ground like tumbleweeds. The tiny ones broke my heart. Wraiths didn't discriminate based on age.

My mind was always churning, always thinking about survival. When millions of people died in just a few months, they left plenty of supplies around. The stores were deserted, but in some cases, there was a good bunch of stuff left on the shelves if the place hadn't been looted. I'd take a glass half full over a half empty one any day. I'd need to find a sporting goods store soon for a new pair of boots and some more shotgun shells to reload with salt.

After the sting of leaving home faded, I found that the open road was invigorating. After a while, dodging abandoned vehicles became as routine as staying between the lines on the road. The buggy had a squatty windshield, but no roof. I wore the goggles we'd bought after we painted the buggy fire-orange.

* * *

Another year of survival was under my belt, and I celebrated with a chocolate protein shake while kicking my feet back and forth over the edge of a bridge in Sioux Falls, watching birds fly toward the horizon. It was peaceful. I was glad to be out of the buggy and taking a break from the noise of the motor. Fog churned and consumed foothills, and the air held the sweet smell of rain. It was gorgeous to witness. I checked the long bridge both ways. Nothing seemed to be creeping up on me, so I laid back on the warm concrete with my arms stretched out to either side as the fog threatened the sun.

That's when I felt an odd vibration beneath my hands. It was subtle and had a slow rhythm. I held my breath and then shot to my feet with the Mossberg gripped in one hand. The vibration was footfalls, and they came from my right, which, sadly, was the closest way off the damned bridge.

A figure, just far enough away so I couldn't tell if it was male or female, neared as I heard the slapping of their feet on the pavement. They would be on me in less than a minute.

"Help!" It was a man, and he was running for his life. Two wraiths streaked above the road behind him, shades moving in for the kill. It didn't appear as though they'd tried to mist him yet, which was weird. Still, this guy was as good as dead. I leveled my shotgun right at his head as the first of the wraiths overtook him. I lowered the weapon, thinking better of wasting a shot and drawing their attention. It was too late to save him from the misery of being eaten. Both wraiths misted him, and he went down, clawing at asphalt. The closest of the wraiths jumped him and began feeding, tearing at his chest and abdomen.

The other wraith attacked it. I was shocked; I'd never seen one turn on another. But it made sense. They were starving. Luckily, they continued to tear at one another with their claws and were so engrossed in the fight they didn't notice me. They were a tumble of black smoke. They screamed, a predatory sound that resonated bone deep since I was a prey animal on that bridge. I had heard it before. It reminded me of the sound of coyotes calling in the plains out back of the house back in Minnesota. Also like the coyotes, the smaller of the two wraiths tumbled free of the larger one and slunk away. That's when the buffet started for real.

I began backing away, feeling for the buggy as I went, as quietly as I could while the thing ate. I needed to put space between us. What was one hungry wraith would soon be two unless the dead guy was sick or whatever, and a wraith couldn't spawn from his remains.

That's when the other wraith returned and attacked the wraith that was feeding. It was fascinating to watch them fight. It was even more enthralling to watch the winner actually devour the loser.

That's how I learned that wraiths would eat one another. I wondered if that made the winners any different? Maybe stronger or smarter or something? I didn't hang around to find out.

Finally, my hand brushed metal. I spun and tossed the shotgun into the passenger bucket seat and dove behind the wheel. I was certain my dune buggy could outrun anything that decided to follow me. Nothing did.

My heart was stung, and my spirits sank. The only other person I'd seen in years, and he was gone. Maybe staying out of big cities was a better idea than driving through them. I gritted my teeth and kept driving, wondering if a new wraith had spawned back there.

The wraith that turned my dad had almost gotten me too. I thought that wraith had, at one time, been one of the neighbors who owned the farm up the lane from us. The Buchanans, I think it was. It had been one of the biggest wraiths I'd seen to this day, and the dad over there had been a giant of a man. The bigger the human, the bigger the wraith that took its place.

The hours on the road were exhausting. I hadn't checked the map in a while, but the road beckoned me ahead, so I kept going. There were mountains in the distance when the sun set, so I knew I was headed west. That's what mattered. I hated to do it, but I had to get some sleep so I could stay sharp. The next off ramp came into view, and I left the freeway. I turned down an alley in Nowhere Town, USA, behind a row of old brick buildings and stopped with the nose of the buggy under a fire escape. I grabbed my gear and hustled up the metal ladder all the way to the top. The moon was bright, so I had a decent vantage, watching from safety as a cluster of shades came apart from the shadows below.

They'd likely been tracking me since I pulled off the freeway. I counted five. They were all over my buggy, nudging at it and creeping beneath the chassis. Their buzzing made the hair at the back of my neck pull tight. I hated that they defiled something I would be touching in the morning. One by one, they tired of searching and drifted off to look for someone else to eat. I moved in near silence as I rolled out my sleeping bag and chewed on a dinner of out-of-date beef jerky.

Although the creatures were fast and shuffle-hovered along the ground on all fours, sort of like a cross between the Grim Reaper and an oily iguana, they were dumb as a box of hammers and about as aware of their surroundings as a rutting bull elk. When they were locked onto a meal, they gave less than two shits about what was going on around them. The buzzing hum they made was the worst. Enough of them in the same space sounded like a heard of freshly hatched katydids. My ears were always tuned in to that sound.

Sleeping under the stars was something I enjoyed when we'd gone camping back when I was a kid. It took a while to fall asleep, but eventually I got some rest.

I woke with buzzing in my ears. My mind was lost in a hypnogogic state, and I wrestled with grogginess as my eyes focused, wondering if I was only dreaming. I hadn't moved; I was still lying flat on my back. I gripped the Mossberg's pistol-grip but didn't move as I listened.

The buzzing was close, but I couldn't tell which direction it came from. I turned my head, looking in all directions, but the rooftop was empty, except for me and my makeshift camp. I rolled onto my belly and crawled toward the ladder, inching my way just enough so I could look down. The buzzing was louder. I pushed forward with my toes and looked down the ladder and straight into the face of a wraith that had somehow climbed almost to the top of the fire escape, just a few feet from my face.

I'd never been so close to one. It had eyes, two of them, and they were a sick shade of yellow in oozing sockets beneath the cover of the thing's cowl-like appendage that hung over the head. An oversized maw gaped below the eyes.

It shrieked, and I jerked backward, but it reached so fast that its claws caught in a few thick strands of my hair that had fallen over my shoulder and hung down. It yanked hard, rapping my face against the tarpaper rooftop. The pain was unreal as I gathered my hair at my scalp and tried to free myself from the wraith's grasp. More buzzing erupted. It felt like the weight of the thing dangled by my hair, which began to snap. A huff of dark mist shot upward past the edge of the building, coating my hand. The skin there erupted in white hot pain as if I'd shoved my hand into a bank of hot coals.

I got one knee under me and then came to my feet. At some point, either the wraith let go, or my hair tore free, but I got away. I lunged for the shotgun and flattened onto my belly, made a tripod with my forearms, and waited for the thing to come into view.

It didn't make me wait long, buzzing ferociously. One arm quested over the top, claws grasping the edge of the roof. I drew steady breaths. The wraith fearlessly heaved itself upward, hovering inches above the surface. As it turned toward me, I put a bead on the head and blew the top off, sending black dust into the air, three stories off the ground.

More buzzing erupted from the ground. I stole a glance at the next wraith, which was a good way down the ladder. I hung over the side of the building and shot the next one off the fire escape, wondering how I could have been naive enough to think they wouldn't be able to climb up to get me? The buzzing stopped.

Mental note: wraiths can shuffle-hover their way up ladders.

The grip of my left hand grew weak enough that I nearly dropped the shotgun. I went to my sleeping bag and sat, cradling my arm in my lap.

The sky was lavender to my right. Stars fought for the last moments of darkness to my left. My wrist and hand burned badly, and I trembled so hard that the slick fabric of the sleeping bag hummed from the vibration. I adjusted my seat until I sat in silence, feeling the first of many tears begin to fall. I stayed that way as the sun broke the flat horizon in the east. Only then did I look at my withered hand.

My left wrist had taken the brunt of the blast. There wasn't any blood, but the flesh of my forearm and the top of my hand had pulled back somehow, kind of like atrophy. The fingers were drawn into a loose fist. I could move my thumb somewhat. I was thankful for at least some remaining use of my left hand.

I withdrew a canteen and extended my arm, dousing it with cool water from the well back home. The thought of Sleepy Eye was enough to start the tears up again. I scrubbed tears from my face angrily, for the first time doubting my decision to leave home.

Maybe my quest was foolish. Perhaps I would get myself killed.

But what was the alternative? To live and die by myself, locked away below ground in a root cellar?

That was no life. I could always go back home. I wouldn't always have the means to quest on.

* * *

I'd been driving for nearly two days. I'd bandaged my wrist so tightly that the wrap acted as a splint. The pain faded into a dull throb that was almost something I could ignore.

The road narrowed. I drove until the mountains held clear detail and then kept driving through some of the most beautiful forests I'd ever seen. There was still snow on the ground in some places. The air smelled crisp—so clean it almost made it seem like a place where there could never be something deathly hunting my species. But I knew they were out there. The wraiths owned all the places, even those of such beauty.

I stopped in the road and checked the map. True to my fears, I was off course. I'd dropped south, driven past Denver, and was near the small town of Redmond, Utah. Salt Lake City was just north. I figured I might as well check it out, so I headed into town.

Redmond was quaint and surrounded by deserted farm buildings and forest. I drove by a small lake where there were too many deer and Canadian geese to count. It was a place that would have been nice to live in before the fall.

I killed the motor and sat still, listening and checking my surroundings. My bladder was screaming at me. I got out with my shotgun and walked to the rear wheel, reaching for the button of my jeans. I handled my business quickly, vigilantly searching for the multitude of wraiths that I knew had to be out there.

It was odd that I hadn't seen more of them in the hours and days since I left home. They must have been starving to death a little faster than anticipated but—

Something that was fast enough to move in a blur darted to the other side of the buggy. I was so startled, I dropped the shotgun, and it smacked against the asphalt and skidded a few feet away. I dove for it and came to my feet, realizing there'd been no dark mist. No buzzing. I sprinted to the other side of the buggy and leveled the gun at a man who crouched there.

A startled, twentyish, Asian guy glanced up at me as I readied to shoot him in the face.

"What the hell?" I yelled. The taste of coppery blood coated my tongue from where I'd bit the inside of my cheek in the shuffle to recover the shotgun and protect myself.

He put his hands up defensively. "Shhhh," he hissed.

"You attack me and then shush me?" The sound of my own gravelly voice was a shock. "That's some nerve, buddy." I cleared my throat.

Psst. I glanced to my right at the sound, and I saw a young, black woman crouching next to a burnt out car. She tried waving me over.

I wasn't budging. I hadn't seen another person up close for too long. I would not simply lower my weapon and get friendly.

The guy next to me started whispering. "I'm sorry I scared you. I was afraid you'd scream or something if I just walked up to you."

"I'm no screamer," I whisper shouted back at him.

"Put the gun down, please?" he asked.

I backed off, keeping them both in my line of sight. The girl stood up, showing me her palms.

"I'm Baxter," the guy said as he came to his feet. "That's Sarah."

"What do you guys want?" They didn't seem much like the Welcome Wagon type.

The girl's eyes darted to my buggy. I looked between them and took a step toward my ride. "I will absolutely put a hole in whichever of you two tries to steal from me." They didn't need to know the shells I had loaded were full of salt. If I shot one of them, it would hurt badly enough to change both their minds.

"Hold on," said Sarah. She took a step toward me. I turned the barrel her way, extending the arm-length weapon with deadly control. She stopped fast. Maybe she wasn't a complete dolt. "We're doing the Lady's work. We aren't going to steal anything from you."

My eyebrows shot up. I looked at Baxter. "So, the Lady told you to run up on me?" This lady and I needed to have a few words.

"I saw the gun and panicked," he said. "Sorry."

"The Lady welcomes all," Sarah interjected. She looked at my bandaged wrist. "You're hurt."

"Keen powers of observation." I was still shaken from nearly having my ass kicked by the two wraiths on the rooftop. I wasn't going to get back to sleep after that. I was exhausted, in pain, and honestly, feeling very grumpy.

I lowered the shotgun. "Back off." I stepped toward the driver's seat, and Baxter stepped back to give me plenty of room.

Sarah's face was incredulous. "You're leaving?"

I nodded, taking my seat. They just stared at me. "Look," I sat up, gripping the roll bar. "You'll be fine. Rock salt kills them." I plopped back down, settling the gun next to me.

"No kidding," Sarah said. I sensed a lot of sarcasm.

"The purge will pass," said Baxter. "It is written." His expression told me he was being genuine with me.

"Purge? Written where? You mean this apocalypse was forecasted somewhere?"

They looked at one another. "The Bible maybe?" said Sarah.

I stopped in the process of starting the buggy. I was no Sunday schooler, but I had gone to church with my dad when I was a kid. There had been forty days and forty nights. They were plagues. There had been no lessons on a "purge" that I recalled. And then there was this thing with the "Lady" they mentioned. They watched me like they were ready for me to call them out. I did.

"I studied the Bible. This sounds a lot like horse shit."

"It is newly found scripture. And you might try some respect."
Sarah crossed her arms. "Maybe it's better that you leave."

When the decision was mine, it felt fine to leave. Now that it was someone else's suggestion, not so much. I shrugged it off and started the buggy.

Baxter stepped into my path. "Please, wait."

"Ugh," I groaned, letting my head fall back against the headrest. I stopped the motor.

"Come with us. We'll show you the way. You can meet Lot. Then you'll understand."

"Lot?" He wasn't helping their case.

"The very man. He can teach you. Then, if you still want to go, I won't step in." He smiled.

I considered it. I'd left the safety of my home to find people. I found two, and they knew where there were more. I had a weapon and transportation. I'd watch my own back and stick close to the exit.

"Lead the way."

Baxter ran around the side of the buggy and jumped in.

I looked at him. He smiled.

"That way," he pointed forward, to the road ahead.

"I'll get the others. See you soon." Sarah didn't even look at me. *Whatever.*

I started the buggy. "Don't try anything dumb. I will toss you out and back over you for good measure."

"Are you always this violent?" He looked around the cockpit. One hand came up as he began to reach toward the console.

"Don't even."

Baxter dropped his hand. "Understood."

"How far is it?"

"Five minutes north of here."

I started down the road.

Five minutes went by like lightning. Baxter guided me to a left turn off the road to the tallest chain-link gates I'd ever seen. The fence continued out of sight along the road in both directions. He got out to open it, waited for me to pull through, then closed it up again behind me. He got back into the seat and instructed me to continue along a dirt road to the north.

We meandered through hills of white gravel. Huge, yellow haul trucks lined a flat lot to our right. We rolled right up to the entrance to an actual cave that was big enough to drive one of those trucks into. I hit the brakes.

"Is this the only way in?"

"I'm not sure. Why? I mean, it's huge in there. I think there's another entrance like this one."

I narrowed my eyes at Baxter, looking for the truth in his answer. He babbled. That wasn't a good sign.

"So, if just one wraith gets in here with us, we're done. With no way out. And you're okay with going in there, knowing that?"

"It's a salt mine. Relax. The Lady provides."

Baxter was an interesting person. His heart was in his words. He truly believed the Lady would protect him inside the cave. The one thing the cave had going for it was that, unless Baxter was lying, there was salt inside. Somehow, Baxter and company had managed to survive.

I wanted to meet those people. On some level, their knowing I existed made me real. I went on a leap of faith and continued into the yawning darkness inside the cave.

Baxter wasn't lying when he said the cave was huge. Echoes of light stretched farther than I could see. I stopped the buggy next to a line of golf carts in the first small room we came to, which was simply a widened part of the road. We got out just as Sarah pulled up beside us, driving one of the carts. They'd apparently mastered bio-fuels and rigged up generators to run on biofuel as well as the carts. Another female and two men got out of the cart with her. That was the first time I noticed they all wore white shirts and dark blue pants.

Baxter and I followed them along a trail around a curve once I gathered my bag and weapon.

"You won't need that here," Baxter whispered.

"It's comforting." I didn't take my eyes off the others as we tromped along, our shoes crackling on white rocks.

What they led me to was an amazing community of people living in underground wooden sheds. Beside some of them stood rounded greenhouses that were lit up inside. We passed groups of others who smiled at me as we walked on.

At the end of the large cavern was a building that was a little larger than the sheds. It was coated in textured white paint. A giant cross stood on top. The door stood open. The six of us walked in.

A slight man in overalls sat behind a desk at the end of the room. We walked down the middle, through rows of pews. He wore wire-framed glasses below a set of caterpillar eyebrows. When he looked up, a smile spread wide across his face. I guessed him to be about fifty years old. Not an old man, but he was distinguished and grey.

Sarah and the others sat in a pew to the right, and Baxter scooted into one opposite. I sat on the end beside him. The guy at the desk put his head back down and continued writing. The room was quiet and awkward. I nudged Baxter.

He looked at me.

I gave him a look that said, "What's going on?"

He held up a finger and nodded with a small smile.

I sat back, allowing myself to rest. It seemed like I'd been on edge for my whole life. Time ran on. I considered getting up and leaving.

Finally, the guy set down his pen and closed the book he'd been writing in. He left the desk, came toward us, and sat down on the altar. His feet were bare and dirty.

"Baxter, who do we have here?" He spoke well, but his voice was high and a little nasally.

"This is, um…" Baxter looked at me. "What is your name, anyway?"

"June Bug Dempsey. It's nice to meet everyone."

"Excellent, Miss Dempsey. The Lady welcomes you." The man turned to the back wall and gestured toward a white statue of a woman who had her hands thrown up protectively around her face. It was hardly flattering. Sodom and Gomorrah came to mind.

"My name is Lot."

"People call me Bug. Called me, I mean," I stammered. *Lot? Really?*

"What happened to your arm?" He inclined his head toward my bandaged wrist.

"A wraith sprayed me. I've learned to fight faster. To hit them before they can hit me."

"Ah. Is it bad?"

"No. It's small. Could've been worse."

"Good. And where are you from?" he asked.

"Sleepy Eye, Minnesota."

His eyebrows shot up. "How did you survive there?"

"I went underground. Stayed in the root cellar and learned to fight them." It sounded like tough talk, but it was really how I'd made it through.

"What brings you west?"

"I was looking for other survivors," I said. My voice sounded young. Childlike. I wasn't sure I liked it. "I got a little lost on the freeway on my way to Salt Lake City."

"Yes, but why Utah?"

"Salt." I didn't much care for the third degree. I fidgeted in my seat.

"And where did you encounter this wraith that sprayed you?" he pried.

"A couple hundred miles back." I looked at Baxter.

"You should see her vehicle," Baxter interjected. "It's very...rugged."

"You have a vehicle?" Lot perked up.

"I haven't been walking all this way." I took a deep breath. "Look, it's been a long couple of days, and I'm not feeling great. I'm still messed up after nearly being killed last night, and I'm afraid I don't have the patience for all the questions."

"Of course," he said. "I didn't mean to make you uncomfortable, Bug."

I relaxed slightly. "Thanks." I looked over at Sarah and the others. "What were you guys doing out in town earlier?"

"We patrol for two things. One is to find other survivors like yourself, and the other is to track wraith activity as our footprint grows," answered Lot.

"Footprint?" I asked.

"Our safety zone. We've been steadily pushing back, gaining ground," he responded.

"So, you think there are no wraiths in town?"

"Almost. Redmond is nearly clean. The wraiths are much like alligators. They're all appetite with no reason."

"I used to think so, too."

"What do you mean by that?" asked Sarah. She stared across the aisle at me without a smile.

"I mean, I'd never seen a wraith climb a ladder before last night. Before, they just hovered along the ground, eating anyone who didn't see them coming first."

She huffed. "Wraiths don't climb anything. They can't. They don't have the brain to do anything like that. They forget what they're doing in about thirty seconds and move on. She's lying."

"Screw you," I said, incredulously. "What reason do I have to lie?" I sat back again, keeping my eye on her.

"So, if they climb so well, how do our fences keep them out?" Sarah's tone was accusing. Maybe she thought I was trying to impress Lot with my claims.

"I don't know. I don't have all the answers. Maybe it's because they're beginning to evolve."

Lot burst into an abrupt belch of laughter. He recovered quickly. "Oh child, they cannot evolve. Wraiths are simply a non-sentient purge, brought down on men who lack faith. They're incapable of reason."

"And women lacking faith," added Sarah, looking right at me.

"And women," agreed Lot. "The chosen shall endure until the purge dies out. It is written."

"By whom? She said it was in the Bible," I said, gesturing to Sarah. "It isn't."

"The Lady provides, Bug. Don't forget. She is loving to all her children and has saved scripture for us when we need it most."

"You can't simply rewrite the Bible." I hoped I didn't offend too badly, but it needed to be said.

"I am Scribe to the Lady Edith," said Lot. "We commune daily, and she provides her gospel. Her prophecy is righteous word. She is our provider and protector. Her wrath will be mighty."

I stared. I was a little crushed. The first people I found were a bunch of religious nuts, holed up on top of a huge stockpile of the only ammunition I knew to work against wraiths, which I'd confirmed were evolving. They were starving and eating each other. It appeared they grew smarter as a result. "Lot" had everyone believing the Lady, or Edith, was a deity. In the Bible, Edith was Lot's wife, and she'd been turned to salt for not listening. He'd best hope she carried a big stick when she showed up to protect them.

I reached for my bag. "It's been nice meeting you all. I'm going to continue on to Salt Lake City like I planned." I looked at Baxter. "Thanks for the kindness." I wanted to shake him though, rather than just tell him goodbye. If he placed his faith in reformed religion with a belief that they'd be protected from wraiths, rather than realizing wraiths had the resources to take them all down, he was in big trouble. I slung my bag over my shoulder and picked up my shotgun, then stepped into the aisle.

"So sad to see you go," said Sarah.

I didn't bother responding.

"The Lady beckons her scribe," said Lot. He stepped up toward his desk, ready to write more into the Bible. "Sarah, Baxter, why don't you and the others walk Bug to her vehicle and show her to the gate?" asked Lot. "And best wishes to you, child."

"Thanks, but I know the way out." I started walking.

"I insist." Lot wasn't smiling anymore.

"Fine." I kept walking.

Baxter caught up to me. "No convincing you to stay, huh?"

"Not a chance," I said. Then I dropped my voice. "Wraiths are evolving. Do you understand? You're not as safe as he'd have you believe."

"But the Lady..." he started but drifted off. He sighed loudly. "I understand. You're not familiar with Her ways."

"All I'm saying is, if a wraith can make it up a three-story fire escape to come after me, a wraith can climb a fence to get to you."

"We have weapons and plenty of salt. I mean, if one of them really did find a way in."

"It only takes one. They'd multiply too fast. One could wipe you out in a half hour."

We'd made it back to the lot where my buggy was parked next to Sarah's golf cart. The four of them talked among themselves as they got in. Baxter took the passenger seat in my buggy as I got settled.

The laughter and talking stopped abruptly. It was weird and eerily quiet. I looked up and saw why.

A wraith hovered in front of the golf cart and another climbed from beneath it. They'd obviously held onto the undercarriage, stowing away to be brought in when Sarah returned.

So much for non-sentience.

"No," Baxter said.

Everything after that happened fast but appeared to be in slow motion. The wraith howled, leaned inside the cart, and misted the two young men in the back. Sarah screamed and dove out of the cart. The girl in the passenger seat wrestled with the door handle and kicked it open. She tried to run, but the wraith at the front of the cart blew mist and jumped on top of her. She screamed and clawed at the ground, but the shade was on her, consuming and goring her body with its claws.

I was horrified. There'd been no warning. No buzzing. I started the buggy as Sarah sprinted into the cavern, yelling for Lot. Baxter opened the door to get out but stopped short when the wraith who'd misted the two in the back of the cart slammed both clawed arms down on the hood of my buggy.

"Get down!" I yelled, just as the thing blew a thick cloud of mist straight at both of us. The cloud of deathly fog swirled against the short windshield and dissipated. We knocked heads, trying to get out of the way quickly. The other girl stopped screaming, finally sucked dry. I put the buggy in gear and hit the gas without looking up. The nubby wheels thump-thumped over the wraith and lurched, roaring ahead a few feet until we smashed into the granite wall.

My good hand was already wrapped around the stock of the Mossberg as I bailed out. "Baxter!"

He didn't reply, and I didn't have time to check on him. I had five rounds ready, one good hand, and two wraiths bearing down on me. I dusted the first and shook a new round into the chamber, leveling the barrel at the second wraith, which blew my mind by skittering away.

"Baxter! Now's a good time to get the hell out of the buggy!" I yelled, running after the wraith. Baxter sat up as I sprinted past, head lolling a bit, but he focused on me quickly. I planted my feet and took aim, but I couldn't fire.

Lot, Sarah, and about ten other people were running straight into the path of the wraith. When they saw it coming at them, they stopped. Sarah screamed. Again.

"Get down!" I yelled, keeping the wraith in my sights. It veered toward Sarah, likely because she was so loud.

I was so scared. Not for my own safety. Not really for the safety of the people clawing over one another to run away. I was terrified of missing the one shot I had at dusting that wraith. A miss meant the end of a colony of survivors. I didn't know how many people were holed up in the cave, but it had been three years. That likely meant kids. Babies.

I steadied and tucked my hair behind an ear, hearing my dad's voice telling me to breathe out. "Don't squeeze the trigger until you're ready," he'd said.

I was ready. The shot echoed in the cavern, and the wraith disintegrated in a burst of black powder. Lot helped Sarah up from where she'd fallen on her stomach when she tried to run.

"I see you," he called.

I didn't know what he meant by that, but I didn't have time to ponder all the crazy. I had to get back to the buggy where I'd left Baxter, punch drunk and trying to get out. I turned and sprinted the few feet around the curved path.

I skidded to a stop. Baxter was out of the buggy, kneeling over the shriveled husk of the girl who'd been killed. He was in danger of being in range when the new wraith spawned. His face was warped with terror and grief.

"Get back, Baxter! The remains are a gate to below ground. Another one's coming!"

It was far too late. Baxter yelped and backpedaled on all fours as oily claws burst upward, barely missing him. The rest of the shade rose up, a vertical cloud of death, ready to claim lives.

"Hey!" I yelled. "Over here!" I waved my free arm to get the thing's attention. The head turned slowly as it zeroed in on me.

My chest was tight with fear. I seated a new round of salt, ready for death to try again.

But it didn't come at me. The wraith turned to the golf cart, lowered to the ground, and slithered into the back seat where two fresh meals waited. It went to work digesting, and I ran toward the cart.

Lot ran to Baxter and helped him up. I couldn't hear what they were saying, but out of the corner of my eye, I saw Baxter run into the cavern. That made me happy. I liked Baxter and wanted him safe.

Three shots remained in the magazine. I took aim and stopped, realizing the salt would blast to bits against the metal cart unless I found an unobstructed line of fire. Rock salt was a killer, but it was also weak material that wouldn't pierce much. I hated to do it, but I ran straight at the wraith.

It finished with the first body, sucking it dry quickly, and hovered against the ceiling of the cart instead of coming to get me. I picked up a handful of gravel from the ground and whipped it at the cart, trying to antagonize the beast, and ran up to the windshield. It held ground, safely behind metal and glass. If I didn't get to it quickly, I'd have two wraiths to deal with instead of one, which was much more manageable.

So, I opened the door.

A thick beam of dark mist shot from inside the cart. The shade was waiting for me, ready to blast me into a state of paralysis so it could go to lunch. I dropped to the ground, small rocks digging into my kneecaps and then my thighs and belly. I rolled to my side under the open door and shoved the gun upward into the darkness circling there and fired with a hell of a lot of hope that I'd hit the wraith. Thankfully, a cloud of black dust huffed out of the cart and everything went silent. I hid my face from the remains as they drifted to the ground.

I rolled onto my bottom and sat crisscross apple sauce with a loaded shotgun in my lap for about three minutes. I sensed people behind me, heard whispers, but I kept my attention trained on the back seat of that golf cart.

First came the buzzing, then the head and claws exploded from the dried-out human remains. I dusted the new wraith before it could get out of the cart. Everything was so silent. No one spoke. I didn't get up, just rested the Mossberg in my lap and shook my hand out to stop the sting from the recoil. My mind whirled, but I was so damned tired.

So, this is life.

Lot's voice brought me back to the moment. "You see, the Lady, Edith, she has come, just as prophesied," he said. "She comes from the darkness and brings the sun with her! She who was lost and led astray is found! She, our Lady, our provider, our warrior goddess and protector! The prophecy is fulfilled!"

I'd come from the safety of my root cellar, far to the east. I'd gotten lost on the freeway but found purpose. I'd honed my skills at turning wraiths to dust and managed to save a bunch of people. It was my life, and I'd live it. I turned to see him standing with his back to me. Light from the artificially generated bulbs mounted to the cavern ceiling filtered through his sparse hair. Clusters of people, too many to count, grouped together behind him.

He twisted, gesturing right at me. "She has come!" he declared. "From the darkness and into the light!"

The crowd repeated his words, vigorously shouting and raising their hands. "She has come! Out Lady Edith is risen! We are saved!"

My jaw dropped, but my heart swelled, and a sob broke free.

I was June Bug Dempsey from Sleepy Eye, Minnesota.

And I'd found my tribe.

* * * * *

Marie Whittaker Bio

Marie Whittaker is an award-winning essayist and author of horror, urban fantasy, children's books and supernatural thrillers. Writing as Amity Green, her debut novel, Scales, the first in her Fate and Fire series, debuted in 2013, followed by Phantom Limb Itch in 2018. Her supernatural thriller, The Witcher Chime, was a finalist for the Indie Book Awards in 2017. She is the creator of The Adventures of Lola Hopscotch, which is a children's book series concentrating on getting sensitive childhood issues out in the open between children and adults. Many of her award-winning short stories appear in numerous anthologies and publications.

Marie enjoys teaching about publishing, writing craft, and project management for writers. She works as Associate Publisher at WordFire Press and is the Director of Superstars Writing Seminars, a world-class writing conference concentrating on the business of writing. Marie is a proud member of the Horror Writers Association and keeps steady attendance at local writer's groups.

A Colorado native, Marie resides in Manitou Springs, where she writes and enjoys renovating her historic Victorian home. She spends time hiking, gardening, and indulging in her guilty pleasure of shopping for handbags. She is fond of owls, coffee, and all things Celtic. A lover of animals, Marie is an advocate against animal abuse and assists with lost pets in her community.

# # # # #

Dust to Dust by Jamie Ibson

I do not know what weapons World War III will be fought with,

but World War IV will be fought with sticks and stones.

- Albert Einstein

The steam 'motive chuffed into Coldhearse Station, brakes screeching, fit to wake the dead. Russell "Rusty" Tailor held a pre-printed card in his hand. He'd never met the woman, but seeing as she was Mister Lippi's daughter, he needed to make a good impression. The squiggles on the back, theoretically a description of the lady he was there to greet, were no help since he'd never been taught his letters as a kiddling.

"Miss Suzanne has red curly hair but no freckles, blue eyes, blue specs, and a big black cat named Otis," Kendall had said as he scribbled the words down. *"She arrives on the noon o'clock train from Lake Winterpeg to formally take possession of the 'stead."*

As usual, the rail 'motive had run a bit late, per the dial on the platform, but it weren't like Rusty had anywhere else to be, and everyone knew the rail timings were pretty "ish." He stood dutifully, patiently, with the sign in his hands near the end of the station where the private cars were attached. Miss Suzanne's father, Dino, owned farms, factories, and a sizeable chunk of the rail industry, making him one of the wealthiest men in that region of the flats. He would have reserved a private car for her and the cat for such a long trip.

The public cars up near the locomotive began disgorging their passengers, many of whom turned toward the rear-most exit of the station, and in moments, he was surrounded by all manner of petticoats, three-piece suits, dapper caps, and dainty fascinators. Most of the men towed wheeled steamer trunks, and many of the women did too. Brass-reinforced trunks gleamed in the afternoon sun as their owners trundled through to the rail station exit or moved to the other platform.

When the sea of people parted, Tailor caught sight of a sole passenger who could only be Miss Suzanne.

Red curls tumbled out from beneath the white cowgirl hat that protected her pale skin from the midday sun. Her shimmering velvet skirt glinted crimson and was scandalously cut with a slit to her mid-thigh. The slit revealed a hint of teal paisley tights and a proper pair of brown riding boots that came nearly to her knee. She wore a broad, brown, leather belt that rode high on her right hip and low on the other. A stamped holster hung on her hip, opposite the skirt's slit, with the shootin' iron's pearl grips easily at hand. Her gloves matched the belt, which matched the leather of her corset-vest, buckled across her abdomen, framing her curves in a way Tailor ignored as hard as he could. Beneath the corset-vest, a high-necked silk blouse gleamed white. Dainty, black, wire goggles holding blue glass perched on her nose and completed the look.

It was one helluva look, Tailor concluded in an instant.

Aside from the hint of a neckline, she was covered from neck to toe in an utterly modest ensemble that would have the savviest saloon girl asking for fashion tips and leave not-so-gentle-men drooling. Tailor was having a hard time not gawking, but four years in the militia had taught him a thing or three about self-discipline. Miss Suzanne scanned the platform, and when she spied Tailor's sign, her face lit up with a smile. The platform was emptying rapidly, and after glancing around, she looked back into the train car and chirped.

"C'mon, buddy," she said and took a few steps forward. Rusty blanched as Otis descended from the train car behind her. Otis was no simple, black housecat. Otis looked more like a hunnert-n-twenny pounds of *panther*, on a black-and-gold woven rope attached to a night-black leather harness. Silver rivets and D-rings shone against the inky-black leather that covered his neck, back, throat, and chest, leaving his shoulders bare. Miss Suzanne strode forward to meet Rusty, the great cat padding forward at his mistress' heels.

"Good, uh, afternoon? Miss Leepee?" Rusty guessed. "Ah'm Rusty Tailor. I take it this terrifying beast is Otis?"

"Please'ta meetcha," she agreed. "And yes, he is. If you'll kneel and offer him the back of your hand, he'll say hello, and you'll be fast friends."

Rusty swallowed hard but did as he was bidden and got down on the cat's level. He smiled nervously and asked, "I'll get me hand back?"

Lippi flashed him a grin and nodded. Rusty couldn't tell whether the pounding in his chest was because of her smile, or the panther's stare. *Both,* he decided. *Definitely both.* Otis' golden eyes narrowed suspiciously, but Rusty offered the back of his hand as he would to introduce himself to any animal. Otis sniffed a couple of times, paused to consider, then rubbed the side of his muzzle and whiskers along the side of Rusty's hand. Rusty shivered as adrenaline coursed through his veins.

"See? Piece of pie. Otis is the smartest cat you'll ever meet, Mister Tailor, and he gets along with people fine, so long as they have manners. People tend to be right polite when he's about."

"I'll be sure to be ever the gentleman," Tailor promised as he straightened back up. "To be fair, my instructions did say he was a large black cat, but that's like saying the flats is "big.""

"And had Thomas told you he was a jungle cat, you wouldn't have believed it anyway. Not to worry, Otis has that effect on people. I'm rather impressed you introduced yourself. It wouldn't have been the first time someone refused and turned tail. It's one of many reasons I bring him with me any chance I get. Now, I presume there's some kind of transport laid on?"

"There is, ma'am. I'll show you to the stage and retrieve the rest of your baggage in a jiff."

"Please." She nodded.

The rail platform was little more than an elevated ceracrete dais with shelter from the elements, a restaurant, public toilets with running water (!), an info board with a map of Coldhearse, another one of the broader region, and the ticket kiosk. As they passed the maps, Miss Suzanne paused to study them.

"Home is… here?" she stabbed a point on the map. Rusty paused. He wasn't literate in the slightest, but he recognized map symbols. He searched the map, starting with the rail line, following it to the station, then west outta town, up to the bridge, and over the Old Man's Crick, to where Suzanne's finger rested on the map.

"That'd be it, Miss Lippi," he said. "Ole Man's Crick is the north boundary, and the Moon River is the south. Where the two come together is the eastern edge. The house is on the north side near the bridge, and the entirety of the property is nearly twenny-five hunnert acres."

"That's a lotta dirt." Suzanne studied the map further, absently scratching Otis' neck as she did so. Several passersby eyed the cat warily, but he didn't deign to acknowledge them. A moment passed and then, as though woken from a reverie, Lippi started and looked sheepish.

"I get distracted easily, 'pologies. Let's get Otis situated before anything else, Mister Tailor."

Rusty guided her and her cat out of the station and out to the waiting coach. Like most coaches, a skeletal frame of an ancient 'mobile had been repurposed since they lacked the materials to make a new one. The panels had rusted away decades ago and been replaced with oiled, stained wood. Simple, solid iron axles replaced the ancient complicated things that had been there before, supported on heavy wooden wheels, and the rest of the heavy metal parts were long gone to lighten the load for the team up front.

The horses chuffed warily, unnerved by the scent of the predator, but their blinders kept them from panicking entirely. The lithe black cat leaped up into the 'mobile and climbed over the mid-bench to stretch out on the rear one. Miss Suzanne tied his leash in a neat half-hitch to the window pillar and petted him on the forehead. Rusty returned to pick up her baggage, and the porter had the trunks loaded onto a sturdy dolly with well-oiled granite wheels. Rusty rolled her steamers out to the rear of the stage, stacked them in the boot, and was surprised to find Lippi had chosen to ride with him.

"I'd rather ride shotgun if that's alright?" she asked. "You do *have* a shotgun, don't you?"

"I do," he said and pulled an old four-shot pump from the sheathe on the side of his door. He passed it to her, and Miss Suzanne expertly checked the exterior of the scattergun, verified the safety was on, performed a slide-check, and confirmed the chamber was empty. She racked the action aggressively to chamber a shell and rested it on one knee, barrel up. Tailor raised an eyebrow before passing her the bandolier of buckshot from where it hung on a peg on the front pillar. Lippi thumbed a paper shell from the leather loops and slid it up into the tube to replace the one she'd just chambered.

"You seem to know your way around weapons, Miss," Rusty said, impressed.

"Father sent me to an excellent finishing school," she said. "The best in Lake Winterpeg. *Ain't no daughter of mine gonna get dusted in a fight*, he usta say. I'm a fair hand at skeet and three-gun." She smiled and drew the revolver from her holster. With a flick of her wrist, she unsnapped the cylinder and passed it to Tailor butt-first. He admired the wheelgun, a well-loved, long-barreled forty-four. She kept it oiled and rust-free, and the smooth pearl handles probably cost more than Rusty had ever seen in his life.

"Very nice," he stammered, returning it.

She snapped the cylinder back in and holstered it. "That said, I wasn't able to ship the rest of my arms with me from Winterpeg and sold them instead. Is there a gun store we could stop at? I'd like to put in an order."

"Absolutely," Tailor agreed. He knew just the place. Rusty snapped the reins, and the team pulled the coach away, leaving a trail of dust in its wake.

* * *

Mister Tailor was intriguing, even if he wasn't very learned or even literate. He was a wealth of knowledge about the area and chatted about the different farms and ranches on the edge of town. As they clattered down the dusty road, Rusty pointed out how certain kinds of animals got along well with each other or didn't, as the case may be. He was clean-shaven, about her age, maybe a touch younger, fit, and didn't shrink away from Otis. His button-up plaid shirt revealed well-muscled arms, used to heavy work, and a militia tattoo rode low on his forearm. He sported a heavy, black, canvas utilikilt that showed red plaid between the pleats, a repeater similar to her own on his hip, and a brown, leather cowboy hat. All to the good. He'd accepted her sidekick with aplomb and hadn't been surprised when she asked to stop at the gun store. It was essential to establish she was no wilting flower or dainty damsel. She supposed, if Mister Kendall had told him anything about her, that shouldn't have been a surprise. Thomas Kendall was her closest uncle in every way but blood. When Father purchased the estate, for a very inexpensive price, he'd sent his top lieutenant west to oversee the deal and get the rougher parts prepared for her eventual arrival. That had been two long years ago, and she was excited to see him again; he'd taught her the fundamentals of three-gun shooting, and she was anxious to carve out a chunk of the acreage for a competitive range.

Speaking of shooting, she heard the store before she spotted it. The large marquee over the front plate glass read *Mike's Alcohol, Tobacco, and Firearms*, and she'd heard slow, steady gunfire for at least a block. It was right on the west edge of town, with one of the region's few hills acting as a backstop for the range. Tailor pulled the coach to a halt, and Suzanne hopped down, still wearing the bandolier and carrying the scattergun. She leaned into the interior. "You just wait here, Otis." She pulled the drapes inside the 'mobile shut and scratched the panther between his ears. He rolled onto his back, accepted a brief rub on his chest, then appeared to doze off.

"He gonna be awright like that, Miss?" Tailor asked, his concern for the panther evident.

"He'll be fine. He's clipped in, so he can't get out. With the drapes pulled, he'll just nap. It's warm, and he's a lazy bum, most of the time."

Rusty led the way into the store, conveniently arrayed into three broad sections. A sign at the back indicated the way to the range, where concussive snaps rent the air every few seconds. She took a moment to appreciate the display to her left; the "alcohol" portion of the store consisted of crystal decanters and fancy bottles with liquids ranging from clear to amber, burgundy, and sapphire blue. The counter was long and stretched deep into the storefront. It appeared they even had a cold storage room: one of the panels on the wall advertised a list of porters, lagers, and stouts. A pair of scrimshawed oxen horns rested in wrought-iron stands beneath the signage. A tall man, wearing a plaid T-shirt, jeans, an apron, and a nametag bearing the word *Chris* approached.

"I've not met you before, welcome to Mike's A-T-F."

"Please'ta meetcha," Suzanne replied. "Suzanne Lippi, new in town."

"She's the new occupant of the old Cortez homestead," Tailor supplied.

"That so?" Chris replied with an arched eyebrow. "Care to sample something as you browse?"

"The chocolate porter sounds interesting," Suzanne replied. She motioned to the horn with knotwork carved into its surface, surrounding a cat's face. "Are the horns for sale as well?"

"They are. The horns are from local oxen. We clean them, scrub them, cure them, and decorate them ourselves. Those two are for serving, but we rinse them before and after each use, and Mike isn't one to turn down a sale. We also have braided leather frogs to carry them if you need."

"I'll take the frog, the cat horn, and the chocolate porter," Suzanne agreed. "Is this all homebrewed?"

"It is," Chris replied proudly. "Mike originally just sold firearms, but over time, he expanded. I brew the beer and distill the spirits. John handles the cigars and tells tales, and Mike is your expert for anything you might want to shoot or stab someone with." Chris added some figures together in an accounts book. "The horn and frog come to forty-two chits. First drink's included in the sale."

Suzanne produced a billfold and handed over a fifty-chit from a stack of fifty-chits. He accepted the large bill and thanked her when she refused the change. He took down the drinking horn and disappeared into the cold room. She became aware of a much quieter clacking interspersed between the repeated gunshots. She noted an older gentleman behind the far end of the counter who was rapid-fire typing away at a brand-new typewriter. He had a greying pony-tail, specs, and an unlit cigar clenched between his teeth. When he finished a sheet, he placed it next to him on a stack.

"Whatcha workin' on now, John?" Rusty asked.

"New idea of mine," the gentleman replied. "Monsters from space, arriving on great airships. Our heroes need to pin them in place so their bombards can dust them wholesale. It'll be great."

"Don't let me interrupt then," Rusty said. He turned away and whispered conspiratorially, "*When John gets rolling, he gets rolling. He was a bombardier a dog's age ago and comes up with the most amazing stories. I don't know my letters myself, but he spins a great yarn if you catch him in a storytelling kinda mood. He's even got a contract for his story, once it's done. They's gonna print off copies down at the new press in Diamond City and sell 'em as books!*" Rusty looked away, shame crossing his features. "Not that I'll be able to read 'em." He cleared his throat and started fresh. "Having said all that, I'd be careful flashing about a stack of chits like that. Chris, Mike, and John are good people, deal with upscale clientele, and don't suffer fools gladly. But elsewhere in town, that'll get you rolled if you're not careful."

"That's why I carry an iron on my hip," Suzanne agreed, "and why Otis watches my back. Father wanted me to have some liquidity when I came out this way," she explained. Rusty nodded in under-standing as Chris re-emerged and handed over the horn, now full of a near-black, fragrant beer that reminded Suzanne of Ecksmass chocolates from her childhood. She sipped and smiled. "Lovely."

"We can supply all the liquidity you need," Chris said with a knowing twinkle in his eye. "We have some very nice scotch, bourbon, rye, sapphire gin, a plain vodka we use to cure the horns that mixes well with fruit juices, and a strawberry vodka that's very popular…"

"Tempting," she said, "but I'm actually here to secure some new firearms. Thank you," she said. Chris nodded politely and excused himself. A moment later, a man, perhaps in his forties, with short black hair and a neatly trimmed mustache, came out to the counter with Chris. He wore a plain black shirt, loose trousers, and safety specs, and he pulled a beeswax earplug from one ear.

"Welcome! Chris says you're the new owner of the old Cortez farmstead?" he asked. "Wow. You've come to the right place. What can I do for you?"

"I am. Suzanne Lippi, please'ta meetcha." Her eyes took in the long guns and sidearms on padded hooks hanging behind the counter, and she smiled broadly. "Rusty tells me you're the place to shop for firearms; clearly, he understated matters. I had to sell much of my collection back east at Winterpeg since it would have filled several trunks. So, I have some"—she grinned—"liquidity, and I'd like to place an order."

Mike produced a notepad from a pocket and picked up a quill from its inkpot.

"I'm going to want a pump scattergun, mag fed, with an interior polish and trigger job. Shorter is better, and several layers of ten-ounce leather at the butt for cushioning. Four stiff, leather mag carriers, and ninety shells to start, evenly split between bird, buck, and slug." Suzanne sipped the porter, then ticked off the points on her fingers as she went. "A lever carbine, Marlin or 'Chester in thirty-thirty would be ideal, with four speed-tube loaders, a clean breaking lever, trigger job as well, and a saddle holster. Another hundred rounds."

Mike had fallen behind as she dictated her needs, and he looked at Rusty with one raised eyebrow.

"She shoots three-gun?" Rusty asked, but "Miss Lippi" was on a roll and continued.

"And something for distance and hunting. Maybe another 'Chester, but in thirty-ought-six. Folding bipod, two spare mags, and fifty rounds. Do you by chance do optics?"

Mike was chuckling by the time she finished. "We do." He withdrew a drawer loaded with finely made scopes. He lifted one gently from the padded slot it rested in and offered it to her. She slipped the still-half-full horn into its frog on her belt to free her hands and exhaled a held breath in deep appreciation.

Each scope was a miracle of modern technology; the lenses were clear, without fogging or scratches. The outside hull was free of blemishes or warps, and it was smooth to the touch. The crosshairs were perfectly straight, perfectly centered, and on this one, there were small hash marks on the vertical post below the crosshairs.

"Human gauge?" she asked, and Mike gave an approving nod. If a standard human fit between the top and bottom hashmark, he was three hundred meters distant. If he fit between the *middle* hashmark and another, he was six hundred meters distant. It was a rough and ready guesstimate, but for putting lead on target, getting the range right was essential.

"They're gorgeous," she breathed. They were, perhaps, the pinnacle of modern firearms technology and made a rifleman vastly more precise at longer distances. She reverently returned the scope, and Mike returned it to its space in the drawer. "I'm reluctant to ask…"

"They range from six hundred to a thousand, Miss," Mike said. "At a rough guess, your scattergun and the two Chesters, with improvements as requested, plus ammunition, will be near eleven hundred as is."

"Rats," Lippi cursed. "My budget is fifteen hundred. That's fine. I'll take what I've got for now and will get the scope once the farmstead is operational, and I have a bit more discretionary funds. Can I get you a draft from the bank?"

"Please," Mike said. He took down three long guns from padded hooks on the wall and laid each on the countertop, actions open. "Will these do?"

Suzanne checked the weight and feel for each, nodding in approval. "Do you have an idea of how long it will take to make the modifications?"

"About the middle of next week," Mike estimated. He consulted a log and nodded. "Half now, half then?"

"Excellent," Lippi said and offered her hand. "Very pleased to have met you, Mike."

* * *

They backtracked to the bank, where Suzanne confirmed her funds had arrived in her local account. There were two transfers—the first, rather more considerable sum, was to get the 'stead up and running proper. The second was the proceeds of her own armory's sales. The banker, Mister Wortheringham, practically tripped over himself in a clumsy attempt to ingratiate himself when he saw the account balance. The atmosphere chilled several degrees when she told him she was the new owner of what everyone called "the old Cortez farmstead," and yet more so when she instructed him to write two drafts, six hundred chits each, to Mike's Alcohol Tobacco and Firearms. Then she wanted another three hundred in small bills. By the time she left, he seemed practically hostile.

His attitude shift puzzled her, but Mike accepted the down payment gratefully and promised the firearms would be ready in a week. Chris was pleased to sell her a keg of the chocolate porter and loaded the wooden barrel into the rear of Rusty's 'mobile. With the most pressing business taken care of, Tailor hopped back into the wheelman's seat and gave a sharp *hyah!* to get the horses moving at a good clip.

Lippi was rapt, absorbing every detail of the trip, even though the ride into town had quickly gotten dull over Tailor's several months of traveling to and fro. He pointed out several of the landmarks—the Coldhearse Legion, adjacent to the schoolhouse, where most of the militiamen gathered on weekends to socialize and tell tales. The scorched forest, a copse of tall, barren pines that had died ages ago but still stood proud in a field where nothing grew anymore. Then, the broken ceracrete that had once been the Number Three, carving a bare path from the northwest to the southeast. Three klicks northwest of town, Tailor guided the horses down a long slope to the river valley floor and then rumbled over a makeshift bridge.

"Question," Suzanne said suddenly. The 'mobile coach was approaching a set of switchbacks that cut its way up the face of the escarpment.

"Answer?" Tailor replied.

"Chris, Mike, *and* that Wortheringham banker gent all seemed surprised I was moving into the farm. Why?"

"Uh…" Tailor swallowed awkwardly. "I'm not sure I'm the right person to answer that. Mister Kendall will explain when we reach the house."

"That's…ominous."

"Omin-what?"

"Foreboding? Sinister?" Tailor continued to wear a blank, uncomprehending look on his face. "Nervous-making?"

"Oh. Yeah, I suppose so. The farmstead has…a rep. Locally. Nothing to be afraid of, just…folk gets scared. Superstitious. This part is a bit complicated Miss, if you'll just give me a moment?"

Suzanne sat back in her seat, but she gripped the pump scattergun a bit more tightly. The horses knew the route, and Rusty expertly guided them back and forth until they crested the ridgetop. They'd gained a fair amount of elevation, enough that she could look out Rusty's window and see Coldhearse, some klicks distant, and the curving, meandering valleys carved by the two rivers below them. Then she looked to her left, and her new home stole her breath away.

The "farmhouse" was less "farmhouse" and more "palatial estate." It perched above the escarpment, set perhaps fifty meters back from the edge. Roughly rectangular, a broad porch surrounded it on the two sides she could see, supported by well-lathed white columns. A half-wall enclosed the porch up to waist height, and white lattice acted as a windbreak. The walls were evenly divided with windows—and the windows were sealed with frosted glass. The second story was near-identical to the first, but double doors over the front doors opened onto a balcony. Hitching posts out front were bare, at the moment, and fences subdivided the yard into an incomprehensible maze of paths and paddocks. A small herd of white, brown, and painted...llamas? waited out front, chewing their lunch. A larger flock of sheep grazed around their feet.

"Oh, my goodness..." she said and squealed as one of the llamas moved out of the way to reveal *baby* llamas, tiny, fleecy, and adorable.

"Mister Lippi's instructions were that the farmstead ought to be as self-sufficient as possible," Tailor explained. "Mister Kendall's been busy buying up as much breeding stock as we can source here, in the flats. Lotsa folk have more critters than they know what to do with. The alpacas and sheep make for good wool, babies especially. It gets mighty cold here in the winter and ain't nothin' warmer than baby alpaca thermals. We've got—sorry, *you've* got about two hundred cattle out in the back forty, twenty goats, on the far side of the house, and there's a coop out back for rabbits and chickens. We've had better luck with them, so we're planning to double it and move the chickens back from the house. Chickenshit's kinda...stinky, Miss. Pardon my language."

"Amazing," she breathed. "What did you call the llamas?"

"Not llamas, Miss," Rusty corrected her. "Alpacas. Related, but smaller, and their wool is nicer."

An older gentleman exited the front door to the house, and Suzanne's face lit with a wide smile.

"Thomas!"

She didn't wait for the coach to come to a stop before she flung the door open, bounded out, and crossed the dusty front yard. She engulfed the older man in a hug, and he laughed and returned it.

"Welcome home, Miss Suzanne," he said. "I think your father would be pleased with what we've accomplished here. Has Rusty taken good care of you so far?"

"Absolutely," she agreed. "I've already met Mike at the gun store and have two rifles and a shotgun on the way next week. There are baby"—she looked at Rusty for a second, and the word came to her—"alpacas in the yard, and the house is gorgeous."

Suzanne reached into the rear of the coach and unclipped her snoozing panther's leash. He opened one sleepy eye, slow-blinked, then clambered over the central bench and lit down onto the dusty ground. He leaned back, stretched, and yawned.

"Hey stranger, how you been?" Thomas Kendall asked, kneeling and scratching under the big cat's chin. Before they'd gone into business together, Thomas and her father had served together in the Cameron Highlanders' Feline Reconnaissance Corps. They'd been working with war cats since before Suzanne was born, and Thomas had taught her much of what she knew about the care and feeding of panthers. Otis' raspy tongue flicked out, and he gnawed on Kendall's knuckle for a moment, before catching sight of the alpacas in their enclosure and wandering out to the end of his leash. Suzanne tugged on it to tell him not to go any further, but the funny, long-necked creatures strode purposefully away to the far end of the paddock. Kendall chuckled. "Yeah, it'll take a bit for them to get used to him. Let's go inside and get you situated."

* * *

I f anything, the interior of the farmhouse was more beautiful than the exterior. Many precursor structures in Winterpeg had been repaired poorly, if at all. Most had just been patched up over and over until, eventually, a stiff breeze knocked over the rotten wood. Out here, the structures seemed solid. Newly made. Nobody was building on the bones of the precursors, save perhaps that rickety bridge below the house, and clearly, that was to the good. Coldhearse had skilled craftsmen if Mike and his staff were any indication. The floors inside the home were smooth, wood planks, not thin, flattened sheets of wood peeled like an onion. Deep pile rugs covered the floors in each room, and Suzanne was pleased to learn much of the rug wool came from the very alpacas Otis had disturbed outside. The doors closed well, and she noted they'd been lined with leather to keep out the draft. A positively heavenly scent permeated the air. Kendall laughed when she asked, and reluctantly admitted the bacon grease-and-beeswax candles came from the butcher's in town.

"I'm gonna excuse myself, and go water the critters, Mister Kendall," Rusty said and tipped his hat to her. "Miss."

"I have a question…" she began. She wasn't quite sure how to phrase it. "Several of the folk in town reacted…strangely to the news that *I* was to be the new inhabitant of the Cortez farmstead. The bank manager was downright rude. Rusty didn't want to tell me, said to ask you. What have I stumbled into?"

Kendall poured them each a drink from the fresh keg, raised his glass in a salute, and drained half his glass in one gulp.

"The Cortez's were popular folk around here as best I can tell. Somebody killed 'em all one night, every one of 'em. No idea whodunnit, or even how. You remember, when you were five, and I caught you and your brother Johnny roasting ants with a magnifying glass?"

Suzanne choked a bit on her drink and gave him an incredulous look. Her brother had had a thing for studying the big, ugly bugs. Most ants only grew to the size of a fingerbone, but the biggest and boldest of them would fill her palm. They were a right pain in the tuchus, and Johnny had shown her how the bigger ones' carapaces were much thicker, much tougher than the wee ones. "I do, but Johnny was the one scorching holes in them. How is that relevant?"

"The Cortez's were killed with something that scorched holes in them too. Holes in their chests you could poke a finger through, in one side and straight out the other. The meat all around the wounds was cooked. No one round here has any idea what coulda did such a thing. It ain't like any regular gunshot wound anyone here's ever seen. That, and their hired help lived on-site and didn't hear nothin' that night. It's a mystery, one the sheriff and his deputies failed to solve. They were anxious to blame one of the ranch hands, on account of he'd disappeared that same night, but no one in a hunnert klicks have seen hide nor hair of young master Leonard. Actually, that's not quite true. One of Mister Cortez's daughters disappeared with the boy. Probably some star-crossed-lovers mischief gone tragic."

"So, someone…what, snuck through the house and *burned* holes in them with an enormous magnifying glass in the middle of the night? With no *sun* to focus? That's ridiculous," she said. "And two people missing?"

"It may be ridiculous," Kendall replied and threw back another swallow of beer, "but it gets weirder 'n' that. I've spoke with Sheriff Barber, Sergeant Moss, and Deputy Isaacs. Ain't none of them will deviate from their tale one smidge. With the Cortez's gone, their staff abandoned the place. Found work elsewhere. Not sure when exactly, but at some point, their whole place burned to the ground. Dino bought the site shortly after."

"It burned down? The whole house?"

"It did, Miss. The house was at the very eastern corner of the property above the river junction. They could see the flames from Coldhearse proper, and tweren't nuthin but charred lumber by the time the deputies came out the next morning. And it's lay fallow since, something the realtor failed to disclose when he sold yer Father "twenny-five hunnert acres of prime farmland." It was evident from Kendall's tone that he didn't think much of the realtor's deceptive sales tactic. "I had a right awkward talking to when I got here. Sheriff Barber's a good man, and I think you'd like Sergeant Moss. She reminds me a bit of you. Same red hair, same fierce "I'll take on the world" attitude. I got the hairy eyeball when I arrived, but they were just motivated to figure out whodunit. Since it weren't me…it remains a mystery."

"And you've built this entire home since you arrived?"

"We have, Miss. You know how much your father prizes efficiency. We were living out of lean-tos and tents to begin with, but there's plenty of timber and folk keen for the work. The dozen aurox I purchased dragged much of the charred remains to the cliff's edge, and we heaved it into the valley to get washed away with the spring melt. Had a whole crew up here, went like cogwork."

"And now, if you like, we can let that great beast of yours stretch his legs, and I'll show you around the property. That'll take most of the rest of the afternoon—it really is quite a bit of dirt—and then we can tuck into some grub and call it a night."

Suzanne got to her feet, and Otis stretched again before following her. "Whaddaya say, buddy? Shall we go see our new home?"

Otis sawed contentedly, the much larger panther's version of a housecat's purr, and followed his mistress out the door.

* * *

Suzanne's mount, an elegant black beauty named Naomi, slowed to a canter as she reached the escarpment. A full week of exploring all the corners of the farm, making notes, and discovering the second house they'd built as a "staff barracks" since it wouldn't do for her to be living in the same home as two men, being married to neither…people would talk. She'd helped with critters around the house growing up, but Father had always done the butchering. Now it was her turn to learn; it all made for a busy week. But now it was Saturday morning, and she had carved out a little time for herself.

The pistol range will go here. She laid out pegs in the ground for the 25-pace range. Lanes for six, overhead protection against weather, blocks-and-tackle to haul target stands out to the proper distance, the works. *And that canyon will work nicely for jungle lanes.* The canyon, with sheer walls, descended to the river valley floor. Once she and Naomi walked perhaps a quarter of the way in, she was completely invisible from above. She'd trade for junk, stuff she didn't mind shooting holes in, and would build up a course full of pop-up targets that changed each run-through thanks to Father's cogwork devices.

At the lower mouth of the canyon, the sheer slopes cut by the river opened wide. The Moon River joined Old Man Crick in a Y-junction. She'd lay out more cogwork targets along the valley floor and up the walls to train for distance shooting. She grumbled to herself a bit that she couldn't afford one of Mike's well-honed optics; ladder sights simply required one to be a better shooter. As a teen, she'd hunted with her father outside Lake Winterpeg, and he'd dropped a feral swamp donkey from nearly a klick away. He'd been using a ladder sight, and when they got close, she was stunned at how massive the beasts were. Their palmate antlers were as wide as she was tall, and the meat had fed the entire household for a month.

The rivers were shallow here, and she stripped off her boots and left them on some rocks by the riverbed. It wouldn't do to get them soaked. Suzanne measured off paces from the base of the canyon and pinned little flags in place as she went. When she returned to put her boots back on, a glimmer of sunlight reflected brightly off something in the grass near an overhang. Curious, Suzanne investigated and found a muddy, rusty revolver in the grass. She rinsed the long-barreled forty-four in the river, then opened the cylinder. All six cases' primers bore divots, indicating they'd been struck, but she couldn't see through the chamber, and a twig down the barrel showed it plugged. The wood grips were well-lacquered, in surprisingly good shape, and bore the letters "R E C" engraved in a stylish cursive script. *Strange.*

She tucked the rusty thing into a saddlebag and rode back up the canyon and returned to the house. "The boys" were out in the shop, shaping the wood that would be water troughs. She'd discussed her plans with them, and they'd agreed. A water tank, no minor undertaking, would go adjacent to the house, and a steam pump would draw water up from the river. The tank would provide fresh water for the house and troughs for the aurox, the horses, the goats, the sheep, and the alpacas. Her father prized efficiency above all, and his engine-seers continually developed and refined new devices to increase his factories' production. Father was a genius who employed geniuses, to the never-ending delight of the people of Lake Winterpeg. His industrial advances saw greater productivity and generated more wealth than they had in living memory. Her task, therefore, was to start with the farmland—twenty-five hundred acres was a lot of dirt—and build it into something self-sustaining. She had enough planted land to feed all the critters, expand the herds, and eventually move into more substantial industry.

But, before any of that could come to pass, she needed to make dinner. She smiled to herself as she peeled taters—she'd be heading into town tomorrow to pick up her new firearms and was looking forward to turning a few chits into smoke and noise.

* * *

IBSON & KENNEDY

Suzanne tacked up her "Help Wanted" sign on the Cold-hearse jobs board. She'd gone over the plans for the water tower after dinner with Thomas and Rusty, and they'd agreed it was a substantial task, well worth hiring some of the crew who'd helped build the houses. The wages spent would be worth the time saved; more importantly, she missed the indoor plumbing she'd had at home. She placed another order with the grocer—it would be some time before her garden was producing enough—and then she was off to Mike's again.

Chris waved as she entered. "Welcome back, Miss. Wet your whistle?"

She laughed. "Not this early, thanks. Unless you have some sweet tea, perhaps? Is Mike around?"

"I do, and he is," Chris said and went to the back room. Both men emerged with long guns in their hands, and Suzanne's face lit with pleasure. Mike was grinning too and laid them on the counter next to a frosty iced tea from the cold room. She tested the action of each, and they were oiled and smooth like well-churned butter. He took her to the range behind the shop, where she fired off several dozen rounds for each and found them very much to her liking. The magazine-fed shotgun was particularly sharp. She hadn't spent much time with guns with detachable box magazines, but being able to reload six rounds by simply swapping boxes was vastly better than feeding them singly into a tube or cylinder. She took her purchases outside to Naomi. She wore the 'Chester repeater over her back and slipped the other two rifles into scabbards on Naomi's saddle. But when she went to load her saddlebags with the ammunition she'd purchased, she found the old revolver from the valley. She returned inside immediately.

"I completely forgot—I found this down where Moon River joins Old Man's Crick." She laid the pistol on the counter and pointed to the initials engraved on the grip. "Any idea who it might have belonged to?"

Mike's mood darkened the moment he saw it. "I do." He went to a drawer and rifled through a stack of old weeklies. There must have been a hundred or more of them, but he eventually found the one he wanted.

"CORTEZ HOMESTEAD MASSACRE!" was printed across the top in bold letters. It was the biggest news story of the week. Suzanne was confused until Mike stabbed the final paragraph with his finger.

Regina Emmalina Cortez is missing, and Antonio Gomez is wanted for questioning related to this heinous crime. Anyone with information is asked to contact the Sheriff's Office.

"No one saw Miss Cortez or Master Gomez after that night," Mike said. "This pistol was hers. I made the grips for her; they were a gift." He riffled back through the stack of dailies, then pulled out a second sheet. "The house burned down a week later. Actually"—he checked the date—"I stand corrected. It was the following night. But they were killed the day before it went to press, and their place burning down was the night after. So, there was a delay. Where did you say you found it?"

"In the valley east of my place, under an overhang. Right where the Moon River and Old Man's Crick join."

"Just below where their house used to stand. Hmm." Mike checked the barrel and tried to clear it.

"It seems plugged," she said. Mike got out a metal cylinder that slipped inside, barely, and tapped it with a hammer. That failed too. He increased the force he was using until it became clear the barrel was well and truly jammed.

"May I?" he asked, gesturing to his foot-pumped belt sander.

"Of course," Suzanne agreed. "It's not mine." Mike clamped the pistol into a vice on an armature and locked it so the barrel would press up against his belt sander. He pumped his foot on the pedal, raising and lowering a piston, getting a flywheel spinning. When it reached a certain RPM, he shifted a lever, pumped his foot harder, and the belt flew even faster. He got it up to speed, then levered the armature forward. Sparks flew as he ground away a chunk of the barrel for several minutes until he finally stopped and pulled the gun back.

"Hah. Thought so," Mike said. The gun was hot, under that kind of treatment, but removing part of the barrel's wall revealed six bullets all compacted inside, one flattened against the other, with just a thin jacket of copper separating each round.

"Who would she have been shooting at?" Suzanne wondered aloud.

"Theory goes, she'd been kidnapped by Gomez, who killed her family and then came back the next night to torch the house and hide the crime," Mike said. "Couldn't say."

"Well, thank you once again, sir," Suzanne said and departed.

* * *

aomi slowed to a trot as a gunshot from the south rent the air, and Otis' ears flattened against his skull. Suzanne waited for a long moment, but when there were no further sounds of distress, she spurred her horse forward into a fast canter. Otis padded along beside them in a loping jog. She'd selected Naomi as her preferred mount as she was the only horse who hadn't panicked at the sight of the lean, black panther. A horse ride was one of the only ways she could ensure her bodyguard got any proper exercise. Two crests later, Thomas Kendall waved to her from atop his mount. Rusty was dismounted and on one knee, inspecting a dead coyote.

"This might be one of the critters what were pawin' at the coop, Miss," Rusty said. "Not sure yet where they're hidin' out. I'd lay in traps, but they'd catch as many cattle as coyotes. I need to find their den before they do too much damage. Or set up an ambush with bait." He patted the fur down and sifted through it carefully. "This'll make for a nice cold-weather lining, though. He's clean, no mange…just have to wash the fur for fleas or parasites. Go on you," he said as Otis nosed around the carcass and tasted the dead scavenger's blood. Rusty tied all four of the coyote's legs together with rough twine and hung it off his saddle for skinning later. "Something we can help you with, Miss?"

"Did you live in the region before Thomas hired you, Rusty?" Suzanne asked.

"I did, Miss; grew up in Diamond City but met Mister Kendall in the militia. Why?"

Suzanne showed them the revolver she'd found, and the cutaway portion of the barrel. "I aim to do a bit of investigating. Something isn't right. How would Regina Cortez's revolver wind up in the river valley, a klick from the house and jammed up with a squib load, if she and her boyfriend had just run away?"

Rusty frowned. "You ask hard questions, Miss. Might maybe you wanna talk to Sheriff Barber about that?"

"I might, eventually. But I don't want to bother him if it's nothing. Awkward way to meet someone."

Rusty mounted his horse and nodded. "Lead the way."

They followed the cliff's edge east from the house until they reached the spot Suzanne intended to put her "jungle lanes" and descended to the river's edge. She doubled back, following the banks west to the overhang where she'd found the revolver, and dismounted. Suzanne rolled her eyes as Otis immediately went to the waters' edge to fish.

"What're we looking for?" Kendall asked. He half-heartedly kicked at some grasses with his boot, then stopped and put his hands on his hips.

"No idea," Suzanne replied. "But we'll know it if it turns up."

They moved slowly, searching the grasses for any artifact that might hold secrets, when a splashing commotion behind her made Suzanne jump. She whirled and breathed a sigh of relief when a very proud Otis trotted away from the rivers' edge with a huge, struggling walleye in his jaws. She rolled her eyes but then frowned. Otis jogged directly away from the river to the overhang—and then scrambled up the wall *under* the overhang and disappeared from view.

"What—hey! Where d'you think you're going, mister?" she asked and cautiously approached. The overhang was not an abrupt rock face, as she'd believed. There was an inky black cave opening concealed behind the front of the overhang, and judging by the wet paw prints, Otis had disappeared inside to eat his catch in private. The two men followed her to investigate. Rusty lifted the hat from his head and scratched, confused. "I have lived near here my whole life. Ain't nobody ever said there was some kinda cave down here."

"Gimme a boost?" Suzanne asked, then paused. She returned to Naomi and pulled her new scattergun from its scabbard. She looped two spare magazine carriers on her belt and returned to the cave. "Okay, *now* give me a boost?"

Rusty sat against the overhang's face and cupped his hands. Suzanne scrambled up to join her cat and lowered her hand to haul Rusty up after her. Rusty pulled Kendall up, and the trio turned and discovered a dry, dusty path of rocks and hardy grasses that disappeared down into abrupt darkness. Suzanne took three slow, careful steps and confirmed that the cavern's footpath sloped away from the cave entrance, lit only by the reflected sunlight from outside.

"Wait," Rusty cautioned, then swore. He drew the iron at his side in a flash and pointed it down the tunnel. Suzanne led with the barrel of her scattergun and followed his gaze.

Just inside the tunnel, maybe twenty feet or so, two human skulls grinned up at them. They rested atop metal rods, and what looked like femur bones crossed beneath them with a slim pin no thicker than Suzanne's pinky. She approached them, nervously, and leaned down.

"Thomas, when you said someone shot the Cortezes with something that *cooked* them," Suzanne whispered, "is this what you meant?"

Both skulls had perfectly round holes in their foreheads. The holes lined up with matching ones at the base of the skulls. When Suzanne leaned down just the right way, she could see clean through the other side. The bones were dry, dusty, and bleached, but the bone surrounding each hole was scorched.

"I think we ought to go, Miss," Rusty said. "Not that I'm afraid. More, concerned. And I think we ought to bring the sheriff."

"I think you're probably right," Thomas agreed. "I think we ought to come back with lamps. And more ammo."

* * *

Diamond City was a ways northeast of the homestead; she'd passed it on the locomotive on her way to Coldhearse. It hadn't looked any different than any of the dozens of tiny towns that followed the rail line. A saloon/tavern/inn, a gun shop (although Thomas warned her the owner was sketchy and not well respected), and a few houses, but Diamond City held one crucial difference.

Thomas, Rusty, and Suzanne halted their mounts outside the county sheriff's office and looped the reins around the hitching post outside. Kendall led the way inside.

"Sergeant Moss," he said, doffing his hat as he entered. "How'd you do?"

"I'm afraid it's Sheriff Moss now," the fiery-haired woman replied. "Griff retired two weeks back. His daughter in Glenwood just had her third, and he's moved down thatta way to play grandpaw. Who's the young lady?"

"I'm Suzanne Lippi, Sheriff, please'ta meetcha."

"Oh, this is your adopted niece, Thomas?" Sheriff Moss stood up and came around the desk to shake Suzanne's hand. "Pleased to meet you as well. To what do I owe the visit?"

"It's about the Cortez…massacre, I guess," Suzanne began. She produced Regina Cortez's revolver from her pack and offered it to the sheriff. "I was exploring the property and was plotting out my shooting range. This was in the grasses down in the river valley below where their house stood."

"Okay," Sheriff Moss replied. "And I take it Mike has confirmed it belonged to them?"

"He did," Rusty replied. "But that's not all we found. There's a cave hidden down in the valley, near where that gun was sitting. Entrance is tucked up above ground level, six or seven feet. Can't see it unless you're right up against the entrance. We checked it out…"

"…And found two human skulls inside," Kendall finished. He reached into his pack and pulled out one of the skulls.

"Now wait just a minute—" Sheriff Moss exclaimed, her hand falling to the butt of the revolver on her hip, but Kendall set the skull on her desk and pointed to the scorch mark on the forehead. She relaxed, a smidge, and sat back down to examine it.

"They were mounted on poles, and they have the same kind of holes and scorch marks that killed the Cortezes, Jules," Kendall said. "There's somethin' down in that cave, and it's bleedin' dangerous."

Moss examined the skull from several angles, put it down on the desk, and blew out a deep breath. "You don't have to tell me twice. For that matter, Ricardo Cortez and his family weren't the first ones to die up there, either."

IBSON & KENNEDY

"What?" Kendall and Suzanne demanded in unison.

Moss raised her hands in protest. "Lots of folk die. On a long enough timeline, everyone does. But I remember Griff said something about the homestead was cursed when we rode up there. The first time was when he was a new deputy himself; had him spooked somethin' fierce. I think he put a copy of the old report in with the Cortez one. Hold up."

Moss disappeared down a hallway past the holding cells and returned with a thick sheaf of papers in a folder. After scanning through the stack of documents, she pulled out a yellowed, handwritten report.

"I swear, Griff's handwriting is worse than a doctor's. Okay. He copied this report over. It's dated…nineteen years ago." She scanned the document and pointed to a section on the third page. "Same basic thing. Three adults dusted with the same kinds of wounds. Cauterized holes clean through."

"Clearly related," Kendall said.

"Clearly. And once we've figured out what the hell is in that cave, I'm going to write to Griff and let him know. Because I know the Moon River Massacres ate at him for years." Moss took the report to the back and returned with a bandolier of rifle bullets on one shoulder and her rifle over the other. "Well, it seems my Saturday has gotten more interesting. Let me round up a couple of deputies, and we'll go have a gander." She took another look at the skull on her desk. *"Well-armed* deputies."

* * *

The afternoon sun cast stark shadows beneath the overhang, and Sheriff Moss let out a low whistle when she moved beneath it and found the cave, just as described. "I have to admit—I didn't quite believe you, Tom," she said. "That's pretty grim."

"On one hand, ouch, Jules," Kendall replied. "But on the other hand, I suppose I can't blame you." Moss rolled her eyes but grinned, nonetheless.

"Alright, deputies, which of you likes whiskey?" Moss asked. Deputy Louis' hand shot up in the air first, but Newfield knew better. "Very good. Louis, you get the lantern. Tim, take the ladder." Louis realized he'd been suckered and cast his eyes heavenward as he dismounted from their horse-drawn 'mobile. Newfield loosened the rope securing their step ladder and carried it to the overhang.

At Sheriff Moss' insistence, she and her deputies would lead the way into the cavern—she didn't want things disturbed any more than they already had been. Deputy Louis scrambled up the ladder with a kerosene lantern in one hand and his revolver on his hip. Newfield followed him with a pump scattergun, and Sheriff Moss was third.

A moment passed, then another.

Moss's face appeared over the lip of the cavern. "Alright, come on up." Her staff clustered around the skull and crossbones. "You've convinced me."

Thomas, Rusty, Suzanne, and her faithful sidecat, Otis, followed the Sheriff's posse deeper into the cavern. Rusty carried one of the kerosene lanterns as well, but the yellow light from the two lanterns was a poor substitute for the daylight outside. Otis tasted the air and wrinkled his nose distastefully. The stink was palpable, a stale miasma where the odor of mold competed with burnt metal like you got off a grinder. The path was surprisingly unbroken, but there was no doubt they were descending as reflected sunlight behind them gradually diminished. The path they were following bent to the right, and Louis' boots *clanged*.

The six of them froze in place, and Rusty lowered his lantern. The rocky ground abruptly gave way to shiny, corrugated metal stairs, and the walls fell away, replaced with simple waist-high railings. Suzanne swallowed hard; the degree of individual welds to make even one such stair would take days. There were dozens of the stairs, disappearing away into the darkness below them.

"Keep moving, Louis," Moss ordered. There was no hesitation in her voice, just grim determination to figure out what, or who, was killing folk in her jurisdiction. Louis swallowed hard and continued his descent. The stairs reached a platform and kept descending off to their right.

A high-pitched whining sound was the only warning they got, a half-second before a blast of light dazzled Suzanne and thunder rent the air. Louis fell with a hole in his chest, and the lantern he held tumbled from his grasp. It plummeted over the edge of the stairs, shattered on the rock surface below, and the kerosene ignited. Flames from below licked up at them, but Moss snapped her rifle to her shoulder and fired, racked the lever, and fired again. Newfield was lower on the stairs and opened fire too. He charged down the stairs past the downed deputy, everyone else on his heels.

The muzzle flashes of whoever was shooting illuminated the cavern, leaving disconcerting afterimages etched into her retinas. Despite the blinding flashes, echoing booms, and the overwhelming stench of ozone, Suzanne knew that to remain still was to die, and she raced forward, following Rusty and Kendall. They were in a fatal funnel, and the only way out of the ambush was to fight through.

The stairs bottomed out, and Rusty charged past Moss, tapping her on her left shoulder on his way by. The sheriff snapped the muzzle of her repeater upwards; Rusty dove behind a protruding rock, made himself small, and Moss resumed firing. The lantern had sloshed during his mad dash and had gone out, but there was a dim glow from some kind of lighting ahead. Suzanne tucked herself in behind another rock to her left to get out of the line of fire. Then a black shadow bounded past her, Thomas Kendall's long coat flapping behind it, and the high-pitched, whining gunfire abruptly ended and turned to unintelligible screams. Suzanne popped up, her mag-fed scattergun at the high ready.

The dim lighting ahead, and the rapidly dwindling flames of the lantern behind, let her see a raised metal platform just two steps above the rough surface. The platform was maybe ten feet deep and had a short half-wall of similarly riveted metal liberally perforated with holes courtesy of their counter-fusillade. At the rear, a wall of flattened sheet metal loomed as high as the lighting would let her see, riveted in place. It reminded her of an all-metal version of her home's porch and front door. Thomas was on the platform and fired an insurance round into a prone target while Otis chewed on something. *Someone?* She waved her hand to indicate that she was going forward and stepped out to join Thomas on the "porch."

Two humans—at least, she thought they were human—lay prone. Otis had gone for one's throat, and his black, furred muzzle was shiny with blood. He met her eyes for a moment, licked his lips, and went back to feasting. The second was dead, but she couldn't tell what had felled their target from a glance. Thomas' insurance shot had been right into the target's nasal cavity, messily evident, but the kill shot was not.

Both wore one-piece, faded grey jumpsuits, with armored plates strapped onto their shins, thighs, chest, shoulders, and arms. Their heads were bare, covered with short blonde stubble so fine it was nearly invisible, and skin so pale it seemed translucent. They held strange weapons Suzanne hadn't ever seen before. They were smooth, all soft curves like a finely polished table leg, made of some kind of material she'd never seen. It wasn't wood, it wasn't metal, but it was rock solid. The armor plates appeared to be made of the same smooth material. Four rails ran down their length, so tight to the barrel, she couldn't fit her fingers in between. A red glowing indicator read *101*. Even the trigger was where she expected it to be.

Moss joined them with a grim look on her face.

"Did Louis…?" Suzanne asked, but Moss shook her head.

"No."

"This is goddamn *archaeotech*," Thomas cursed. "I shoulda known."

"Archaeo-what?"

"Archaeotech," he repeated. "Ancient, precursor stuff, squirreled away underground and sealed to survive when civilization got dusted. We, scouts, in the Feline Corps, used to clear routes for archaeo-excavators into the ruins. I'm no precursor buff, but your father understood a lot of it. That's one reason his industrial advances are developing so quickly." Thomas glanced at the door set into the metal wall. There was a vibration in the metal under their feet, as though dozens of feet were running in their direction. "And I think we've done kicked a hornets' nest of Morlocks. At least, that's what your father called them. They're the descendants of the precursors."

"From before civilization got dusted?" Moss repeated. "Oh my…"

Rusty hefted one of the big, boxy firearms. "We're committed now; they know we's here. Fire inna hole!" He aimed the gun back up the stairs, sighted down the barrel, and squeezed the trigger stud. The device hummed for a moment, then lightning sizzled down the rails, and a blinding bolt streaked across the cavern and *melted* through one of the stairs, leaving a perfectly round, glowing circle where it passed. The readout on the side now read *100,* and Rusty wore a slightly unhinged grin on his face. "I think this'll do nicely."

Newfield picked up the second blaster gun, which read *76.* Thomas began pawing through the dead archaeo-peoples' jumpsuits until he came up with two objects. The first was a cylinder with a ring on top and a lever on the side. The second, a flat, white object about the dimensions of a deck of cards but thinner. "The precursors used talismans like these to access doors." He held the talisman up to a block protruding from the wall, adjacent to the door, and it beeped. Thomas popped the door open a bare inch and glanced around to make sure all were ready. Suzanne was next in the stack and had Otis at her heels. Thomas threw the door the rest of the way open and lobbed the strange cylinder after it. *"Banger out!"*

"What's a—" Suzanne asked, but was interrupted by a deafening crash and blinding light from beyond the door. Then Thomas was gone, racing into the next room, rifle up and blazing. Suzanne followed, close on his heels, but went to the opposite side of the door, her shotgun up and ready. Otis bounded right up the middle, and the rest followed.

The cavern on the far side of the door was vast, so large Suzanne would have thought it would reach the surface. Structures lined both sides with suspended walkways above them. More armored Morlock-people lined the catwalks and doorways, placed to defend their bunker. The interior was much better lit, with bright lamps mounted high on tall poles and more strung between cavern walls. She had no trouble picking them out. Their blasters hung from slings or clattered to the floor at their feet. Many covered their eyes or had their hands clamped over their ears.

Thomas wasted no time. He opened fire immediately, potting three Morlocks who held rifles. Suzanne dropped one armored figure who staggered from a doorway to her left, then shot at another blasting wildly at them from a corner up ahead. Her buckshot skittered along the wall, struck him in multiple places, and he collapsed. She ducked behind a metal crate as cover for a moment. The cavern was so large, her buckshot was going to be useless, so she swapped her magazines to slug, and started drilling .70 caliber holes in targets.

Otis dashed forward, leaping from rock to wall to rooftop to Morlock. He caught the rifleman by the neck, mid-leap, and the cat whipped his body so hard the man flew, limp, with a broken neck. The black panther jumped and clamped onto an armored shoulder and raked with his back paws, spraying a torrent of blood.

Rusty was third in the door and knelt next to Suzanne. He didn't try to pick off the exposed bits of flesh; he just started firing through their 'cover.' His gambit worked, and by the time his shot-counter reached 81, he'd plugged at least eight, maybe ten, targets. It occurred to Suzanne that perhaps her metal crate didn't provide as much cover as she'd initially thought. It was time to go.

She tapped Rusty on the shoulder and pointed to the doorway to her left. Rusty nodded his understanding and put three more rounds into each side of the door before she moved. It was a good thing, too, because one of the armored Morlocks slumped out from behind the doorway with a hole burnt through his rib cage and a rifle trapped under his torso.

Suzanne burst through the door and blasted a second armored form. This one had a different kind of firearm. Rather than a long barrel with four rails, this one was compact and boxy, with only the hint of a barrel. She knew her shotgun was no good in the cavern's vast open space, so she slung it and picked up the smaller weapon. She pointed it out a second door and squeezed the trigger.

It clicked, and a stream of bolts spewed forth. They were inaccurate, but the blasts from the gun were plainly visible and easily reached the far side of the cavern. Suzanne hadn't fired tracer rounds before, but she'd seen some once, and they looked sort of like that. The range this blaster thing had made it more useful than her scattergun. Better yet, it had iron sights, and she knew how to use iron sights. She leaned out the second door and hosed down a three-story structure opposite their entryway. One of the Morlock riflemen sniped down at the entrance, but the glowing bolts betrayed his position. Suzanne's burst of fire left glowing blisters where it hit the wall; she'd never fired the thing before, and she missed. Rather than killing the shooter, he ducked away for just a second. He popped up and fired twice more, but something hit him, and he slumped forward. His limp form tumbled over the railing and thumped heavily to the rock floor head-first, thirty feet below.

Suzanne gradually became aware the shooting was over, and she didn't see any more of the Morlocks moving about.

"I'm comin' out!" she yelled from the first door, but she couldn't hear herself talk. The repeated gun blasts in such close quarters had rendered her deaf. When she returned to the entrance, she gasped.

Deputy Newfield was dead. His face and torso were scorched black, and shrapnel had completely taken one arm off. Blood oozed from shrapnel wounds, but the ragged hole near his throat meant he was gone. Scattered parts suggested his Morlock blaster gun had exploded in his hands. Maybe it had been shot and whatever powered it had detonated?

A short distance from Newfield, Rusty sat against the entrance bulkhead. He was moving, clutching his arm, and then Suzanne saw it. His forearm, the one bearing the militia tattoo, lay in the dust at his feet, and he was cradling a cauterized stump. He'd wrapped a tourniquet around his bicep, and he grimaced in pain, but she couldn't hear him moaning.

She didn't know where Sheriff Moss or Thomas Kendall had gone. "Thomas?" Suzanne shouted. "Thomas!" She took a breath and calmed herself. She knew this. Finishing school had covered the kinds of injuries one could suffer working the farm, and that included traumatic amputation. Despite the tourniquet, Rusty's stump was still bleeding. It was certainly better than nothing, but his plaid shirt was stained, and a pool of black mud had formed under his wound.

Suzanne took the big blaster rifle and stepped back out the front door onto the porch. She fired one bolt, then another at the stairs' railing support. She'd missed, but it was close. Panic threatened at the back of her mind, but she locked that down, took another shot, and then she blasted free a two-foot-long length of steel. She jabbed the hot ends into the Morlock Otis had killed, where the tips sizzled until they'd cooled enough, then she returned to her downed partner. She slipped the bar between the belt and his skin and rotated it once to clamp the belt down harder. The bleeding stopped, but Rusty groaned in pain. She could hear him this time; her hearing was coming back. Otis found them, and he licked Tailor's face, worried. Since he'd just been *eating* the Morlocks he'd killed, the cat-kisses left morbid, bloody streaks across Rusty's visage that made him look even worse than he was.

Suzanne checked his pulse and found his skin clammy and drenched in sweat, but he was cold to touch. "You're going to go into shock," she yelled. She realized she was shouting and forced herself to lower her voice. "You're going to go into shock," she repeated. She flicked open her pocketknife and sliced away the hem of her wool skirt down to the slit. Rusty's eyes widened in surprise—he wasn't so far gone that he didn't react to her cutting her clothes off—but then he nodded in understanding when she wrapped the wool tightly around his shoulders as a shawl, to conserve body heat. She still had her striped tights on, after all, so she was still decent.

Thomas returned, armed with one of the short, rapid-firing blasters. He'd been in the largest of the underground buildings, a massive structure four stories tall that disappeared into the rock face. She had to concentrate to hear him, but the more he spoke, the better she understood him. "…you need to see this!" he shouted and got an arm under Rusty's shoulder to help him to his feet.

560 | IBSON & KENNEDY

"He's hurt!" she protested.

"I know! Trust me!"

Sergeant Moss was holding the door open, and Thomas seemed to know where they were going, so she went with it. Inside, down a corridor, she read a lit sign that hung from the roof.

Medical Wing

An idle part of her mind noted, curiously, that the signage was legible and in English.

Inside the room, she found ten tables arranged in two rows of five. Strange plates of black glass surrounded each on armatures that extended from the wall. "Lay him on the table," Thomas instructed. Suzanne helped Rusty onto the table, which had the same seamless metal-and-something look of the guns, and Thomas tapped one of the black glass plates. It lit up at his touch.

"*Auto-Doc, initiated,*" a hollow metallic voice said. It had a funny accent, but Suzanne could understand the words even if she didn't know their meaning. "*Do you wish to assume manual control?*"

"No," Thomas replied with some authority.

"*Analyzing. Respiration: high. Pulse: rapid, weak. Blood pressure: low. Administering aid.*"

A flexible arm snaked out of the wall and pressed against Rusty's chest. There was a hiss, and Rusty gasped, but his features relaxed. "Oooh…that's kinda nice," he murmured. "Do that again…"

"*Repeated administration of pain relief narcotics is contraindicated in such a short time period,*" the voice replied. "*Analyzing. Trauma—left arm— amputation, full, recent. Query: Is the severed limb available?*"

"Yes," Thomas replied.

"*Place the limb below the amputation point and stand clear.*"

The armature retracted into the ceiling above them, and a large shell descended, enclosing Rusty from the neck down like a clamshell.

"*This will take some time,*" the voice warned. Suzanne glared at Thomas.

"You've seen this before."

Thomas had the decency to look sheepish. "I have. Or something like it. Scouts get into mischief sometimes. Sheriff Moss?" Moss may well have been in shock, herself. Whatever she'd been expecting, a gunfight with Morlocks in a hidden underground cavern wasn't it. Nor had she expected both her deputies to be killed and another member of the party to be wounded. "Would you remain with Rusty? You've known him the longest. Can you hold the door while we clear the rest of this place?"

Moss nodded and adjusted the grip on her carbine. "I can do that," she said. Thomas led Suzanne and Otis from the Medical Wing back into the main cavern.

"How're you doing, kiddo?" he asked Suzanne.

"Scouts out, Sergeant Kendall," Suzanne replied. "Hooah." Not that Thomas had been a sergeant in a long time, but he had been when she was a child, and it seemed appropriate. She wore a grim smile on her face, determined to see things through.

"That's my girl. Three things. One, there may be children. There must be children for any Morlock population to survive. Two, they may be cannibals. Back east, underground bunkers like this one trended that way, I've…seen a few. And three, don't touch anything, you don't recognize. I don't want you looking like poor Deputy Newfield back there."

"Understood. Lead on," she replied.

Thomas led them to the three-story structure where the rooftop rifleman had tumbled over the balcony. The two humans and the panther cleared from room to room, finding more precursor tech, but nothing either of them recognized until they entered a long, broad room. The room had a sign hanging from the ceiling that read, *HYDROPONICS*, but Suzanne had no idea what the word meant. Inside, the air was hot and humid, and fans circulated. Row upon row of glass tanks lined the floor, with some kind of solution bubbling through them. The tanks were full of greenery—Suzanne recognized beans, carrots, cabbage, and other vegetables in several stages of growth. That boded well, at least on the cannibalism front.

They pressed on, reaching a set of stairs leading up, and on the second-story landing, Thomas studied an ancient paper map taped to the wall. He'd been silent, using nothing but hand signals to communicate. He padded forward silently again. Or maybe he wasn't silent, and she just couldn't hear? It was hard to tell. They worked their way back to the front of the building again. Many of the side rooms were small, with bunks for one or two and small storage compartments. They reminded Suzanne of the private room she'd had on her train from Lake Winterpeg—there was just enough room for someone to survive with some privacy, but little more.

The second story ended in another stairwell, and they climbed higher again. Another rooftop sign read, *FABRICATION.* Thomas entered and drew up short.

Three adult Morlocks—two women and one man—stood between Thomas and a huddled mass of children, their ages somewhere between "infant" and "teen." The lone man out front brandished a metal club. He had the same, so-pale-as-to-be-translucent skin, long stringy brown hair, and wide eyes with pupils so dark they appeared wholly black. But none of them wore the armored plates—their jumpsuits were unadorned, and he squinted as though he had trouble seeing clearly.

"Whatchew wan'?" he demanded. "Gittout!"

Suzanne moved to the side to cover him with her acquired blaster, while Thomas lowered his.

"I don't want to hurt you," he said.

"LIAR!" the man shouted and swung the bat with all his strength. The muscles in his arms, however, were flaccid and weak from growing up underground, and they were utterly unused to manual labor. Thomas caught the bat with his bare hand and stopped it cold. He clamped on with his iron grip, and he gently, deliberately passed his blaster to Suzanne. He took hold of the bat with his second and began twisting. The Morlock struggled and kicked him in the shins, but Thomas was impassive. He wrenched the club out of the other man's grasp and flung it away to the corner.

"Sit. Down," Thomas commanded. The man's spirit broke, and he and the women slunk away and sat on the floor with the children.

Thirteen. Suzanne counted thirteen of them seated on the floor. The utter absence of sun, the diet, and the lack of anything physical to do had left them skinny, malnourished wretches. Her heart broke for them, locked away, trapped here beneath the ground, living off cabbage and beans and who knew what else. Their guns were terrifying, insanely powerful, but once disarmed…they were pitiful.

The room they'd taken refuge in was huge. An enormous metal box as big as eight 'mobiles, two wide, two tall, and two long, dominated most of the floor space. There was a hopper in one end, but what they put in it, she had no idea. Thomas stood at another one of the strange black glass plates, tapping on it and swiping across the surface.

"We have to help them," she said.

"What?" Kendall put a finger in one ear, wiggled it, and turned back to look at her.

"We have to help them," she repeated. "We just…killed the rest of their clan, we've destroyed their way of life; they're dead unless we help them."

Kendall frowned. "They're Morlocks."

"They're children," she argued. She couldn't believe what she was hearing. She couldn't believe "Uncle" Thomas Kendall was this callous. "They're no threat to anyone!"

Kendall shook his head angrily and turned back to the glass plate. "You're wrong, miss. They killed the Cortezes and the family before them. They hate surface dwellers, and they'll kill you in an instant if they think they can get away with it."

"They probably thought they were under attack!" Suzanne argued hotly, then stopped abruptly. "Just like now."

"Doesn't matter," Kendall said. "You're in luck—you can ask Father yourself."

He tapped another command, and one of the walls illuminated.

"*Father?*" she gasped.

"Hello, sweetheart," her father answered. This wasn't possible. Father was days away to the east. But there he was, on the wall, like he was right there in the room with them.

"It was where you thought it would be, sir, more or less," Kendall reported. "It's actually directly under the farm. I was worried I'd need to figure out how to link the systems, but we're in luck—they're already networked. I just had to open the link from this side."

"Perfect," Dino replied. "Any troubles?"

"No," Kendall answered.

"*Yes!*" Suzanne cut in.

Father frowned. "What's wrong, Suzie?"

"What's wrong? No trouble*?"* She glared at Kendall, incredulous at the bald-faced lie. "Father, two of the sheriff's deputies are dead, Rusty Tailor had his arm shot off, we had a gunfight with a dozen or more of these…Morlocks, or whatever you call them, and the last ten Morlock children were hiding in here. There is exactly one adult man remaining and two women, and between them, they had a single club. We most definitely had troubles! Not to mention that it sounds like you two knew this place was here. You didn't deign to tell me I was moving to a farm on top of a precursor bunker?" She glared at Kendall.

Father cocked one eyebrow and focused his attention on Kendall again.

"Thomas?"

"I didn't want to worry you, sir. Yes, we have two dead deputies, and yes, Rusty lost his forearm to a bolt in his bicep, but he's in the med bay with an auto-doc patching him up. I would have…handled, the survivors."

Suzanne most definitely didn't care for the way he said that last part. "We must help them!" she cried. "We've just invaded their home, killed nearly all the adults, and now it sounds like Thomas wants to put them down like an ant colony or something!"

Father nodded. "Of course, sweetheart. I understand. Thomas, are they salvageable?"

Kendall looked at the kids for a moment and shook his head in the negative. "I doubt it. It depends on how heavily they've been indoctrinated, sir."

One of the Morlock women opened her mouth to speak, but she was shushed by the second.

"Suzie, sweetheart, let me explain?"

"Please do," she said coldly.

"You know Thomas and I served in the Highlander scouts together. We had long wondered just how it was that the Feline Corps' cats were so smart, so trainable, so…well, not domesticated, but how they worked so well with us. House cats certainly don't have their personality, nor do mountain lions or any other cat you care to name. Some of them are complete assholes. A year or so before I retired, we, scouts, escorted a team of archaeo-engineers to some precursor ruins in the flats northeast of you. We learned the ruins were once named Suffield, in part because the ruins there were still functional. And that function, we learned, was to grow cats, like your Otis, in glass tanks. Precursor engineers selected and refined the cats for certain qualities, like the way a Percheron horse is a heavy workhorse, but your Naomi is a riding horse. They edited these cats' makeup in a way we still can't begin to understand. But tests in their medical bays showed one thing for sure—our cats with the Highlanders were special—they were the descendants of the military's cats from before civilization got dusted."

Suzanne was fuming inside. Damn Father and his secrets! But she let him continue, uninterrupted.

"The second, and more important thing we learned inside that facility, was there was a device known as a Fabricator only a short distance west of Winterpeg, in another precursor base called Shilo. And that, my dear, was where we hit the motherload."

"I fail to see what any of this has to do with ten orphaned children, Father," Suzanne retorted stubbornly. "Morlock or not."

"Please, sweetheart, hear me out. Shilo had a Fabricator, just like the device in the room where you now stand. It can make anything. Cogs. Rail lines. Cold weather clothes. Irrigation systems. Pumps. Pipes. Electricity! Firearms! The railgun you hold in your hands at this very moment! Add enough of the right kind of raw material at one end, select the function on the control panel, and get finished goods at the other end."

It clicked.

"And that is the basis for your industrial 'advances?'" she asked.

"Of course. We have learned *so much* these last few years, but the Shilo Fabricator was damaged, corrupted, and its information stores were incomplete. With an intact information base? We can rebuild the precursor civilization. But, of course, we won't allow ourselves to be dusted like they were."

"What do you mean?" Suzanne asked, confused. Everyone knew civilization had ended; the precursor ruins were proof of that. But how the end of the world had come about was more mysterious.

"They had... machines, sweetheart. Tiny machines, invisible to the naked eye. They called them "nanites." They were miracles of engineering and formed the basis for all precursor tech. Imagine the smallest speck of dust you can see. Divide it in half, then again, and again, and again five more times. Those machines break down the materials in the fabber and rebuild them into whatever it is you need, in whatever shapes you require. But something went wrong. Someone made nanites that could make more of themselves, and they lost control. Once you have enough nanites, they resemble a dust cloud, and they ran rampant. Nearly everything and nearly everyone turned to dust, broken down into their tiniest component pieces by the runaway nanite clouds. They killed the precursors and stripped civilization to its very bones.

"A few of the precursors cast their hope into the future though. Writers and artists with imagination had foreseen all the ways the world could end, and a wise few sequestered these fabbers away underground. They scattered them all over the globe under or around military bases, schools, industrial centers, and they sealed them against the exterior and made them self-sufficient, so they could re-emerge when the time was right. When the nanite dust clouds weren't a threat anymore."

The woman who'd opened her mouth to speak was nodding, and Suzanne held up a hand to interrupt her father. Her head was spinning, trying to absorb everything he was disclosing, but she needed a moment.

"Stroo! Stroo!" the Morlock woman said, and this time she wouldn't be shushed by the others. "Da holee 'cator cares fer us, our erry need. Sumfin breaks, the holee 'cator provides, shall provide, til de dusts be gone an' da world be new. So say da holee Youzer Gaid!"

"The dusts are gone," Suzanne said. "They have been for my whole life, and their lives too," she said, pointing to Kendall and her father.

"Dey gone?" she asked, her eyes wide.

"They're gone," Kendall confirmed. "But evidently, no one below the surface has gotten the message."

"Indeed," Father agreed. "Too few, *far* too few of them have re-emerged. Since Thomas and I secured the Shilo fabber, we've had a guide map to go by. It's rough; they don't give precise instructions, but we have some ideas. I purchased that farm thinking you would get it functional and become a local figure of some importance with your resources, education, and natural talent, sweetheart. Meanwhile, Thomas would quietly work in the background, and once he found the fabber, he'd help you "discover" it. When the time was right." Father checked his timepiece, an intricate pocket watch he'd had as long as she could remember. Now, Suzanne suspected it came from this *Shilo fabber* thing. "I certainly didn't expect you to find it your second week, sweetheart; we're not in a hurry. Rebuilding civilization takes time, and if the secret of these fabbers gets out? It will just cause more and more bloodshed. You, and me, and Thomas and everyone else in on the secret will become targets for anyone with a hint that they exist and the will to kill over them. They're a link to the past and a bridge to the future. Anyone who gains control of them controls the future. So we have to keep our agenda a secret. For now."

Footsteps coming up the stairs behind them caught Suzanne's attention, and she whirled with her repeating blaster raised.

"It's us!" Rusty's voice came from beyond the doorway, and he entered the fabber room with his hands raised. Sheriff Moss followed.

Suzanne did a double-take.

His hands, plural, were raised.

"Well, I'll be damned," he said, taking in the enormity of the fabricator room. "Uh, howdy, Mister Lippi. Miss." He lifted his hat to Suzanne. Suzanne threw her arms around him, thrilled he was alive and somehow intact. She hadn't entirely realized just how much Mister Tailor had come to mean to her, and before she knew what she was doing, she kissed him squarely on the cheek.

When they separated, Father cocked his eyebrow again. "Mister Tailor, you're looking well for someone who lost his arm," he said dryly.

"I'm not quite sure what to think, sir," he said and rolled up his tattered sleeve to reveal a pink scar connecting his upper arm to the lower. He wriggled each finger in sequence. "It itches like the dickens, but it works, so...yeah, I'm doing pretty good." He leaned aside to Suzanne and whispered, "These must be some crazy medicines that auto-doc gave me, to have me thinking I'm talkin' to Mister Lippi right now. Cray-zee!"

"This is all a lot to take in, Father. I wish you'd told me this, say, two years ago when you purchased the farm. But I'll say this. I want Thomas gone." It stung to say the words, but she had to say them now or never. "I cannot trust him anymore, not with the secrecy and the lies, and your agenda. With as much land as I've got, I can show these poor Morlocks that yes, the dusts are gone, and the world is ready to be made new. If this fabricator is as miraculous as you say, I can build them homes, above ground, quickly, so they can enjoy the sun on their skin for the first time in their lives, and watch the stars at night. So they can enjoy steak, and lamb chops, and bacon, instead of vat-grown cabbage and soy beans. And they can see that their years underground were not a waste."

She looked at the children again. These skinny, wretched, pathetic waifs were scions of the precursors. They'd kept the tech alive for so long...but now they were orphans, huddling behind the last three adults, the only people they'd known their entire lives. She wept. They weren't cannibalistic monsters, they were just people, protecting their home. "I wish more of them were here to see it."

* * * * *

About the Editors

Jamie Ibson is from the frozen wastelands of Canuckistan, where moose, bears, and geese battle for domination among the hockey rinks, igloos, and Tim Hortons. After joining the Canadian army reserves in high school, he spent half of 2001 in Bosnia as a peacekeeper and came home shortly after 9/11 with a deep sense of foreboding.

After graduating college, he landed a job in law enforcement and has been posted to the left coast since 2007. He published a number of short stories in 2018 and 2019, and his first novel came out in January 2020. He's pretty much been making it up as he goes along, although he has numerous writer friends who serve as excellent role-models, mentors, and, occasionally, cautionary tales. We Dare: Semper Paratus is the second anthology he's edited, and he will probably keep doing annual, themed anthologies as long as Chris will let him.

His website can be found at https://ibsonwrites.ca/. He lives in Abbotsford, British Columbia, is married to the lovely Michelle, and they have cats.

A Webster Award winner and three-time Dragon Award finalist, Chris Kennedy is a Science Fiction/Fantasy/Young Adult author, speaker, and small-press publisher who has written over 20 books and published more than 100 others. Chris' stories include the "Occupied Seattle" military fiction duology, "The Theogony" and "Codex Regius" science fiction trilogies, stories in the "Four Horsemen" and "In Revolution Born" universes and the "War for Dominance" fantasy trilogy. Get his free book, "Shattered Crucible," at his website, https://chriskennedypublishing.com.

Called "fantastic" and "a great speaker," he has coached hundreds of beginning authors and budding novelists on how to self-publish their stories at a variety of conferences, conventions and writing guild presentations. He is the author of the award-winning #1 bestseller, "Self-Publishing for Profit: How to Get Your Book Out of Your Head and Into the Stores," as well as the leadership training book, "Leadership from the Darkside."

Chris lives in Virginia Beach, Virginia, with his wife, and is the holder of a doctorate in educational leadership and master's degrees in both business and public administration. Follow Chris on Facebook at https://facebook.com/chriskennedypublishing.biz.

* * * * *

The following is an

Excerpt from Book One of The Psyche of War:

Minds of Men

Kacey Ezell

Available from Theogony Books

eBook, Paperback, and Audio

Excerpt from "Minds of Men:"

"Look sharp, everyone," Carl said after a while. Evelyn couldn't have said whether they'd been droning for minutes or hours in the cold, dense white of the cloud cover. "We should be overhead the French coast in about thirty seconds."

The men all reacted to this announcement with varying degrees of excitement and terror. Sean got up from his seat and came back to her, holding an awkward looking arrangement of fabric and straps.

Put this on, he thought to her. *It's your flak jacket. And your parachute is just there,* he said, pointing. *If the captain gives the order to bail out, you go, clip this piece into your 'chute, and jump out the biggest hole you can find. Do you understand? You do, don't you. This psychic thing certainly makes explaining things easier,* he finished with a grin.

Evelyn gave him what she hoped was a brave smile and took the flak jacket from him. It was deceptively heavy, and she struggled a bit with getting it on. Sean gave her a smile and a thumbs up, and then headed back to his station.

The other men were checking in and charging their weapons. A short time later, Evelyn saw through Rico's eyes as the tail gunner watched their fighter escort waggle their wings at the formation and depart. They didn't have the long-range fuel capability to continue all the way to the target.

Someday, that long-range fighter escort we were promised will materialize, Carl thought. His mind felt determinedly positive, like he was trying to be strong for the crew and not let them see his fear. That, of course, was an impossibility, but the crew took it well. After all, they were afraid, too. Especially as the formation had begun its descent to the attack altitude of 20,000 feet. Evelyn became gradually aware of the way the men's collective tension ratcheted up with every hundred feet of descent. They were entering enemy fighter territory.

Yeah, and someday Veronica Lake will...ah. Never mind. Sorry, Evie. That was Les. Evelyn could feel the waist gunner's not-quite-repentant grin. She had to suppress a grin of her own, but Les' irreverence was the perfect tension breaker.

Boys will be boys, she sent, projecting a sense of tolerance. *But real men keep their private lives private.* She added this last with a bit of smug superiority and felt the rest of the crew's appreciative flare of humor at her jab. Even Les laughed, shaking his head. A warmth that had nothing to do with her electric suit enfolded Evelyn, and she started to feel like, maybe, she just might become part of the crew yet.

Fighters! Twelve o'clock high!

The call came from Alice. If she craned her neck to look around Sean's body, Evelyn could just see the terrifying rain of tracer fire coming from the dark, diving silhouette of an enemy fighter. She let the call echo down her own channels and felt her men respond, turning their own weapons to cover *Teacher's Pet*'s flanks. Adrenaline surges spiked through all of them, causing Evelyn's heart to race in turn. She took a deep breath and reached out to tie her crew in closer to the Forts around them.

She looked through Sean's eyes as he fired from the top turret, tracking his line of bullets just in front of the attacking aircraft. His mind was oddly calm and terribly focused...as, indeed, they all were. Even young Lieutenant Bob was zeroed in on his task of keeping a tight position and making it that much harder to penetrate the deadly crossing fire of the Flying Fortress.

Fighters! Three o'clock low!

That was Logan in the ball turret. Evelyn felt him as he spun his turret around and began to fire the twin Browning AN/M2 .50 caliber machine guns at the sinister dark shapes rising up to meet them with fire.

Got 'em, Bobby Fritsche replied, from his position in the right waist. He, too, opened up with his own .50 caliber machine gun, tracking the barrel forward of the nose of the fighter formation, in order to "lead" their flight and not shoot behind them.

Evelyn blinked, then hastily relayed the call to the other girls in the formation net. She felt their acknowledgement, though it was almost an absentminded thing as each of the girls were focusing mostly on the communication between the men in their individual crews.

Got you, you Kraut sonofabitch! Logan exulted. Evelyn looked through his eyes and couldn't help but feel a twist of pity for the pilot of the German fighter as he spiraled toward the ground, one wing completely gone. She carefully kept that emotion from Logan, however, as he was concentrating on trying to take out the other three fighters who'd been in the initial attacking wedge. One fell victim to Bobby's relentless fire as he threw out a curtain of lead that couldn't be avoided.

Two back to you, tail, Bobby said, his mind carrying an even calm, devoid of Logan's adrenaline-fueled exultation.

Yup, Rico Martinez answered as he visually acquired the two remaining targets and opened fire. He was aided by fire from the aircraft flying off their right wing, the *Nagging Natasha*. She fired from her left waist and tail, and the two remaining fighters faltered and tumbled through the resulting crossfire. Evelyn watched through Rico's eyes as the ugly black smoke trailed the wreckage down.

Fighters! Twelve high!

Fighters! Two high!

The calls were simultaneous, coming from Sean in his top turret and Les on the left side. Evelyn took a deep breath and did her best to split her attention between the two of them, keeping the net strong and open. Sean and Les opened fire, their respective weapons adding a cacophony of pops to the ever-present thrum of the engines.

Flak! That was Carl, up front. Evelyn felt him take hold of the controls, helping the lieutenant to maintain his position in the formation as the Nazi anti-aircraft guns began to send up 20mm shells that blossomed into dark clouds that pocked the sky. One exploded right in front of *Pretty Cass'* nose. Evelyn felt the bottom drop out of her stomach as the aircraft heaved first up and then down. She held on grimly and passed on the wordless knowledge the pilots had no choice but to fly through the debris and shrapnel that resulted.

In the meantime, the gunners continued their rapid fire response to the enemy fighters' attempt to break up the formation. Evelyn took that knowledge—that the Luftwaffe was trying to isolate one of the Forts, make her vulnerable—and passed it along the looser formation net.

Shit! They got Liberty Belle! Logan called out then, from his view in the ball turret. Evelyn looked through his angry eyes, feeling his sudden spike of despair as they watched the crippled Fort fall back, two of her four engines smoking. Instantly, the enemy fighters swarmed like so many insects, and Evelyn watched as the aircraft yawed over and began to spin down and out of control.

A few agonizing heartbeats later, first one, then three more parachutes fluttered open far below. Evelyn felt Logan's bitter knowledge that there had been six other men on board that aircraft. *Liberty Belle* was one of the few birds flying without a psychic on board, and Evelyn suppressed a small, wicked feeling of relief that she hadn't just lost one of her friends.

Fighters! Twelve o'clock level!

* * * * *

Get "Minds of Men" now at:

https://www.amazon.com/dp/B0778SPKQV

Find out more about Kacey Ezell and "Minds of Men" at:

https://chriskennedypublishing.com

* * * * *

The following is an
Excerpt from Book One of the Salvage Title Trilogy:

Salvage Title

Kevin Steverson

Available Now from Theogony Books

eBook, Paperback, and Audio Book

Excerpt from "Salvage Title:"

The first thing Clip did was get power to the door and the access panel. Two of his power cells did the trick once he had them wired to the container. He then pulled out his slate and connected it. It lit up, and his fingers flew across it. It took him a few minutes to establish a link, then he programmed it to search for the combination to the access panel.

"Is it from a human ship?" Harmon asked, curious.

"I don't think so, but it doesn't matter; ones and zeros are still ones and zeros when it comes to computers. It's universal. I mean, there are some things you have to know to get other races' computers to run right, but it's not that hard," Clip said.

Harmon shook his head. *Riiigghht,* he thought. He knew better. Clip's intelligence test results were completely off the charts. Clip opted to go to work at Rinto's right after secondary school because there was nothing for him to learn at the colleges and universities on either Tretra or Joth. He could have received academic scholarships for advanced degrees on a number of nearby systems. He could have even gone all the way to Earth and attended the University of Georgia if he wanted. The problem was getting there. The schools would have provided free tuition if he could just have paid to get there.

Secondary school had been rough on Clip. He was a small guy that made excellent grades without trying. It would have been worse if Harmon hadn't let everyone know that Clip was his brother. They lived in the same foster center, so it was mostly true. The first day of school, Harmon had laid down the law—if you messed with Clip, you messed up.

585

At the age of fourteen, he beat three seniors senseless for attempting to put Clip in a trash container. One of them was a Yalteen, a member of a race of large humanoids from two systems over. It wasn't a fair fight—they should have brought more people with them. Harmon hated bullies.

After the suspension ended, the school's Warball coach came to see him. He started that season as a freshman and worked on using it to earn a scholarship to the academy. By the time he graduated, he was six feet two inches with two hundred and twenty pounds of muscle. He got the scholarship and a shot at going into space. It was the longest time he'd ever spent away from his foster brother, but he couldn't turn it down.

Clip stayed on Joth and went to work for Rinto. He figured it was a job that would get him access to all kinds of technical stuff, servos, motors, and maybe even some alien computers. The first week he was there, he tweaked the equipment and increased the plant's recycled steel production by 12 percent. Rinto was eternally grateful, as it put him solidly into the profit column instead of toeing the line between profit and loss. When Harmon came back to the planet after the academy, Rinto hired him on the spot on Clip's recommendation. After he saw Harmon operate the grappler and got to know him, he was glad he did.

A steady beeping brought Harmon back to the present. Clip's program had succeeded in unlocking the container. "Right on!" Clip exclaimed. He was always using expressions hundreds or more years out of style. "Let's see what we have; I hope this one isn't empty, too." Last month they'd come across a smaller vault, but it had been empty.

Harmon stepped up and wedged his hands into the small opening the door had made when it disengaged the locks. There wasn't enough power in the small cells Clip used to open it any further. He put his weight into it, and the door opened enough for them to get inside. Before they went in, Harmon placed a piece of pipe in the doorway so it couldn't close and lock on them, baking them alive before anyone realized they were missing.

Daylight shone in through the doorway, and they both froze in place; the weapons vault was full.

* * * * *

Get "Salvage Title" now at:
https://www.amazon.com/dp/B07H8Q3HBV.

Find out more about Kevin Steverson and "Salvage Title" at:
http://chriskennedypublishing.com/.

* * * * *

The following is an

Excerpt from Book One of the Revelations Cycle:

Cartwright's Cavaliers

Mark Wandrey

Available Now from Seventh Seal Press

eBook, Paperback, and Audio Book

Excerpt from "Cartwight's Cavaliers:"

The last two operational tanks were trapped on their chosen path. Faced with destroyed vehicles front and back, they cut sideways to the edge of the dry river bed they'd been moving along and found several large boulders to maneuver around that allowed them to present a hull-down defensive position. Their troopers rallied on that position. It was starting to look like they'd dig in when Phoenix 1 screamed over and strafed them with dual streams of railgun rounds. A split second later, Phoenix 2 followed on a parallel path. Jim was just cheering the air attack when he saw it. The sixth damned tank, and it was a heavy.

"I got that last tank," Jim said over the command net.

"Observe and stand by," Murdock said.

"We'll have these in hand shortly," Buddha agreed, his transmission interspersed with the thudding of his CASPer firing its magnet accelerator. "We can be there in a few minutes."

Jim examined his battlespace. The tank was massive. It had to be one of the fusion-powered beasts he'd read about. Which meant shields and energy weapons. It was heading down the same gap the APC had taken, so it was heading toward Second Squad, and fast.

"Shit," he said.

"Jim," Hargrave said, "we're in position. What are you doing?"

"Leading," Jim said as he jumped out from the rock wall.

* * * * *

Get "Cartwright's Cavaliers" now at:
https://www.amazon.com/dp/B01MRZKM95

Find out more about Mark Wandrey and the Four Horsemen Universe at:

https://chriskennedypublishing.com/the-four-horsemen-books/

* * * * *

Manufactured by Amazon.ca
Bolton, ON